H RINK

RIDING THE WOODEN HORSE

THE FALL OF TROY

authorHOUSE®

AuthorHouse™ LLC
1663 Liberty Drive
Bloomington, IN 47403
www.authorhouse.com
Phone: 1-800-839-8640

Published by AuthorHouse 01/22/2014

ISBN: 978-1-4918-3564-7 (sc)
ISBN: 978-1-4918-3565-4 (e)

Library of Congress Control Number: 2014900911

Contents

❧ 1 ❧

On the Beach

It was a peaceful morning in early autumn. The sun was up in all its glory; in fact, it was unseasonably hot for this time of the year. What is it humans call this sort of weather? Indian summer or the dog days[1]. What do the Indians have to do with it? Or the dogs, for that matter. Don't know.

Beyond the breakers, the waters of the Ægean Sea gleamed and twinkled under the sun's rays: the sea was calm and white surf lapped gently onto the sandy beach, which stretched for miles. In the bay, off Tenedos isle, the Greek fleet rode at anchor, sails furled, oars stowed, ships rolling gently with the lazy swell of the waves. All was quiet and picturesque. High in the sky, white fleecy clouds lazed about. Just at elevenses, a pleasant breeze sprang up, blowing off the Ægean and cooling things down a bit.

I am a cat with pretensions to Siamese descent. Not many humans are cat wise enough to tell the difference between the real thing and a moggy. Be that as it may, I came to Troy for the weekend and should have left about a month ago but my

---

[1] Indian summer: summer in autumn; dog days: combined heat from the sun and the dog star, Sirius

travel agent said I could stay on if I liked—at no extra cost. In exchange, I promised to write glowing comments on my stay for his Internet blog.

Turning my back to the sea, I looked inland and my eyes wandered to the city on the hill—Troy of song and legend, its massive walls built for eternity and its tower reaching for the sky. I could see, with my sharp cat's eyes, tiny figures marching backwards and forwards along the ramparts; otherwise, all was quiet. It hardly looked like the scene of a war that had lasted for nine years and cost I don't how many lives that begs the question: Was anyone counting? Yet the ravages of war were clear wherever I looked. Nothing lived beyond the city wall. No little villages, no orchards of olive trees, no herders with their sheep. On the slopes of the hill tufts of grass clung stubbornly to the soil. A few olive trees, stunted and dusty, hung their heads as if in shame. All gone. Only the city remained.

To the west, beyond the battle plain, I could just glimpse the Greek City States' camp. I didn't have to go there to know it was filthy, slovenly and muddy. Husbandry was not the Greeks' strong suite. Besides, after nine years of war, most Greeks were oblivious of their surroundings. As for guards, I couldn't glimpse a single one. But then guard duty was something the Greeks never took particularly seriously.

War had wreaked havoc with both sides. The last great battle—*the battle at the Greeks ships*—took place some thirty days ago and had cost Troy its mainstay and inspiration, Hector, master of horses and Priam's oldest (at that time) living son. The Greeks had lost Patroklus and, although the Greek High Command had had no high opinion of Achilles' best friend, they had to acknowledge that Patroklus saved the Greeks' bacon that night. Later, the funeral pyres burned merrily, sending the dead to their well-deserved rest in Hades; I could still sniff a tang in the air from burning wood and flesh.

Although, to the casual observer, both city and camp looked peaceful and at rest, a feline isn't your casual observer. He sees with his eyes and feels mood through scent, smell, vibes—good or bad—and taste, of air, sea and terrain. I could sense that peace and quiet was only on the surface; below, everything was different and nothing was the same.

Troy's Hector was no more and there wasn't another Hector to be had for love or money; Troy's standard—white horse on a red background—fluttered at half-mast from the colossal tower, the city still mourning its fallen Hero. However, in Hector's lifetime, the Trojan leadership had been riven this way and that on how to conduct the war, what to do about Helen, queen of Sparta, at the moment resident in Troy, or how to rid Troy of the Greeks. Any proposed solution was challenged for or against. King Priam listened to everyone, heard no one, dithered about and nothing was done. Now, without Hector, my mind boggled at what could be going on in the Trojan High Command. The wise say doing nothing is a good strategy but not, I think, when the enemy is camped outside your front door. That said, the Trojans might be down, but they weren't out, not while they stayed behind their city's massive walls.

In the Greek camp, only the standard of Phtia, Achilles' fief, was at half-mast, mourning Patroklus, Achilles' great friend, fallen to Hector's sword during the *battle at the Greeks ships*. Patroklus, although a nice guy, wasn't high on any of the other Greek City States' lists of the top ten fallen heroes. The Greeks still had their most important asset: Achilles, nonpareil[2] when it came to stabbing and slashing and causing mayhem. For a time, Achilles and the Greek Commander-in-Chief, Agamemnon, king of Mycenæ, had had a falling out and Achilles had retired to his tent to sulk, refusing to take part in further battles and, fatally, letting Patroklus take his place at the *battle at the Greeks ships*. The death of Patroklus brought Achilles out of his tent with a vengeance. After murdering Hector, he spent his time lamenting his lost friend to anyone who cared to listen. Achilles as an ally was an unknown cypher. When push came to shove, would he or wouldn't he?

---

[2]   Equal to non

The Greeks had other troubles besides Achilles; disunity and jealousy within the command structure may have been the main cause of their inability to achieve a decisive victory over Troy.

City and camp were, therefore, eerily quiet, as if both sides had, so to speak, declared bank holidays, to take stock, lick their wounds and decide on what to do next.

It was now lunchtime and I considered whether to go to *The Sign of the Greek Olive Tree,* the only watering hole available to the Greeks, with the advantage of being right on the beach. Despite this attraction, I wasn't too keen to mix with the Greek High Command who would be there in strength: Agamemnon, king of Mycenæ, the richest and largest of the Greek City States, on the plain of Argos in the Peloponnese. As king of Mycenæ, Agamemnon was the natural leader of the Greek Expeditionary Forces. Menelaus, Agamemnon's brother, was king of Sparta, or Laconia, on the west bank of the river Eurotas, through his marriage to Helen, the cause of everyone's present troubles. Odysseus, prince of Ithaca, an island off the west coast of Greece, was by far the ablest of the Greeks commanders. I was scared witless of Odysseus. Nestor, an ancient warrior and a firm adherent of Odysseus, ruled Pylos, a city on the west coast of the Peloponnese. Then there was Idomeneus, ruler of Crete, an island in the Mediterranean southeast of Greece and south west of Asia Minor. Diomedes was the leader of the men of Argos and Tiryns, although I never heard that he had any official title such as king or prince of whatever. I don't really have to say anything about Achilles of Phtia in Thessaly. Everyone knows about Achilles, although not everyone loves him. In fact, since he had no quarrel of his own with Troy, it was debatable what he was doing with the Greek Expeditionary Forces. Me, I think he just liked a good fight. Last but not least, Ajax from the island state of Salamis. Ajax was all brawn and no brains. Like Achilles, a killing machine. And he enjoyed every minute of it. War to Ajax was not about looting, rape or booty but about killing.

There were of course other Greek City States but their leaders had either been killed or just gone home.

Not that I'd ever mingled socially with these gentlemen but, still, what I'd seen of them would last me a long long time. So I stayed quietly on the beach thinking of this and that and how soon the powers-that-be would take themselves off for their post-prandial snoozes, as they soon did. Once they reeled off, I made my way to the bar and jumped up on my usual spot closest to the beach. Eurybates, owner of the establishment, a client of Odysseus of Ithaca and my good pal, came up with my usual water and tuna snacks.

"Hey, Gaius," he greeted me, "how's the cat?" I stopped scarfing tuna for a bit and replied:

"This cat is doing just great. How are all your most important customers?" Eurybates sighed:

"Well, Gaius, unfortunately they're as bad as ever. They're now divided into three camps . . ." I pricked up my ears:

"Three? What do you mean?" Eurybates scratched his ear then started counting on his fingers:

"The first wants to fight it out—for the honor of the Greek City Sates." I sighed:

"Don't tell me—Agamemnon and his ilk." Eurybates sighed too and continued:

"The second: the time for battles is over and a new strategy needed." I shook my head:

"Odysseus and Nestor." Eurybates lifted his eyebrows.

"Of course. And the third: everyone else, hanging around waiting to be told what to do—Diomedes and the rest of them."

"Tell me," I asked, "where does Menelaus come in? What camp does he belong to?" Eurybates shook his head sadly:

"Poor Menelaus! I think he would just like to go back in time and marry the local milkmaid—or anyone but Helen." We both shook our heads in commiseration. I think everyone had a soft spot for Menelaus. He married the most beautiful woman in the world and became king of Sparta. If he could, he would give it all back and start life again as a lowly peasant.

5

I lazed away the afternoon on the beach. Come Happy Hour, I decided to go to the Other Place, Happy Hour at *The Greek Olive Tree* being fraught with tension and peril as the various factions battled it out for dominance, drinking permitting. So off I went to Troy.

◟ 2 ◞

On the Town

The Trojan Horse, just off Priam Square, was a café rather than a bar. The tables were not too close together ensuring clients a modicum of privacy. It was still early when I arrived and the place was pretty quiet. I checked it out. The board listing Troy's top scorers had not been updated since Hector's death; neither had its neighbor, the day's specials. Marianne, the proprietress, ensconced behind the bar, had taken Hector's death hard and probably didn't think updating either board made any sense now that he was gone.

Customers were huddled around their tables, clinging to their mugs as if the Greeks were about to pounce and take their drinks away. I recognized Deiphobus, now Priam's oldest son. No one, not even Deiphobus, thought he would take over Hector's mantle. Helenus, his brother, and Æneas, a leading Trojan aristocrat, completed their table. They all three looked glum. The Trojans may have carried the day in the battle at the Greek ships, or so they said, but it had been at best a Pyrrhic victory[i], since it cost them Hector. There were other Trojan noblemen among the clientele but I didn't really know any of them.

My thoughts went to Paris, another of Priam's lads. I don't know if I'm right but he may have been one of the first guys to be offered a bribe he couldn't refuse. As a lad, Paris was taken to Mount Olympus and told to judge which of the goddesses— Hera, Aphrodite or Pallas Athena—was the fairest. Of course, as in all elections, bribery was rife and each goddess made Paris an offer. The first: he would rule all Asia. The second: he would be victorious in every battle. Third: he would be given the most beautiful woman in the world.

Paris' choice is common knowledge but, hang on, of the three, was the most beautiful girl in the world really the best option? I know I'm a cat but cats aren't stupid. A beautiful lady cat or rule over the whole cat kingdom? No contest. I mean, OK, Helen's good looking but, to have her, Paris gave up being king over all of Asia, and put himself in the way of losing all his battles. Which begs the question: was the Trojan War lost the moment Paris made his choice on Olympus? What if Paris had taken Helen off to, say, the Caribbean?

I take *the world [being] well lost for love*[ii] with a grain of salt. Although I'm sure Mark Anthony, the Roman general, was fond of Cleopatra, the Queen of Egypt, and all that, I doubt he'd gone as far as he did—marriage and a civil war—if she'd been a shepherdess or an upstairs maid. And if Anthony had been an ordinary footslogger in the XV Augusta or whatever, Cleopatra wouldn't have looked at him once, let alone twice. Further, I'd bet a fresh salmon to a sardine that Cleopatra would have shopped Mark Anthony to Octavianus (Cæsar so-called heir) after the debacle at Actium, a disaster Cleopatra blamed on Anthony, had he, Octavianus, given her the least chance.

Yes, Paris' choice tells us tons about Paris.

2.1 Cassandra

I was so deep in my own thoughts I didn't notice somebody sitting down next to me. I looked up. It was Cassandra, also one of Priam's brood. Pretty girl, must be getting on for 25. Beautiful soulful dark eyes—rather spoilt by their wild look—with lovely long lashes. Oval face, high cheekbones, thick brown hair in permanent disarray. Nice figure, too. If I were to find fault, it was with her taste in clothes that tended to flowing, not to say billowing, layers of draperies.

"I've seen you around," she said.

"I," was my dignified response, "am Gaius Marius, a Siamese cross, if you like. You, of course, are Cassandra, the prophetess." Cassandra nodded; she looked bitter.

"I suppose you know all about me. Everyone knows all about me." She turned on me quite savagely. "Don't you tell me I'm crazy! I know what I see will happen! I know it! I know!" Poor girl. A terrible gift indeed, the gift of prophecy along with the curse that no one would ever believe her; punishment, you know, because, after saying 'yes' to the God Apollo, she said 'no'. A bit of overkill. Men are such sore losers and most have no scruples or morals. I said soothingly:

"Yes, I do know all about you. And I know you're dead right. The end of Troy will be just as you say." Cassandra looked at me; it wouldn't be an exaggeration to say her jaw dropped. She squeaked:

"You believe me? You really believe me?" I drew myself up:

"It's not a question of belief, Cassandra. I know." None of us can withstand the temptation to swank and show off. "But tell me, how much detail can you actually see? You say that Troy will be destroyed by fire and it will." No one would believe us, of course, a lady who should have been in the loony bin and an upstart cat. "Who dies and who doesn't? How and when will it all happen?" Cassandra shook her head sadly.

"I can't see that, Gaius Marius, I can only see the horror, the despair. Blood, rivers of blood. And flames. I can see the city enveloped in flames." She stopped and stared as if it was happening before her eyes. "People cut down as they try to flee. Dead and dying on the temple steps, in Priam Square, within the palace, in the streets and alleys. Children, old people." Of course, this is all in a day's work in wartime, no matter when or where, the only question being which side would be on the receiving end.

No doubt, the art of prophecy is fraught with peril. And, frankly, in the present case, knowing the future wouldn't do anyone all that much good. So what if my fellow bar flies knew Troy would be destroyed and how? No one knew when. Tomorrow? Next month? Next year? When would it be time to head for the hills? Further, all that fire and blood pointed to the Greeks getting into the city. But how? That's the rub, you see. The devil, as they say, is in the details.

Cassandra had ordered tea that the aged waiter attached to the establishment now brought over; she sat there stirring it listlessly. She started to cry.

"You don't know what a comfort it is to have someone believe in you," she said between sobs. "I wish I'd paid attention to you earlier. Yet how was I to know? You are, after all, just a cat."

"My dear," I answered, slightly offended by the word 'just'. "I think you were given a real bum deal by Apollo. OK, he gave you a gift but attached a curse. Well, that's the official version. However, to my mind Apollo's real curse was that you would prophecy only bad news. That's why no one believes you. The future, as we all know, is awful enough when it arrives; knowing about it beforehand doesn't really do anything for anyone. Sufficient onto the day is the evil thereof and all that stuff." I patted her hand with my paw. "Now," I continued, "if you were to prophecy, say, that it will be a nice sunny day tomorrow or that the Greeks are going home a week from Tuesday, everyone would love you." Cassandra sniveled. Of course, she didn't have a handkerchief—do women ever? I asked Marianne for a napkin. As Cassandra wiped her tears and blew her nose, I went on:

"You were born in the wrong century, culture and country. Another 3 000 years and on another continent, you'd have had it made—when good news is no news and bad news is great news." Cassandra sniffed.

"That Apollo, he's a right bastard. Is that a way to treat a lady?" I shook my head in commiseration:

"Honey, in 3 000 years, there will be laws that say a lady has every right to say 'no' even if she said 'yes' first. Why, you'd be able to sue and dun that Apollo for millions!"

"Perhaps I will sue," said Cassandra, cheering up slightly, "when all this is over." I drummed my claws on the table.

I had just realized the difference between a seer and a prophet. Now, a seer uses knowledge of the past and present to predict the future. A prophet, on the other hand, has visions that are quite unsubstantiated and impossible to validate. The seer has real-time value in developing strategies leading to positive outcomes while the prophet sees only the outcome. Prophets will never get good press. I turned back to Cassandra who looked slightly miffed and returned to her own predicament.

"What you're saying that my prophecies are no good and people are right not to listen to me." Embarrassing, but that was my point. Then it came to me. Who was it that said:

No man is a prophet in his own town [iii]

Well, something like that. And it made perfect sense. Because if Cassandra emigrated to, say, Sparta or Krete, went into the marketplace and prophesized the fall of Troy, everyone would believe her. She'd probably get her own TV show and be feted by the glitterati. However, in Troy, she was unpopular with everyone who, starting with her family, would like her to disappear. I looked at her sideways. Should I suggest she emigrate? However, I felt this would complicate matters, so instead I said:

"Sorry, love, it's all very frustrating. If the Trojans believed you—as they should since you are dead right—they would head for the hills—now." I crossed my paws in front of me and asked her: "Think, Cassandra, before all the blood and fire, can you see anything? Or, to put it another way, how does all the blood and fire come about?" Cassandra looked at me in annoyance.

11

"I've told you, over and over again, I don't know!" Yes, and that was the rub.

2.2 Helen

"Well, my young sister-in-law. Out on the tiles?" We both looked up. There was Helen, known throughout the ages as Helen of Troy, for reasons I can't fathom, since she in reality was Helen of Sparta. She wore a wispy blue dress with silver trimmings, golden sandals, gold hoop earrings, gold necklaces and a gold bracelet or three, her blue shawl interlaced with gold and silver threads. She looked like a million drachmas. But then, Helen dressed in rags would look like a million drachmas. She made poor Cassandra, with her sweet looks and floating Trojan draperies, positively tatty. Ten years with Helen, Cassandra had learnt nothing from that paragon of women.

Helen was quite tall for a woman in those days, slender, great poise, carried herself like a queen, which, of course, she was. Long blonde hair, lovely waves with golden lights here and there, done in the usual Grecian style; some locks pinned up, others falling around her face and shoulders. She could be going to either a bath or a ball. However, Helen always looked as if she was going to a ball, even on the way to the shower. Blue eyes, in fact, a lot like mine. However, the most remarkable thing about her was her total, absolute and complete self-confidence.

> *'I am that I am and that's who I am.*
> *Bothers you, live with it or move on*
> *I am Helen and Helen means me.'*

Personally, I think her beauty was based on fantastic bone structure; believe it or not, structure is everything, whether you are a castle or a human being. Now, how old was Helen at that time? 18? 30? 50? Impossible to say. Based on her conversation and mindset, she sure wasn't 18; besides, if she were, she would have been about 10 when she left Sparta. She might be any age. Needless to say, I hadn't the guts to ask. Did I say she was graceful? She was. Every movement seemed learned and rehearsed but was not. Helen was born, well, perfect. Ageless and timeless.

Helen sat down without waiting to be asked and without bothering with introductions. She looked at me. "Seen you around, my friend the feline." So much for a cat's invisibility. I stuck out a paw.

"I'm Gaius Marius." I got a finger tap. Helen waved her hand at Marianne and called out:

"Wine and water and go easy on the water." Marianne smiled back and got her act together in a hurry. Royalty is royalty but some are more royal than others. Helen turned to me. "You have to be careful; who knows, the water could be contaminated and not fit to drink." True. Acid rain or bronze dust. In addition, leaving it out of the equation, gives one the chance to drink undiluted wine and get pissed that much faster.

Someone approached our table. I looked up. It was Deiphobus. But before he could open his mouth, Helen waved him away with a scowl. Did I say Helen looked great with a scowl? Well, she did.

"Get lost. No men tonight, except for the tom. I've had enough of men. Piss off!" The poor guy walked back to Helenus and Æneas like a whipped cur. "Men!" continued Helen through gritted teeth. Oh, and she had great teeth too, perfectly shaped and pearly white. Her smile? Sorry, hadn't seen that yet. She turned to me: "Do you know of a country where there aren't any?" I shook my head sadly. Marianne herself brought Helen's drink. She had combed her hair, repaired her makeup and freshened her lipstick. Perhaps she was a candidate for Helen's man-less nation. Would toms be allowed?

"Sorry," I said. "Not on this planet." I was going to suggest Helen join the *Enterprise* and go star trekking with Captain

Kirk and Spock.[3] Surely, there was an empty world somewhere she could have. Gaius, you're losing your marbles. I shook intergalactic travel out of my head. Now was not the time. I continued: "That doesn't mean you couldn't start a man-less nation yourself. Perhaps not a country but an island—an empty one; bound to be one around somewhere." Helen lifted her cup and drained it, waving at Marianne for more:

"Empty?" she sneered. "If it wasn't, I'd soon see to it." We all brooded on this for a bit. Cassandra said, almost timidly.

"I suppose you mean a society only of women, like Penthesileia and her Amazons." Helen leaned backwards, pushed her hair away from her face and sneered:

"Penthesileia, that loser! What is she but a woman who wants to be a man, to win a place in the world by adopting a man's values—fighting wars, killing. Smash and slash. There're plenty of men for that kind of work—and, sorry, sisters, they do it better than we ever could. A warrior woman—useless. Mortifying!" Having thrown Penthesileia under the bus, Helen continued:

"Women should be proud to be women and not pretend they're men. They should do what they're best at— manipulation." We looked at her with blank expressions. She added impatiently: "You know, he gets to decide who wins the Trojan War but I decide where we live, what we wear and eat." Talk about domineering. Poor Cassandra shrank into silence. But Helen wasn't done yet. She continued, looking straight at Cassandra. "And I don't mean getting married or otherwise spreading her legs. That's the road to nowhere." Well, Helen should know. She went on, leaning forward while poor Cassandra cowered into a hypothetical corner: "You're supposed to see the future. Find me an empty island." Cassandra gave her a scared droopy-eyed look:

"After so long in Troy," she answered sulkily, picking at the table cloth, her eyes lowered, "you ought to know that I see what will be. I cannot see what is." Helen sighed impatiently:

---

[3]   *TV series Star Trek*

"Hair splitting, as usual! As for your gift, all you say is that this affair will end badly for Troy. I can tell you that without promising sex to Apollo and then crossing my legs. Troy is on the way to Hades in a handcart." Bit coarse, our Helen. She sighed, leaning her elbows on the table and her chin on her hands. "What you need to predict is how to get us out of this mess." Cassandra opened her mouth but Helen waved her hands. "I know, I know, that's not the way it works. Much good you are to anyone." The conversation sort of died. Cassandra sulked and Helen pondered. To break the silence, I turned to Helen:

"Well, Helen, you could end all this here and now. Why don't you just walk out of Antenorides and down to the Greek camp? Then the Greeks could sail home and that would be that." Cassandra brightened up at once.

"What a lovely idea, Helen. Shall I help you pack? Can I carry your suitcase?" Helen looked down her Grecian nose at the pair of us.

"You wish! Do you really think this war is about me? What simpletons the two of you are!" Cassandra didn't react; she'd probably heard worse. I swished my tail in anger. Who did this broad think she was? Calling me, ME, Gaius Marius, a simpleton. But Helen was oblivious to my ruffled fur and continued: "So you think I could just march down to the Greek camp. I'd go up to Menelaus and prostrate myself before him." She lifted her arms towards the sky and declaimed:

"I have recklessly forgotten your glory, O my husband, and among sinners I have scattered the riches which the gods gave me. And now I cry to you as the Prodigal; I have sinned against you, O merciful husband; receive me as a penitent and make me as one of your hired servants!'

"Menelaus would reply:

'This is my beloved wife, who was dead, and is now alive again; she was lost and now is found.'

"Agamemnon would fall on his knees, arms towards the sky and add:

> *'There shall be more joy in Olympus over one sinner that has repented than over ninety and nine that need no repentance.'* [iv]

"Everyone would cry:

> *'Hallelujah!'*

"And we'd kiss and make up right there and then. All the Greek princes would gather around to share our happiness. Then we'd all go off to the . . . what's the name of that bar on the beach? I can see it from the ramparts."

"*The Greek Olive Tree,*" I answered sourly.

"Right. *The Greek Olive Tree.* They'd kill the fatted calf—providing of course they could find one—and we'd have a great party. You're both invited. Then," she continued, "once we'd recovered from our hangovers, we'd get the ships ready and sail away, back to Greece, where there would be general rejoicing." I frowned. It sounded somewhat familiar. [v] She stopped, then went on: "And we'd all live happily ever after." She turned to us. "Is that the scenario you had in mind?" Well, if ever a lady could ride a tiger, Helen was that lady. Cassandra stared at her, open mouthed. She whined:

"Are you serious?" I sneered at her:

"Of course not, she's having us on." Boy, there was a lot more to Helen than met the eye. I turned to her:

"What you're saying is: even if you were to return to Menelaus, the war would still go on." Helen smiled a feline smile and tweaked my ear. It hurt. I wanted to scratch her but didn't dare.

"Aren't you my clever pussycat! Spot on."

"Well," I continued thoughtfully. "I always suspected there were wheels within wheels, so to speak, but I've not been able to put my finger on it." Helen became more feline still:

"Have you ever looked at the geographical position of Troy on a map?" I said I had but couldn't quite remember. "Well, my sweet puss, if you do, you will see that Troy sits right smack overlooking the Hellespont, the strait that links the Ægean to the inland Sea of Marmara."

"The Dardanelles," I mused. "There will be a very horrible battle there in about 3 000 years[4]. Lots and lots of soldiers will die." However, Helen's only interest in the Hellespont was what would happen there in the next month or so. She ignored future wars and casualties—sufficient onto the day is the evil thereof— and went on:

"Now, a lot of trading is done on the northern shore the Sea of Marmara. There are copper mines and I don't have you tell how significant copper is in this day and age." I was starting to get her drift—all the warriors, Greek and Trojan, wore bronze armor and carried bronze weapons. "My darling Papa-in-law or, if you prefer, Priam, has been lording it over the Hellespont for decades. No one goes in, no one comes out without his say so and his say so depends on payment of a hefty fee. To add insult to injury, all ships entering the straits had to take on a Trojan pilot—at a cost. More money in the kitty. And don't forget taxes on imports and exports. In fact, the Hellespont is a cash cow." She leaned across the table: "What do you think the Greek take is on this?" Now I did see. For the Greeks, it was clearly a matter of DELENDA EST TROIA [vi]—Troy must be destroyed. Cassandra got huffy:

"Traders could come ashore along the coast south of Troy and reach the Sea of Marmara by going overland," she said but Helen just sneered:

"Yeah, they would beach their vessels a long way away to avoid the Trojan patrols. I can just see my darling husband and his brave brother, to say nothing of our other valiant Greek boys, slogging it through Anatolia. It's hot in summer and cold in

---

[4]   *Battle of Gallipoli, World War I, 1914-1918*

winter. There are mountains. And, believe you me, it's a damned long way."

"So, you're telling me," I said, "that the Greek occupation of Troy is the ultimate objective of that lot down on the Dardan plain? And they're not leaving until Troy is Greek and they control the Hellespont and collect the loot?" I could hear the Greek cash registers going full throttle. Helen continued smiling:

"My, you're a fast learner." I rested my head on my paw. I could see what Helen was aiming at but there were still problems with her theory. I extrapolated:

"But if it's all so obvious, why do the Trojans keep insisting it's all about you? They could just negotiate with the Greeks and come to some sort of compromise." Helen answered pensively, her nails tapping on the tabletop:

"I'm not too sure. Trouble is, Troy doesn't have an Odysseus; Hector's strongest suit—forgive the pun—was doing battle in the old way—thrust and stab. Hector, bless him, was short on brainpower." She continued thoughtfully. "Perhaps neither side wants to confess it's all about greed—keep the masses keen on the honor and glory business and a wronged lady." She pointed to herself. "That's me." My, I would never have guessed. "But now that Hector is no more, I don't think this lot knows which way is up or what to do next." She turned again to Cassandra. "What good did it do your Daddy to have fifty sons if only one was of any use at all?" Cassandra started to cry. Marianne came running with another serviette. Cassandra sobbed into it.

"You're so mean about my family. And we've tried to make you feel welcome and give you a good home and look what it's cost us." Helen fanned herself with her hand.

"Spare me. I came here under duress—well, sort of. Your mother hates me, and who can blame her? Andromache thinks I'm a tramp and you think I'm a curse from Apollo." Andromache was Hector's widow. We all pondered for a bit. Cassandra continued sniveling. She was not really into geopolitics, political economy or political sciences. I didn't think she was much good at abstract thought at all. With Cassandra,

18

it was all personal. I waved at Marianne for drinks all round—one tea, one designer water—scratch that, I needed something stronger at this point, two wines-and-water. When we'd all been served, I said to Helen:

"Now, I agree that everything you say is very relevant but I don't think we can forget or ignore your part. After all, you are the daughter of a God." For a moment, I thought she was going to throw her wine in my face but then decided it would be wasting tolerable wine on cheap revenge. Instead, she sneered. A great sneerer, our Helen.

"Don't tell me you buy that crap." I twitched.

"Not really, but I thought you did." She threw up her hands.

"It's unbelievable. Every Tom, Dick and Harry in Troy and Greece are descended from a God. Why, at that rate, the gods would have to spend their entire time begetting." Well, those people in the Old Testament did, too. It must be a God-thing. Helen continued in outrage: "So many idiots want to raise themselves above the common herd. No way is Achilles going to admit his bloodline's no better than the scurviest of his camp followers. What arrant nonsense! I have no patience with such pretensions." Well, here was a lady with a chip on her shoulder for sure. She continued drumming her fingers on the table. I asked carefully:

"What about Leda and the swan?" Helen laughed.

"If a gal wants to cheat on a boring husband, what better way to cover her tracks than talking about the Gods? I can hear Ma saying to Pa when he got back from one of those eternal wars: 'My dear, I had the most curious encounter with this swan. You'll never believe it.' The husband would go around preening himself that he was the adoptive father of a God's offspring. What an idiot!" Julius Cæsar would not have liked Helen. Descent from Aphrodite was central to his creed. Silence fell as we applied ourselves to our drinks.

Then Helen resurfaced: "Let me tell you what it's like to be a beautiful woman. You do think I'm a beautiful woman, don't you?" She asked. I answered cagily:

"Well, everyone says you are and I take everyone's word for it. However, you need to understand that to a cat beauty takes on other forms. For instance, I don't like your ears. They're in the wrong place and the wrong shape. Also, your nose is enormous; a cat has a cute little button that, to my taste, should be black and covered in white fur. Also . . ." But Helen cut me off.

"OK, OK, point taken. From the purely human point of view, I am beautiful and my ears and nose are perfect. Do you know what happens to a beautiful girl?" I shook my head; I was sure I was about to find out. Helen leaned back and went on. "When I was in my early teens, Theseus abducted me. Why? Because I was clever? Spoke five languages? Understood Euclid's' theorem? A wonderful conversationalist? None of the above. The one, the only, reason: I was beautiful. I was an object of desire, a trophy, a Praxiteles sculpture, a prized possession; I gave a man status if he happened to own me. Fortunately, Theseus had business in the underworld and while he was away my brothers rescued me." She continued thoughtfully.

"I came home to Sparta. My Dad was not happy to see me. He said I was more trouble than I was worth and he was fed up with protecting me from lecherous men." Helen drummed the fingers of one hand on the table, the other holding up her chin. The she continued in a Freudian vein: "It's so nice to have parents who really care about you. Dad said he would get rid of me by marrying me off." Curious how it always comes back to the parents. However, one can only sympathize with poor old Dad. A beautiful daughter may be as difficult to get rid of as a plain one. Helen continued: "Of course, all the princelings in Greece came running. Did you ask why?" I hadn't but humored her:

"Why?" Helen shook her blond locks back.

"It might have been my skill at weaving or because I was a thrifty housekeeper. Or even my perfect embroidery. Not that I had any of these or other household skills. Why bother teaching a beautiful girl to keep house? After all, she's beautiful. What else does she need?" She took a swig at her wine, waved her mug, calling for more. "It was an added plus that I was the heir to Sparta, my brothers having gone off on adventures the Gods only know where." She grabbed the mug from Marianne's hand, took a swig and went on: "I wasn't given an education. What for? I didn't need to read or write or think. I would make a splendid marriage. To have men admire me was the only skill I needed." I signaled to Marianne to leave the jug on the table. Helen went on, somewhat dreamily. "There is a positive side, you know. I don't have to please men. They have to please me!"

"It must have been very frustrating for you," I said soothingly.

"There's no greater curse for a clever woman than to be beautiful. You can take my word for it. Anyhow, everyone wanted to marry me except Agamemnon—thank the Gods— what an idiot that man is; he married my sister Clytemnestra and may they have joy of each other. Odysseus, of course, was married to that drip Penelope." She stopped. "I wouldn't have minded Odysseus. He's the cleverest of the whole bunch." Tell me something I don't know. "So, in the end, I got stuck with Menelaus. So much for a splendid marriage. He, if you please, became King of Sparta. I should have been queen regnant and he prince consort. He reigned, if you please, while I stayed with the children. And, mind you, a woman's lot in Sparta is a sight better than in the rest of Greece."

"So," I said, "when Paris turned up, you decided to give it all a miss and follow your dream of love." I thought Helen was going to rip my head off. Instead, she guffawed and almost choked on her wine. Once she caught her breath, she laughed until she cried. Having sort of collected herself, she said.

"Dream of love? You gotta be joking. That idiot boy who fancies himself because he thinks he's good looking, every girl's idol! Oh, he's OK as a toy boy, not bad in bed and so on but pure concrete from the nose up. Try having any sort of conversation with him that isn't about his looks, his horses or his dogs. And," she added with a sideways glance, "he doesn't like cats." My heart was about to break but then I remembered I didn't like him

21

much either. Helen continued: "And, I'm sure you've figured out I didn't expect the arrangement to be permanent. More like a month's holiday to which I thought I was entitled."

"Well," I said, "you could have gone somewhere with Menelaus, couldn't you? Week at the seaside with the kids? Why take off with some moron? And did you leave a note?" Helen looked at me as if I had come in last in the spelling bee.

"You don't know much, do you? Husbands never take their wives anywhere. No, and I didn't leave a note." She laughed. "I can just hear Menelaus if I said I wanted to go on holiday: 'Honey, how would you like to come along on our next campaign? It'll be such fun, you'll see muddy fields and men pushing against each other',"—like Sumo wrestlers?—"'in the good old hoplite fashion'." Helen sighed and spread her arms. "I wanted to see the world, to meet different people, to learn of cultures beyond my own which, let me assure you, is nothing to write home about." She looked dreamily into nowhere. "To sit at the feet of the great philosophers and drink in their wisdom." Sorry, honey, they haven't been born yet.

"And then," continued Helen bringing us back to the real world with a bump, "before you could say Jack Robinson, Troy is besieged and I'm stuck and it seems I'll be here to the end of days. I'm sick of Troy. I've seen everything there is to see twenty times over and I've exhausted all possibilities of meaningful conversations!" Cassandra looked up:

"Considering," she said with the first bit of spirit she'd shown, "the size of my family, it doesn't seem possible you've run out of people to converse with, even in ten years."

"Yes," agreed Helen nastily, "but they're dying at such a fast rate it's impossible to form a lasting relationship." Cassandra sniffed and Helen went on: "To tell you the truth, I despise all men. I've never known one I wouldn't happily put through a meat grinder. So here I am in Troy—and what does it matter anyway? One needs to be somewhere, after all. In addition, I've had the chance of making the Trojans miserable—for daring to say they abducted me—as if they could—as well as the Greeks for belittling me. A plague on both their houses."[vii] She turned to Cassandra: "Just you wait till the city falls. You will survive. Good-looking girls always do; you'll become a sex slave for some depraved Greek." Cassandra didn't look as if she thought this would be a good career move.

"I think I'd rather die," she said mournfully.

"Well, you won't," was Helen's brutal answer, "but you'll wish you had."

So, there it was: the gospel according to Helen. Mind you, I'm not saying she didn't have a point or even three. And if it was revenge she wanted, she sure was getting it in spades.

2.3 *Laodicea*

As we sat brooding and drinking, there was a sniff next to us. Not a Helen sniff signifying disdain or a Cassandra sniff meaning she hadn't finished crying. It was a disapproving sniff. I looked up. There stood what humans would call a statuesque blonde. Tall, curvy, arms akimbo, staring down at our little party. Helen reacted first. She smiled nastily as only Helen can. Turning to me, she said:

"Gaius, I don't believe you've met my sister-in-law, Laodicea." Another of Priam's output.

"Seen her around," was my answer. But Laodicea wasn't interested in introductions. Turning to Helen, she said, her voice dripping displeasure:

"Really, Helen, I would have hoped to see you behaving with a bit more dignity. If for no other reason, to avoid shaming my royal father who has shown you every consideration and has treated you like a daughter." Helen cocked her head:

"Izzatso?" She leaned, one hand on the table, the other elbow over the back of her chair and looked up at Laodicea. I could see the rage behind Laodicea's cool façade. She went on haughtily:

"You are not behaving like a lady. Coming out in public with that . . . that . . . disreputable . . . animal!" Helen and I laughed until we almost choked and Cassandra had to pat me on the back. "And," continued Laodicea trembling with rage, "bringing my pure virginal little sister with you!" Helen waved an arm at the waiter and he came running with another chair.

"And, oh," said Helen to the waiter, "bring some more wine, water on the side." She forced Laodicea to sit. "If you don't," she threatened, "I'll make such a rumpus they'll hear it down in the Greek camp." Laodicea looked close to tears but held them in.

"You wouldn't," she said in a low voice. "Have you no pride?" Helen poured her a mugful and laughed some more:

"No, sweet Laodicea, I haven't. And let me tell you, the time for pride is over. Drink up, my sweet, for next week we will die. It may be next month, if you like, but doomed we are; ask you little sister." Seeing no way out, Laodicea sat down and downed her allowance of wine. I looked at them. Both blonde, with perfect bodies and beautiful faces. Was Helen more beautiful than Laodicea? I pondered. Then it came to me. Laodicea was all ice while Helen was fire and ice, with very little in between. This gave Helen an interior glow that Laodicea would never have. And that made all the difference.

Our meeting broke up shortly thereafter, perhaps as the wine jug was empty again. Anyhow, there didn't seem to be anything left to say. I walked them back to the palace steps and saw the three of them go up. Nice girls all. No fault of Laodicea's if she seemed to have swallowed a poker. As I walked away, I thought that, had either the Greek or Trojan side put Helen in charge, this thing would have been over long ago. A song kept going through my head but the words seemed to have curiously changed:

She came up from Sparta with Paris to Troy
More for the thrill not so much for the boy
Well, ev'ry woman is entitled a toy
That's why the lady is a tramp.
Doesn't go clubbing with Trojans or Greeks

C'mpany of men is not what she seeks
In fact, she'd be happy not to see one for weeks
That's why the lady is a tramp[viii].

That was the burning question: was she or wasn't she? Well, five thousand years on, they're still arguing. Messieurs, Mesdames, faitês vos jeux. Rien ne va plus.[5]

---

[5]   *Roulette*: the wheel is spinning: no further bets

❧ 3 ☙

Profiling for Success

Next morning, as I lay quietly beneath my tree getting my twenty hours, an unpleasant odor invaded my sensitive nostrils. Human, I knew at once. Unwashed clothes and other unwasheds it wouldn't do to think about. I cocked an eye. And there was Odysseus, inflicting his company where it was certainly not wanted. Despite my cool non-welcome, he sat down next to me, knees up, arms around knees. I eyed him askance. We stared at each other; since he had sought me out, he should speak first. The silence went on for a few minutes. Then he gave in and said, not without some pride:

"I," hand on his chest, "am Odysseus, Lord of Ithaca." I answered, not less haughtily:

"And I am Gaius Marius,[ix] nine times consul of the Roman Republic and imperator[6]." Well, it might have being eight but who'd be counting? Odysseus raised his eyebrows and I could read his thoughts: 'Some animal association or other. Nothing to worry about—I hope!' We sat in silence for a bit. The conversation seemed to have died away. Although I wanted to

---

6   *Roman army troops in the field would proclaim their commander imperator after an important victory.*

know what business the Prince of Ithaca could have with a cat, I sure wasn't going to ask. Again, Odysseus blinked first:

"Seen lots of cats,"—well, not surprising since there were a fair number in and around Troy—"but you sort of stand out." I sat up as straight as I could, nose in air:

"That," I answered haughtily, "is because I am a cat of Siamese descent—look at my blue eyes and the curious dark patches on my white coat. Also, I am fairly large for a cat." I looked straight at him—top that, you plebe! Odysseus scratched his beard—not been trimmed for some weeks. Then he decided to forget about the niceties and get down to business:

"Well, Gaius, let's cut to the chase. We are having this conversation because all my human confederates have turned out to be wanting—in one sense or another. Oh, stalwart fellows, all. Most just have a few screws missing in the upper story. Nurture or nature, who's to say?" He sighed. It was now my turn to raise my eyebrows—was the nurture or nature concept this ancient?

We fell silent and communed with ourselves on the travails of family life. With cats, of course, Dad does his bit then disappears and Mum takes care of the kids until she's fed up when she throws them out to fend for themselves. Most do o.k. There are enough human bleeding hearts around to care for lots of sad eyed cute irresistible kittens. Odysseus continued thoughtfully:

"Diomedes and Idomeneus are o.k. but they'll never set the Aegean on fire. Tell them what to do and they'll do it to the best of their abilities. No direct orders, they'll just sit on the beach. Now, Menelaus, a good fellow, stout heart and all that but he carries too much baggage . . ." Odysseus added as an afterthought: "And the less said of Agamemnon, our Supreme Leader, the better." A tad longer silence. The he continued: "And the less said about Achilles and Ajax the better." I nodded and added:

"I am an outsider, but it seems to me the only strategy you Greeks ever had was to kill Hector and, there you have it, Hector is dead! Your aim achieved, why haven't you won the war?

27

Why are you still here?" I sneered at him. "What will your next strategy be? And will implementation take another nine years?" Odysseus laughed silently and mirthlessly.

"Don't smart ass me!" His voice wasn't pleasant. I got defensive:

"Well, what's the alternative? Or did you think once Hector was goners, Priam would just hand the Greeks the key to Antenorides and welcome you all in?" Odysseus looked at me sideways rather nastily:

"I hope you know what happens to smart-alley cat!" I sneered in turn:

"Considering your track record so far, I'm not worried. After all, I have nine lives. Hector only had one. So, based on past statistics, killing me would take 9x9 attempts, or about 81 years." I laughed myself sick and had a nasty coughing fit. Odysseus looked at me with a marked lack of sympathy, merely rubbing his hands. He said:

"I must confess I'm not too thrilled with our past and present stratagems and strategies . . ." I interrupted him:

"You've put all your eggs in one basket, the Achilles basket; dangerous, you know; once that basket is empty, you've no alternatives." Odysseys ground his teeth:

"No one can out-Achilles Achilles though many have tried. He's a pest and a nuisance and totally untrustworthy. But while he's around, the Greeks are unbeatable. Yes, Achilles, pain though he is, has his uses." I sneered:

"You don't really believe Achilles will eventually hand you victory on a silver platter. One man—no matter how strong and skilled—is not the key to success." Odysseus looked as if he were about to start pulling his hair out by the roots:

"I know it, you know it, but the rest of my pals still believe Achilles will save the day." I curled my lip:

"It might still happen. Who knows? Wonders will never cease." I countered: "But one day Achilles will fall. Where then will the Greeks hang their helmets? What will keep them going?" Odysseus grounded his teeth, got up and left. I didn't miss him. I curled up and went back to sleep.

Of course, it couldn't last. One afternoon, a few days later, as I was snoozing under my tree I was suddenly and unreasonably prodded in the ribs by a dirty finger. I shook myself and opened my eyes cautiously. It was, of course, Odysseus. Back again. I hadn't missed him.

"We will win this war," he announced, poking at me again, "with the most formidable weapon known to man—or cat, for that matter: information!" I felt a bit fogged as I tried to drag myself out of the haze of sleep. I was also feeling grouchy:

"What do you mean?" I asked in a surly voice. "Information? About what?" I shook my head and continued: "Do you want to know how many warriors are left in Troy, how many allies they still have or who's going to take Hector's place and is that guy going to be any good?" Odysseus shook his head, and answered emphatically:

"No, no, no! Aren't you listening? We don't need military information, we've got that in spades and it's never done us any good." Another prod. "Really, Gaius, I thought you would understand. We are entering the realm of psychological warfare. What I want is a psychological profile of the Trojan man-in-the-street: how does he see the war effort—or lack of it. What is his breaking point, the moment when he just can't take anymore? What is the straw that will break the camel's back?" He stopped and added glumly:

"I thought it would be Hector's death but I was wrong. Everyone cried and flocked to the funeral but nothing changed. Rather disappointing," he concluded sadly, adding: "I bet there was an open bar after the funeral." I know what he meant, of course, but his mistake was confusing Trojans with Greeks. Greeks will do anything for a free drink while the Trojans truly loved and mourned Hector. I sat up, cleaned the sand off my paws, and asked:

"So, how do you propose to set about gathering this information? I suppose you'll send in spies, clever fellows in trench coats who lurk about, make notes and send up flares." Odysseus looked at me in a pitying sort of way.

29

"You've been around long enough; haven't you noticed a marked shortage of brain power among the Greeks? Whom could I use? Diomedes? Ajax?" I sniggered. Ajax as a secret agent? Wearing a tuxedo and ordering martinis—stirred not shaken? As if he could tell the difference! I could just hear him saying: "Salamis. Ajax of Salamis," pulling his shirt cuffs down. It would be such fun. I warmed to my subject.

"You, for instance. I'm sure you'd make a superb spy." Odysseus sighed and said, as if he hated to admit it:

"Been there, tried it. Didn't work." After another deep sigh, he went on: "Falling back on that well-known maxim: *if you want something done properly, do it yourself*, I dressed myself in rags and, looking like a dirty old man, actually got into Troy. I was there for a week. No good. The problem is that no one talks to dirty old men and what information, rumors or gossip I picked up on the street just hanging around was useless. So, no, I need someone who is invisible, who can get in anywhere. Who is never out of place, whether in a palace, temple, hovel or street—in short, a cat!" I frowned, as best a cat can and lifted a paw in what I hoped was dignified protest:

"Wait a minute, hang in there. You're asking Me to help You? Why should I? Don't you know anything about cats? They walk alone. They don't do anybody's bidding. They care for no one. They have no loyalty." It sounded terrific. He was sure to give up. On the contrary, it just egged him on.

"But don't you see?" he cried. "That's just the point. As you say, a cat has no loyalty. You can hang around, snoop everywhere and into everything, as you've been doing with the Greek High Command, for that matter, don't think I haven't noticed you. It just proves my point; no one thinks anything of it and if they do, they'll think you're stealing food. They'll say: 'It's a cat. Give him some milk and he'll go away'." I hissed and raised my hackles in displeasure. This sort of profiling really pisses me off. I hate milk. Never touch it. I pursed my lips as a sign of disapproval.

"I suppose you think you're very clever," I sneered, "trying to make me your cat's paw. For starters, I have no idea what you're on about! Psychological profiling? What's that when it's at home with its feet up? And how will knowing what the cobbler, the baker and the candlestick maker—to say nothing of the little boy who lives down the lane—think of it all help bring down Troy?" Odysseus sneered back at me but in a friendly way:

"Cute, aren't you?" He looked at me thoughtfully, then continued: "all those days you were hanging about *The Greek Olive Tree* I actually thought you might be a Trojan spy. And you know what? Had you told anyone in Troy what you heard, perhaps the lot of us would be sailing home at this moment." Or feeding the fishes. It was my turn to sneer, but not in a nice way:

"Don't try to butter me up, pal. Why should I tell anyone what I hear or see? As for the outcome of this buffoonery you Greeks and Trojans are putting on, I don't care one little bit." But Odysseus was far away:

"Cats," he continued with enthusiasm, "are just perfect for intelligence work: they are sneaky, evil, cruel and completely amoral."

"Yeah," I drawled. "And we have many other fine qualities as well."

"No, doubt, no doubt," answered Odysseus. "So what do you say? Have we got a deal?" I held up a paw.

"Don't forget," I cautioned him, "I know lots of people in Troy. No way I'm the invisible cat you want." Of course, he wasn't listening; he just went on:

"First, let me brief you on intelligence. There are three stages:" He held up his hand, ticking dirty fingers off as he went through the list.

"Acquisition: visual and auditory surveillance, and/or interception of data. Delivery: agent (you) to handler (me).

"The faster information reaches the handler, the more valuable it is. I'm not interested in what Priam had for dinner two months ago, while what he had yesterday could be pertinent.

> *"Validation: I must be able to trust the information I get since*
> *I won't be able to verify whether any of it is true."*

Well, isn't that my clever little Greek. He went on:
"The next two stages are not your concern:

> *"Interpretation—how the data can be used strategically*

and last but not least:

> *"Implementation of the strategic plan developed based on the data."*

He waggled a finger at me. Odysseus was a great finger waggler.

"Remember: you don't judge what may or may not be relevant." That might be very true but in actual fact he'd only hear whatever I chose to tell him. You hires a cat, you takes your chances. He went on blissfully: "I need to know everything that's going on in the city. No detail is too small or too unimportant." Talk about being over-confident. He clapped his hands.

"Ok, let's get this show on the road. What do you need: slate and stylus?" I shook my head. I didn't tell him about the voice-activated recorder or the return ticket in my back pocket. He continued: "Do we have a deal?" He stretched out his hand. I hit it with a closed paw. Deal? You make deals with cats at your peril. However, I did make one condition:

"This is just between you and me," I said sternly. "I don't want anything to do with that gaggle of geese you hang out with. I see any of them, I'm out of here." He laughed as if I'd come out with a clever joke.

"That's just great. I don't want a gaggle of geese around either. They honk at all the wrong times, and are useless when it comes to intelligence gathering. For that, two is the perfect number." How cozy; we were all agreed. Odysseus dragged me off to *The Green Olive Tree* and paid for a very c-three tea

Eurybates rustled up. (The Greeks know nothing about tea; in fact, they can hardly be called civilized at all.)

After getting rid of him, I considered the whole proposition. Why should I become Odysseus' cat's paw?[x] Well, that story never did ring true because cats don't like chestnuts and certainly don't do favors that may prove dangerous to themselves. The cat, in fact, is your typical psychopath. It's all about the cat; it does not feel empathy, has no sense of right or wrong or any sensitivity towards other species.

Anyhow, I decided that I might as well go to Troy as not. And why? First of all, I would only do what I wanted to do. Cats have no honor. Of course, there was another underlying reason: curiosity. I did want to know what was really going on inside Troy. Having come this far, I just couldn't leave during the first interval, so to speak. If the Trojans won—what a scoop! And after everything I had learnt from Helen and Cassandra, I thought I might get a deeper insight into Troy and its ultimate fate.

I left the beach just before sundown. I ignored the paved road that curled up the hill to Antenorides and instead ran silently through the grass and weeds towards the great city wall. Having arrived, I considered the walls of Troy. They were thick. They were massive. The foundations, I had been told, went deep into the ground. However, there is no way of making a city impregnable against rats, mice, diverse bugs—and cats.

Just by Antenorides, there was a cunning bolt hole, too small for humans to worry about, drilled by crumbling stone and helped along by centuries of gnawing sharp little teeth. I thought I heard scuffling as I went through. I stopped to listen but the noise ceased. I sniffed. Mice and cats. What else. If mice, to be quite frank, I don't 'do' mice. I don't like the blood or the possibility of chocking on those tiny bones.

~ 4 ~

Cat among the Trojans

Once inside the city, a bit at a loss as to my next move, I walked aimlessly around the residential area of which I had seen little. The place was uncanny in the creeping dusk. Many houses were dark and forlorn and, here and there, obviously empty and noticeably in decay. Gardens were uncared for, dusty and desolate, with weeds running rampant. A few maple trees survived with, here and there, a dusty olive tree. I could smell hopelessness and fear in the air. The toll of war on a community. One way or another, this would soon become a ghost town, all ready for Heinrich Schliemann[xi] to find in about three thousand years' time. Yet, a month or so ago, Troy had been quite an upbeat place, people apparently happy enough, given the circumstances, with the usual hustle and bustle common to city life. But, with Hector's death, reality had set in with extreme severity.

I came to what must have been a fine house in bygone days. Now, its walls were crumbling; the house itself was minus its roof and most of the upper floor had collapsed and a forlorn balcony was about to lose its struggle with gravity. Then I spotted a large ginger cat lying on a part of the outer wall still standing. I sat down on the pavement and we stared at each other for some moments. I was surprised Mr Ginger wasn't hissing or showing himself otherwise territorial.

"If you call me Ginger," he suddenly said, "this will not be the beginning of a beautiful friendship." When I'd recovered from the initial surprise, I said hastily:

"Wouldn't dream of it. I'm Gaius Marius."

"I," said Mr Ginger, licking a paw, "am Cælius. Are you going to give yourself airs and graces because you're part Siamese?" As I told Odysseus, there is certainly Siamese somewhere in my family tree and, OK, I am a bit snooty about it. Everyone wants to come from a distinguished family. I like to pretend Cleopatra's favorite cat was an ancestor of mine. However . . .

"Certainly not," I said with dignity, "I abhor pride of any sort."

"True," answered Cælius. "Pride, as they say, goes before a fall." Amazing, there's nothing new under the sun. "So tell me," he continued, "what are you doing in our fair city of Troy?" I looked around.

"It must certainly have been a very handsome city in its time," I said evasively. Cælius replied, with a sigh:

"There's no limit to the mess humans can make once they put what they call their minds to it."

"I came out for the weekend," I went on. "I've had a very exciting time. I was here when Hector died." Cælius scratched his ear thoughtfully.

"Yes, I thought the end had come and was all packed up and ready to be off. But the Greeks seem as stupid as our lot. At this rate, another ten years could be on the books."

At that moment, a dog came running up; I went into attack mode immediately, making my tail twice as thick as it really was, curving my spine, hackles up, baring my teeth and giving my most ferocious hiss. Cælius gave a short laugh.

"OK, Ok, just take it easy. This is Betsy. She's one of our scouts." Betsy wagged her tail, not that she had much of one, sat down and said:

"Hi. New around here?"

"This is Gaius Marius," said Cælius. "He's here for the weekend." Betsy tittered.

"Is that so? It must have been a really cheap holiday package. Why bother otherwise? Did you get a free rental chariot thrown in?"

"Now, Betsy," Cælius waggled a paw at her. "Cut the comedy bit." Then they both looked at me. I looked back, bemused. What was this all about? A dog and a cat on friendly terms? No growling or fighting, no eyes scratched out? Can't believe it—perhaps Darwin's evolutionary theory hadn't set in yet.

"Please forgive me," I said at last, trying to recover my wits. "This has really taken me by surprise. Is this a Troy thing? Have cats and dogs evolved into friends and allies?" Betsy and Cælius almost split themselves laughing.

"My dear Gaius Marius," Cælius said as soon as he could say anything. "I suppose it does look odd, doesn't it? But I'm not going to explain now. Just remember: politics make strange bedfellows. Come along and you'll see for yourself." He jumped elegantly into the street and walked off with Betsy. I trailed behind.

Now, while there's a moment, let me describe my new friends. Cælius was a large cat, his coat light ginger with dark ginger and white stripes. He carried himself with a dignity worthy of Agamemnon. In fact, as commander-in-chiefs go, I was to find Cælius a cut above the worthy king of Mycenæ. Betsy was one of those ugly dogs that, for reasons unknown, are called 'cute'. She was a medium sized boxer, all light and dark browns with a snub squashed-in nose and black muzzle and let's not forget the soulful eyes and floppy ears. But there was nothing soulful about Betsy. I never saw her stop to meditate or even think before she jumped. With Betsy, as I was to find out, it was all go, go, go, never a dull moment. Take my advice and steer clear of her.

We wandered on, crossed Priam Square and, just by the temple steps, turned into an alley, which led to a small square, liberally endowed with bits of broken statues and pediments, columns and what not. Betsy said:

"This is where the temple priest repaired temple property. Obviously, there has been scant enthusiasm for any kind of temple upkeep since the war began and this alley is more or less abandoned. So, we took over the shed." She waved a paw at a rickety building stuck in a corner

We made our way inside and I must say I did not expect to find what I found there.

4.1 An Early Warning System

The shed was crowded with animals of all sorts: more cats and dogs, chickens and a couple of roosters, ducks, geese and swans, a large number of rats and mice, a donkey or two and pigeons, sparrows, crows, seagulls, a few hummingbirds, plus other birds I couldn't put a name to. A number of owls sat in stately fashion on damaged statues or columns. The noise of barking, mewing, cackling, chirping, honking, hooting and braying was deafening.

Cælius jumped lightly onto an upside-down sarcophagus, indicating with his paw I should sit in front of him so I faced the crowd. He then waved a paw for silence.

"Hi, everyone," he called. There was a chorus of answers. "This," pointing a paw at me, "is Gaius Marius. He's a tourist. Please don't bite, kick, peck or nibble him. After all, you know how important it is to encourage tourism." When the laughter had died down, he continued, this time to me: "And the same goes for you, Gaius Marius; no scratching, biting, hissing or eating." As if I would. A street cat I am not.

"Now," he went on, "before we begin, a few words of explanation for our guest." Everybody settled down comfortably. Cælius stroked his whiskers and began: "You will know, if you are an educated cat, Gaius Marius, that when there are earthquakes or tsunamis or a besieged city falls, in fact, before any natural or manmade disasters, the animals will have left long before the first blow strikes. In the early days of this war, besides a couple of minor earthquakes no one took seriously, on a number of occasions we thought the end had come for Troy. We all headed for the hills, only to find that, at the end of the day, the Greeks where still on the plain and the Trojans in the city. So we all went back home again.

"After three times or so, we decided we were not acting but reacting. If we didn't get organized, we would be spending the rest of the war packing and unpacking, going and coming back. Further, all the allarums and excursions were getting on our nerves. We needed a new strategy that would ensure we left only when essential. We needed to be able to predict, with fair warning, when the city was about to fall." Cælius took a sip of water from a bowl next to him. He continued:

"The war has now dragged on for nine years. The Greeks bring siege towers, huge ladders and such up to the walls and make a great deal of noise. They shoot arrows, incendiary and otherwise, that fall short of the ramparts. The Trojans don't need siege engines, of course; they throw stones and burning oil and stuff from the ramparts on the Greeks below. In fact, Gaius Marius, the city isn't fit for beast or bird. Trojan and Greek arrows have killed a number of dogs, cats and rats, to say nothing of the boiling oil and stones raining from the ramparts. A couple of our elderly have died of heart failure. Very sad." He paused, shaking his head. Dead silence as the audience waited for him to continue.

"So, all the free animals of Troy entered into a covenant to safeguard their mutual interests and increase everyone's chance of survival. Rule one: no inter-species fighting; two, food and other necessities shared, according to each individual's needs; three, setting up an early warning system so we know when the end is near and can get away. We are, in fact, an escape committee, if you like. Each animal has his or her specific task.

"Our strategy is based on past events that prove the Greeks will never be able to scale Troy's walls. That leaves the gates as the weakest links in Troy's chain of defenses and it is there we are concentrating our efforts. At each, we have a team of observers: a cat in overall command, mice and rats to gather information, a dog for security. Other dogs do general dog's body work—no offence meant to our doggie friends. Dog runners carry messages between HQ—me, wherever I happen to be," he added, trying to look modest, "as well as other errands." Betsy whispered:

"Yeah, getting snacks and that sort of thing." Very proper, I thought. Cælius went on:

"There's also an air patrol coordinated by the seagulls. Donkeys roam the streets of Troy and wander in and around the Greek camp, checking troop movements. Horses act as military advisors as they have actual battle experience." He paused and said directly to me: "OK, I hope this is clear, Gaius Marius." As mud, thought I. Cælius then continued: "Now, for our debriefing: as I call each gate and cat, please give an update on the situation at his—or her—station.

"Tymbria, Palamedes." Tymbria was the gate nearest the cliffs overlooking the Hellespont; Palamedes was a medium-sized black and white tom.

"Well," drawled Palamedes, "the Greeks at the camp up the hill got a bit noisy last night. Couldn't imagine what they were up to. Dirty songs and all into the wee hours. I thought it might be a diversionary tactic before some really nasty attack; so I sent a few of the rats to check it out." He stopped and glared at the rats on his left. "They came back with the milk and went straight on the sick list with upset tummies—from overeating." Despite his nasty looks, the rats pretending this had nothing to do with them. Palamedes went on sternly: "I am still considering disciplinary action." Cælius raised his eyebrows:

"As it turned out to have been just a party after all, I would forget it if I were you." The rats looked pleased but Palamedes frowned. Cælius passed on to the next point on his agenda:

"Helia, Daphne." Helia was a small gate on the north side of the city and Daphne a white lady cat dotted with black spots. Daphne seemed extremely laid back. I'm not sure she hadn't been snoozing as I saw a rat prod her when Cælius called out her name. She said:

"We had the usual comings and goings," stretching lazily. "Mostly at night. A few couriers from the cities inland arrived and some Trojan families left, hoping to sneak across the Greek lines in the dark. They didn't come back and we heard no hue and cry so they probably made it OK." She stretched out again, her head on her paws. Cælius waited for a moment or so but it seemed Daphne was done. He cleared his throat and said:

"Perhaps Lysandra, the palace cat, will have more to say about the couriers." I wondered who Lysandra might be but no clarification seemed forthcoming. Cælius called out:

"Chetas, Herakles." Chetas was one of the smaller gates to the southwest and Herakles an elderly tom, a bit the worse for wear; ragged coat with half an ear missing. I was surprised he was in charge of a gate, given his obvious age. As he got to his feet, I also noticed a distinct limp. Betsy whispered:

"I know what you're thinking. This cat should have gone to pasture long ago, digging in his garden or looking after the grandkittens. But old soldiers never die; they hang on and on until all you can do is to hope either for thrombosis or a fulminating heart attack." She snickered. "Cælius just couldn't get rid of Herakles. Before he got his own gate, he used to go around all the others with stupid suggestions and haranguing poor Cælius for hours on all the mistakes he—Cælius—was making. At last, Cælius could not take it any longer and put him in charge of Helia. We are all crossing our fingers for nothing of consequence to happen there. One of our best dogs—Attila— is posted at Chetas and keeps an eye on things." Betsy pointed to a large fierce looking black Rottweiler, the hound of the

Baskervilles'[7] elder brother. Attila? A curious name for a dog in ancient Greece. Herakles got to his feet importantly:

"Fellow animals, cats, dogs and other beasts, furred or feathered," he began, puffing out his chest and limping up and down in front of his audience. "We at Chetas have not been idle, no, indeed. Idleness is next to godslessness. Indeed it is. I run a tight ship, don't you know, there's no shillyshallying on my watch. I like everything spick and span. No untidiness, if you please. All the rats and mice know they must attend roll call on the dot. Slacking is severely punished. As for going off to parties, that would not be tolerated . . ." Cælius rolled his eyes.

"We all know your virtues, Herakles. Just tell us if anything has happened at Chetas." Herakles strolled up and down.

"Well," he said at length, "to tell the truth, there is no news today at all. It's all so quiet I believe a great push by the enemy is coming." Cælius breathed a sigh of relief as Herakles sat down. Curious, though, Herakles turned out to be dead right. It was indeed the lull before the storm.

"Troien, Antigone." Troien was another smallish gate, right in the center of the south wall; Antigone was a mostly white lady cat with bits of gray here and there and quite an exotic Egyptian look. She also had a really attractive salmon-colored nose. Me, I'm a nose guy.

"We did have a bit of a scare at Troien," she said. "There was a lot of burrowing and snuffling just next to the bolt hole. I got the local dog, Buster, to go out and look around." She laughed a nervous kind of laugh. "It was nothing really, just that mutt from the Greek camp, Rex, burying a bone." Subdued laughter all around. Betsy pointed out Buster to me. A large unkempt dog that might or might not be white or might or might not be grey. It was hard to know without giving him a good drubbing and

---

7   See *The Hound of the Baskervilles*, a Sherlock Holmes mystery, by Arthur Conan Doyle

scrubbing. He had stringy hair sticking up in all directions that hadn't since a brush since the Flood. Cælius pressed on.

"Antenorides, Orestes." Antenorides was the oldest, biggest and most important of the Trojan gates on the east side of the wall. Orestes, a ginger tom with very sloppy markings. Sad that so many cats are yobs. Well, Orestes might be a moggy but he had the self-confidence of a purebred.

"Well, we heard someone sneaking in through the bolt hole earlier today," he said. "It could have been a big rat, a small dog or a noisy cat; whatever, you could hear him a mile off! I even thought it might be a couple of elephants." General laughter and Orestes smirked. Cælius interrupted.

"Cut out the comedy bit, Orestes. You know perfectly well it was Gaius Marius." I felt quite offended.

"I wasn't trying to 'sneak in' as you put it," I said with dignity. "Why should I? I'm a bona fides tourist. My visa and laissez-passer are both in order." Orestes was having a belly laugh.

"I hope you're not thinking of raiding anyone's pantry," he gasped. "They'll be able to hear you all the way down in the Greek camp." I gritted my teeth and started to stretch out. But Cælius interrupted the both of us.

"You two wanna fight, your dime, your time. Stop larking about, Orestes, just bloody give your report." Orestes sat down and looked innocent.

"Nothing to report. Quiet as a millpond." Cælius sighed in obvious frustration and moved on.

"Dardan, Philocrates." Dardan faced due west and Philocrates a very dignified looking tom, all reddish fur and dark brown stripes.

"A few Greek boys were reeling around on the cliff path today," Philocrates said. "Me and my lads made a book on who would make it to the next gate without going over. For a bit I actually thought they were up to something more sinister, it was such an unlikely place to get pissed and disorderly—although I couldn't imagine what it could be—but then one of them did fall over. Saved by a bush. So they were just ordinary or common garden drunks."

"Jonathan, captain of the air patrol," was Cælius' next call. A large seagull flapped his wings. White and grey feathers, the usual curved beak with reddish lower lip. He said:

"Two biremes left today, mostly carrying wounded. Nothing else from the port or the sea; and the owls report no movements on the hills behind the city during the night." Jonathan flapped his wings, knocking a couple of sparrows off their perches. He continued:

"There's a stranger hanging around in the hills above the Greek camp. I've kept a watch on him but he keeps to himself and hasn't tried to communicate with either Greeks or Trojans." I felt a tingling along my spine. A stranger who contacted neither side and kept to himself? This needed looking into. However, Cælius didn't seem to be too worried.

"Well, watch him," he ordered Jonathan. "The situation is complicated enough without strangers sticking their spoons in. Strangers don't have to stay on hills, you know. They can move about." Oh, really. Jonathan flapped his wings, indicating he had more to say.

"I would like to suggest, Cælius, that we station an owl permanently at each of the gates during the night. In case someone—or everyone—falls asleep." Cælius looked a bit skeptical.

"I remember we've had a bit of a rumpus between the owls and the mice," he said. "We can't have any of that. So, what do you say, owls, no mouse pie for the duration." A large, rather scraggy owl spread his wings.

"That's Socrates," whispered Betsy in awe. "A great scholar." Socrates said with dignity.

"Really, Cælius. I thought that misunderstanding was all sorted out. Archimedes, as most owls, doesn't see too well during the day. He swears he thought it was a bread roll he swooped for." Archimedes looked around, who was perched near Socrates, flapped his wings in an apologetic kind of way. "He has said he was sorry, you know." Cælius' whole demeanor screamed: 'Yeah. Tell us another.' But aloud he said:

"Well, we'll need to keep an eye on Archimedes. If he has an addiction to mouse barbecue, he'll need to go into rehab. So the roll—no pun intended—of owls will be: Antenorides—Seneca. Troien—Cleopatra. Chetas—Archimedes . . ." He didn't get any further because there was a general outburst. The cats mewed, the mice and rats squeaked, the geese honked. (It was none of their business but they joined in anyway.) The noise was deafening. Cælius waved his paws trying to get some silence, but it took some time for his audience to settle down.

"Guys," he said, "sorry, and gals, I wish you wouldn't question my decisions. Everything I do is well thought out and for the general good." Well, yeah, I'm sure Hitler said something similar at one time or another. Cælius continued: "I have chosen to place Archimedes at Chetas for three reasons: because the team already know him; Herakles is a fearless commander, does everything by the book and won't brook any nonsense. He is absolutely loyal to the rules of war and knows exactly where each member of his troupe needs to be placed. And, should all else fail," his audience was becoming restless so Cælius raised his voice. "Chetas' dog is Attila." Attila opened one eye and glanced at the row of owls. He rumbled deep down in his throat. His head swiveled from side to side, giving each member of the Chetas team a piercing look. He growled:

"While I'm in charge, Archimedes will have mouse pie only in Hades. He as much as leers at a mouse, I will chomp him and chomp him good. My advice to him is: don't mess about on my watch!" He lay his head down on his paws, closed his eyes and started snoring. As everyone else was silent trying to get over the shock, he waved a paw. "OK. Get on with it." The owls kept a wise silence. Even Cælius looked a bit shaken. It's OK to have elephants in your army but how do you control them? Ask Hannibal[xii]. Cælius went on with the owl call:

"Dardan—Zeno. Tymbria—Marcus Aurelius. Helia—Selene. And, owls, no more funny business," he concluded sternly. "This sort of friendly fire we can do without." Then he moved on.

"Now, ground patrol. Captain of the watch, Betsy, please report." Betsy said:

"Everything in the city is quiet. No troop or other military movements noted." She stopped then continued: "Perhaps our guest, Gaius Marius, can tell us more about the Greek camp." All eyes turned towards me and I felt rather exposed. Cælius said:

"Excellent, Betsy. Hadn't thought of that. So, Gaius Marius, what have you got to tell us?"

"Well," I started. I looked around at all the expectant animal faces. This was after all my own lot—besides, whatever this Escape Committee knew or did would make no difference to the humans. But still . . . I cleared my throat and began:

"There are several distinct currents in the Greek camp. Agamemnon wants to go on as usual waging tried and true warfare: hulking fellows lugging swords, spears and whatnot." I stopped, rather unsure of myself, but the audience was hanging on my lips. So I continued: "On the other hand, Odysseus thinks the time for traditional warfare is gone and that a totally new strategy is needed. Something called psychological warfare. What exactly that is, he either doesn't know or can't explain. And that's about it." Total silence while everyone looked at Cælius who stared at me. So I added: "It all depends who you think will have the final word: Agamemnon or Odysseus." Cælius asked me:

"What do you think?"

"Me? I think Odysseus is the leader DE FACTO[8] while Agamemnon is the leader DE JURE[9]. Odysseus will take over leadership of the Greeks when he is ready—if ever. Until then, he

---

8   Widely accepted.
9   Installed by law.

and the others pay lip service to Agamemnon." Cælius scratched his ear thoughtfully.

"We'll have to keep an eye on both Agamemnon and Odysseus." He looked around. "Anyone want to add something?" Nobody did, so Cælius started winding the meeting down. "OK, then. Both sides seem to be licking their wounds and re-evaluating their position. The Trojans have only one option that I can see: total surrender. Lysandra, what's doing at your end?" Lysandra, who had just come in, was the cutest lady cat around, all salmon (ton-sur-ton, no less) and white, with green eyes. She was really delicate in her movements and had a rather sexy voice. I was impressed. Lysandra combed her whiskers with her claws and said rather languidly, as if all this really bored her.

"Following Hector's death," she said, "the Trojan High Command is in complete denial. A meeting of the High Command is mentioned from time to time but never seems to take place." She looked around. "The Trojans' current strategy is to do nothing so it's all up to the Greeks." She paused, a paw on her lips. "As for the couriers Daphne mentioned, no good news there. The inland kingdoms are exhausted and neither able nor willing to provide further troops. A turnip and carrot once in a while is about the extent of their contribution to the war effort." Cælius said pensively:

"Hopefully the Greeks don't know any of this; if they were to strike now, our boys would roll over like nine pins!" He scratched an ear. "Hypolytus!" This was a silver blue donkey with the usual white muzzle and ears. He lifted his head attentively. I'd seen him grazing in and around the Greek camp. I shuddered. Really, I'd been behaving as if I were on vacation, which of course I was. I needed to shape up. Be prepared, even on the beach. The enemy could be listening. Had Hypolytus seen Odysseus and me in deep confabulation? Cælius continued: "You're out and about. Anything new?" Hypolytus answered:

"Not from the Greek camp. No proper guards are posted and everyone just hangs about." In fact, he might have added, business as usual.

"Hmm," was Cælius' comment. "Still and all, we mustn't be caught napping. The Greeks don't seem to be about to up and leave any time soon. They're the only game in town and need watching." He clapped his paws: "Anyone has anything to add?"

It seemed not, so Cælius summed up: "Right. We need to intensify our surveillance of the Greeks. I want two dogs around their camp, 24/7. Volunteers, please." Two doggy paws shot up. Cælius glanced at the volunteers and did not look too impressed. But needs must, as they say, so he tried to put some enthusiasm into his voice. "Great. Arthur and Antonia, report to Betsy twice a day." Antonia was a yellow mutt, the kind my flat mate, for reasons known only to herself, calls a Neolithic dog. I remembered Antonia from *The Trojan Horse* café, forever begging for tidbits. Dogs have no dignity. Arthur was a longhaired cross between a German Sheppard, collie, spaniel and I guess a can of sardines and a grandfather clock. Cælius continued, with little hope in his heart: "Make sure one of you is in the Greek camp at all times." Both wagged their tails and Arthur said, throwing out a paw in a mock salute:

"Don't worry! Antonia and me'll be all over it!" Cælius gave them a doubtful look.

He turned to Jonathan. "I'd like more flyovers of the Greek camp, too, please. Report to me daily." He looked at the sparrows, now back on their perch. "You lot should carry any messages from the seagulls into the city as you attract less attention." The sparrows twittered and puffed themselves up. Cælius turned to the cats: "Cats at the gates: doubled attention, please, for any signs of tunneling or digging and, owls, a sharp lookout for night-time climbers. Thanks for coming and we'll all meet again next week, same time, same place." The animals started to disperse. Cælius came up to me, followed by Lysandra.

"I'm staggered," I said. "This is really a first rate organization. Neither of the other sides has anything comparable." Cælius purred in satisfaction. He pointed to the white cat next to him.

"This is Lysandra, as I'm sure you've figure out." I looked at Lysandra and she looked at me, rather haughtily. We knocked paws. Good looking but I thought her a bit aristocratic to be acting as a snitch and telltale, a spy within the walls. Introductions over, Lysandra went off to the palace while Cælius and I went back to his lair. Cælius stretched out on his spot on the wall and said sleepily: "These meetings really fag me out. I'm forever putting out fires between natural enemies that now need to be friends and allies to survive. I wish I could go back to the old life."

I found myself a bit of masonry that didn't seem on the imminent verge of collapse and spent an uncomfortable night. Sleep, too didn't come easy since my mind kept wondering back to the stranger in the hills. I considered who it might be. Not Homer: discretion wasn't his style; he'd be everywhere cadging free drinks and scarfing food. As for the poets who wrote about the Trojan War in antiquity—Euripides, Æschylus and so on—they used Homer as their main source. They wanted high drama and memorable lines, and if the truth, the whole truth and nothing but the truth, got in the way, what the hell. So it had to be someone to whom the true outcome of the Trojan War was important. But who? I started to drop off; a name was just under the surface of my subconscious mind. If only I could reach it . . . if only . . .

Next morning, we got up latish. Cælius had milk and bread for breakfast; I had brought some of my cat food with me. Cælius sniffed at it.

"It's full of preservatives. Wouldn't touch it." Suit yourself, pal. "I'd rather have a mouse," he confided, "but a deal's a deal." There was a fountain nearby with nice spring water and we had our morning drink. Breakfast over, I asked:

"I'd like to go round the walls and see how you've set up your surveillance teams, if you don't mind." Cælius shrugged and said:

"Knock yourself out. I suppose you want to see if there's anywhere the Greeks could burrow through." He thought this was a great joke. I gave a watery smile. "Anyhow," he continued more soberly, "should be a good day for it." He looked up at the sky. "The birds are lazing about, which means nothing has happened at the Greek camp overnight. Pigeon pie," he murmured with longing but then shook himself. "Oh, well, better times must come eventually. Betsy will show you around." Eventually, Betsy turned up and Cælius told her what was wanted. Betsy was game at once.

4.2 The Gates of Troy

"We'll start at Antenorides," said she, "and work our way around to Helia, if that's OK with you." Well, it was. One must begin somewhere. The two of us crossed Priam Square. Way up on his column, Tithonius had the company of pigeons who were roosting on his head and shoulders. That's the whole point of statues: pigeon roosts. An entrepreneur was selling little bags of crumbs so the kids could feed the pigeons and, of course, the kids screamed at their mothers to let them buy a bag. No wonder Cælius dreamt of pigeon pie.

It was now mid-morning and life in the city was in full swing: vendors set up stalls, café owners were on the lookout for morning shoppers needing elevenses. Women lugged carrier bags, kids ran around getting in everyone's way and were cuffed by their mothers when the mothers could catch them. There were soldiers loafing around, ogling the girls. Betsy and I gave all this activity a wide berth and in due course reached Antenorides.

This gate was huge: about six meters high and five wide; two wooden leaves opened inwards, each of very hard wood with heavy bands, studs and fixtures, all bronze. The massive sliding bolts were also of hard wood. If a battering ram were to make an impact, it would need to be enormously heavy and allow for a hefty purchase. But where was the wood for such an implement to come from on this barren plain? However, after nine years, the Greeks must have thought and tried all this—as Odysseus had said. Short of using dynamite—or at least a couple of kegs of gunpowder –, I couldn't see how anyone could get into Troy save by invitation.

Orestes, the local cat commander and his gang of rats and mice came out to meet us. Paddy, the German Sheppard, who was sleeping, just opened an eye and closed it again.

"Hi, Betsy, and Gaius," Orestes said, "nice of you to come and see us. It's rather slow here just now but I ain't complaining. The Greeks have given us enough entertainment in the past so a quiet time is nice. On the other hand, they do make such a row every night down at that bar of theirs that our eardrums must be permanently damaged." This was thought a huge joke; the rats and mice squeaked in appreciation. Paddy barked. Selene, the owl, was asleep in a nearby tree.

"This is some gate," I said. "Take a few woodpeckers to get through it." Another joke; more squeaking and barking and mewing. Orestes said:

"It's the oldest of the Trojan gates. I believe it was the first one. As the city grew and the walls extended, new gates were added to avoid traffic jams."

"Not surprising," said Betsy. "Imagine if everything had to come and go through one gate." Another joke. It was going to be that kind of day.

"Before the war," I said, "I suppose the gates would stay open from dawn to dusk." Orestes nodded:

"Seems obvious but can't remember myself," he confessed. "I'm not that old. Better ask Herakles. He may know." Betsy chortled:

"At least, he's old enough. About 15, wouldn't you say, Orestes?" Orestes nodded. I intervened, not wanting any more discussion of Herakles' age, by saying:

"It can't have been opened very often over the past nine years." Orestes demurred:

"Well, the Trojans leave by this gate for all major battles. The gate is closed after them and survivors have to get back in by one of the smaller gates, either Chetas or Helia." Betsy chimed in:

"Some Greek or other might sneak in if a gate this size was left open." I gazed up at the formidable wooden structure:

"I take it the Greeks have already tried to batter it down."

"Well, actually no," answered Orestes. "It's just too solid, you can tell just by looking at it from the outside. And, of course, there are spies and traitors galore in Troy so the Greeks know all about our defenses, strengths and weaknesses." Oh, oh. Hope no one suspects me. However, it was a good point and begged the question: what did Odysseus want me for?

Orestes continued: "A couple of the other gates are less solid and that's where they've tried to use a ram. Without success, but you know that, anyway." I looked at the walls themselves. Huge blocks of stone, roughly dressed but with enough cracks and crevices for a man to find footholds and climb up. I mentioned this to Orestes.

"Yeah, right," he said, "and many have tried—including that Patroklus." He grinned. A grinning cat is an alarming sight. "That's why the ramparts are heavily manned at all times." Another grin. "So it's a case of keeping the oil burning, fellas, and stones handy to discourage any would be heroes." I looked at my bolt hole a meter or so to the right of the gate. Orestes watched me and sniggered:

"Yeah, I've seen you come through plenty of times, you know. A cat can fool a human and a dog—no offence, Betsy, Paddy—but not another cat." The mice squeaked in merriment. I almost took mouse pie back to Cælius. I gave a half smile to show I appreciated the joke. Heaven help me—there were another five gates to come. I answered:

"Good for you. On the other hand, I come and go quite openly. After all, a cat is a cat is a cat and who cares? I had to wait until the company got its breath back. I took up the conversation again: "Haven't the Greeks tried to tunnel under the walls?" More shrieks. I was starting to feel like a member of the USO, entertaining the troops. Orestes said:

"Sure they have. It was very good exercise, too, enough to keep them fit and out of the public houses. You see, Gaius Marius, Troy's walls were built on solid rock foundations. I don't know how far down the rock goes but, believe you me, it's a ways. So, should anyone be stupid enough to try, they'd continually hit hard rock. Troy was built to last." I nodded:

"I can see that," I said. "But tell me: if this place is so impregnable, why have you lot—I mean, you animals—set up these surveillance teams? You should be quite safe inside the city." This time Betsy answered:

"No city is totally impregnable, Gaius. There's always a weak spot." She continued: "These gates are strong, that's right, but there's always fire, you know. The Greeks have tried to burn down most the gates in turn, without any luck so far, mostly due, I think, to constant Trojan surveillance. From the ramparts, you can see far into the distance. No one sneaks up on Troy."

Orestes continued: "There's always the unknown factor. Something you haven't thought of. And that is what will bring the city down." Sounded dramatic.

"I won't bother to ask what it is," I said, "since if you knew, you'd tell us." That's the kind of boasting bastard you are, thinks I. Orestes waved my comment away with a paw.

"That's no secret, Gaius. Treachery. That'll be the city's undoing. It's the form it will take we don't know. Troy will fall by treachery. If we don't keep constant watch, we could wake up one morning and find the city in flames around us. So it's up and doing, my friend, 24/7, to quote our fearless leader." I mulled for a bit.

"I know there's a cat at each gate," I said. "Do you have shifts? Two cats for every gate, 12 hours on, 12 hours off? 24/7 is OK but no one can stay awake 24/7, especially a cat. Some of us need 20 hour naps." Orestes replied:

"Very true. But, no, it's one cat per gate. We have a Rota system; for a given number of hours during the day, the local dog takes over while the cat naps. It's a good system since cats sleep by day, dogs by night. And, of course, we have plenty of mice and rats for logistical and intelligence support—and to keep us all on our toes." The mice and rats looked downright proud. "They're very helpful indeed. Couldn't do without them." Orestes patted a few heads.

"Still," I said, "It's a bit hard kudos on the Trojans not being able to use their main gate." Orestes shrugged:

"Such is the way of the world," he said languidly. "Once outside the city, the Trojan warriors are on their own. Antenorides is only opened if a truce is called so both sides can collect dead and wounded." Orestes looked quite sad. "Not many Trojans wounded, I'm afraid, they need more funeral directors than doctors."

Now this was an interesting remark. All in all, the Greeks had the advantage of leaving the battlefield whenever they felt like it while the Trojans had to be let in as convenient. Rather a Greek soldier than a Trojan, thinks I. But it further proved Odysseus' point. The Greeks could kill as many Trojans as they liked on the battlefield but no battle could force open the gates. Treachery was the only game in town. I thanked Orestes and his minions and Betsy and I went on our way.

Troien, where that cute white cat, Antigone, was in charge, was one of the newer gates. The workmanship was shoddier and the whole thing looked a whole less solid than Antenorides. Antigone told me the Greeks had tried to burn down this gate. The signs of scorching were plainly visible. I looked at the damage. Must have been a close thing.

"It wasn't fun," Antigone told me. "Of course, we saw it coming and I got my troops out—mice first, then the rats and the support dog, Buster. My tail was slightly singed—you can't see it now as the fur fortunately grew back. To make matters worse, before I got clear, men came running up with buckets and threw water on the flames. Boy, did I get wet! It was most unpleasant. I had to ask Buster to stand in for me while I found a sunny spot to dry off on." A real lady, our Antigone. "Then the lads on the battlements got their act together. What they'd been up to all this time I don't know. However, they were clever enough not to use burning oil—that would have made a splendid fire—but threw down the biggest stones they had and managed to beat back the Greeks." Buster added excitedly:

"At that point, Hector led a cavalry sortie out through the Chetas gate and the Greeks ran right smack into it. Talk about being between a rock and a hard place." We all tittered politely. "It was not a good day for the Greeks." Now, this was all very interesting and I was glad to have heard all about it. However, it wouldn't be news to Odysseus. We waved goodbye to Antigone and Buster and pushed on.

Next, we came to Chetas, the fief of the old duffer Herakles. Built even later than Troien, it was a lot less sturdy. Sad to see how the level of workmanship fell off over the years. Herakles came limping up to meet us, all spit and polish.

"My dear Gaius," he enthused, "and Betsy," as an afterthought. "Welcome, welcome!" As if we'd come from over the sea. After paw knocking and all that, he said pompously: "You will do me the honor of inspecting the troops." I looked at Betsy. She sniggered. The rats and mice were obviously used to the drill; they lined up, rats first then mice, tallest to smallest. I felt a real chump walking down the line. At the end, the large Rottweiler, Attila, was less than spick and span. Herakles frowned and said angrily:

"I'm placing you on report!" Attila carefully moved a flea and growled a deep growl that just about scared me out of my fur.

"The day will come," he said to Herakles, "when I will tear you limb from limb." He slobbered. "I can hardly wait." But Herakles seemed unfazed and unafraid. He threw up his paws:

"You see what we've come to? No respect for senior officers. Plain insubordination. When I was young, the likes of him would have been court-martialed!" Betsy poured oil on this particular spot of troubled waters:

"The Greeks tried to ram this gate, you know, Gaius. Isn't that right, Herakles?" Herakles forgot about Attila immediately. Attila was already asleep.

"Yes, indeed," he said. "A sight to be seen, I do assure you. Can you believe they brought the ram all the way from Greece— there's no wood around here suitable, you'd have to go high into the mountains for a trunk thick enough and, if and when you found one, drag it all the way down to the coast. Easier to bring it in by ship." He arranged his tail with military precision before going on. "But one day, there they were: ram, undercarriage, kit and caboodle. I saw them pushing the thing up the hill." Betsy took over, much offending Herakles:

"A slog, I can tell you; half the Greek army pushed, the other half pulled. The whole of Troy was on the ramparts for the entertainment." She giggled: "You should have heard them; calling the Greeks offensive names and egging them on." Herakles elbowed Betsy aside and took up the tale:

"Now, Chetas is the weakest link in the Trojan gate system, as the Greeks well know," he continued. "The problem is the slope before it is steeper than at any of the others." Humm. Perhaps this was the reason why the Trojans hadn't bothered overmuch when building Chetas. Why waste time, materials and effort that could be better employed elsewhere? I asked:

"How did they manage to swing the ram?" Visions danced in my head of the Roman pulley system. Herakles answered:

"The usual way. Pick it up, run and ram." I almost gagged.

"Uphill?" Herakles and his underlings laughed and slapped their thighs.

"You should have seen it! No discipline, no tactics, no one seemed in command! The ram had five hand poles on each side, so it needed ten Greeks to pick the thing up, gain momentum by walking then trotting, then running up the hill and slam the ram into the gate. Of course, they never got anywhere near Chetas, but collapsed halfway up the hill. Any commander worth his salt should be able to see the thing was totally unfeasible. Sloppy warfare, that's what I call it." He walked up and down then said firmly: "In my young days, no commander would have put up with being made to look so stupid." He shook his head. "Naturally, the really strong Greeks, Ajax and Achilles, say, weren't about to work like field hands. An officer is, after all, a gentleman. Stiff upper lip, you know, and all that." Yeah, tell me about it. Many a battle has been lost because the upper class wouldn't get its hands dirty. In the meantime, the rats and mice rolled on the ground in mirth. Herakles watched them indulgently. As an aside, he said: "Funny isn't it. In the past, the only place I wanted to see a rat was on the dinner table with a grape in its mouth. But I'm quite fond of the little fellows now. I'll probably keep them as pets once this is over. Why, they're like family."

"You could breed them," I said, nastily. The herd glared at me, their feelings clearly hurt. Not funny. He soothed his crew: "Don't listen to him, he's an uncouth moggy." He turned to me and continued haughtily. "A commander's first duty is to his men but then what do you know about loyalty among comrades in arms, one for all and all for one?" Sure, I thought, that's why so many die in action. Can't stand these military types. I sneered at him:

"And no mouse left behind!" Herakles glared at me.

"That," he said loftily, "goes without saying." Betsy tried to break this up before things got bloody.

"I was on the battlements that day," she said. "And, besides having a good time, the Trojans were taking other measures, such as organizing burning oil. In addition, the archers were busy at it, too. They're good, the Trojan archers."

"Anyhow," continued Herakles, somewhat mollified. "It was a no-win situation for the Greeks. Too many aspects to keep in mind: ram, slope, Trojan arrows and burning oil. No, not a good day for them. In the end, they let the ram roll down the hill and went back to their camp." Eurybates and *The Greek Olive Tree* must have done a roaring trade that night.

"Amazing," I said. I looked at the gate. Herakles said:

"They only got close once. You can just see a bit of splintering on the outside of the gate." He shook his head. "I think the Greeks might have broken through given better odds." I shook my head:

"All things considered, one wonders the Greeks haven't given up long ago."

"Well," said Herakles, "there is no limit to human folly." I looked at him:

"It was at this gate Patroklus tried to break through, wasn't it?"

"Of course," exclaimed Herakles. "I'd almost forgotten. Yes, the outside wall is at an angle and the poor chump thought he could just run up it." I mused on this and my comment was:

"Had it been possible, someone would have done it ages ago."

"Very true," came the answer. "That Patroklus, he really was a waste of space. Hector was standing in the shadows of the gate, you know, and it was here he killed Patroklus."

"Yeah," interposed Betsy, "Hector thought he'd killed Achilles. When he saw it was Patroklus, boy, was he pissed off." Poor Patroklus. When even the cats and dogs don't have a good word to say for you, it's time to leave.

Herakles, rats and mice saluted smartly as we turned to go, all acrimony forgotten. Just as we were leaving, I saw something scurry across the ground. I was about to reach for the bug spray when it ran up Herakles' leg, on to his back and hid behind his left ear. I started to point. But Herakles just smiled a sort of tender fatherly smile.

"This is poor Phillip," he told me. "He's never gotten over being mistaken for a bread roll. I can hardly get him to go outside. Hey, little guy," he said. "It's OK. Old Herakles will look after you." He glanced at Attila snoring under a tree and then looked upwards. On a high branch of a neighboring tree, Archimedes was asleep, as if this remark had nothing to do with him. Attila emitted a low growl. He looked after us thoughtfully as we left. That was one fellow I hoped never to meet once the animals' covenant expired.

Next stop was Dardan where Philocrates, all dignity and shiny coat, held court. I never saw a cat sit up straighter. And his rats and mice were beautifully groomed. Even the bolt hole was spick and span. Dardan was an old gate; I imaged it was built not long after Antenorides. Wonderful workmanship, fancy bronze fittings. Made sense. Antenorides looked west; Dardan was almost on the direct opposite side of the city, looking east. It was the last gate before the cliffs and the drop to the Hellespont. I couldn't see much action happening here.

"You're right," Philocrates said before I had opened my mouth. Philocrates oozed self-confidence. "We have a very quiet time here. Not much the Greeks can get up to so close to the cliff." Betsy broke in:

"The Trojans make a lot of cavalry sorties from this gate," she said. "With so little space for maneuvering, there's small chance the Greeks can cut them off."

"But it did happen," said Philocrates. "The Trojans got over confident—I think it was that hothead, Troilus. Got no time for him. Be that as it may, the Trojans got cut off by a Greek cavalry contingent. There weren't many Greeks and the Trojans could probably have broken through. However, it was just too dangerous to open the gates as the Greeks could have reached them at the same time as our lads. It was head for the hills for our lot. I believe they eventually shook off the Greeks but they had to camp out for a day or so before sneaking back in through Helia." Philocrates tapped his front paw on the ground. "Hector was not pleased." I bet. We said our goodbyes and went on.

Betsy suggested we go to Tymbria via the outside path so I could have a look at the cliffs and the drop to the Hellespont. I really didn't fancy this but I just couldn't lose face in front of a lady dog.

We slipped out through the bolt hole at Dardan and found ourselves on a narrow path that skirted the city walls and followed the cliff edge. I'm not much of a walker and this walk was one I could have done without. The path was wide enough for three cats to walk abreast but, still, this cat needed to keep his wits about him and concentrate on where to put each paw, no daydreaming tolerated. A gust of wind could sweep a cat like me off the cliff if I forgot what I was about and got too near the edge. Halfway around, we reached the base of the tower; I looked up; I could hardly make out the ramparts far above. There was no gate leading into it. On we went and believe me I was glad to see the bolt hole at Tymbria and get back into the city.

Tymbria was a smallish gate, but judging by the workmanship, quite old. Once inside, Palamedes, the black and white tom, met us. I asked:

"So you can't leave the city through the tower but have to use Tymbria or go all the way to Dardan. I suppose they didn't want people rushing out of the tower in a panic and spilling off the cliff."

"Well, if you really want to leave by the tower," drawled Palamedes. "You could knot sheets or get a rope ladder." Another jokester. Must come with the job. Of course, the rats and mice loved it. I ignored him and went on:

"What about secrets passages from the Tower to the countryside?" Palamedes shook his head.

"We've had the rats and mice check every centimeter—nothing. And none towards the city either. I believe the ground's just too hard." I thought about this.

"So, there's no way out of the city except through the gates."

"Only if you're a bird." I thought about the two cats in Kilkenny[xiii] and tips of their tails. However, a cat fight would not go down well and Cælius would be pissed off in no uncertain terms.

"On the other hand," I said, "you could hole up in the tower and defend it for months."

"That's probably true," said Betsy, "but I don't know what good it would do in the long run. You could be starved out or disease get you. You'd be caught like a rat in a trap." The rats frowned at her. She said: "Sorry, guys, nothing personal. It's just a metaphor." I doubt they knew what a metaphor was but it's a nice impressive word and they relaxed. Betsy went on: "All your enemies need to do is camp by the front door and sunbathe. No, I'm not sure what the point of the tower is. Lookout, or just to say you have one." I asked Palamedes:

"What kind of action have you had around here?"

"Not so dramatic, I'm afraid, as at the other gates," he said. "This gate was built, I think, more or less at the same time as Dardan. It's mainly for communications inland, to bring in produce and other merchandise. Troy's client kings and allies also use it for courier and minor troop movement." He had a bit of a stretch.

"Of course, the Greeks soon found that out and set up a small garrison to our rear. This has real nuisance value; each time the gate opens, a Trojan cavalry contingent needs to be on hand to keep the Greeks busy. So we have a lot of skirmishing going on. At one point, the Greeks got another cute idea. You must have seen that the plain starts sloping gently upwards just outside the gate. That means if you are on the hill, gravity is on your side." Betsy took up the story.

"The Greeks decided to roll boulders down the slope to smash Dardan. That created havoc, let me tell you. They almost got through, too. The gate had to be reinforced." I looked at it. There was indeed a lot more bronze than on the other gates and some of the beams had been reinforced, too. What they needed were iron fixtures, of course. If I'd had any to sell, I could have made a killing.

"What actually saved us," continued Palamedes "was that, after a while, there were so many rocks lying around they essentially protected us. Of course, the Trojans had to go out at night and clear some away so as not to complete obstruct the gate. Go out and have a look: there's almost an avenue of rocks running back towards the hill." I slipped out of the bolt hole. And indeed, there were enough rocks around Tymbria to build a new Troy. OK, so that's an exaggeration. I looked up at the sparsely wooded slope. Not many rocks left up there. It seemed that, besides having unwillingly helped to protect Tymbria, the Greeks had run out of missiles. Gotta hand it to them for sheer tenacity. I went back inside. Palamedes continued: "I lost some of my rats and mice to the rocks. Very sad, you know. But we had nice funerals for them."

We left and I walked on thoughtfully with Betsy. This war was more complicated than I had imagined.

Helia was quite a narrow gate; it was to the left of the palace, while Antenorides was to the right. Betsy said Helia had been an afterthought, built once the conflict had started and it became dangerous to open the main gates for minor comings and goings. She continued: "Helia is mostly for pedestrian traffic. A man and horse can get out as long as the guy leads the horse as the couriers do. However, there are always Greeks on the lookout, on the off chance of picking up a courier or a pedestrian or so."

We found Daphne, the white cat with the curious black spots, sunning herself on a convenient rock. She opened half an eye when we arrived. Called upon for further information, she answered lazily, licking a paw:

"Watching Helia is mostly a waste of the Greeks' time. If you look closely, you'll see that Helia practically blends right into the wall. In fact, at night it's difficult to see whether the gate is open or closed. A clever man can slip out without the Greeks being any the wiser. More difficult if you have a horse, of course. Horses are so big."

She yawned and started washing her face then continued. "This is a most comfortable billet. Wouldn't change it for anywhere else. Me and my rats and mice get on really well and I can always get one of them to run into town to get me a snack since Priam Square is real close by."

I looked at her troops. Most of the rats were just lazing about; the mice were playing some kind of bean game. There was an assortment of kittens running about, a couple definitely ginger. Hmm . . . Daphne didn't pay much attention to her offspring, as there were rats on babysitting duty. Daphne then dozed off, ignoring us completely. Yeah, be a deadbeat Mom; leave the kids to the babysitter. I looked at Betsy. She said:

"That's it. You've now made a complete circuit of the city and seen all the gates. Want to go up through the tower and see the ramparts?" I thought: why not? Might as well do the full ten-drachma tour. Of course, I'd been there before but under rather different circumstances. Perhaps I would learn something new.

"Sure," I said. Betsy then suggested we get some lunch, have a bit of a rest and then be off. I'm not much of a lunch guy but Betsy was for sure a lunch gal. I had a couple of tuna snacks, tuna being definitely my favorite fish; Betsy had everything she could lay her paws on. She'd have had my cat food too, if I'd given her half a chance. After that, we went to Priam Square and napped under a convenient shady tree.

Mid-afternoon, Betsy was up and doing and off we went. There were flights of steps leading to the ramparts next to each gate, except Helia. Betsy and I decided to use those next to Antenorides. I looked up and sighed inwardly.

"What about the Tower?" I asked, more to postpone the start of the ascent than any need for information. "Can we get onto the ramparts through the tower?" A lift, I thought, would be nice. Or perhaps an escalator. Betsy answered:

"The Tower is mainly for the accommodation of foreign troops; there are also munitions rooms, you know, where they keep bows and arrows, extra lances and swords, shields and stuff. Masses of that, seeing men die while their hardware is left behind." I know, I thought cynically. Waste not, want not. Betsy went on: "The ramparts run right around the top of the walls and through the tower. The Tower has underground storerooms for foodstuff, grain, wine and so on, built long ago and hewn out of the living rock. These storerooms are huge, which explains how Troy has survived a nine-year siege." Betsy made a motion of starting to climb but I stalled again by pondering aloud:

"I see there are plenty of wells in the city, besides that huge fountain in Priam square. Must be quite a network of underground streams in these parts." Betsy nodded.

"I suppose so, although I don't know the details. Have to ask the rats. The city also has a good sewage system. If not, we'd all have died of the plague long since." Yeah. Everything I wanted to know about Troy but wouldn't have bothered to ask.

There was nothing else I could think of that could delay the 100 steps, so we set off. We played a silent game of 'who's fastest'; I won by a short head. Dogs, of course, have longer legs. But cats are lighter and faster. That's how the cat climbs the tree before the dog catches the cat. Elementary, my dear Watson.

Like all ramparts, at least those I've seen, these were crenulated for the purpose of shooting arrows or throwing things down on the enemy, with merlons for protection. I jumped onto a crenulation between two merlons while Betsy stood with her back paws on the ground and her front paws next to me. Dogs do not have good heads for heights. We looked out. The sun had passed its zenith and was slowly sinking into the west. In front of us lay a panorama stretching all the way to the Ægean;

Tenedos was a halfway mark, where the Greek ships bobbed about like so many cockleshells.

It was a perfect afternoon; a blue sky with the odd drifting cloud. Waves lapping gently on the white sands and tiny figures moving on the beach. The sea stretched out before us until it disappeared over the horizon. Birds whirled overhead, screeching and cawing. Wish I'd brought my digital camera. A large seagull dived towards us and, for a moment, I thought I was going to become dinner. But when he perched elegantly on the merlon next to me, I saw it was Jonathan and breathed easier.

"Being a bird," I said by way of greeting, "sure has some advantages." Jonathan stared in surprise.

"What are the disadvantages?" he asked in wonder. However, I wasn't about to go down that road.

"I can't see the Greeks getting up to anything at all without your knowing all about it." I buttered him up.

"Well, hardly," he answered complaisantly. "The problem is, I can see what they do—moving troops or war engines or whatever—but I don't know their purpose until they act. For instance, I saw them dragging that enormous battering ram towards Chetas; Herakles must have told you about that. Of course, I know a battering ram when I see one, so I sent the crows as fast as their wings could carry them to warn Herakles and he made sure—as far as possible, of course—that his staff was out of the way. He sent all non-combatants and non-essentials to safety in Priam Square." How like Herakles. Everything by the book. Jonathan flapped his wings.

"We got Cælius up here as fast as we could, and had the sparrows on standby in case a complete evacuation became necessary." He flapped some more. "Cælius knows more about strategy and tactics than anyone else including, I suspect, old Priam. Of course, a horse would have been better since horses have battle experience but most can't handle the steps. We kept one on the ground as a military advisor with a couple of pigeons to act as couriers."

My head started to swim. This escape committee beat anything I'd ever heard of. However, it was all in a day's work for Jonathan who went on, scratching his head with a claw: "Who was the horse on duty that day, Betsy? Do you remember?" Betsy thought for a moment.

"As far as I can remember it was Polyneices. I could be wrong. All horses look the same to me."

"Well," continued Jonathan. "Cælius briefed Polyneices on developments via the crows. Polyneices answered immediately: 'It doesn't sound too serious, guys; the uphill terrain is against them. So chill out.' The rest, as you know, is history". Indeed. Not the Greeks' finest hour. Of course, I know nothing about strategy except that, if under attack, keep very very quiet and move very very slowly and run away at the first chance; if you must; pounce when the enemy least expects it. This is a sound cat tactic, honed to perfection over millions of years, but it wouldn't work here, not with the Greeks in their open camp and the Trojans behind their impregnable walls. Stalemate.

I looked around. There was plenty going on. Although the city was in a more or less relaxed state, on the ramparts there was a guard every two meters or so and a continuous stream of humanity moving this way and that. The three of us hung out watching the tiny figures moving about in the Greek camp below. Just as we were getting bored, a sparrow landed next to Jonathan, an anxious look on its face. It chirped and flapped its wings. Jonathan looked pensive. The sparrow flew off.

"What was all that about?" I asked Jonathan. He ignored me.

"Come on," he said urgently, "we need to go and see Cælius right away. Meet you there." And off he flew. Betsy and I scrambled down the steps and headed for Cælius' lair. We found Jonathan perched on the wall next to him. Jonathan ruffled his feathers and looked important:

"The sparrows report the ravens inland have seen a group of horsemen heading our way, out of the north." Cælius raised his eyebrows:

"A group is it? How many do the ravens consider a group to be?"

"Well," answered Jonathan, "Montrose thought about a baker's dozen." He looked uncomfortable as Cælius glared at him. I explained hastily:

"A baker's dozen is 13." Betsy enquired:

"If you mean 13, why not say 13? A baker's dozen, indeed!" I wasn't about to explain and Cælius had moved on anyway.

"How far from Troy are they? Are they for the Greeks or the Trojans?" Betsy scratched her ear in a thoughtful sort of way then said:

"Well, I can't see the Greeks desperate enough to need 13 horsemen. But Troy is desperate for anything so my guess is they're coming here." At that moment, Lysandra, the palace cat, came haring up, quite out of breath:

"You've got to come to Priam Square right away!" She panted. "Horsemen have arrived." Jonathan flew off and Betsy claimed she had business elsewhere so Cælius, Lysandra and I hotfooted it all the way to Priam Square.

◦ 5 ◦

The last Battles

5.1 Penthesileia

Although night had fallen, Priam Square was lit up as if it were high noon. We walked slowly down a side alley, keeping to the shadows and peeked out carefully when the Square came in sight. The whole of Troy seemed to be there and the uproar was deafening. People where dancing in the streets. Fireworks in all colors of the rainbow lit up the sky in the form of falling stars and comets. We crouched in a dark corner behind a bronze lion.

Then trumpets blared, the cheering redoubled and into the Square pranced a superb horse, all black, its bridle and saddle adorned with accruements of gold and silver. It held its head high and snorted in the approved warhorse fashion. The rider also held his head high; his corslet was black but the gleaming of many precious gems gave it a rainbow radiant effect. From the helmet streamed a wild mane of golden-glistening hairs. I could see his scabbard of ivory and silver. He was not lacking other weapons; I counted two javelins besides the sword, of course, and a huge halberd; as for the shield, it was so large it seemed to block out parts of the square.

Other horses now entered, milling about in the crowd; I counted them. Then I whispered, raising my eyebrows:

"Here we have Montrose's baker's dozen. Who are they?" Lysandra shrugged and Cælius was obviously grasping at straws when he suggested:

"Do you think Hector has come back from the dead?" We both turned to look at him. He felt foolish so he added: "After all, Hector was master of horses." Lysandra sniffed:

"Highly unlikely," she said and I had to agree with her. I craned my neck for a closer at the lead rider. I murmured:

"Whoever he is, he has long hair." However, this didn't get me anywhere much since in antiquity many men had long hair. "I also find him somewhat overdressed. Why, not even Agamemnon to these extremes. Then I heard Lysandra gasp:

"Look" she squeaked excitedly, then cleared her throat and continued in her normal voice. "It's a woman!" Cælius and I stared, our eyes goggling. A woman! We looked at each other, shaking our heads. Lysandra said wistfully:

"She's very beautiful—in a human sense, of course."

"Well," I added, "It's not Helen since Helen is blonde while this one is dark and I don't think Helen would be caught dead on a warhorse. Could it be one of Priam's daughters come back from parts unknown?" Lysandra shook her head as girls do when they consider the males with them to be perfect idiots.

"Helen," she sneered, "of course not. That dead white skin only goes with really black hair." I considered. She might be Irish. "However," continued Lysandra thoughtfully, "her upper body a bit too muscular for my taste. I bet she lifts weights; not Helen's thing." She continued: "As for Priam's daughters, they are all accounted for." Well, having exhausted our speculations, we continued to stare. Lysandra was very impressed. "Look at her helmet and that mane and the corslet is to die for. And the boots . . ." Lysandra ran out of words and her eyes shone. Cælius and I looked at each other. Whatever the species, ladies are ladies. Show them a high-class outfit and they fall all over themselves—admiration or envy, take your pick. I couldn't resist saying:

"Yeah, you'd look great in those boots, Lysandra." Her head snapped around and she hissed before answering:

"And why not? I wouldn't be the first cat to wear boots." She tossed her head disdainfully. Right. The original Puss'n Boots. I said thoughtfully:

"I bet this is her on parade outfit. I'm sure she has another for everyday use that's easier to launder." Lysandra looked at me in contempt but I ignored her and continued thoughtfully: "Of course, if this is to be her last battle, she'd want to look her best and ruining her outfit wouldn't matter."

Lysandra clicked her tongue in irritation. I turned on her sharply:

"Don't click your tongue at me. She's obviously a warrior. Look at her sword: the hilt is encrusted with pearls and jewels, as is her shield." My head span. Perhaps she was a model for a war poster: 'Priam wants you!' sort of thing to get the recruits to sign up.

The cheering increased. And there was old Priam hobbling down the palace steps as fast as he could manage, other members of the royal family following behind him. As Priam approached, the lady warrior jumped off her horse and fell into his arms, almost sending him backwards and almost crushing the poor old creature to a pulp. But Priam took it all in good part. The lady held him at arm's length.

"Great Priam, king of Troy, Penthesileia, queen of the Amazons, salutes you!"

"Penthesileia, my beloved kinswoman," he managed to wheeze in reply. "What has made you cross the river Thermodon and come to my poor kingdom?" I heard Lysandra hiccup.

"Penthesileia," she breathed, "the queen of the Amazons! She's a living legend and I'm actually seeing her!" Cælius looked equally impressed. However, some dim memory filtered back to me and I sneered—I love sneering about people who thrive on being famous.

"Penthesileia; isn't she the gal who mistook her sister for a wild boar and killed her?" Lysandra flared up angrily:

"A stag, you ignoramus, not a boar."

"Still," I insisted, "not a mistake easily made, is it? Given that a stag is a lot bigger than a woman, has four legs and antlers which I have never known a woman . . ." Lysandra interrupted me, quite rudely I thought:

"Oh, you! Like all males you just hate it when a female makes a name for herself in a man's field!" She snickered. "As for horns—that's more a male thing, isn't it?"

"Is it?" came my retort. "I'll have to ask Menelaus." Lysandra and I glared at each other. Cælius hissed:

"Will you two stop bickering! I want to hear what they're saying." Penthesileia now greeted the other members of the royal family. I looked in vain for Helen but she wasn't around. Neither was Cassandra, but that I could understand. Penthesileia continued in a loud voice; she never spoke when shouting would do as well.

"My Lord," she cried. "Let me introduce my handmaidens." She named each one. Clonie. Polemousa. Derinoe. Evandre. Antandre. Bremousa. Hyppothoe. Harmothoe. Alcibie. Antibrote. Derimacheia. Thermodosa. They stood proudly by their horses heads, their armor and weapons gleaming; each beautiful, with long hair running from dark brown to golden but none outshone their Queen. Penthesileia was obviously skilled at selecting subordinates. Priam, the old fool, quavered:

"But where's Hippolyta, my dear? Hasn't she come with you?" I sniggered. Hippolyta, the murdered sister. To cover Priam's gaffe, everyone started talking at once, while Hecuba whispered in Priam's ear; his eyes and mouth opened into round 'o's. Hecuba gave him a shake and waved a finger in his face. I looked at Penthesileia carefully. There was something terrible about her perfect face; the raven black hair gave her a hard and unyielding look, her eyes, dark as night, were cold and merciless. I wouldn't like to meet this lady in a dark alley. However, the beautiful and terrible creature ignored the remark regarding Hippolyta, and went on:

"Priam, I and my Amazons have come to Troy eager for cruel war and glorious battle. To win renown by our prowess in arms, redress the wrongs Troy has suffered at the hands of the Greeks and avenge the death of the incomparable Hector." She pulled her sword out of its sheath and, holding it aloft, cried: "Death! Death to the Greeks! I will annihilate them totally, from Agamemnon down to the meanest footslogger." There she stood, in all her splendid beauty; her handmaidens all drew their swords, pointing heavenwards, echoing:

"Death to the Greeks!" Soon the whole crowd in Priam Square was shouting. "Death to the Greeks! Death to the Greeks!" Then: "Hear! Hear!" and "Three cheers for Penthesileia!" The multitude threw their hats and caps into the air. Well, the lot of them was making enough noise to be heard in the Greek camp and beyond. I wondered what Odysseus was making of it all. Of course, I should have hotfooted it out of Troy had I been a proper little spy; on the other hand, this was too interesting to be missed and I decided Odysseus could wait.

Priam now gave Penthesileia a more careful hug. He said:

"Penthesileia of the Amazons, the Trojans have prepared a banquet to honor you and your warrior maidens. Come, let us feast and be merry for tomorrow is another day." He led Penthesileia up the palace steps followed by the higher ups, while the hoi polloi raced to get the best tables in the bars around Priam square. In a besieged city, every event, no matter how insignificant, called for a party.

Lysandra, Cælius and I looked at each other. Lysandra said quickly:

"Well, I'm the palace cat so I must be there." I said:

"I'm right behind you." I got a nasty look but not even that would keep me away from this festivity. Cælius said he'd leave us to it and would await reports back at his lair.

Lysandra took off and I was right behind her. She ran lightly up the palace steps while I galumphed behind. (Lady cats run lightly up stairs, jump gracefully onto parapets or whatever, like a feather borne on the wind. Male cats are not so graceful. They thud up stairs. They need to scramble with their hind legs to get onto a ledge or anything high.) We reached the main courtyard in no time. Impressive, all mosaic floors, Doric columns and fancy pediments. There were almost no guards so no one bothered us; we were, after all, just a couple of cats.

Lysandra led the way into the palace proper, through a number of brightly lit halls awash in multi-colored marble floors, bronze and marble statues of the Gods, painted in gay colors. I sat down and stared at a marble statue of Zeus. His helmet was gold, his cheeks ruddy and he wore garishly colored clothes and gold sandals.

"What are you staring at?" hissed Lysandra. "Never seen a statue before?" I answered:

"I'm used to them in pristine white marble. This one—well, it looks rather tacky. All those gaudy colors! So primitive. No pastels. No ton-sur-ton." Lysandra purred in mirth and waved her paw.

"Really, Gaius, I don't know what you're on about. White marble statues! Who ever heard of such a thing? Why, they'd be boring and offend the Gods. Come on."

On we went, through many halls adorned with frescoes, one of Leda and the swan. Most appropriate. We reached a terrace that ran the whole length of the palace and I jumped on the balustrade and took a moment to get a view of the city. Troy lay spread out beneath me; torches cast a red glow over the city; I shivered. Someone walking on my grave or somebody's grave. I scampered down and followed Lysandra into the great hall; here were more wonderful mosaics depicting Troy in all its glory poised over the Hellespont, flag flying proudly, its gates open to the world. Well, that was then. Once inside, Lysandra and I split up. I melted into the shadows behind what I guessed to be Priam's great chair.

Servants streamed in, bearing linen table clothes, silver and gold goblets and plates. An enormous bronze vase, gaily inlaid with figures of the Gods, stood in the center, held a beautiful arrangement of flowers and autumn branches. Soon the company entered, Priam leading Penthesileia, followed by Hecuba and Deiphobus, then the rest of the gang: Priam's surviving sons, a gaggle of daughters. (Cassandra still conspicuous for her absence; I wondered which turret they'd locked her in.) The Trojan nobles, army commanders and so on and so forth with their wives. I did not see Helen.

First, there were many toasts, and I nodded off after the third. You've heard one toast, you've heard them all. Then the food arrived. I suppose Troy's allies must have made them proud for it was a banquet indeed. I shuddered at the stuffed swan still wearing all its feathers; as for the roasted dormice, I wouldn't have touched one for a pension. The wine flowed and flowed as if there was no tomorrow—as indeed many would not see one. Desserts came, blancmanges, puddings of all sorts, fruit and cheese and so on. I suppose coffee and tea and liquors were served, but I had been sound asleep since dessert. I woke up when Penthesileia rose to speak. When Penthesileia spoke, no one slept.

She raised her goblet, sweeping her arm first left then right, so as to take in all those either willing to die with her or just there for a free meal. Then she spoke, and her voice was charming; her lovely dark eyes sparkled like black pools reflecting far away stars—or do I mean black holes? How she managed to hide her strength and resolution under this divine maidenly grace and a modest maidenly blush I can't tell. The Trojans hung on her words.

"My friends and kinsmen," she said, ignoring that she had as many kinsmen down in the Greek camp as up in the city. "I am Penthesileia, daughter of Mars, the God of war. And these," with another a sweep of her hand, "are my handmaidens. I do not have to name them for each is famed throughout Troy and the known world for her deeds and valor." I call that downright cheating but people cheered and applauded wildly and the girls smiled prettily. I felt sick. A little bit of patronage and we are all on our backs with gratitude. Penthesileia continued: "May I, first of all, give thanks to our host, Priam, king of Troy . . ." loud and long cheers, "for his munificent welcome . . ." more cheers and the Amazons all joined in and would have sung the national anthem if Penthesileia hadn't put a stop to it. She went on:

"We have come to save the Trojans from imminent doom!" I raised my eyebrows. Not very diplomatic and some of the other guests frowned. But Penthesileia went on: "We will perform such deeds that no man could hope for. And, as I stand here I swear to you: I will destroy the Greeks; and I will kill Achilles! This I will do!" More cheers and applause. I looked around at the revelers. A few looked a tad doubtful, including Æneas and Andromache. I heard her mutter to Aeneas or maybe just to herself:

"Oh, my Hector. While you lived, you were both your parents and my glory. Why did I not die and lie in the earth before the breath left your body? Hector, you left me nothing but grief unutterable, widowed of my hero-husband, doomed to live in bitterness for the rest of my days." She started to rise but Aeneas got her to sit down again. Well, I felt sorry for Andromache and all that but it's never any good bewailing the past; what is done is done and cannot be undone. However, here was someone who would not be cheering Penthesileia on to victory!

The party went on and on. Everyone who was anyone was loud in praise of the visitors, and Priam heaped presents and more presents on Penthesileia and her handmaidens.

Suddenly the hall fell into darkness and silence; the light fled to the great open double doors, illuminating a figure in the doorway. My eyes goggled. Blimey if it wasn't Helen. Like a heroine on stage, she stood in a halo of light. She radiated beauty: the golden stresses, the white white limbs, the perfect features and those blue blue eyes. Then she spoke:

"Penthesileia, most valiant and beautiful. Why have you come?" Penthesileia opened her mouth but Helen stretched out a hand, palm outwards, silencing her. "You wish to right Troy's wrongs! Unhappy woman! Where in your arrogant heart have you found such pretentious words? Do you really believe you have the strength to confront, fight and best Achilles? You mock yourself with such dreams; for doom is upon you and your death at Achilles' hands shall be cruel and swift. I pity you for the madness that has taken possession of your soul.

"Don't you understand that Hector had the strength to wield his spear that you, a woman, have not? Yet, despite his might, courage and love of country, he was slain, his death a bitter grief for Troy, whose people consider him a God!

"Take care, for the Gods will not be mocked. Death stands beside you and doom hangs over you and your maidens. May the gods have mercy on your souls."

The light vanished from the doorway and returned to illuminate the great hall. After a moment of stunned silence, Penthesileia lifted her goblet and cried out:

"Oh, dear Helen! For a moment, I thought it was Cassandra! Come, my friends, one more toast before we go to rest! To Helen!"

Well, had I been Penthesileia I would be heading for the hills! As for confusing Helen with Cassandra, that was just plain stupid. Helen did not prophesy. Helen saw. Between the two of them, my money would always be on Helen.

Soon after, the party broke up. After all the humans had left, Lysandra came over to me.

"Come on," she whispered, "let's go and tell Cælius all about it." However, I shook my head. There was still more I wanted to learn.

"You got ahead," I whispered. "Join you soon." So Lysandra took off while I made my way to the women's wing of the palace, where I knew Penthesileia would be housed. I jumped up on the terrace balustrade and walked silently along. Most of the rooms were dark, except for one; Penthesileia was still up, wearing what I took to be her nightgown, a short filmy black tunic. Very sexy. She was out on the balcony, leaning against the railing, and her face was somber. I lay down in the shadows.

"Helen," she whispered. "The most beautiful woman in the world but also the most terrible. Can she see that my desire for glory in battle will bring grief to myself and the Trojans?" She gripped the edge of the balcony and leaned her head back as far as it would go, eyes closed. Then she straightened herself up: "No! I shall overcome! I am Hector renewed! I shall defeat Achilles and the Greeks and be cleansed of a sister's death!" With that, she walked back to her room. "Tomorrow I will perform mighty deeds and win wide renown." I shivered. Indeed, humans will believe the mocking lies whispered in their ears, luring them onto paths unknown to defeat and despair.

As if by magic, three women took her place, each handsome in her own way. They wore short Greek tunics and golden sandals, their blonde tresses, from darkish to golden, tied up with silver ribbons. The one nearest to me said:

"Well, girls, and what do we do now?" The second one took a swig from a golden goblet and answered:

"As far as I'm concerned, I don't see why we should tire ourselves out when the Greeks will probably take care of it all for us." The third one suddenly saw me and cried:

"Look, girls! A cat!"

"Come off it," came the retort. "What would we need a cat for? We're not witches!" And all three looked at me.

"So, scoot, kitty, you've come to the wrong party! We are not hiring cats." I sniffed.

"I am a cat. I go where I want when I want and do what I want." Laughter.

"So, puss, what are you doing here?" This was embarrassing. So I told the truth and shamed the devil, answering with as much dignity as I could muster:

"To speak frankly, I'm spying on Penthesileia!" All three laughed some more and shouted in unison:

"Curiosity killed the cat!" I answered with a sneer:

"But information brought it back." I was really getting very tired of this line. The lady with the goblet giggled:

"Very true, very true." I continue rather sternly:

"I wish you wouldn't make such a racket! You'll wake everyone up!" More laughter from all three, in fact, they held their sides and just went on and on. I was mortified and expected the palace guards or somebody to come running. At last, the lady with the goblet gasped:

"You are priceless, puss. No one can hear us; no one can see us—no human, that is. Cats are something else. You see, puss, we are the Furies. I am Allecto, this one," pointing to the girl next to her, "is Megære and the one over there is Tisiphone." I looked at them rather dubiously.

"You don't look anything like the furies described in mythology," I said carefully, adding, for safety's sake: "you are too pretty to be . . . furies. Aren't they supposed to be dreadful frightening creatures?" Tisiphone snickered:

"Like this?" Before my very eyes, all three vanished. Violent and howling winds raged, dark clouds and unknown horrible shapes swirled around me. The winds increased to hurricane level. I was so frightened I fell off the balustrade. Megære, now in human form again, picked me up. I shivered:

"Please don't do that again. I must have lost three of my lives."

"Have a drink," Allecto offered me the goblet full to the brim. I looked at it.

"Why, you've been drinking for ages and the goblet is still full!" I shook my head. I was going nuts. "Sorry, of course you would have a goblet that's never empty. Like a cornucopia. But, no, I won't have any wine, it's not a cat thing. Have you got any Perrier?" Allecto shoved the goblet under my nose and I sniffed. Vintage Perrier. I lapped greedily. Having pulled myself together, so to speak, I continued in a conversational sort of way:

"So I take it you don't think Penthesileia killed Hippolyta by mistake?" Tisiphone, who now had the goblet, answered:

"Well, to tell you the truth, we don't really know or care. But somebody above our pay grade thinks she's guilty of murder and here we are." Allecto added:

"We're also supposed to punish perjurers and those who violate the laws of hospitality or supplication." Megære continued:

"To be frank, we just ignore perjury and hospitality issues; otherwise we'd never have any peace. Now, Penthesileia . . ." we all looked into her bedroom, where she lay on her back, perfectly still with wide open eyes. Said Allecto:

"Hasn't slept a wink since it happened." Went on Tisiphone:

"She came here, you know, because she was afraid her own people might condemn and execute her." Megære nodded:

"Better the Greeks get you than your next door neighbor." I mused on all this a bit. I said:

"A murderer needs means, opportunity and motive. Now, she had both means and opportunity. But what was her motive?" Tisiphone shrugged:

"Jealousy, ambition, love, who knows?"

"I mean," I continued, "if you are to be her executioners, you ought to know. What if it really was an accident?" However, all three shook their heads and Tisiphone said:

"That's not our remit. We're not executioners. We hound the guilty until they can stand it no longer and throw themselves over a cliff or something."

"In this particular case, that is, Penthesileia," concluded Megære, "we've decided to wait and see what tomorrow brings. Perhaps our services won't be needed after all."

And, as suddenly as they had appeared, they vanished and I was alone. I stayed a while longer watching Penthesileia. She never closed her eyes. She never even blinked, at least not that I saw. I turned to go. Here was someone who would not be bright eyed and bushy tailed tomorrow.

It was a pensive Gaius Marius that made his way back to Cælius' lair. So in the dark I missed an odd bundle lying on the sidewalk. In fact, I stepped on it and it suddenly came to life, screaming, yelling and jumping about; I nearly had heart failure.

"The Greeks are upon us, the Greeks are upon us!" It cried out and ran off as fast as its legs could carry it. Cælius, curse him, almost died laughing.

"Don't let those guys scare you," he said, wiping tears from his eyes. "They're war veterans who have gone bananas. They've completely lost it and have no direction in life. They live on the street. People feed them out of charity."

"Post-traumatic stress syndrome," I mused. "We've got them at home, too. Don't you have veterans' hospitals or special legislation? A free university education? Or a guaranteed job on discharge?" Cælius shrugged.

"That's not the way we do it here, pal. Of course, they can always enlist again. There's tenure for you. Stay in the army until you die. Come on, curl up and go to sleep." I thought: Troy is not going to last long enough for anyone to get pensions, let alone other entitlements. So I curled up and went to sleep. It had been a long day. Just as I was dropping off, I heard Cælius' voice:

"Tell me, Gaius Marius, what's your take on Penthesileia?" I dragged myself back from dreamland and answered, in an irritated voice:

"What do you mean? Is she guilty of murder or do I want a pair of boots just like hers?" Snarl.

"Don't be stupid! What are the odds she will prevail where Hector failed?" Well, I thought that was a stupid question in itself. But never mind. I considered and said:

"On a scale of 1 to 10, I put her chances at about 4 if Achilles is still in a sulk. If not, zero." No comment. We both went to sleep.

The city of Troy was silent as I sneaked out before dawn the next morning and back to the Greek camp. No battle would take place that morning; mid-afternoon would be my earliest guess. I went straight to my favorite tree, curled up and snoozed until

Odysseus prodded me in the ribs about half an hour later. I was not pleased and frowned at him:

"I've been up half the night on your business," I growled, "can't you let me sleep?"

"No, I can't," sneered Odysseus back. "I want to know what was going on in the city last night. Anyone would have thought Zeus himself had come down to lead the Trojans into battle." I curled up and closed my eyes, murmuring:

"It's only Penthesileia with about 12 other girls. What harm can they do against the whole Greek army?" A prod from Odysseus' foot sent me spinning off my root into the sand. I got to my feet, shook myself and looked at him in anger. "Will you get real, Odysseus," I snarled, showing my incisors, "you have an army and Priam has 13 girls! Do tell me how this is going to shift the balance of power!"

"Idiot cat!" snarled Odysseus, we were a right pair of snarlers. "The 13 girls are nothing but their very presence may fill the Trojans with hope and fire and courage. When do you think they'll attack?"

"Considering the hangovers," I answered, curling up again, "I would guess sometime in the afternoon." I added as Odysseus started striding off. "Are you going to tell the others?"

"Not just now," came the answer. "They'd just get in the way. I'm going to make sure the troops are fairly sober and alert." Good luck, thinks I before going back to dreamland.

I was at *The Greek Olive Tree* by lunchtime. Eurybates brought me my usual tuna snacks and designer water. After concentrating on food for a bit, I looked up to see who was around. I was not really surprised to see the whole Greek High Command in their usual basic groups, by which I mean Agamemnon and Menelaus; Nestor and Odysseus, Odysseus staring into space with a vacant look on his face while Nestor napped. Ajax was by himself getting as much drink as he could while shoveling his face with moussaka. A growing boy, our Ajax. Diomedes was twiddling his thumbs next to Idomeneus. Diomedes broke the silence:

"Where's Achilles?" Idomeneus sneered.

"Where'd you think? In his tent, wailing because there are no more Hectors to slaughter.[xiv]" Diomedes sniggered and Idomeneus looked pleased at his own cleverness. I looked at him lazily. Actually, I could have told them Achilles was on the beach blubbering over Patroklus' ashes. So all was peace and quiet, everyone relaxed. And the afternoon wore on as afternoons do. Odysseus called for some more wine and Ajax for more moussaka. Then, about teatime, all Hades broke loose. There came the sound of running feet, gasping breath and one of Agamemnon's Mycenaean non-coms literally fell into the bar, mouth agape and eyes popping.

"Great King, Great King," he gasped. "The Antenorides gate has opened and the Trojans are streaming out in great numbers! A woman on a great black horse commands them. It is said to be Penthesileia, the Queen of the Amazons." Agamemnon shook his head and closed his eyes.

"Young man," he said, "you must have heatstroke. Come out of the sun and have a glass of water." He leaned back and picked at his teeth. Nestor shook his white head solemnly:

"Women warriors! I'm sure the Mesopotamia Convention does not allow it." Odysseus looked at his nails.

"Well, Nestor, either Priam or Penthesileia or both can't read or don't care in the least about the Mesopotamia Convention. However, I have it on good authority that Penthesileia really is here and that a battle is in the works. So, great King, I suggest you get off your backside and, as Commander-in-Chief of the Greek Expeditionary Forces, do something about it." Agamemnon got up in fury and turned, I suppose, to smite Odysseus. But Diomedes and Idomeneus were already on their feet, staring towards the city on the hill. I didn't bother to lift my head since I already knew all there was to know. Idomeneus cried out:

"Something is clearly going on. Look at the clouds of dust on the plain: horses and chariots. Antenorides is indeed open."

"Come one," Diomedes shouted, "this is no time for lounging about. Whether Amazons or not, something has put heart into the Trojans." Menelaus groaned:

"We should never have allowed Calchas to leave!" Odysseus sneered:

"Too late for that! Move, it's all hands to the pump now!" Ajax, who could never get enough of maiming and killing, sprang up, shouting:

"Goody! Action at last!" The kings and princes vanished towards the Greek camp to arm themselves and join the fray. I stretched, washed my face, and lay down for a nap. I had seen all the battles I ever wanted to see. This one, the Greeks would have to handle without my help.

The sun passed into the west while the noise from the battlefield grew louder and louder. Wounded and stragglers started arriving at *The Greek Olive Tree* for bandages and sustenance, the one provided by Eurybates' wife (whose name I never learnt), the other by Eurybates and his bouncer. At a question from Eurybates, one of them gasped:

"Penthesileia! The Amazon Queen! It really is her. I swear she'll have all our hides before the day is done! Those women are more furious than Hector ever was. The Trojans are all worked up and they're going at it as if there was no tomorrow." Very true, I thought, for many a Greek and Trojan, there would indeed be no tomorrow. Eurybates asked, handing the guy a brimful:

"What about Achilles?" Another walking wounded came in, holding his broken arm:

"Achilles?" He asked bitterly. "Who's Achilles?" Well, there was one thing I could do for the side that would cost me nothing and might even be fun, so I wandered down to the beach where, indeed, I found Achilles moaning over Patroklus' ashes. I sat down next to him, curling my tail neatly around my paws.

"Well may you weep, great Achilles," I said in formal tones, "not only for your friend but for all of Greece." He looked up. Seeing me did not console him. He sneered:

"Always hanging about, aren't you? Scat, go away. Chase a mouse or a bird. Make yourself useful." My tail flicked.

"Oh, I am," I answered, "making myself useful. And you would be well advised to be doing something useful, too. Grieving over the dead is all very well, but not when there's man's work to be done. The Greeks are under heavy attack. They need every man."

"And why should I care?" jeered Achilles. "Let them all perish. I shall dance on their funeral ashes." I inspected my claws and remarked:

"And so it shall be written:

> *the Greek army at Troy was destroyed by a woman,*
> *despite the presence of the great Achilles . . ."*

I got no further. Achilles was on his feet:

"A woman?" he shouted. "A woman? What nonsense is this?" I looked at him guilessly with my big blue eyes.

"Not any woman, Achilles the Great, but Penthesileia, Queen of the Amazons, and her female warriors. She has sworn to kill Achilles, destroy the great army of the Greeks and burn their ships." I gazed at the sky: "She is the daughter of a God while Achilles is the son of a mere water nymph. That may be taken into account when they write your obituary.

> *'Achilles was slain by Penthesileia, the Queen of the*
> *Amazons, not merely a woman, but a goddess!'*

"Listen! Can you not hear her voice?" Sure enough, a high woman's voice seemed to fill the air all around us.

> *"Ye dogs, this day for evil outrage done*
> *To Priam shall ye pay! No man of you*
> *Shall from mine hands deliver his own life,*

And win back home, to gladden parents eyes,
Or comfort wife or children. Ye shall lie
Dead, ravined[ravaged] on by vultures and by wolves,
And none shall heap the earth-mound o'er your clay.
Where skulketh [hides] now the strength of Tydeus' son [Diomedes],
And where the might of Aeacus' scion [Achilles]?
Where is Ajax' bulk? Ye vaunt them mightiest men
Of all your rabble. Ha! they will not dare
With me to close in battle, lest I drag
Forth from their fainting frames their craven souls."[10]

Achilles went berserk. He jumped up with a wild look in his eyes:

"Me? Me? Bested by a woman? In your dreams! And why should I believe you, a mere cat, or a disembodied voice in the wind, for that matter?" I inspected my claws.

"No reason you should believe either," I answered, "just listen to the sounds of war; chariots racing, horses neighing, hooves beating, dust rising from the plain, the moans of the wounded, cries of the dying." And, sure enough, the tumult was now so great it easily reached us.

"We'll see about this," Achilles cried and was off like lightning. "That bitch! She'll soon learn who Achilles is! I'll make her eat her words, see if I don't!" As he ran, he shouted: "Automedon! Automedon!" Automedon was Achilles' charioteer and general factotum.

I lay down besides Patroklus' ashes for a while. The company of the dead can be very soothing. An added bonus: they can't argue or answer back. I said:

"You know, Patroklus, I don't usually interfere in human affairs." Then I declaimed, in as loud a voice as I could, waving my paws for emphasis:

'After all, what am I to Hecuba?'

---

[10]   Quintus of Smyrna translated by A. S. Way (1913)

"Or, for that matter,

'what is Hecuba to me that I should weep for her?'[xv]

Oh, I felt so cultured and clever. Then I stroked my nose thoughtfully. "So why am I interfering this time? I must confess to myself—and to you, Patroklus—that I don't really know. Perhaps," I continued, "I should have left well enough alone and you and Achilles would have been reunited in the great beyond." I rolled over on my back to get sun on my tummy. Vitamin D is good for the system. I closed my eyes, wiggled my toes and soaked up the solar rays.

"When you come down to it, Patroklus, the way you died, well, it must have added to your status in Hades. After all, Hector himself, not a common footslogger, killed you! In addition, wearing Achilles' armor! You died a hero! Who would ever have believed it? That, my friend, was way above your pay grade. A glorious death for Patroklus! Patroklus, a hero!" I stroked my nose in thought. The breeze whistled around me; Patroklus, perhaps, trying to be rid of me. But I continued:

"Truth to tell, Patroklus, all other thing being equal, your death did bring Achilles out of his tent. That was your greatest achievement." Fierce rustling. "O.K., o.k., so in the nick of time you turned the tide down by the Greek ships! True! That was, perhaps, a bit heroic." The wind whistled around me. "But you should have stopped at that, my good friend, not imagined yourself Achilles and try to take Troy all on your own." I shook my head sadly. "If you'd known your place, you'd still be alive today." The rustling became more frantic. Patroklus was getting very tired of my company. But what did I care? Human ghosts? They don't bother me none. Not that I had ever seen any—at the time. To give poor Patroklus a rest, I lay down for a snooze.

At Happy Hour, I was back on my usual place on *The Greek Olive Tree* bar. Eurybates waggled his eyebrows at me. I said:

"Achilles went to join the fray."

"Ahhh," was Eurybates' comment. Then he gave me some designer water and fresh tuna snacks.

Stragglers continued arriving, more or less bruised and battered, all with stories of the fearless Amazons and the havoc they were creating among the Greeks. The Greek body count, it seemed, was up and up. *The Greek Olive Tree* became busy, a kind of field hospital, Eurybates' wife as nurse, Eurybates and his bouncer dishing out booze and food. Just as dusk was falling, a guy with a mangled foot, hobbling along with the help of a spear, arrived:

"Achilles!" He gasped between bouts of pain. "Achilles is on the field. The tide is turning in our favor . . ." and then he collapsed. Thinks I, took him long enough . . . I mean, he was supposed to be Achilles.

And so the long day wore on. The sun sank into the west and, with darkness, the bedraggled Greek High Command returned. They hadn't bothered to wash or change and most of them needed attention from Eurybates' wife. Odysseus was last; he collapsed on an empty chair and called for wine.

"That," he said, "was close. I thought the Trojans really had us this time around. Achilles arrived at just the right moment." Diomedes said:

"You could have knocked me down with a feather when I saw all those mounted women. I mean: how on earth do you handle lady warriors?" Idomeneus added:

"Yeah, I wanted to hold the Antenorides gate open for them but I couldn't get near it." Menelaus said:

"You should have put your name down on their dance cards!" Odysseus gurgled:

"Those were dance cards of another color."

"For instance," snickered Idomeneus, "my name was down for a quadrille with Bermousa; got her right through the heart." Everybody looked embarrassed. Nestor cleared his throat:

"Goes against the grain, having to treat women in this fashion. I really do think Priam overstepped his mark this time. Using those girls as warriors—not playing the game. In complete opposition of the terms of the Mesopotamia Convention." Nestor was really put out. He was nowhere near the acceptance of equality between men and women.

Then, Achilles sauntered in, covered in blood. Eurybates' wife ran forward with whatever bandages she had left, but Achilles waved her away:

"Woman," he said haughtily, "this blood I am covered in is not mine. I have no need of your ministrations." Nestor looked up:

"So whose blood is it?" Achilles looked at his haughtily:

"Really, Nestor, I expected more acuity from you. Of course it's Penthesileia's."

"And her horse's," murmured Menelaus. Everyone stared at him. Achilles sneered:

"You don't think," he said, "I was going to let myself be beaten by a mere woman!" Idomeneus replied:

"A mere woman, I think not. This one must have had the ability, courage and strength of ten warriors. Her girlfriends weren't to be sneezed at either. They bagged many a Greek." Achilles quaffed his wine and said dreamily:

"I'd liked to have taken that Penthesileia home as a concubine or slave or something. A bit of a waste having to kill her, she was absolutely gorgeous. Such curves. Such lips. Such flashing eyes. And such hair! Black as night! Why, I might even have married her—if she'd insisted." Diomedes joined the conversation:

"You'd have taken that hellcat to bed? I wouldn't give odds for your getting up in one piece the next morning." Achilles shrugged.

"A woman," he replied, his voice chilled steel, "is after all just a woman. Her aim in life is to get a husband. Once she gets that, she settles down and worries about pickled onions and cured hams, schools for the children and having better furniture than the neighbors." Odysseus asked:

"How did you manage? I didn't see the actual kill." Achilles guffawed. I had never seen him enjoy himself so much.

"Not surprised, Odysseus. I hardly ever see you when the going gets rough." Odysseus didn't bother to answer. Achilles steepled his fingers and looked heavenwards. "If you want to know, she attacked me first, throwing her spear with great force, I grant you. You should have seen her face when it broke on my shield! I then ran her and her horse through with one fell swoop of my spear." Murmurs of admiration. "A first class kill. Can't remember a finer one! But a real waste all around. I took her helmet as a trophy." He frowned and looked around: "I hope no one has an issue with that?" They all shook their heads. "Yes," he continued in a satisfied voice, "a trophy worth a king's ransom. Solid bronze, encrusted with jewels. Should be worth a fortune." At that moment, Ajax arrived. He'd cleaned himself up. He was all smiles.

"Best battle I've ever been in," he said, sitting down with a satisfied sigh and snapping his fingers at Eurybates, who did not hurry over with his drink. "Kill as many ladies as you like. Beats the hell out of pillage and rape any day of the week, I can tell you." He drank deeply from the mug the bouncer set down before him. "Yes, sir! What a day. What a day!" The others looked uncomfortable. Nestor frowned. I could read his thoughts: Ajax was not a gentleman. But, as the man says, it takes all sorts.

5.2 Eurypylus, Herakles' last descendent

Needless to say, Odysseus sent me right back to Troy and I was happy to oblige—Odysseus was getting on my nerves in no uncertain terms. I was hanging about the battlements with Betsy—she having no urgent business elsewhere—when it was all Déjà vu again! Jonathan swooped down next to us and announced:

"There's an army coming out of the north." My eyes widened.

"An army?" I quavered, then hopefully, "another 13 girls?"

"No, Gaius," Jonathan sounded irritated. "Betsy, you'd better advise Cælius at once." Betsy hared off, not stopping to say goodbye. "Come on," urged Jonathan, "if we get above the Helia gate we should be able to see what's what." He flew off. I ran along the ramparts until I got to Helia and jumped up on a convenient crenellation. What I saw coming down the hill was indeed an army, well, of sorts, marching any old way, singing at the top of their voices. They also banged drums, blew on trumpets and clashed cymbals. There was shouting and laughing and enough noise for 100 trumpeting elephants. These boys were in for a good time. At their head came a big brawny fellow, armed to the teeth and carrying the most enormous shield. He needed a shave and a wash and a change of clothes. The whole company was dressed in animal hides. They all carried the usual ax, sword and shield.

"Blimey," I said, "Troy's being attacked by the Neanderthals." Jonathan, who had alighted next to me, cocked an ear and gave me a surprised look but I wasn't about to elaborate. By this time, there was a stampede of Trojans towards our spot. Jonathan flew away and I made myself scarce, hiding in a convenient hole. Paris and Deiphobus came up, pushing the lower classes away. Then Paris let out a yell and held up his arm with a closed fist, waiving it about with enthusiasm.

"It's Eurypylus and his gang!" He cried excitedly. "Look, they're marching round the city towards Antenorides!" Well, that was enough for me. I hared down the nearest steps, hoofed it to Antenorides, shot through the bolt hole, pushing aside whatever mice and rats got in my way. I shouted to Orestes:

"Get your gang out of here. There's a whole crowd of the unwashed coming your way." Orestes gasped but to do him honor he didn't stop to ask questions but retreated in good order towards the city. Only the owl Seneca was left. He was asleep and I don't think even the last trump could have woken him up.

I got out of Troy just in time, for Eurypylus and his band camped by Antenorides and spread themselves out halfway to Troien.

I ran straight for *The Greek Olive Tree* and only came to a stop when I bumped into someone's legs.

"Hey!" It was Ajax, "someone's killed the cat!" For I confess I fainted for a few moments—I didn't know cats could but I did. Somebody grabbed me from Ajax.

"He just needs a bit of water." That was Odysseus. He put me on the bar and told Eurybates to get some retsina but before this materialized, I went into hysterics:

"They want my hide," I howled, clinging to Odysseus, my claws digging into his arm.

"Will you get a grip?" he shouted, "and get your claws out of my damned arm! You're tearing me to shreds." I wailed:

"Do you know how many ways there are to skin a cat?" Then Eurybates came with the retsina, they held it under my nose; I sneezed and then slowly came round.

"Go get some water with a bit of wine in it," ordered Odysseus. I was going to say I didn't like wine but when it came and Odysseus poured it down my throat, I spluttered, shook my head, and felt better. Odysseus patted me on the back:

"Well, Gaius, what's going on?" I was still out of breath and confused and cried:

"Goths and Vandals![11] Goths and Vandals!" Odysseus gave me a good shaking.

"What are you talking about? Pull yourself together! What's a Goth? What's a Vandal?"

"Never mind, never mind," I said impatiently. "You should see those guys. They're uncivilized. I saw one spit on the road and another piss against a tree. Is that a mark of civilized people? They're all wearing animal hides. Disgusting!" Odysseus chuckled. I looked at him angrily and he wiped the grin off his face.

"Tell me, dear friend," he said soothingly, "did you find out who these uncivilized people are?"

---

[11] The tribes that destroyed the Roman Empire in the West.

"The leader," I said huffily, "is called Eurypylus or some such thing." I started shaking again. "They want my hide—I know it, I just know it! I want to go home!" More pats. Eurybates brought me some tuna snacks and I forgot my terror for a bit.

"Eurypylus," Odysseus rubbed his chin. "That explains much." He turned to Agamemnon. "Isn't Eurypylus a relation of yours?" Agamemnon sneered and answered haughtily:

"Everyone wants to be my relation." Odysseus sighed but then Nestor intervened:

"He is said to be the last descendant of Herakles." Odysseus nodded:

"One of those. I see. His 'gang', of course, are Cetæan warriors from the banks of the river Caïcus. They have great faith in their spears." Very interesting, I'm sure, but I was keeping well away from both men and spears.

They all trooped out of *The Greek Olive Tree* to watch Eurypylus and his horde set up shop between Antenorides and Troien. Even Achilles was there.

"It's an outrage," he shouted in real fury. "All these foreign princelings coming to Troy just to try their luck in defeating ME!" He snarled. Achilles as we know and love him. "Any descendant of Herakles," he went on, "deserves to die by Achilles' sword." Said Menelaus pensively:

"We might rush them now when they are all confused with setting up camp." Odysseus, of course, nipped this right in the bud:

"Bad idea. We want Eurypylus and as far as I can see he isn't there." I said:

"Probably gone to the customary banquet!" Everyone looked at me. I wondered if Troy would ever run out of food. Then Odysseus got up to leave, saying:

"Guys, get some sleep. However, before turning in, see that your warriors have their gear ready, spit and polished. And post guards, in the camps and near the ships." As an afterthought: "And no drinking between now and Happy Hour tomorrow.

Eurybates, close up shop." He walked out, saying: "We'll rise and arm at dawn."

The crowd dispersed to their tents and I slunk down to my tree on the beach. I was hyperventilating and had trouble settling down. Just as I was finally starting to nod off, footsteps approached. Damned Odysseus.

"Gaius," he said in a smarmy voice, "you could consider . . ." I cut him off before he could finish.

"No I wouldn't; go away." I closed my eyes tight and went to sleep.

The next day at dawn, the armies drew up facing each other, their commanders before them: Eurypylus, Paris and Deiphobus for the Trojans, Agamemnon, Achilles and Menelaus for the Greeks. The Greeks stood waiting silently in serried ranks but the Cetæans were in great fettle, jumping up and down and whooping and generally making nuisances of themselves.

Then Eurypylus stepped forward, his sword raised. His shield bore engravings of all of Herakles' 12 labors[xvi] and he could hardly lift the thing off the ground. He cried:

"Men—Cetæans, Trojans and Greeks—the Gods have determined who will die and who will live before this day is over. I stand here before Troy, as is my birthright as a descendent of the mightiest of all warriors, Herakles, and, like him, I have the strength to fight and fight I will. And I take this oath: to vanquish the Greeks and burn their ships. Hear me all—here I shall stay until my oath is fulfilled or I have perished!"

This sounded a bit like Penthesileia but then I suppose there aren't many variations on the theme when you're on destruction bent. Achilles snorted:

"Indeed! Herakles, that great big hunk of nothing. Who mistook his own family for . . . for . . . well, I don't know what but he slaughtered the lot. I hope this guy already has a family for if he doesn't he'll be the last of his clan. Trust me."

Then Paris spoke:

"You are most welcome here, Eurypylus. I know in my heart that, together, we will wipe the Greeks from the face of the earth. So, I extort you all, Trojans and Cetæans: fill your minds with deeds worthy of the great and mighty Herakles. Eurypylus, your leader, is his descendent and resembles him in size and strength. And never doubt that our cause is just!" Everyone cheered. Translation: please come and get us out of the hole we've dug for ourselves! A lousy speech as I'd ever heard but what could be expected from Paris!

Then every warrior girded his loins or pulled up his socks or whatever it is humans do before slaughter begins. I hoofed it back to *The Greek Olive Tree*. Whatever they were about to do they would do without me!

Eurybates and I shared a convivial drink, listening to the noises of battle. The usual stuff, it never varies: screams of pain from both horses and men. Clouds of dust rising from the plain and very soon the smell of blood and guts and despair became overwhelming. I covered my nose with a paw and tried to sleep.

As usual, there was a steady stream of walking wounded coming to *The Greek Olive Tree* in search of bandages and sustenance. Their accounts of the Cetæans agreed with Nestor's—fearful warriors who had never heard of the Mesopotamia Convention—in fact, they were neither officers nor gentlemen. As advertised, they were good with their spears; once these had gone, stones became their weapons of choice, hurled on the premise that one or other was bound to hit something or someone. It was uphill work for the Greeks and Achilles and Ajax were essential in keeping defeat at bay. This was definitely their kind of battle.

The slaughter went on all day. It was late in the afternoon when Achilles pierced Eurypylus' throat with his mighty sword, and fighting came to an end; whatever Cetæans were still standing fled into the hills, while the surviving Trojans slunk back into the city by the Helia gate.

93

The Greek survivors, included all of the high command, were back at *The Greek Olive Tree* by sundown. Happy Hour got into full swing, in spite of the myriad contusions and bruises and cuts of minor or major severity. It was difficult to tell the really wounded from those who were just covered in blood. Of course, Achilles was the hero of the hour, since he was the one to have dispatched Eurypylus. When he walked in, he was such a gory mess that, for a moment, I thought he was a walking corpse. However, I was soon disabused as he rubbed his hands and said with a satisfied smirk:

"That's one of Herakles' descendants who won't bother us again." He snapped his fingers at Eurybates who sauntered out with the required mug. Achilles sighed: "I said to him: 'Eurypylus, you said you would destroy the Greek ships and army, and would kill the lot of us.' A smirk. "But unfortunately the Gods didn't respond. For all your invincibility, my spear has subdued you." He got up and threw out his arms. "The spear of Achilles that no man shall escape, even if he were made entirely of brass." Everyone applauded. Achilles was so pleased he ordered a round of drinks for all, including the soldiers on the terrace.

Odysseus looked at Achilles sort of sideways.

"One more such battle and it'll be curtains for both Greeks and Trojans." Achilles turned to him in irritation but Odysseus continued: "We lost Machaon, you know, I saw him go down. One less Greek physician."

"Can't see what he was doing in the field anyway," scoffed Idomeneus. "Why wasn't he back in the hospital?" Diomedes answered caustically:

"Better dead, perhaps, than trying to handle all those wounded." It was a thought. Being a doctor under the conditions I'd seen could hardly be called practicing medicine. Naturally, Achilles waved away poor Machaon.

"Oh, just collateral damage. He wasn't a particularly good doctor anyway. Otherwise, I can't understand what you lot mean. It was a clear victory for us. Ye gods, Odysseus, don't you ever find anything positive to say about our victories?" Odysseus sneered:

"Victory indeed! The whole thing was so in the balance, going backward and forward, first we had the upper hand then we did not. It only ended when you gave Herakles' grandson or whoever Eurypylus was his comeuppance." Diomedes chimed in:

"You must confess, Achilles, that you really had to work hard for this one. Sheer luck, in my view, your finally managing to gouge him." Achilles was sucking on one finger, a dreamy look on his face, reliving events.

"He can't say I didn't give him fair warning of my intentions," he remarked loftily. He stretched out his legs, and laid his threaded fingers on his tummy. "I said to him: 'Eurypylus, I fancy I heard you say that you could, all by yourself, destroy the Greeks and their ships. Well, I am sorry to have to teach you otherwise—no mortal who comes against me escapes my spear or my sword, be he encased in solid bronze.' Then I let him have it." Deep silence all around. "Then," continued Achilles, "I removed his armor and my lads took it back to our ships." Yep, that's our boy, that's our Achilles. Hope those untanned hides won't smell up the place too much. Odysseus just looked glum. He said to Agamemnon:

"Well, you've had your wish, Commander-in-chief, lots more battles and we're no further along than we were after Hector's death." Agamemnon swaggered about:

"Nonsense, my dear Odysseus. Just another battle—or three or four—and we shall prevail!"

Both sides become busy with the usual post battle housekeeping—burning the dead and tidying up the battle plain. That's the problem when there's only one battlefield, and armies can't just move on leaving the mess behind.

There wasn't marked enthusiasm for further engagements within the High Greek Command, except for Ajax who kept egging Agamemnon on. This continued until one day at elevenses, with everyone there, Agamemnon jumped up, as if he had sat on a nail, and announced:

"My friends, Ajax is right. We must throw off this lethargy and develop a new strategy and plan of campaign. We still have thousands of men and armament and siege weapons. We need to follow up our victories and give the Trojans the COUP DE GRÂCE[12], and wrap this thing up. Let's develop a new battle plan and . . ." He got no further because Odysseus leapt up and interrupted him.

"No!" He said firmly. "No! The time for battles is past! No battle will end this war. I have said so before." Agamemnon looked at Odysseus in puzzled surprise and spread out his hands:

"Then what do we do? We can't continue sitting here just twiddling our thumbs until doomsday!"

"Eurybates," and Odysseus' voice was stentorious. "Drinks for everyone! On the house!" I knew 'on the house' meant: 'chalk it up to the High Command'. The drinks arrived and everyone fell to with a will. Did Odysseus have a new plan or at least a new idea? I felt doubtful. Odysseus twirled on one spot like a lecturer in an auditorium or a whirling dervish. Then he spoke:

"Boys, we need to admit this war will never end in the conventional way; for nine years we have fought endless battles, always thinking this one would be the last one. That has proved a fallacy and here we are in utter stalemate." He strode up and down, pointing at each Greek commander in turn. "We need a new way of thinking. We need to develop a completely new strategy that focuses solely, and I say solely, on destroying the city of Troy the only way it can be done—from within." There was a flutter among his audience but Odysseus held his hand up. "Don't argue. If you think about it, you'll see I'm right." Ajax looked dumbfounded:

---

[12]   Finishing/last stroke

"But, Odysseus, we've tried to get in every way possible, haven't we, lads?" The others murmured their agreement. Odysseus waggled his finger in Ajax' face:

"Not everything, we haven't tried everything. We haven't tried the one that really works." The rest looked stunned. Agamemnon asked:

"And which is that?" But Odysseus just walked out.

I thought this would be a good time to visit Troy again before Odysseus got me involved in another of his nefarious plots. Troy should be safe now. I couldn't see another champion turning up to save the Trojans' bacon.

Cælius and I lay on his wall. It was about Happy Hour but the mood in Troy was dejected not to say defeatist; first, Penthesileia then Eurypylus had proven to be complete washouts. Cælius sniffed:

"The real truth that no one will admit," he said, "is that the Trojans just can't handle this on their own and, I hate to say it, with or without Hector. All this stuff of bringing in famous names and so on is just so much gist to Achilles' killing mill." I had to agree. Cælius went on: "Of course, Penthesileia was a non-starter. I mean, thirteen girls?"

"But a lot of Trojan warriors followed her," I reminded him. Cælius waved his paw as if swatting a fly.

"Be that as it may, as soon as Penthesileia was no more, the Trojans cut and ran." That was undeniably true. I tried to defend them a tad.

"There were a lot more warriors with Eurypylus . . ." but Cælius swatted that away, too.

"Don't you see, my friend, all these battles depended on only one warrior? Once Penthesileia and then Eurypylus were goners, the Trojan offensive collapsed. And that ought to tell you something." I thought about it for a while.

"It tells me," I said, "that the Greeks are still here because they have not one leader but several. And the loss of one would really make no difference." I added: "If, say, you got rid of

Agamemnon, it could only make things better. And if there was no one left but Odysseus, he'd just go home."

"True," answered Cælius, "if you depend on one man—or woman or cat or whatever—to lead you, you're skewered. That's why this idea of kingship—one man in charge of the state—doesn't work." I had to admit he was right but I didn't tell him it would take about four thousand years for humans to accept this truism. Cælius continued: "When Hector fell, Troy was left rudderless. Deiphobus and Helenus are good officers but not leaders. Paris and Troilus you can discount for obvious reasons."

"Troilus may not be too bad," I ventured, "once he masters his temper." Cælius rolled his eyes.

"That," he answered, "won't be any time soon." I said rather sadly:

"I doubt he'll live long enough . . ." I couldn't finish because Lysandra came flying up:

"They're having a meeting—the Trojan High Command, I mean—right now. Are you coming, Gaius?" she cried excitedly. Well, why not? Better than going to the Greek camp and getting the runaround from Odysseus. As we were scooting off, Jonathan swooped down and settled on the wall next to Cælius. He flapped his wings.

"There is news, from the North as usual. The crows have seen a retinue of black men coming this way, not many and one is borne in a sedan chair." We looked at Cælius for enlightenment. He scratched his whiskers:

"Sounds like an embassy to me." To Jonathan: "Not an army, you say." Jonathan nodded.

"Twenty at most, according to Montrose."

"Right," said Cælius, "since we know nothing about this, it's on the cards that the Trojans aren't expecting whoever it is. It could turn out to be important. Better get on with it, you two." I followed Lysandra and, before I could say 'knife', we were in the great hall, deserted and in total darkness, and retreated into the shadows.

5.3 Menon of Ethiopia

Servants came in with torches, pitchers, glasses and such. Then the council members arrived, all dressed in somber colors, as if for a funeral, arms swinging, heads bowed, led by King Priam, his sons Paris, Helenus, Deiphobus, Troilus, Polytes and others I didn't recognize. The Trojan nobles followed: Æneas, Antenor, Adrestus and so on. Then the ladies, also in dark colors, except for Helen who wore light blue: Hecuba, the Queen, Andromache, Hector's widow, Hecuba and Priam's daughters: Cassandra, Laodicea, Polyxena, then other great ladies of Troy.

King Priam sat down in the great chair at the head of the table. At the opposite end, a lone chair was conspicuously empty—Hector's, who wouldn't be needing it, at least not in this life. Priam stared for a long time at the empty chair. At length he said:

"He can never be replaced." No one asked whom he meant. Then Priam wrung his hands. "And we grieve also for Penthesileia and Eurypylus. Oh, my friends, I prayed to Zeus that the Queen and her Amazons would vanquish the Greek host and she would return in safety to my house. But it wasn't to be!" The hand wringing continued. "Then Eurypylus came with the Cetæans. Again I begged the Gods to show mercy to me, I have who suffered so many evils and seen so many of my sons die!" Deep silence. After all that, what was there left to say? I also felt it was a lot of ask even of the God of Gods: take my burdens and have this kind lady and/or gentleman—Penthesileia/Eurypylus—sort things out.

Priam continued piteously: "Our good friends, our kinsmen, all gone." True, thinks I, and in an unworthy cause. Priam broke down and wept, whether for Hector, Penthesileia, Eurypylus or himself he didn't say. Me, I bet these were tears of self-pity. Hecuba and a few of the daughters tried to console him and at length he regained his self-control. He rose, lifted his exhausted and tear-stained face and held out his arms:

"My sons and peers of Troy, let us have a moment of silence in honor of the great sacrifice of Penthesileia and Eurypylus." Yeah, needless and stupid. What good had their sacrifice been? But everyone rose obediently and bowed their heads—except Helen. Next to her, Hecuba frowned but Helen took no notice. At length—it might have been a minute but it could also have been two—Priam sat down and everyone else—except Helen, of course—followed suit. Priam sighed and, turning to Helen, said wearily: "You could show some respect, my dear Helen. After all, Penthesileia and Eurypylus both died in your cause." Helen looked at Priam, a glance that should have killed, crossed her long legs and snapped:

"No, she didn't and, no, neither did he. By dying, neither did me any good. In fact, I said so then and I repeat it now: Penthesileia's arrogance in challenging the Greeks was reckless and stupid. How could she think—how could you think, Priam –, that she would succeed where Hector failed? And, if she had, how would it reflect on Hector's memory?" Hard words. No one wanted to take this discussion any further. Priam sighed deeply and moved on:

"My fellow Trojans, I am afraid I can no longer lead you. I am old and worn out. My heart is broken and in the urn with Hector. My only hope now is to join him as soon as the Gods permit; my son, my son!" Large tears started falling on his trembling hands as they lay on the table. As in all such situations, the men became uncomfortable and looked elsewhere. Hecuba and the daughters looked concerned and some started sobbing, too. Helen's face remained like a block of ice. From where I lay, it seemed that, if no one had any bright ideas, Troy was going to tank. Then Deiphobus rose to his feet.

"Father, even if we shed enough tears to overflow the Ægean, we cannot bring Hector or our kinfolk back. I'm sorry, my dear parents; there is no time for lamentations if our city and its people are to survive. We cannot help the dead. Let us see what we can do for the living." Shocked looks from various sides but Deiphobus was right. One needs to get real, get closure and move on. Priam saw it too because he pulled himself together:

"My son, even if your words are cruel, they are true. We have a higher duty to the living than to the dead. There will be time for sorrow later." True, old man, but not for you. Priam continued: "I nominate you, Deiphobus, my eldest surviving son, and Æneas, as senior Trojan nobleman, to take Hector's place." He sat back. "I leave the fate of Troy in your hands."

Deiphobus and Æneas looked at each other. Clearly, an honor they could well have done without, although Deiphobus had rather asked for it. On the other hand, both Paris and Troilus looked put out. Oh, oh, thinks I. Priam, you may be old and worn out but you still have some wisdom left. You don't want these two scallywags—well, Paris wasn't a kid by a long shot but he still acted like one—making decisions or giving orders. Deiphobus said:

"Father, though Æneas and I have not looked for this, we accept your decision and will do what we can. Æneas, I am sure, will agree with me." Æneas nodded his face somber. So now, if nothing else, Priam had chosen who would take the fall when things went south. Thinks I: the Escape Committee in the shed next to the temple is better organized than you lot. Then Æneas stood up. He leaned his knuckles on the tabletop and said in a somber voice:

"My friends, a lot has happened over the past months. I thought we had reached a turning point at the battle by the Greek ships; the day was ours but, truth to tell, the price we paid, the loss of Hector, was so terrible that victory turned into defeat." Yeah, one more such victory, it'll be curtains for the Trojans. Æneas stopped and looked around the table. Then he continued. "Let us review what has been accomplished over the last nine years; we have not been short of victories, held our own on the battlefield, withstood a siege, our city still intact. However, the Greeks are still with us." Another pause. "So let's be frank. Luck has also been on our side. The greatest of the Greek warriors, Achilles, abandoned the war efforts for a while, giving us much needed respite. However, the death of Patroklus, slain by Hector, brought Achilles back into the fray. In addition, I must agree with Helen: the interventions of Penthesileia and Eurypylus, no matter how well intended, were total disasters and hard for us to live with. In summary, we are still much where we were ten years ago and victory still out of our reach." Deiphobus then took over.

"I agree with most of what Æneas says, except that we are not where we were ten years ago. We were all ten years younger then, stronger in body and feats of arms with a full contingent of warriors. How many have died over the past decade? How many families have moved away, afraid that the future of their sons to be war and death? Have you walked through our city's streets lately? Seen the abandoned houses, falling masonry, overgrown gardens? Troy is dying." Deiphobus paused and then went on: "I believe Troy's walls will stand when all those alive today, whether Trojan or Greek, have departed for Hades. Inside our walls, we may be able to hang on until Judgment Day. But, tell me, please, what good will it do? Our normal lives ceased ten years ago. The Hellespont is blocked and our trade routes closed." Deiphobus bowed his head. Æneas took over:

"My friends, we will not win this war on the battlefield; we have neither the warriors nor the leadership. The allied kingdoms to the North are unwilling and unable to support us and who can blame them? They have no fresh troops to aid us and we must be grateful they still supply us with grain and meat." Troilus jumped up, waving his hand. I thought: here comes a tirade on honor and glory. But Æneas wasn't having it, not just then. He waved Troilus down. "The prosperous villages that once surrounded our city were laid waste and disappeared long ago. Let's say we continue to withstand the siege. At one point we'll run out of supplies, and what would the harvest be? Pestilence, hunger, civil strife and death." Right, Æneas, the Four Horsemen[xvii] will ride again and then you'll be shouting for the Greeks to come back. Better the devil you know than the devil you don't. Troilus now sprang to his feet again and this time Æneas and Deiphobus let him have his say.

"Brother, this is the worst kind of defeatism. Where is the honor or the glory of Troy in such talk? There are other options, we must have other options!" Troilus looked around the assembly. Helenus answered him:

"Name one." However, before Troilus could do so, Deiphobus broke in:

"Whatever honor and glory were to be had from this affair, my dear Troilus, were used up long ago. And most of it belonged to one man: Hector." Well, I must say I agreed in part with Troilus. At this rate, they might as well throw in the towel, give Helen a one-way ticket to Sparta and concentrate on coughing up war reparations. Troilus wasn't done, though:

"If we are in such a bad way, the Greeks are not much better off. Look at the length of their supply lines. They've been stuck out on the Dardan plain for almost ten years. They, too, have lost many warriors." Helenus broke in:

"Very true, my brother, but their home states are safe. Their houses stand, their women weave and sew, peasants grow crops and breed animals. When the Greek warriors leave Troy, they will re-enter their lives as if they had never been away." Well, Helenus might be a seer but he obviously wasn't seeing much just then. He forgot that, while the warriors were away, life in the Greek City States continued without them; things change in ten years: new interests, new relationships, new alliances. No, the Greek homecoming would not be happy. Anyhow, as soon as Helenus stopped to draw breath, Troilus was on his feet again:

"I think we still have a chance of defeating the Greeks in open battle. An all-out effort, a last attempt to drive them into the sea. And we need to do it now before more men and new supplies arrive from Greece. A final battle: would that not be better than a slow death inside Troy?" Who could imagine that Troilus could be so poetic? Hey, man, you might not turn out so bad—if you survive.

A long silence followed. Then Deiphobus spoke:

"Troilus, we have fought our final battle over and over again. Who will lead us next in battle, Troilus? You? Myself? Paris? Æneas? Whom will the Trojans follow? Who will inspire them to fight and win or fight and die?" Dead silence. Troy had run out of heroes. Then Æneas rose:

"Should we decide to throw such resources as we have a last time, it must be soon, very soon, as Troilus says. But remember: our troops are exhausted and whoever we choose as our military commander untried. If we fail, granted Troy's walls will keep the Greeks out, but most of those inside would be women, old people and children. What is to become of them? That we also need to consider." He bent his head to general silence. Even Troilus seemed to have run dry. So Æneas continued:

"If I may sum up our options, I see limited choices: give up Helen and come to a settlement with the Greeks; stay inside Troy until the Greeks go home or we die either of starvation or old age; or one last battle, one last throw of the dice and let the chips fall where they may. What say you all?" Agonizing silence. Horrid situation. If I had a vote, Helen would have been long gone. Then Paris spoke for the first time:

"I will not give up Helen." Deiphobus turned to him and spat out:

"That question, my brother, is not on the agenda. You lost Helen the moment you allowed others to fight for her. If you now say that you will, indeed, stand by yourself against the world to defend Helen, please remember you've never tried it and, brother, it wouldn't go well. Paris, we have moved on. Get with it!" Priam turned to Paris:

"My son, Deiphobus is right; the fate of Helen is no longer yours to decide. It may be that for too long we have allowed the fate of the one to govern the fate of the many."

A servant of sorts sidled up to Priam and whispered in his ear. Priam's eyes and mouth turned into o's and he hurried out. I don't think anyone noticed. Deiphobus waved at the servants for another round of drinks, putting everyone in more mellow and pensive mood and silence reigned until Priam returned, looking ten years younger and almost skipping for joy, followed by a large black gentleman. Priam guided this astonishing visitor to the empty seat—Hector's—returning to his former one. Priam, it seemed, had decided to be king again. He rose and said in a quavering voice:

"My friends, I have superb news for you. This," and he turned and bowed to the tall visitor who rose and bowed in return, "is Lord Tetton, ambassador from the court of Memnon, King of Ethiopia. Lord Tetton, will you please repeat to the Trojan council what you imparted to me in private?" Tetton bowed again. He was wearing a most colorful robe with a golden sash and a fantastic turban topped by an ostrich feather. He then bowed to the ladies.

"My lady Helen," he said to that particular lady; he had a deep and sonorous voice, "you are indeed beautiful beyond words. Your fame does not do justice to reality." Helen inclined her head:

"My gracious Lord," she answered unsmiling, "it is a sad world where beauty is the cause of strife." Well, there didn't seem to be any answer to this so Tetton turned back to the gentlemen:

"My Lords," he said, "I have been instructed by my master, the formidable King Memnon of Ethiopia, son of the Dawn, to bring you this message: he will gladly come to Troy with his armies and put an end to this war; he will destroy the Greek armies and cast their ships into the sea. This he has promised and this he will do." Tetton sat back down. Dead silence followed this little speech. To fill the gap, Priam looked around the table and quavered:

"My friends, this is unlooked good fortune. King Memnon is not only a man of great courage but of vast armies." He paused. Some of the Council shifted uncomfortably in their chairs but no one said anything. The old King tried again: "Come, my friends, let us endure a little longer until King Memnon arrives; it is far better to die bravely in battle than become exiles, living in disgrace in foreign lands." Deiphobus rose. He bowed to his father then ceremoniously to Lord Tetton to whom he said:

"My Lord Tetton, you are the servant of a brave and a great man, a man who knows no fear and who is willing to go to war, expend his army and treasure in a land and for a cause not his own." Deiphobus stopped and bowed his head, leaning his hands on the table. He then continued: "I beg you, my Lord Tetton, not to take amiss what I am about to ask you: I request, in all humility, that you withdraw while this matter, this great offer, is discussed by the Trojan Council in private." He snapped his fingers and a menial of sorts appeared: "Take my Lord Tetton and entertain him royally, see that he lacks for nothing." Lord Tetton bowed:

"I beg you," he said, "to feel free to take as long as you need. Let me have your decision as and when it pleases you. Let it be known, though, that my master is prepared to set out as soon as he receives your answer." He left the chamber, following the menial. Hecuba and some of her daughters left also. Helen didn't move. Priam looked at her.

"Helen . . ." he started but closed his mouth as he caught the look on her face. Deiphobus looked at his father.

"Father," he said, "earlier you called upon myself and Æneas to lead Troy. I now ask you to allow us to conduct the discussion on the offer from King Memnon." Priam sprang up, trembling, his eyes wide:

"Discussion?" he cried. "What is there to discuss? We have an eleventh hour reprieve, we are being offered unlooked-for aid in our greatest hour of need and you want to discuss it? My son, I do not understand." Deiphobus put his hands gently on his father's shoulders and eased him back into his chair. He turned to Æneas:

"What are your thoughts?" However, to everyone's amazement, Helen stood up and walked over to the main table. She faced the assembly who seemed to cower slightly. She slammed her palms into the tabletop:

"I say, and I am Helen, that no more foreign lives shall be laid down for this ignoble and dishonorable cause. Too many have died, Trojans, Greeks and allies, and for what?" She pointed her finger around the table. "If you Trojans want to continue fighting and dying in a worthless, immoral and useless war, so be it. But I say, and hear me well; no more foreign blood will be spilt!" She didn't return to the other women but sat down in Hector's chair. Priam sat there, looking confused. It was Æneas who spoke.

"My friends," he said quietly, "we have been down this road before and our cause is no further along." He looked sadly around the table. "And now, another eleventh hour reprieve. Memnon the king! And his armies! What if Memnon and his warriors go the same way as Penthesileia and Eurypylus? For how long can we expect other nations, in no way connected to this affair except through bonds of friendship, to bleed and die for us? We cannot carry any more guilt! I say that in all cordiality we refuse the offer of King Memnon." Æneas sat down and Deiphobus took over:

"There is only one option upon to us—to return Helen and her treasure and more besides while our city is still intact and under our control. My friends, we have tried honor and glory and find ourselves where we are today. I agree with Helen. No more, I say, no more." Deiphobus fell silent. Of course a hue and cry followed, the ones shouting loudest being Paris and Troilus.

"You are both cowards and weaklings," Troilus voice was heard first as his was the loudest. "I suggest you keep away from the battle field; hide under the skirts of your women. You are sapping the courage and strength of real men." Paris then managed to make himself heard:

"Men's greatest glories are won through deeds of arms; it is women and children who are afraid and run away. Your spirit is like theirs, my brother Deiphobus. Forgive me, but I have no confidence in you as a warrior or a leader." Helen's fury turned towards Troilus and Paris and she cried out:

"Don't you two idiots understand that while Achilles is in the game, Troy will never triumph on the battlefield? Think about it: Achilles has only one real opponent, be it Penthesileia or Eurypylus or King Memnon. Achilles, my friends, can destroy any leader we may send against him. And then, as we have seen, his—or her—followers collapse as do our own Trojans!" Paris and Troilus looked at each other glumly but remained silent. Helen turned towards Deiphobus. "Let this be your answer to King Memnon of the Ethiopians. Thanks but no thanks!" She turned and left the chamber, throwing out a last bitter line: "If I had to sit through any more of those bloody boring formal official hypocritical banquets that last forever, I'll freak out." Helen was a great one for adjectives. Dead silence. Then Æneas spoke:

"So it is decided." Deiphobus nodded. A dazed Priam got up and reached his hands out towards Deiphobus:

"I am still king of Troy! My son . . ." But Deiphobus replied sadly:

"No, father! This is no longer your call." Deiphobus looked around at his peers; one by one they stood until only Priam, Paris and Troilus remained seated. "The offer from King Memnon is declined by a vast majority of the Council. Æneas and I will carry the decision to the king's ambassador." And that was that.

Lysandra and I left after the gang had dispersed.

"I must say," was Lysandra's comment. "Helen surprises me more and more." I concurred:

"And so does Deiphobus, standing up to good old dad like that. I always thought him a bit of a wet blanket. But perhaps not. Come on, let's do some more snooping." Lysandra hesitated and then followed me slowly. A cat with moral scruples! Lord of Cats, save me.

We left conference chamber and ran quickly down the stairs to the public chambers on the ground floor. The double doors to an especially grand one were open and there sat ambassador

Tetton at his ease on a couch with lots of pillows, a table near him with quantities of wine and fruit; soft music played in the background. Lysandra stopped.

"I've never seen a man like that," she said shivering and then firmly: "I'm not going in." And she literally turned tail and ran. I, on the other hand, went in, jumped up on a convenient marble balcony and ran along until I was almost dead behind the ambassador. His full concentration was on a papyrus he was reading. I took a peek. It had strange scribbling all over it. OK, so I'm illiterate. I sat down and said:

"My Lord Tetton, why is your master looking for a war?" Poor old Tetton jumped almost a meter, coming down with oomph on the pillows. He looked one way, then another way, then a third and then behind him. His mouth opened like a fish out of water then closed again. He managed to stammer out:

"A feline!"

"Surely," I said with dignity, "you've seen cats before?" Tetton nodded, hand on his heart.

"The ones we have back home are larger, much larger, and they don't live in people's houses." I answered musingly:

"Lions, I suppose. No, you wouldn't want them around the home. They take up a lot of space to say nothing of what they eat." The ambassador's heartbeat being back to normal, I repeated my initial question: why was his master so keen to find a war. Tetton looked around him carefully, making sure, I suppose, no one listening. Then he said in a low voice:

"If you must know, and this is just between you and me; my lord king thinks we have too many young bucks in dire need of employment. Unfortunately, there are no wars around our neck of the woods at the moment so my master had to look elsewhere."

"Humm," I said, "and the Trojan War seemed a good bet. It's been going on forever with no end in sight and, all things being equal, you are guaranteed getting rid of a good number of your young bucks. The Greeks are awesome fighters and they have Achilles, who is not to be sneezed at." Tetton nodded his head.

"That is so. At the last minute, my king will unfortunately say he is not able to come but will send his armies to Troy." We fell silent. Yes, what do you do with your superfluous male population? Of course, you can do as the Egyptians and build pyramids. That kept lots of Egyptian lads busy. The Romans never ran out of places to conquer or to occupy and never seemed to have enough footsloggers. However, once you've hit rock bottom after trying youth clubs where the lads consume drugs and alcohol all day and at night break into people's houses, rape the local girls and generally make nuisances of themselves, you can't beat the draft.

Footsteps sounded along the corridor and Æneas and Deiphobus entered. They stopped before the Ambassador with low bows. Tetton got to his feet and bowed, too. Deiphobus spoke:

"My Lord Ambassador, the most generous offer of his Majesty, your Master, has been discussed in Council and it is the majority opinion that it should not be accepted." Deiphobus bowed again and Æneas continued:

"This has been a long and costly war, Mr Ambassador, and the many friends who have aided us paid for their generosity with their lives and treasure. We, the Trojans, do not wish to see more of our benefactors die for a cause that is ours alone." Deiphobus again:

"Take our most grateful thanks to his Majesty and tell him that, both morally and ethically, we cannot accept his generosity." They bowed, turned and left. As soon as they were gone, Tetton gritted his teeth and slammed his hand down on the table next to him.

"Damn," he said fervently. "And how am I going to explain this to my master? The Trojans have moral and ethical scruples! Did you ever hear the like?" I felt quite sorry for him.

"You'll have to find another war," I said. "How about a tribal conflict somewhere close? Civil wars, now, tend to be popular, the upside being that everyone who dies will be from the same

country. That should reduce the number of your young bucks."
Tetton shook his head sadly as he got up.

"I'll have to think about it," he said as he collected his bits
and pieces. "However, civil wars always leave a mess that needs
cleaning up. My master prefers doing his fighting elsewhere and
leave the tidying up to others." He turned and bowed to me.
How very civil of him. I didn't know what to do since cats aren't
constructed to bow. But I dipped my head. He said:

"Thanks for your advice. What did you say your name was?"
Well, I hadn't but answered politely.

"Marius. Gaius Marius." And so we parted on the friendliest
of terms, he shaking his head gloomily and muttering:

"My master is going to be that pissed . . ."

I met Lysandra on the palace steps. She said in derision:

"So they agreed that they wanted no more foreign help but
what else did they decide? Nothing!" I murmured:

"No decision is actually a momentous decision." I considered
further: "I must agree with Troilus: they need to get off the fence.
Time is fast running out and further delays could prove fatal to
Troy." I thought of Odysseus; what he needed was time, which
the Trojans were kindly giving him. I inspected my claws and
continued: "The Trojans may be damned if they do but they are
certainly damned if they don't. If you'll excuse the platitude, at
the moment they are in a lose-lose situation." We crossed Priam
Square heading back to Cælius' lair. When we arrived, Cælius
looked at us enquiringly.

"Well?" He asked. Lysandra answered:

"They haven't decided anything except that they will not
accept help from the king of Ethiopia. It was his ambassador
the ravens saw." Cælius stroked his whiskers. He looked at me:
"What do you think?" After consideration, I answered:

"Well, on the surface, the Greeks don't look that much better
off than the Trojans. However, I do feel the Trojans need to move
before that non-parreil Greek schemer, Odysseus, comes up
with a plan the Trojans won't like or can't figure out. Odysseus
thinks too much and such men are dangerous. And there is

that paragon of fighting men, Achilles to contend with; time is definitely not on the side of the Trojans." I swished my tail a bit, it helps my thought process. "Be all that as it may, if something doesn't happen soon, everyone will get so desperate the Trojans will throw themselves off the ramparts and the Greeks will drown themselves in the sea." Cælius nodded:

"I think you're right. The only recourse the Trojans have is to continue fighting and hope for the best." I shook my head:

"Odysseus and Helen both think that the time for battles is over." Cælius raised his eyebrows:

"Oh! And when have they discussed it?" I shook my head.

"Well, they haven't. But there is a meeting of minds." Cælius scratched his ear.

"Decision-making is an art and the Trojans don't seem to have the knack for it." He stretched out, indicating that the discussion was over and he was ready for his nap. "Right. I'll discuss our own options with the committee tomorrow. We need to finalize our plans. We need to be ready to move." I didn't fancy bedding down in Cælius' uncomfortable quarters so I told him I would go back to my tree on the beach. But in the morning I was back in Troy. I wanted to steer clear of Odysseus for as long as I could.

I went back to the beach for the night; on my way to Antenorides, I passed by Cælius' wall as had become my habit. Cælius looked at me and asked:

"So, what's new?" I thought for a bit before answering:

"Difficult to say. The Trojans are torn about seven ways to Sunday." Cælius raised his eyebrows.

"What do you mean?" I shrugged.

"Their best option is to negotiate with the Greeks about access through the Hellespont to the Sea of Marmara, which is what this is really all about. But they've got themselves so convinced that the trouble is Helen and nothing but Helen they're unable to move any other way." I added: "In fact, they can't see the wood for the trees."

"Humm," was Cælius' comment. "I'm not sure I understood your last comment but never mind, I'm too tired to go into it." He yawned, which I thought was very rude, then continued: "So you think the Trojans are done. Damn," shaking his head and scratching his claws along the wall. "I find moving a real hassle."

"Sadly," was my reply, "bar a miracle, the Trojans seem destined for the rubbish heap of history." So we parted in all cordiality. I wasn't worried as I was sure Cælius and his gang would be all right, come what might.

~: 6 :~

The Roman Poet and the Roman General

The next morning I got up feeling moody and out of sorts. I decided I would like nothing better to go for a walk on the cliffs. I climbed at a leisurely pace, up and up. As usual, it was a fine morning. Do they ever have high winds and rain or storms around here? I suppose what was to come should be storm enough for anyone, no need to add abominable weather.

I reached quite a high spot with the inevitable Ægean spread out below me. Forgive me, Lord of Cats, but the Ægean was starting to bore me. Birds whirled above but then, when didn't they? Then with a whoosh, Jonathan landed next to me.

"Hi, there, Gaius Marius," he said. "My, you sure get around for someone who has to walk." I looked at him.

"I've become very tired of humans," I answered sulkily. "Up here I'm free of them for a bit. How are things back in the city?" Jonathan shrugged.

"No change. It seems each of the higher-ups wants something different. Troilus wants a battle, Priam pretends the Greeks aren't there, Hecuba wants Helen thrown out, Æneas wants to discuss terms, Paris wants to keep Helen—I don't know why since she never looks his way, or speaks to him. Lysandra says they've got separate bedrooms." That Jonathan! What a gossip!

"What does Helen say?" I asked. Jonathan sniggered.

"Helen? I swear I don't think she cares one way or another." Sounded like Helen to me. "She says she'll be happy to walk down to the Greek camp if that's what they want. Or she'll be happy to stay where she is if that's what they want. Whatever, you know. Me, I think she's got a thing going with Deiphobus." Well, I suspected she had a thing going with someone, though I hadn't thought Deiphobus a likely candidate. Not quite her type, much too placid. Anyhow, she'd dump him soon enough. Men in Helen's world were definitely expendable. Jonathan broke into my thoughts.

"Have you got any news for us? Message for Cælius?" I licked my paw and washed my face.

"Not really." I pondered. "The way the Greeks are behaving, they might be on holiday. The way the Trojans are going, they are right on the path to self-destruct."

"Right," said Jonathan, flapping his wings. "Just business as usual." He was gathering himself for lift-off when he paused: "Oh, look, there's that human I mentioned at the meeting in the shed. Just below you. I can't figure out what he's all about." He flew off with a "see you around."

I looked down. Indeed, there was a guy sitting on a rock. I'd spent considerable time trying to figure out who it might be but, with everything else that had been going on, I'd quite forgotten about him. I slowly started to descend towards him for a closer look. There was something about him neither Greek nor Trojan. First of all, his clothes looked different. He was wearing a tunic and lace up boots. Then it hit me. Could it be . . . a Roman? What would a Roman be doing this far away in time if not in space? What Roman would give a rat's ass on the outcome of the Trojan War? They'd just accept Homer's version. But then . . . of course . . . It could only be . . . I jumped up on a nearby rock.

"Pùblius Vergilius Maro[xviii], the Roman poet, I presume." Pùblius Vergilius Maro turned and looked at me. A tired looking sort of guy, no bounce in him at all. Of course, he would never see forty again. Wispy hair brushed forward, in the Julius Cæsar style, a must, to this day, for the hair challenged. He stooped a little, as if the load of life was too much for him. He said with a marked lack of interest:

"And you are Mr Cat."

"I'm Gaius Marius." He raised bushy eyebrows and shuddered.

"Well, I never met the original," he said. "Fortunately he was dead before I was born. But all reports of him are pretty bad, you know. Definitely not a role model for anyone, except tyrant wannabees. Sorry you got saddled with his name."

"That's OK," I answered cheerfully. "I don't mind. Not many people know who he was, anyway. I forever have to explain he was a Roman general—and consul a zillion times." Vergil raised his eyebrows: I hastened to correct myself: "Well, that may be a slight exaggeration. Let's says 7 or 8 or perhaps 9." I snickered. "And it could be worse, you know! It could have been Cornelius Sulla[xix]." Vergil shuddered.

"All those generals," he lamented. "They wanted power and more power! And see where it got us!" I remonstrated:

"Don't forget how they got that power. Troops, my dear Vergil, troops who were loyal not to Rome but to their generals, the provider of loot, slaves, what have you." Vergil sniffed but said nothing. Why I should be expounding on Roman history to a Roman I can't fathom—pride, pride, I suppose. I continued: "It was on the cards that Octavianus would come up on top in that last tangle with Mark Anthony. Actium, and who ran away— Antony or Cleopatra?" Vergil shrugged:

"And who cares?" It's how you arrive that counts, not how you got there." I went blithely on:

"Augustus,[xx] as Octavianus was to become, put paid to all those rivalries and, frankly, I can't see he was worse than any of the other contestants."

Vergil didn't look pleased. He sniffed.

"And who," he asked, "is going to put paid to Augustus!" Well, what could one say?

"I'm afraid," I answered, "you're stuck with him until death do you part."

"Yeah," he answered, "but whose—his or mine?" That was an embarrassing question since I knew Vergil would take the high road while Augustus was still on the low road[13].[xxi]

"Anyhow, if I may ask," I continued, "what's your beef with Augustus? You should be grateful; he ended all that nonsense of the civil wars and introduced the Pax Romana." He looked at me askance.

"Obviously you don't know His Mightiness—or his family." Vergil sighed. "I suppose if it was only him one could put up with it but there's his whole ruddy family. Augustus was Cæsar's heir but who is Augustus' heir?" Too true, as I knew from the history books. Augustus' heir was whoever of his male relations managed to survive until he, Augustus, died. No prizes for guessing the winner—Tiberius[14], courtesy of his mother, Augustus' wife Livia (but not Augustus' son). Which goes to show that Mother love is a terrible thing and that even a monster such as Tiberius can be loved. I shook my head. I had no use at all for heirs—anyone any good will certainly not live to inherit. I changed the subject.

"I bet you've come here for inspiration for your immortal epic poem *The Æneid*, the greatest of your works." I thought this would please and flatter him but Vergil groaned and buried his face in his hands. Oh, dear, I'd stepped in it. He got up and walked up and down, wringing his hands.

"I was happy, you know, writing bucolic poems about milkmaids and buttercups –you must have read my *Eclogues*." He struck up a pose and I knew I was for it:

---

[13] If you take the high road you are dead and can fly on the wings of angels; if you take the low road, you need to slog all the way.

[14] Tiberius Claudius Nero, 42 BC-37 AD, Augustus' stepson. See endnote xix

You, Tityrus[15], 'neath a broad beech-canopy
Reclining, on the slender oak rehearse
Your silvan ditties: I from my sweet fields,
And home's familiar bounds, even now depart.
Exiled from home am I; while, Tityrus, you
Sit careless in the shade, and, at your call,
'Fair Amaryllis'[16] bid the woods resound.'"[17]

He stopped, looking well pleased with himself. Fortunately, he didn't want an opinion for I just wouldn't have known what to say. Who is Tityrus? Silvan I take it means woodland in general. He went on, almost in ecstasy: "And my *Georgics*, a manual on farming." Another pose:

"What makes the cornfield smile; beneath what star
Mæcenas[18], it is meet to turn the sod
Or marry elm with vine; how tend the steer;
What pains for cattle-keeping, or what proof
Of patient trial serves for thrifty bees;-
Such are my themes.
O universal lights
Most glorious! ye that lead the gliding year
Along the sky, Liber and Ceres mild,
If by your bounty holpen[19] earth once changed
Chaonian acorn[20] for the plump wheat-ear,
And mingled with the grape, your new-found gift,
The draughts of Achelous[21]; and ye Fauns

---

[15] The shepherd in Virgil's *Eclogues*, or Virgil himself.

[16] *Amaryllis belladonna*. "Fair Amaryllis", the shepherdess in Virgil's *Eclogues*: "sparkling, beautiful lady."

[17] Text by Vergil translated from the Latin by John Dryden (1631-1700)

[18] Gaius Mæcenas (?-8BC) Roman, trusted counselor to Augustus. Patron of poets, including Vergil. .

[19] Archaic past participle of the verb Help

[20] Acorns. From oak trees of Chaonia or Dodona

[21] Patron deity of the "silver-swirling" Achelous, largest river of Greece

To rustics ever kind, come foot it, Fauns
And Dryad-maids together; your gifts I sing.

There were quite a few words and references I couldn't place but I would not live long enough to hear Vergil's explanations if I were fool enough to ask. Ignorance is bliss. So I applauded:

"Wonderful! Very thematic!" He cheered up a bit.

"I got rave reviews, you know. My mother collected them all and pasted them into a scrapbook; but of course it's back in Rome." Thank the Lord of Cats for that or I should no doubt have had to read the lot and make intelligent comments. He sat biting his nails for a few minutes then said through his teeth:

"Of course, it couldn't last. Augustus, that s.o.b. and an s.h.i.t. of the first order, demanded, yes, demanded, that I write a patriotic epic. He wants to give the Romans a sense of togetherness, unity and common destiny, instead of continuing to be obnoxiously individualistic, forever complaining about the government and griping about their taxes." A deep sigh. "You know the sort of thing: one people, indivisible under the gods." Well, I suppose these mottoes keep cropping up. Trust the Americans to swank about boasting they'd thought of it first. If I looked closely enough, I'd probably find E PLURIBUS UNUM[22] on Alexander the Great's standard.

"Patriotism," I said thoughtfully. "The last refuge of the scoundrel.[23]" Vergil brightened:

"Now, that's a great line," he said. "D'you mind if I borrow it?" I shrugged.

"Knock yourself out." Then I added: "If you like that sort of thing, here is something else:

Take up the White Man's burden—
The savage wars of peace—
Fill full the mouth of Famine
And bid the sickness cease.[xxii] "

---

[22]   From many, one.
[23]   Samuel Johnson, 1709-1784.

"Good, very good," said Vergil enthusiastically, "sounds like something Octavianus/Augustus would like too. In fact, I have some lines that are quite similar." He drew himself up:

> *Romans, let your concern be to command the nations;*
> *your skills shall be these: to impose the rule of peace, to*
> *spare the submissive and to crush the proud.*

He looked as pleased as the cat that ate the canary. Metaphorically speaking, of course. I applauded. Pop Kipling probably loved it—and may even have indulged in a spot of plagiarism. "So," Vergil continued with intense curiosity, "there are other empires besides Rome?"

"You bet," I answered, "but they won't last as long as Rome." Vergil asked hopefully:

"D'you think any of them will invade Rome soon?" I shook my head:

"Sorry, pal." I hated to disabuse him. "Not in the foreseeable future." He ground his teeth:

"Personally, I think this whole epic thing is a load of horse manure. It starts out with Æneas leaving Troy; he travels to Italy and, after killing off the local inhabitants, founds Rome and becomes ancestor of the Romans. Absolute tosh, especially as most of the ancestors of today's Romans are the result of empire and the slave trade.

"On top of that, Octavianus/Augustus wants to strengthen Æneas' legitimacy as the son of Venus and ancestor of the gens Julia to prop up Cæsar's claim to divine descent.[24] To be frank, the very idea makes me want to open my veins." Well, at least Augustus didn't claim Æneas had been born in a log cabin. (Which begs the question: was Lincoln really born in a log cabin?) Nowadays, one snobs down not up. However, Vergil wasn't done complaining: "He wants the epic to include all of

---

[24] The 'gens'—family—Julia took its name from Iulius, (Ascanius in the *Iliad*), son of Æneas, descendent from Aphrodite or Venus or whatever.

Rome's remarkable achievements, with special emphasis on his—Octavianus/Augustus—remarkable achievements." For sure, poor old Vergil had a problem. I asked:

"Who made up this story about Æneas going off to Italy and founding the Roman Empire? Did you?" Vergil frowned ferociously.

"You offend me. Would I come up with something that stupid? It's in *The Iliad*." Homer again. I might have guessed. Vergil continued: "You obviously haven't studied the classics properly." Oh, all right. So what if I just read the summaries! He continued: "In Book XX, Æneas and Achilles are fighting it out and it's on the cards that Æneas is for the buzzards when some God or other—I forget which—says:

> '*It is fated, moreover, that he [Æneas] should escape,*
> *and that the race of Dardanus [Trojans] . . . shall not perish utterly*
> *without seed or sign.*

> *. . . . Æneas shall reign over the Trojans, he and his children's children*
> *that shall be born hereafter.*'

Vergil concluded: "The God snatches Aeneas away, leaving Achilles wondering what hit him." Tough luck. I knew Achilles hated seeing a quarry escape. However, Vergil was already on to the next thing. He asked: "Have you met Æneas?" I nodded.

"A few times."

"What kind of a guy is he?" I considered.

"Just ordinary. Tries to do his best. A decent sort." I mused. "He's none too chipper at the moment. Priam can't handle this thing any longer. Now Æneas and Deiphobus, Priam's oldest surviving son, share the Trojan High Command. Well, sort of, since the old man won't stop meddling." Vergil nodded but his thoughts were elsewhere:

"Octavianus/Augustus can force me to write a patriotic epic but I'm still master of what goes into it—up to a point. I'm not going to make it all cakes and ale, you know; I'm going to show just how horrific the fall of a city can be and how evil and cruel

121

humans are. I'll show there's no glory or honor in war. Everyone suffers: the conqueror and the conquered. The noble and less noble. How some are caught up in the fate of others, brought down by no fault of their own.

"Also, Æneas is not going to be a symbol of propriety and virtue. He's going to put self-interest above everything else as he travels towards Latium." Vergil came closest to a smile I had yet seen. "Naturally, he'll claim all his bestialities are the will of the gods." Helen and Vergil would have gotten on for sure. Homer, on the other hand, would have been much offended. "So there goes Octavianus/Augustus' super hero if I have anything to say about it. I don't like Octavianus/Augustus." I blinked. Really! I would never have guessed! He paused. "Have you been inside Troy?" I nodded.

"I have. Pretty bleak at the moment. They were doing OK until Hector died. But now it's all falling apart."

"Helen still there, I take it."

"You better believe it. That's one tough lady." Vergil sighed. I continued: "But, tell me, Vergil, what on earth are you doing here? All the information you need is in *The Iliad*. And the rest you can just make up." Vergil shook his head and looked crafty:

"If you must know, I harbor a hope that the Trojan War, in spite of Homer, did not end with the destruction of Troy. After all, Homer was writing for a Greek audience so the Greeks had to win. Now, imagine if they didn't! What if the Trojans, somehow, swept the Greeks out to sea and drowned the lot?" I looked at him doubtfully although I confess I'd occasionally had the same thought.

"It doesn't seem very likely," I said slowly. "Don't let me rain on your parade, but I can't see the Trojans victorious over an army of cats much less the Greeks." Vergil wilted like a cabbage someone had forgotten to water. I've never seen anyone that sad. He really believed that the next chapter in life would be worse than the last. I continued: "Can't you just tell Augustus to bugger off and write his own patriotic epics?" Vergil gave a mirthless laugh.

"If I do, he'll get at my family. I don't have a wife and children myself—that at least is something—but there are other relatives around." I see. Vergil didn't want to wake up one morning with his favorite niece's head on his pillow. Mafia tactics have much earlier origins than we think.[25] "But," he continued, looking at me craftily. "I'm making arrangements to have the manuscript burnt as soon as I'm dead. Then we'll see where he'll get his bloody patriotic epic." That made me feel sad, as I couldn't tell Vergil that Augustus would not only get his mitts on the manuscript, he would edit it. Vergil went on: "I haven't written much so far, just a bit of the beginning. D'you want to hear?" Well, I didn't but, as I'd already learnt, if a poet wants show off his verses, all one can do is sit down and look interested. In fact, Vergil didn't wait for an answer but began:

> *Arms, and the man [Æneas] I sing, who, forc'd by fate,*
> *And haughty Juno's[26] unrelenting hate,*
> *Expell'd and exil'd, left the Trojan shore.*
> *Long labors, both by sea and land, he bore,*
> *And in the doubtful war, before he won*
> *The Latian realm, and built the destin'd town;*
> *His banish'd gods restor'd to rites divine,*
> *And settled sure succession in his line,*
> *From whence the race of Alban fathers[27] come,*
> *And the long glories of majestic Rome."*

I felt an icy tingling down my spine. The whole thing smelt of destruction of the locals, their gods and their civilization to make way for Æneas' people, gods and civilization. Well, shit happens—again and again. I applauded. Anything to keep the man happy. It was a pity, however, that Vergil hated Augustus so

---

[25] See The *Godfather*, part I, Francis Ford Coppolla.

[26] Juno is the Roman name for Hera, wife of Zeus (Jupiter to the Romans)

[27] Rome's 'founding fathers'

much he was going to ruin poor Æneas' reputation as a man of integrity. Life sucks.

"One thing I do wonder about, Vergil," I said conversationally. "*The Iliad* ends with Hector's death and as far as I know Homer then followed up with *The Odyssey*, where Helen is back in Sparta, a contented hausfrau with nothing on her mind but butter and fresh bread." Vergil looked at me.

"You mean," he asked frowning, "you haven't read Homer's book linking *The Iliad* and *The Odyssey*?" I raised my eyebrows:

"I didn't even know there was one." Vergil looked shocked.

"Honestly, Gaius, of course there is. Would it make sense to write about a war and stop at the death of one of its characters? Why, there'd be lynch mobs going after Homer—the sequel or else!" I thought of Sherlock Holmes and poor Conan Doyle[28]. Vergil went on: "Homer would have had no choice. So a sequel there was."

I was flabbergasted. What could have happened? There are reams of documents from Ancient Greece and Rome around, and even if the Goths and Vandals (or the Turks, for that matter) had burnt every single copy extant, there should still be references somewhere in all the accumulated correspondence from antiquity. I said as much to Vergil. He shrugged.

"Can't answer your question; but *The Troiad* was the basis for all the books, plays, essays and so on written on how the Trojan War ended."

"Oh," I said in disappointment, "so there doesn't seem be to any real possibility that the Greeks didn't burn down Troy and return home as conquering heroes!" But Vergil shook his head:

"Of course there is, MEA CATTUS AMICOS,[29]" he insisted. "You've met Homer, haven't you?" I couldn't deny it. "And did

---

[28]   Arthur Conan Doyle (22 May 1859—7 July 1930) author of the Sherlock Holmes detective books, got tired of Holmes and tried to kill him off. There was such a popular outcry that Doyle had no option but to bring the fellow back to life.

[29]   My feline friend

you find him unswervingly truthful?" I shook my head. Vergil looked quite lively now. "And where is Homer now?"

"He said," I answered, "that he was going to see his literary agent in Krete. That was just after Hector's funeral. Haven't seen him since." Vergil laughed, showing that at least he knew how.

"So there you go! Who says old Homer didn't just stay in Krete and write *The Troiad* from a balcony looking over the MARE NOSTRUM[30], making the whole thing up?" I gasped. He continued, well pleased with himself: "Ergo; if I can prove that the Greeks were humbled or that Helen dumped Paris and went off with, say, Achilles; Æneas was killed in battle or ran away with a barmaid, why, puff . . ." He threw up his hand, opened his chest and blew air through his mouth. "Octavianus/Augustus' dream of descent from the Gods goes up in smoke!" He got up and danced about, singing: "Oh, happy day . . ." for a bit, then sat down. "Actually, just the possibility keeps me sane." I looked at him thoughtfully and combed my whiskers.

Having collected my wits, I said, getting back on track:

"OK, Vergil, so let's see where we are. According to Homer, the Trojans attacked the Greek ships; Patroklus put on Achilles' gear, saved the Greeks and was killed by Hector, after which Achilles killed Hector. I can attest to all this since I was an eyewitness. What happens in *The Troiad?*" Vergil thought for a bit then said:

"Well, Penthesileia joins the war on Priam's side, she and her lady warriors . . ." He rose and quoted in a very dramatic posture:

> *"And there, leading her Amazon band in a fury . . .*
> *was Penthesileia, a flame of fire amid thousands, a woman of war . . .*
> *Daring to join in the battle, a maiden among men."*[17]

D'you like it?" Helen would have hated it but one must be polite.

---

[30] Our Sea - The Roman name for the Mediterranean

"The verses are fine as long as you're not trying to tell the truth, the whole truth and nothing but the truth." Vergil looked pained:

"Where have I got it wrong?" I fidgeted:

"I wouldn't say wrong, Vergil, but you give Penthesileia a buildup that doesn't tally with the clobbering she got from Achilles." Vergil sighed:

"Oh, well. Nothing in this life is perfect. Poetry has to sound good, you know, and if what sounds good is not quite true, who cares? Truth is not the object of poetry." Oh really! If he hadn't told me, I would never have guessed! But I let it slide. Life is too short.

"Then what?" I asked. Vergil scratched his head.

"King Memnon of Ethiopia and his armies arrive to support Priam . . ." I interrupted him.

"Not the king himself, actually, his Ambassador came. But Helen scotched that idea. Æneas and Deiphobus supported her. Priam was truly pissed off. So no Ethiopians for Troy." Vergil wrinkled his nose. He continued:

"Next come Achilles' death and funeral games." I exulted:

"In fact, Achilles is alive and well and as obnoxious as ever. Next." More head scratching:

"Ajax goes mad and commits suicide." I was gob smacked! Ajax eating his own spear! I laughed so hard I fell off my stone and Vergil had to pick me up. When I stopped laughing, I said:

"I've never known anyone less likely to commit suicide than Ajax. Also, he's too stupid even to go mad!" Vergil glared at me but went on:

"Death of Paris!" That should make Helen happy. Actually, I'd wondered why she hadn't murdered him herself long ago. However, I held up a paw:

"You seem to have forgotten Eurypylus, descendant of Herakles, who also came in aid of the Trojans." Vergil frowned:

"Eurypylus! Can't remember anything about him." I chewed my lower lip and answered pensively:

"He was all cock-a-hoop, but descendant of Herakles or not, Achilles made mincemeat of him in next to no time. You can't fault Helen's thinking vis-à-vis foreign aid for Troy; with Achilles around, becoming Troy's ally was just a shortcut to Hades." By this time, Vergil seemed up in the clouds. I pulled him back. He said:

"Whatever! I'm not adding Eurypylus. If he was in any way related to Herakles, he must have been a most unsavory character." I nodded:

"And unsanitary." I added. "So what next?" Vergil went on, counting on his fingers:

"Indecisive skirmishes around Troy, the Wooden Horse and the sack of Troy. Those are, as far as I can remember, the main points." He scratched his chin. "I suppose we will just have to wait to see."

"How do Achilles and Paris die?" I asked. Vergil answered without interest:

"Oh, they're both killed by vengeful Gods for being uppity." I smirked and said:

"I have it on good authority that the Gods on Olympus are not going to interfere in this war. An order from Zeus himself!" Vergil looked at me doubtfully but I continued regardless: "Now, what we need is a timeline!" Vergil stared:

"A what line?"

"Timeline," I repeated irritated. "Every author needs a timeline so action takes place in the correct order." Vergil scratched his head. "For instance, what if you wrote that Dido killed herself when she saw Aeneas' ship coming towards Carthage and not sailing away?" He snorted:

"That would be ridiculous!"

"Exactly," I said authoritatively. "Hence a timeline. Give me your slate and stylus. I suppose you have them?" Vergil sneered:

"Of course! Would a writer go around without?" I didn't bother to answer but made the following list:

- Death of Hector
- Death of Penthesileia
- Death of Memnon

- Death of Achilles
- Suicide of Ajax
- Death of Paris
- Fighting around Troy
- The Wooden Horse
- Fall of Troy

"Well," said Vergil, "I see what you mean. But I think we need to list things as you tell me they actually happened." Vergil continued speculatively: "I think we need a timeline that doesn't follow *The Troiad* at all." He took the wax tablet from me and studied it carefully. Then he said:

"I've forgotten one item—the arrival of Neoptolemus—Achilles' son. That would be after Achilles' death and before the Wooden Horse." I wasn't too impressed. Achilles was a bastard with a bitch for a mother[31]. How would a son with such genes turn out? Vergil smoothed the wax and started a new list: "OK, this is what we know has happened."

- Death of Hector;
- Death of Penthesileia;
- Death of Eurypylus;
- Memnon of Ethiopia does not come to Troy.

Then I got an idea. "Vergil," I said, "it seems that the linchpin or keystone or central event in this contest between Greeks and Trojans is the Wooden Horse." Vergil considered this:

"You may be right . . ." I didn't let him go on:

"Odysseus says the war cannot end except by the fall of the city. And I think we can agree," I continued, "that the city can only fall from within. The Greeks have tried everything and nothing has worked." Vergil rubbed his cheeks.

---

[31] Achilles' mother was a neriad, a water nymph, Thetis, daughter of Neptune, old man of the sea.

"Have you, in your time with the Greeks, heard the Wooden Horse mentioned?" I shook the noggin'.

"Noo," I said slowly. "Odysseus is trying to dream up an alternative solution—he asked me to make a psychological profile of Troy—whatever that is." Vergil shook his head.

"But it still doesn't follow that he will come up with the Wooden Horse." We sat quietly for a bit, each in his own world.

"You're right, Vergil! The only source we have is Homer and we both agree he is not trustworthy. So it's an open case and all bets are still on." *In fact, it ain't over 'til the fat lady sings.*[32]

Then Vergil said, slapping his hands:

"Well, Gaius, you'll just have to keep your ears open and pay attention to what goes on around you. If the Wooden Horse rears its head, we'll know which way the wind is blowing." I got up.

"I'll keep you posted." As I turned to leave, I said as an afterthought: "You ok here?"

"Oh, yes," he replied, "brought my campaigning outfit—every Roman has to have one; mine was in mothballs." So we parted in perfect amiability. I was glad Vergil wasn't going to share my olive tree root. Nice guy and all that but life is sad enough without living with someone who complains all the time.

As I walked down the hill, I couldn't help thinking of the uncanny similarities between Vergil's and Kipling's take on imperialism. The time span between their worlds would be 2 000 years, give or take. However, the essence of their times were the same. Bash people about and call it fighting for peace and freedom. Invade your neighbors and say they're getting civilization. And so it goes. Your empire just grows and grows until it is so big as to be unsustainable. No matter how one turns it, Vergil, and Kipling and their ilk are to blame for blatant nationalism. Oh, well. Everyone has to eat. What comes around goes around.

---

[32] Colloquialism referring to the end of Wargner's *Ring Cycle* operas that takes over 6 hours to perform.

⁓ 7 ⁓

Cat comes in from the cold

Back under my tree, I slept through the night. I know cats should prowl at night and sleep during the day. However, life during the Trojan War didn't work that way, even for cats. The next day, after a bit of breakfast, I went down to my favorite spot on the beach. I didn't bother to look for Odysseus. He'd turn up sooner rather than later.

It was now mid-autumn but still seemed like summer: agreeably warm; soft breezes from the sea; waters as calm as a lake; birds whirling overhead. I looked at them askance. Who knew what they were up to. The dogs Arthur and Antonia were on duty in the Greek camp and appeared to have become great favorites, getting pats and tidbits galore. Talk about mixing business with pleasure. Or perhaps I should call it multitasking. There were a couple of crabs fooling about at the water's edge. I wondered whether they were part of Cælius' committee.

I thought about Vergil, too; it is the fate of artists—painter, poets and what have you—to be dependent on sponsors for their daily bread; if patrons suddenly turn nasty and/or homicidal, that goes with the territory. Ask Leonardo da Vinci. Ask Michelangelo. Ask Mozart.

However, I wasn't left to my own thoughts and ruminations for long. About midmorning, there was Odysseus.

"Well, Gaius Marius, you're a great one for watching the sea." That was a NON-SEQUITUR[33] so I didn't bother to answer. Odysseus continued: "We've been having an exciting time here while you were lazing about in Troy. Everyone is at sixes and sevens." I looked at him sideways. As if this had ever bothered Odysseus! Management by chaos, that's our Odysseus. He cracked his knuckles. "But, tell me, how are things in the fair city?" I'd been thinking about what to tell him. I'd decided to keep myself strictly to the human element. After all, it had been my time, my dime. Even so, most of what I'd seen and heard wouldn't change much for the Greeks and Odysseus actually already knew what there was to know in one form or another. So I summarized:

"The Trojans are not happy campers. They are at a total loss without Hector. Priam has abandoned ship and Æneas and Deiphobus are captain and pilot. Trouble is, Priam keeps sticking his oar in. I also had a long chat with Helen." Odysseus raised his eyebrows. Why do humans do that?

"Oh?" he said. "And what does our fair queen have to say?"

"She says the war is not really about her. She hates all men for being hypocritical misogynists and is going to start her own country—ladies only." Odysseus laugh wasn't very hearty.

"Dear Helen, such an imagination! We all miss her at our musical evenings!" I drove on relentlessly:

"She says that, if she were to stroll into your camp this afternoon, you'd all be embarrassed because it would wipe out your excuse for pursuing this war and show the lot of you up for the greedy grubbing savage capitalists you are whose ultimate goal is to take over the Hellespont for gain and profit."

If Odysseus had been wearing a suit, this would be the moment when he'd loosen his tie. Since he wasn't, he scratched

---

[33] Non-sequitur—statement that does not follow logically from what preceded it.

his face and looked silly. But I went on. I wasn't in the mood for exculpatory explanations from Odysseus.

"Look here, Odysseus, I don't really care one way or another." He had Homer on his side so he would be all right as far his future reputation went. I was feeling miffed. "Frankly, I still don't know what you wanted me to do in Troy. I heard all about your spies and failed tactics and no-win stratagems; you know as much about what goes on inside the city as I, had I lived there for five years." Odysseus fiddled with his belt, cracked his knuckles again then confessed:

"What I want, what I need, is the general mood in Troy. What are people thinking? How do they feel? How has Hector's death and the Penthesileia and Eurypylus disasters affected the man in the street?" I sneered:

"Bit of a tall order, wouldn't you say? And we've been through all this!" I twitched my tail about—a sure sign I wasn't pleased. "I'm a cat and you're asking me to profile another species. You need to be human to understand humans; you need to be a feline to understand a cat." However, Odysseus wasn't buying it.

"Au contraire," he said—where he picks up these expressions, I don't know. "People are just big lumbering egocentrics always looking at their own navels. Cats, on the other hand, have evolved over millions of years to gauge atmosphere—'am I being stalked?' 'am I in danger?' 'is it safe to drink the water?'" I stared at him. He waved his hands. "OK, but you know what I mean. Smell, too, cats can smell mood. 'This place is going up shit creek and it's time I moved on' sort of thing." Well, I like a bit of flattery as well as the next guy, so I decided to humor him.

"Odysseus, the mood in Troy is not the calm before the storm. They are so far gone they aren't even thinking about storms. The air is alive with despair, hopelessness. 'Will anything ever be as it was before?' 'Will this war never end?' Don't forget these people have been cooped up in that city for over nine years. No holidays abroad. No chariot parties to the seaside. No picnics on the cliffs. They can see the ocean from the ramparts—those that bother climbing up all those steps. But they can't take a dip in the sea, their kids can't build sandcastles.

"They've been with the same people for years on end and the only change is when someone dies or is born. They get news when a courier comes from a kingdom next door and these are now few and far between because the neighbors, too, are exhausted." I stopped to get my breath. Odysseus sat quietly and waited for me to go on.

"As for the high command, the best of Priam's sons are dead. It's against nature, you know, that the strong die while the weak are left to procreate. War is contrary to evolution." I couldn't discuss evolution with Odysseus so I went back to what he could understand. "There are no heroes left in Troy—and no strategists. Anyway, Hector was a superb warrior but strategy wasn't his forte." I scratched long lines in the sand with my claws.

"As I see it, that's one of the problems. The whole of Troy believes that if Hector had survived he would have led them to victory. Without him, all hope seems lost." I scratched the other way and played noughts and crosses with myself. "But the truth is, Odysseus, Hector could not have stopped the fall of Troy." I sighed: "Hector was like all other crown princes—brought up to be nothing so as not to threaten daddy. Hector knew all about battles and killings but absolutely nothing about management and administration." I shook my head. "Not that Priam is any good at that either."

"So you are telling me Troy's fate is sealed," was Odysseus' comment. I nodded:

"I believe so, Odysseus. However, I don't know whether you Greeks are up to the task. Perhaps some other tribe and leader will come along after you've given up." Odysseus sniffed. He didn't like that. For a moment, he blew air through his nose like a bull and looked downright dangerous. He poked me in the ribs with a finger. I hissed. He held up a finger:

"Don't hiss at me, pal, and write this down on your little slate. We the Greeks will finish off Troy." I looked at him in a supercilious manner and asked:

"How?" Odysseus shook his head:

"I don't know—yet!" So he was silent while I concentrated on my noughts and crosses. Finally, he said, as if he hated to admit it:

"That was pretty good evaluation, Gaius. But then, I didn't expect anything else from you." I smirked. It's nice to be appreciated.

"Well," I said. "I don't know what else I can add or how any of this can be of use. Truth to tell, I can't see you lot having all that many options either. Don't expect Helen to do the right thing. She wouldn't know what it was if she fell over it in the dark. I'm afraid her motto is: 'Happiness for the clown is when the circus burns down'." Odysseus might not know what clowns were although he must have been acquainted with circuses. Then his demeanor changed and he looked at me through slit eyes:

"What is this I hear, about an embassy from Ethiopia?" I waved a paw.

"Oh, that!" He narrowed his eyes.

"You might have told me about it."

"Whatever for?" I asked in mock surprise, "you seem to know all about it already. Anyhow, it didn't float—Helen put a kibosh on the whole thing. So, no Ethiopian warriors for Troy." Odysseus chewed on this. After a bit, he said:

"You've given me much food for thought, Gaius. You've done well." Oh, really! "And I think I have the glimmering of an idea—based on the psychology of the individual—in this case, everyone inside Troy." He got up: "I want to go and think about it for a bit." He walked off and I looked after him. Odysseus' ideas usually boded no good for anyone. Just as well I wasn't inside Troy.

Odysseus turned up again the next day. I gave him a snide look:

"Well," I asked, "what have you dreamed up for the Trojans delight and entertainment?" As usual, he rubbed his chin and looked out over the sea. The he said:

"My plans are not fully matured." Ya don't say! He looked incredibly serious.

"I want you, Gaius, to help me in a preliminary phase." I arched my back, extended my claws and he hastily corrected himself: "what I would like you to do, what I would request you to consider," he amended hastily, "is to set up a court of arbitration." I gasped, almost swallowing my tongue in surprise.

"You gotta be kidding me, pal. First you're considering how to obliterate Troy and then you're into arbitration?" Odysseus looked at me with big innocent eyes. Come off it, I know that look. Cats hold the patent.

"But, Gaius, all options should be kept open. Why, if arbitration proves successful, it could all be over." I sneered:

"Don't tell me; I know you, Odysseus. You're just playing for time and giving the Trojans the run around." Odysseus tweaked my ear; I hate that and responded by clawing his wrist. He withdrew his hand in a hurry. Once he'd staunched the blood, he continued: "Now, Gaius, you're turning into a cynic; I could say it doesn't suit you but it does. Cats make great cynics." He sighed and looked heavenwards:

"I want to give peace a last chance! Stop all this killing and whatnot. A peaceful solution—I'm sure we can reach one that will satisfy both side." He gave me that cat look again: oh, be kind to me, I'm so defenseless! I turned my back on him.

"I'll consider it," I said, "for the sake of humanity. Now, go away. I want to nap."

Next morning, I watched Jonathan the seagull coasting on the warm air currents while the dogs Arthur and Antonia fooled around on the shore. I ignored them as I'd other things to occupy my mind. I was considering Odysseus' arbitration wheeze. Of course, he turned up way before I was ready for him. I looked at him askance and said:

"You know, Odysseus, to have an arbitration, you need an arbitrator, some impartial being to ensure fair play, keep the sides within the rules and hold both to the final outcome." Odysseus opened his eyes wide:

"Naturally, Gaius. And I thought of you right away. Who else?" Really, this Odysseus was too presumptuous by half. I sneered back:

"Don't be daft, Odysseus. A cat can't arbitrate in a human dispute." Odysseus looked at me—there was that innocent look again I was coming to detest.

"Why not? It seems ideal to me," he said. "Being of another species, a cat would be totally impartial."

"Except that the cat would probably get bored and fall asleep. Get real, Odysseus, the Trojans may not be rocket scientists but they're not complete fools." Odysseus didn't ask what a rocket scientist was. I continued, now well and properly pissed off. "I don't know where to find someone impartial in these parts. All of mainland Greece and the islands are Greek allies and all the kingdoms inland are either on the Trojan side or wouldn't take either side if their lives depended on it." Odysseus gave me a few pats.

"I'm sure you'll come up with something!" And he just walked off. Well, I never . . .

I was so fed up I took myself off to Troy for Happy Hour. I sat in the corner of *The Trojan Horse*, skulking and feeling used and let down. Really, why did Odysseus think I cared at all for his stupid schemes. And this one was a lulu. I mean, arbitration after nine years?

I was quietly toying with my designer water when who should come up: Æneas and Deiphobus. I scowled. Really, where can a cat get some peace in this place? However, they sat down at my table anyway. Marianne came running up and took their order for wine and water. After they got their mugs, silence reigned. Then Deiphobus found his tongue. He gave me a hard stare. Oh, my! The day I'm scared of Deiphobus will be the day I turn in my cat membership card!

"What's with you?" he asked. "You're always hanging about." I looked at him sideways. These humans are such busybodies. What's it to them what I do? But if I must, I must, so I looked at him all innocence:

"I'm a tourist. Hanging about is what tourists do." Æneas scratched his chin.

"If you weren't a cat, I would think you were a spy." I called for more designer water, retsina on the side, and snickered at him:

"A cat as a spy? You must have lost your marbles. Might as well suspect the dogs and horses." Deiphobus said bitterly:

"Don't think we haven't! However, it's hard to pin anything on them. You think you have a lead but when you get there, the horse is browsing or the dog is scratching its ear." He was quite serious. I tried hard not to laugh.

"Well, you guys must be pretty desperate. But you're absolutely wrong. Animals wouldn't spy for the Greeks or for you, come to that. They have other agendas. They're wired to survive and, as we all know, a spy's lifespan is severely limited. Also, spies need to be true believers or get paid huge amounts. Animals don't have faith, not in humans at least. In addition, what have you got they'd want? If anything, they'd just steal it. So, don't worry. If you meet a dog or a horse, just give it a few pats."

I thought this was clever but it didn't make the other two happy. They dipped their beaks into their mugs in a pensive sort of way. Then it came to me that this was a good time to learn the Trojan side to the war question. I had Helen's, of course, but that hardly seemed to count. "So," I asked, conversationally. "What are your plans?" Deiphobus looked up, puzzled:

"About what?" Jeez, they'll never beat the Greeks at this rate.

"About the war. The situation. What are the latest stratagems?" Æneas shook his head sadly.

"We are at an impasse." You don't say. Good vocabulary, though. He continued: "We should really return Helen; I don't know why we want to keep her. She and Paris are hardly on speaking terms. But Troilus foams at the mouth if it's even mentioned." Deiphobus added:

"And Paris won't accept or acknowledge that Helen has literally dumped him. He continues going around looking snooty and saying he won't give her up." Well! The presumptuous bastard! However, all this gave me an opening.

"Do you think," I asked cautiously, "that giving Helen back would settle the matter? Would the Greeks just take her and sail away?" Deiphobus looked up, startled.

"Why, of course! That's what's it's been about all along. They want Helen back."

"Well, and her treasure," added Æneas. I asked:

"Surely they'll want war reparations as well? Payment for all the aggravation, treasure and time wasted?" Æneas clinked his mug on the table. Marianne came running with a refill. He said, scratching his chin thoughtfully:

"It's not really been discussed, you know. We've always thought they just wanted Helen and her belongings and, as neither has been on the cards, we've not explored other options. Also, why should we have to worry about what they've spent on the war? We didn't start it. And what about what we've spent?" Well, this was all open to discussion although I didn't think the Greeks would consider the Trojans entitled to a single drachma. Truly, this lot was hopeless. I continued:

"Before all this Helen business came up, what were your relations with the Greeks?" Deiphobus scratched his head. I moved slightly away. If he had lice, he could keep them.

"It seems so long ago, it's like ancient history," he answered. "Was there a relationship between our countries before Helen? I suppose there must have been." He fell silent. Truly, Deiphobus was unbelievably clueless. However, Æneas said thoughtfully, as if pulling at memories from the long ago past.

"There was a spot of bother, you remember, Deiphobus, about the rates we were charging for Greek shipping to pass through the Hellespont and import and export taxes on goods from and to the Sea of Marmara area. The Greeks wanted both reduced and have their own pilots navigate the straits. I'd clean forgotten about all that. Why, that was the reason for Nestor and Odysseus' embassy about twelve years ago!" A class action. Very up-to-date. "But no agreement was ever reached. You remember, Deiphobus. Although a Trojan delegation went to Sparta for further discussions."

"Of course," answered that gentleman, slapping his hands on his thighs and coming alive, "You went, Æneas, Hector and Helenus, and father sent the kid Paris along, too, because he thought travel might broaden what there was of his mind and that he'd be a hit with the ladies as indeed he was . . ." He stopped. "That's how it all started." He sighed; they both sighed; they both looked gloomy. Not surprising. I think they would have given much to be able to turn the clock back and leave Paris behind or, if not, that he'd stolen a Praxiteles Venus, a bronze Poseidon or the Winged Victory instead of Helen.

I pressed the point away from Helen: "At the moment the Hellespont is closed to all shipping. A nuisance for everyone and you lot must have lost a mint over the last ten years." The more I see of the Trojans, the more I think the whole lot belongs in a loony bin.

"You're right as to the revenues," growled Deiphobus. "The Greeks' first act was to blockade the Hellespont. No one goes in. No one goes out. Damned nuisance!"

"So," I continued, "how is everyone managing?" Æneas answered with a sigh:

"As the straits are off limits, merchant ships have to sail between the islands of Eceabat and Samothrace to the Gulf of Limnos where there's a makeshift port." Indeed, the same tactic the Western allies were to use in World War I. PLUS ÇA CHANGE . . . [34] "Trouble is," he continued, "that means everything then has to be lugged overland." He shook his head sadly. "No one is happy." I bet. The Trojans had really made a mess,

---

[34] Plus ça change, plus c'est la même chose. The more things change, the more they remain the same.

focusing on Helen without looking at the economic side of things. If they'd negotiated earlier, they might have reached a deal with the Greeks everyone could be comfortable with. In fact, I'm not sure Agamemnon wouldn't have let Helen stay on in Troy if she'd insisted. Now, of course, the Greeks were too pissed to accept anything but total surrender and a lengthy Greek occupation. Oh, dear, the strategy of the World War II victors. PLUS ÇA CHANGE again?? Deiphobus sighed:

"It's too late now!" I could smell the despair on him. "We'll just have to gird our loins and take our medicine!" What a pair of knuckleheads.

"Guys," I said as harshly as I could, "you're missing the main event!" They looked at me, total incomprehension on their faces. "Lads," I started again. "Now that you've realized it's not all about Helen, you're in a position to negotiate with the Greeks, agree on some sort of compromise and get out of this hole you've dug for yourselves." Æneas said slowly:

"I suppose we could call a meeting of the Council and discuss it." I would have scratched him but before I could, Deiphobus shook his head sadly.

"Father would never agree." I bristled:

"As far as I understood, Priam gave up the reins of government to you two. So what do you care whether he agrees or not?" Deiphobus continued:

"And there are Troilus and Paris." I was ready to tear my fur out by the handful.

"This is no way to run a city or a war," I snarled. "You're running in circles. The buck has to stop somewhere. You can't govern by committee that only moves on unanimous vote. You'll get roasted!" Æneas patted me in a kindly sort of way.

"You mean well, Gaius, but you're a cat, you know. You'd never understand." And the two got up and left together sadly. I looked after them and in my frustration felt that, whatever was coming their way, would be well deserved.

All things being equal, the idea of arbitration was a non-starter. Who was there to make these two sides sit down and discuss things in a rational way? Not me; besides, no one would take me seriously. It had to be someone with clout, with attitude, with gravitas . . . I stopped. Someone who had no ties to either side and whose chief interest lay in a peaceful solution to the conflict so he could snooker his boss. Vergil! Gaius, you are brilliant!

~: 8 :~

Legal Eagles

Vergil stared at me.

"Are you serious?" He obviously didn't think so. I explained a bit more and he said: "Ohhh . . ." After turning it over in his mind, he muttered, chin in his hand: "As a Roman, I have some legal training, at least in rhetoric, even though I wasn't any great shakes at it." I interrupted, assuring him:

"Vergil, we're dealing with a bunch of yokels. I don't know how their legal system works but I wouldn't want to go on trial for robbing candy from a baby in this time and place. No matter how mediocre you are as a lawyer, and," I hastened to add, "I'm sure you're selling yourself short, you can probably run rings around the lot of them." I continued ingeniously: "I'd not be surprised if their system of justice was to include tying a parricide in a sack with a cat and a dog or some such thing and chucking the sack off the Hellespont.[35]" Vergil smiled for the first time.

"Gaius, for a cat you are extremely smart. OK, you got yourself a deal. Set it up here, right on the cliff. The Trojans probably wouldn't let us into the city . . ." I interrupted him:

---

[35] In fact, this was the Roman punishment for parricide—murder of a father.

142

"Perhaps that was Odysseus' intention all along. Come into my parlor and all that . . ."[xxiii] Vergil shook his head:

"Not even Odysseus could be so naïve as to think that would work." I had to agree. "So, neither city nor camp but here." I nodded firmly.

"Quite right, Vergil. In addition, of course, I haven't much faith in Odysseus' quest for a win-win solution to the war; I know—and you know—that he's one slippery bastard. I presume his intention with this wheeze is to waste as much time as possible so he can perfect his other nefarious plots, whatever they are." We sat silently, both thinking, no doubt, of Odysseus' shortcomings as a chap to be trusted. Then I continued:

"But, think, Vergil, there is a chance, just a chance, that arbitration could work and we would beat him at his own game. If the Trojans and Greeks could agree to terms that are even halfway sensible without either side giving up too much, it would be difficult even for Odysseus to ditch the outcome. And with you as arbitrator . . ." I was getting quite excited. "Think of the implications: no fall of Troy." Vergil scratched his chin. I looked at him sideways like: "Your *Æneid* would need extensive re-writing." Vergil looked thoughtful.

"If, and I say this cautiously, this works, there would be no *Æneid*; I'd write a pastoral epic instead. Æneas stays in Troy and runs a farm or market garden. White flocks, shepherds playing pan pipes, fields with spinach and tomatoes and meadows of golden corn."

"Sounds wonderful!" I enthused. "Æneas living happily ever after, surrounded by sheep and vegetables!" Vergil cheered up.

"It would put paid to Augustus and his patriotic epic poem." Hope is contagious. So, for Vergil, was the thought of Augustus not getting his own way. He got up and started dancing about, singing:

"No Dido, no Latium, no . . . ." We finished the sentence in chorus:

"No Roman Empire." I added:

"No Vergil, no Gaius Marius but I'll probably still be a cat in my own time and you a human in yours, but what different worlds they would be." We sat in silence for a bit. I asked. "Would you mind very much?"

"Me?" cried Vergil, still jumping about. "Not at all! No Augustus! Oh, joy!" Vergil continued dancing about on the hillside for a bit then sat down:

"Now leave me if you will. I need review what I can remember of my legal training." I scampered off and returned to Troy.

I was getting a lot of incredulous stares that day. Æneas lifted his eyebrows:

"I don't believe it." How original. At least Deiphobus kept silent. Had he said anything, he would have said: 'I don't believe it'.

"Guys," I explained, "this is a one-time offer. Think of it. You have nothing to lose because, if it doesn't come off, you'll be no worse off than you are now. But at least you'll be doing something; it'll be good for the city's morale."

"Not if we don't get anywhere," said Deiphobus. That was true. There are many bridges to cross in life; let's take them one at a time.

"Guys, this is a very simple matter. The Greeks are here. You don't want them here. What will you pay to get rid of them?" Æneas and Deiphobus looked at each other.

"I hope you don't mind, Gaius," said Deiphobus, "if we go and discuss this in private. We also need to consult some of the others." I was all affability.

"My friends, I understand entirely." Right. Lysandra will take notes. "I'll be on the battlements when you want me."

So to the ramparts I went looking forward to a nice quiet nap. I had just had a good stretch and was curling up all comfy when who should appear but Hecuba. A stately lady, matronly perhaps but with a great deal of dignity. Her hair was grey; not surprising seeing the miserable life she'd led but it was beautifully coiffed. Being miserable is no excuse for letting oneself go to pot.

"Why doesn't she go away?" Hecuba asked. I knew who 'she' was. If you meant Andromache or Polyxena or Cassandra, you said so. 'She' was Helen.

"Perhaps," I answered, wondering why people kept talking to me. "She loves Paris." She answered, shaking her head sadly:

"I don't think Helen can love anybody." Well, no prizes for guessing that. On the other hand, one might excuse Helen who'd been so used, abused and misused she'd probably lost the ability. Hecuba went on: "Husband, children, family, she left them all and never looked back." Hecuba sighed. "If she had any love or pity in her heart, she'd go down to the Greek tents now and spare Troy this final agony." Hecuba might have my full sympathy but still . . . I said:

"Sorry, but, you know, I don't think at this stage what Helen does will make much of a difference." Hecuba seemed not to have heard. She looked out over the sea.

"So beautiful," she said wistfully, "I have always loved this view." Indeed.

When every aspect pleases and only man is vile[xxiv].

There's really nothing one can say to a grieving mother. It's best when they're religious and get comfort from 'it was the will of the gods'. One might think that a woman with as many kids as Hecuba might not notice if half-a-dozen or so went missing. Gaius, don't be cynical. Let Hecuba grieve. She would have a lot more grieving to do soon enough. Still . . . I said:

"Paris shares the blame, surely, along with Helen." Hecuba shook her head and excused her offspring as mothers have done from time immemorial. She said:

"He was just a boy and she was a married woman. She led him astray." She then wandered off, to go and be sad somewhere else. I settled down. Peace at last. So I thought.

145

Helen pounced on me:

"What," she asked me, "is that knave Odysseus up to? What's this I hear of arbitration? " I looked at her innocently.

"Why ask me? I'm just a cat."

"I love," she said with that nasty smile that was her chief trademark, "being lied to."

"By the way, Helen, as a matter of curiosity, do you love Paris?" I got the gimlet eye for my pains.

"I advise you," she answered coldly, "to stop guzzling that retsina. It seems to be addling your brain." She stalked off. Back home, they say: 'Asking is not an offence.' But then, they probably haven't met Helen.

Well, after Hecuba and Helen, I was settling down again when somebody else came up. This time, an adolescent girl, 16 or so. Polyxena, Priam's youngest daughter.

"Hello," she said and sat down next to me.

"Hi," I answered. One needs to be polite. She continued:

"I've never seen a cat quite like you."

"That's because I am a Siamese. You can tell by my blue eyes. Only Siamese cats have blue eyes." Well, it might not be true but Polyxena wouldn't live long enough to find out.

"Do you know," she said, changing the subject, "I can't remember ever having been outside the walls of Troy?"

"But you must have been," I objected. "After all, what are you, 16? So you were about six or seven when the war started." She continued in a dreamy tone:

"When Helen arrived, I thought she was a fairy princess. So beautiful. I wanted to be just like her. She used to let me play with her jewels." She looked down sadly at her hands. I shuddered. Two Helens! The Gods forbid! "She was nice to me. Said I looked like her daughter, Hermione, who was back in Sparta. But now, I don't know. She looks cross all the time and hardly ever speaks to anyone." I commiserated.

"It's this war that just drags on and on," I said. "No wonder everyone's out of sorts. They all want to be doing something else and getting on with their lives." Polyxena wasn't listening.

"When I was a little girl," she continued, "I was promised in marriage to Achilles. But of course that's off now." I shuddered. I said with feeling:

"Count yourself lucky, Polyxena; I can guarantee Achilles would have made a lousy husband. Anyhow, he's old enough to be your grandfather." That Achilles! Always going to marry someone but never getting around to it. Think of Agamemnon's daughter, Iphigenia, brought to Aulis supposedly for her wedding and then sacrificed to the Gods so the Greeks could get a proper wind and sail for Troy. Being engaged to Achilles can be hazardous to a girl's health. Polyxena sighed:

"The only one who wants the war to continue is my twin brother, Polytes. Father won't let him become a warrior until he's 18 and he's afraid the war will be over by then."

"Well, let's hope it is," I countered. Polyxena sighed again, got up and left. I felt awful. It's dreadful to see a human of 16 with no future.

I was happy in dreamland until Lysandra came running up and shook me awake. No naps for Gaius or so it seemed.

"Things are really moving," she panted. "They've had a terrible row in the High Command. I thought they were going to tear each other to pieces." Well, that would have been another solution to our problem. If someone killed Æneas, Vergil would really be pleased. "It was all about who is to represent Troy at the arbitration—is that the correct word?" Yes, sweetheart, move on. "Of course, Æneas and Deiphobus thought they should go— having been given joint command by Priam. But Troilus threw a fit—he said they would sell out to the Greeks—and Paris backed him up.

"Then someone actually asked Cassandra how this would play out—but of course she started raving about fire and blood, which wasn't any help at all." The Trojans had to be truly desperate if they were looking to Cassandra for advice. Problem with prophets is that one must decode, as it were, what they say or, rather, see. Moreover, Troy has never had anyone really good since Calchas went over to the Greeks. But he had gone to Greece and was thus not available. Whatever, lots of clever people over the millennia have decoded prophecies the wrong way. Remember:

If you go to war, a great empire will fall[xxv].

Poor old Croesus went to war and a great empire fell—his own.

However, there was another side to this and my heart sank. If Cassandra continued seeing fire and blood, the arbitration might be doomed to failure. Oh, well. Hope, as they say, springs eternal—who knows, it might be all right on the night.

"So," I asked, getting back to the issue at hand, "what did they decide?" However, Lysandra was not to be hurried; she was going to give the news in her own way. So she continued:

"This just went on and on. Troilus shouted that he should go—because he had Troy's real interests at heart—together with Paris who, after all, was a chief interested party because he was, so to speak, the 'owner' of Helen." Oh, oh, that spelt trouble.

"Helen was furious. She said she would decide whether she stayed in Troy or went back to Sparta. So would they please leave her out of the equation; in fact, she said, since she was the main interested party, she should go." Wonderful. What side would she represent? "Priam tried to intervene but the shouting got so loud and raucous that his frail old voice just couldn't be heard. Then someone suggested that all four should go—but that, Æneas said, would not be acceptable. Two representatives from each side only." I hadn't realized this would become so complicated. I wondered how the Greeks were getting on. Perhaps Odysseus, too, was having his problems. Lysandra continued:

"Someone suggested putting it to the vote. But Æneas put his foot down. He said that, as representative of the Trojan aristocracy, his inclusion should not be in question. One aristocrat, one representative from the royal family." Oh, my, I almost couldn't bear the suspense. "So a vote was held for the second representative—and Troilus won." I shook my head.

"Æneas and Troilus," I said. "Can't believe it. They might as well call the whole thing off here and now." I jumped down from my perch. "You've done great, Lysandra, come along to *The Trojan Horse* and I'll treat you to a cream tea." Ladies love being asked out to tea so off we went.

I later found out that the Greeks had indeed had the same problems as regards representatives. They'd ended up with Odysseus and Agamemnon. My heart sank further still. On the other hand, this would be right up Odysseus' street if his purpose was to merely waste time. No matter how I looked at it, the whole arbitration exercise seemed doomed before it even began. I decided not to tell Vergil. Wait and see, that's my motto.

8.1 Arbitration

Odysseus had some Greek lads dragged up a table from *The Greek Olive Tree*, plus five chairs and a stool—for me—up the cliff. When Vergil and I arrived, we found the others waiting for us. Agamemnon in full commander-in-chief regalia, Odysseus in a battered non-too-clean tunic, Æneas looking every inch a Trojan aristocrat. What can I say about Troilus—his chief attire seemed to be attitude. Vergil was turned out in a toga—now, that made the others stare. I wasn't surprised. If I live to be a hundred, I shall never know what the point of the toga ever was. It looked hot, uncomfortable and difficult to put on and keep on. That said, Vergil looked impressive. Vergil and I had discussed how he was to be introduced and we decided omission to be the best policy. He was just a passer-by from somewhere or other. I patted him down before we joined the others, just in case he had a knife and was planning to murder Æneas. Vergil took the seat at the head of the table. I jumped up on the stool.

"My friends," I said, "this is Vergil, a visitor from a far land who has been kind enough to agree to act as arbiter in your quarrel. Vergil has had experience in the law courts of his country and is therefore fully qualified to lead arbitration."

Vergil looked around at them. I could see he was not too impressed. Of course, his gaze rested longest on Æneas. Oh, dear. He opened the session.

"You have come here to try and settle your dispute in a non-violent fashion," he announced. "I commend you on your good sense." Which begged the question: why hadn't they done it nine years ago? However, Vergil continued: "I want you all to understand what arbitration is:

> *A proceeding in which a dispute is resolved by an*
> *impartial adjudicator whose decision the parties to the*
> *dispute have agreed will be final and binding.*

Is this clear and acceptable to both parties?"
General nodding. Vergil continued:
"Allow me to stress:

> *Arbitration is a consensual process; parties who take their case*
> *to arbitration have agreed to do so. And further: the decision*
> *reached at arbitration cannot be appealed to a higher court."*

Even Odysseus was impressed and a wee bit worried. He looked at me and I could almost read his thoughts: 'where did you find this bloke? He's too good. I was expecting a dog or donkey or something.' Sorry, Odysseus, you're not the only one with brains around here. But Vergil went on: "I also want you to understand, and accept, the role of the arbiter:

> *Who will not necessarily judge according to the strict letter of the*
> *law but chiefly consider the principles of practical politics.*

Is that also understood and accepted?" There's something about a Roman nose that inspires respect. Add gravitas, which Vergil had in spades, and it wasn't likely anyone would object or, in fact, say anything. "Now," said Vergil, "will each party introduce itself and nominate who will speak for it." Agamemnon responded at once:

"I am Agamemnon, king of Mycenæ and leader of the Greek Expeditionary Forces. I speak for the Greeks." If I hadn't already been sure that Odysseus wasn't serious about this whole affair, I was now. "This," continued Agamemnon grandly, "is Odysseus, prince of Ithaca." Vergil looked towards the other side.

"I am Æneas," said that gentleman, "the leader of the Trojan aristocrats. I speak for the Trojans." Well, good luck and I hope you can keep Troilus under wraps but wouldn't bet on it. "This is prince Troilus, a son of king Priam."

"Very well," said Vergil. "Now, which side is the plaintiff and which the defendant." There was an uneasy silence. Then Agamemnon declared:

"The Greeks are the plaintiffs. They are the injured party." Of course, Troilus flew up.

"They are not. We are the plaintiffs, they are the defendants." Well, this was not a hopeful beginning. Vergil held up his hand for silence.

"Since there is disagreement on this point, I will rule on it after I have heard each side's arguments." This lot needed a firm hand. "Prince Troilus, since you do not speak for the Trojans, I ask you to remain silent until you are addressed directly." This was not popular with Troilus. He glowered at Vergil who ignored him and addressed Agamemnon. "King of Mycenæ, state your case for the Greek side." Agamemnon cleared his throat, drew himself up and began:

"We have for a number of years been attempting to negotiate with the Trojans more favorable terms for passage of our ships through the Hellespont to the Sea of Marmara and also to reduce the rates on import and export of goods passing through the straits. Several Greek embassies have been to Troy, with no success. The Greeks feel," Agamemnon look at his adversaries from under lowered brows, "that the Trojans acted in bad faith, with no serious intention of reaching an agreement." Troilus flew up but subsided when Vergil held up his hand. Not surprising the Romans became masters of the world.

"Your turn will come, Trojans. Continue, King Agamemnon," he said.

"In a further attempt to broker a deal," Agamemnon continued, "we invited a Trojan embassy to visit the Greek City States and participate in sporting events in Sparta. To cut a long story short, we were repaid for our goodwill and hospitality by the abduction and ravishing of Helen, queen of Sparta, by Paris, son of Priam." Vergil lifted his eyebrows:

"Are you telling me," he asked, "that the queen of Sparta was raped and then murdered?" That would have been a case for the Special Victims' Unit. Agamemnon almost looked sorry to have to admit that Helen was still alive and kicking. Yeah. Emphasis on kicking. "Please go on," said Vergil. Agamemnon continued:

"The Greeks demanded the return of Queen Helen, which the Trojans refused out of hand, as they refused further discussions regarding access to the Hellespont. The Greek City States then called together a coalition of the willing and an expeditionary force sailed to Troy to retrieve her by force, if necessary. After nine years, the Trojans continue to refuse to hand Helen over or come to terms." A lousy case if I ever heard one. Vergil said:

"Is that your whole case?" he asked.

"It is." answered Agamemnon. Vergil looked at Odysseus.

"Have you anything to add, Prince of Ithaca?" Odysseus shook his head:

"I do not. The case is as stated by the king of Mycenæ."

"Very well," said Vergil. He turned to Æneas. "Please state the case for Troy." Æneas looked embarrassed as well he might. As far as I could see, the Trojans didn't have much of a case. However, Æneas pulled himself together and plunged into it:

"The case for Troy is: it is true that the negotiations between the Greek City States and Troy regarding the Hellespont never reached a satisfactory conclusion. We, the Trojans, thought the Greek terms to be ridiculously low and we wished for extensive revisions. However, talks broke down after Helen, queen of Sparta, by her own free will, came to Troy. She was in no way coerced or forced. Although we have made this clear to the Greeks innumerable times, they remain on our shores with their engines of war and have laid siege to our city for nine years. We wish them to cease and desist and leave Troy." Well, overall, Æneas had done as well as could be expected. Vergil said:

"Having heard both sides," as if he didn't know all this inside out, "it is my ruling that the Greeks are the injured party and therefore the plaintiffs, while Troy is the defendant." In a fit of rage, Troilus shouted, standing up and pointing directly at Vergil.

"How much have the Greeks paid you for this treason?" Oh, dear, this boy will come to a bad end. Vergil looked down his nose at Troilus, quite a feat since he was sitting while Troilus was standing. His voice was icy:

"If you are suggesting that I have accepted a bribe," he said, "you will need to substantiate your accusation with evidence. Have you any?" Troilus sat down. "I thought not. Let us proceed." He looked around at the assembly. "Since the lady seems to be central to the question, perhaps we should have her testify in person."

"Rhm." I cleared my throat. All eyes turned on me. This was sort of embarrassing. But there was nothing for it but to plough on. I said: "I have here a power-of-attorney—duly notarized—whereby Queen Helen authorizes me to speak for her." The document passed around for everyone's inspection. "Queen Helen," I continued, "has asked me to say, on her behalf, of course, that she will take no part in these proceedings, nor will she corroborate any issue or support either side. She will, however, abide by the final decision of the arbiter." Well, that for sure stunned the lot and it took a moment or two before Vergil went on:

"That is, I suppose, the lady's prerogative. We will have to come back to this matter at a later stage. Let us pass on. I would like the positions of each party clarified. Greeks first, if you please. What terms will you accept?" Agamemnon said:

"We want the return of the lady and her treasure; we want war reparations and compensation for defamation and moral injuries the Greek City States have sustained by Troy's infamous behavior." Vergil nodded to Æneas.

"Troy wishes the Greeks to lift the siege of our city and leave our shores. And we wish to retain the lady until she herself expresses a desire to leave."

"Well," said Vergil raising his eyebrows. "The matter of the lady must be left to the last. Now, in the matter of war reparations, what is Troy willing to offer?" There was a bit of a silence. Æneas and Troilus exchanged glances. At last, Æneas said:

"We are willing to offer the Greek City States one-third of the income from all vessels passing through the Hellespont in either direction as well as one-third of the rates and taxes on imports and exports from and to the Sea of Marmara for a period of twenty years." Vergil looked at Agamemnon who said:

"That is not sufficient. The Greek City States want two-thirds of rates and taxes in perpetuity." Well, perpetuity was for sure a long time and two-thirds represented a lot of Troy's income. Not even the British would prove that greedy. Vergil said:

"As arbiter, I suggest that the split be fifty-fifty over a period of 100 years." The Trojans looked horrified.

"Fifty years," suggested Æneas in panic. "And we'll accept the fifty-fifty split." Agamemnon nodded. Amazing! Were they really coming to an agreement? I could hardly breathe I was so tensed-up. Vergil continued:

"Then, if these terms are acceptable to both sides, it is so agreed." Odysseus now spoke for the first time.

"Then we come back to the lady," he said. Agamemnon looked at him haughtily.

"That matter will be settled by the lady returning to her lawful husband." Troilus completely lost it. He jumped up, shouting:

"No! The honor of Troy will not accept such a decision. We will fight to the death to keep her, to the death, I tell you! We will not admit she was abducted, we will not admit she is with us under duress."

"Well," began Æneas; but Troilus was now out of control.

"There is no agreement if Helen does not stay in Troy." And off he stormed. Vergil looked at Æneas.

"You speak for Troy. You can override him if you wish." However, Æneas shook his head sadly.

"No," he said simply, "I'm afraid I cannot." He got up and walked slowly down the cliff. The rest looked at each other. I thought Odysseus was smiling secretly as if he had never been in doubt of how this would end. Agamemnon spoke to Vergil:

"Stranger, we thank you for the trouble you have taken and are sorry it has come to such an unsuccessful conclusion. We wish you a pleasant journey back to your homeland. Come, Odysseus."

Off they went, leaving Vergil and myself in the debris of the arbitration. We said nothing for a while, each ruminating on what might have been.

"For a moment there," Vergil said pensively, "I thought we were going to swing it. The money bit was easy to sort since it's only cash with no honor or glory involved." I was full of sympathy.

"Vergil, no one could have done it better than you. But with that arrogant Agamemnon on one side and the impetuous hothead Troilus on the other, one should have foreseen what the harvest would be."

"I suppose," remarked Vergil glumly, "my only option is to write my epic and then burn it. Better keep my matches dry." I mused:

"Perhaps we were over optimistic, Vergil. You just can't come back from the future and change the past, at least not on the scale we were proposing. You know, che será sera."

We looked over the Dardan plain at the dark blue Aegean. I sighed and became quite morose. I must have felt pretty bad because all I think of was poetry. I quoth:

> *The Moving Finger writes; and, having writ,*
> *Moves on: nor all your Piety nor Wit*
> *Shall lure it back to cancel half a Line,*
> *Nor all your Tears wash out a Word of it.*"[36]

Vergil listened, brooded then shook his head. "A bit defeatist, don't you think? In fact, not like you at all. When did cats become so fatalistic? When did they begin to believe in fate or kismet or karma?" I shrugged.

"Sorry. But it just occurred to me that what is done is done and cannot be undone." Vergil shook his head and, raising a finger, admonished me:

"Gaius, this moving finger of yours . . . well, once it has moved, yes, it cannot be erased. But has the finger moved beyond the fall of Troy or, rather, the end of this war?" I chewed on this for a bit then brightened up once I saw where Vergil was headed.

"You're right, Vergil, we mustn't give up hope." We both felt better at once. I invited Vergil to *The Greek Olive Tree* for Happy Hour. However, he'd had enough of Greeks for the present. And Trojans, he added before I could suggest *The Trojan Horse* in Priam Square.

I wandered slowly down to my favorite spot on the beach and looked out over the sea. A voice behind me said:

"There you are." I ground my teeth. Would no one rid me of this troublesome Greek? Odysseus sat down. I snarled:

"I am."

"I suppose," he continued, "you're pissed off because the arbitration didn't work out," he said.

"That," I replied with dignity, "is one reason."

"Well," said Odysseus, "live with it. Did you really think, with Agamemnon and Troilus there, it could have ended differently?" I answered:

---

[36] Omar Khayyam, Siamese poet, AD 1048-1122

"It might if you'd left those two bad news bears at home." Odysseus shook his head sadly:

"Now, Gaius, in all fairness I can't be held responsible for Troilus. And only by skewering him with a nice sturdy lance would Agamemnon have stayed away," he said in his own defense. "In fact, my dear cat, you almost got Agamemnon and Menelaus." I thought about that.

"The proceedings would have been a lot shorter than they actually were," was my comment; then I sighed and admitted: "I suppose it wasn't really your fault. Although I bet you were counting on it being a frost and getting nowhere." Odysseus nodded sheepishly:

"I confess that, yes, you're right. On the other hand, had we reached an agreement that would have been OK, too." He speculated for a bit. "Perhaps I should have given more attention to reaching a positive outcome. We could all have been heading home by now. Yes, it was a mistake, I admit it." I seethed inwardly. He agreed with me, did he, now that there was no going back. Then he suddenly laughed out loud, giving me quite a turn. "I liked the bit about Helen. Couldn't believe it, you know. That lady is something else. What a fool Menelaus was for not appreciating her. But then, Menelaus can always be counted on to be Menelaus."

Odysseus got up and strode away. I looked after him. I felt depressed me, I had a migraine and Odysseus had just made it worse. I wanted was to be alone to sulk.

~: 9 :~

On the Hellespont

I decided it was time to take a personal day. So the next day I walked up the coast to where I could look down on the Hellespont.

Homer was a great poet, no doubt, but, really, one has trouble separating his Trojans from his Greeks. It's obvious that multiculturalism wasn't around in his day and he wasn't worried about political correctness. So to Homer, everything was much of a muchness. There must have been vast differences between Troy and Greece and Trojans and Greeks but don't look for it in *The Iliad* where everyone speaks the same language, worships the same gods and, as far as I can tell, wears the same clothes. Except for helmets: one had a horse hair tail and the other didn't. So, when you got down to it, *it was all Greek to Homer."* I tittered at my own cleverness. No East and West for him!

That brought to mind another poem by Kipling:

Oh, East is East, and West is West, and never the twain shall meet,
Till Earth and Sky stand presently at God's great Judgment Seat;
But there is neither East nor West, Border, nor Breed, nor Birth,

When two strong men stand face to face, tho'
they come from the ends of the earth![37]

In the real world, Troy was well to the east of the Greek City States. The Greeks developed the basis of what today is western civilization. So the War in Troy may have been the first of many confrontations between East and West. The traffic over the Hellespont since then and for the past three millennia has been intense.

Darius I of Persia, also known as the Great King, didn't go himself but sent seven armies across, first in 492 BC and then in 490 BC. To get across, Persian troops built bridges of boats lashed together. Neither campaign was successful; the first because the Persians couldn't find the Greeks; the second ended at the battle of Marathon (490 BC), which didn't go the Persians' way. The Greek warrior Philippides famously ran from Marathon to Athens (125 miles) to bring the news to the Athenians, which begs the question: why not take a chariot or at least a horse? Be that as it may, running a Marathon has been popular ever since[xxvi]. Humans are strange.

Another famous moment during that particular war was when the King of Sparta and 300 of his warriors tried to stop the Persian advance at Thermopylae; they were skewered by the Persians, of course, but not through defeat but treachery. Considering the opposing numbers, Sparta made Persia pay dearly for the privilege. The Spartans won immortality, also worth something. I do admire their epithet:

Go tell the Spartans, thou who passest by,
That here, obedient to their laws, we lie.[38]

Xerxes I of Persia, Darius' son, crossed from Asia to Europe in 480 BC and actually sacked Athens. However, he got his comeuppance at the naval battle of Salamis that same year when

---

[37] *The Ballad of East and West*. Rudyard Kipling (1865–1936)
[38] Simonides, Greek poet (556–468 BC)

the Greeks beat him to a pulp. When he got home, a member of his staff murdered him. This should happen to all unsuccessful generals.

In 330 BC, Alexander the Great went the other way, on conquest bent, what else. Why people don't just stay at home and watch television or read a good book I can't fathom. Everyone knows all about Alexander; just let me say that another Persian King, Darius III, got on Alexander's wrong side with the result that the Persian army was utterly destroyed in 333 BC and Persia ceased to exist.

When the Greeks couldn't find a willing foreign foe, they went for each other. Athens and Sparta fought what became known as the Peloponnese war in about 400 BC that went on for four years, with everyone very busy on both sides of the Hellespont. The city of Byzantium, founded in 667 BC, was captured and recaptured repeatedly by both sides.

The Romans were here, too, couldn't keep that lot out: the Roman Emperor Septimus Severus laid siege to Byzantium in 196 AD.

The city of Constantinople was founded by Constantine I in 330 AD, who, famously, made Christianity the Roman state religion. He claimed he saw a cross in the sky and heard a voice: IN HOC SIGNE VINCERAS[39]! That's when hearing voices started becoming popular. But he may just have been bipolar. Later on, in or around 420 AD, the Huns invaded Europe by crossing the Hellespont hanging onto their horses' tails. Lazy bastards.

Constantinople became the capital of Byzantium, the Eastern Roman empire and, against all odds, lasted for over a thousand years after the Western Empire was no more. Many willing hands—including other Christians, who should have been its friends and allies, engendered Byzantium's demise. In April 1204, Western European crusaders[40] invaded and conquered Constantinople. This was seen as the last straw and led to the

---

[39] In this sign you will be victorious
[40] The **Fourth Crusade** (1202–1204)

Great Schism between the Eastern Orthodox Church and the Roman Catholic Church. Constantinople fell to the Turks in 1453, and was renamed Istanbul. The Greeks, however, still call it Constantinople.

During the Napoleonic wars, in 1817, Russia blockaded the straits and, in 1833, forced the Turks to close the Hellespont to non-Black Sea Powers. The French and British used the straits to reach the Crimea in 1856, with the objective of protecting the defenseless Turks from the Big Bad Russian Bear. The Crimean War is best remembered by *The Charge of the Light Brigade*, a poem by Alfred Lord Tennyson (1809-1892). Although the Light Brigade was virtually destroyed due to a stupid mistake by the English upper class commander, Tennyson still saw the disaster as a great moral English victory.

The British are good at this and pulled the same spin in 1940, with the withdrawal from Dunkirk during WWII, where the British had been cut off from their Belgian and French allies and corralled by the Germans on Dunkirk beach. The Germans decided not to attack and the British managed to get most of their troops back to England. Another moral victory for Britain! I'm sure someone wrote a poem about it but I haven't read it.

The Hellespont's most infamous moment came during World War I or, as no one at the time knew there would be a second edition, the Great War. This naval battle, known as Gallipoli, was a British attempt to reach Constantinople via the Hellespont and beat the hell out of the Turks. The action lasted from April 1915 to January 1916 and cost 336,930 lives—over half Turkish. I hope someone got court marshaled but probably not. Wisely, Turkey kept out of World War II.

Perhaps there's something to be said for ancient warfare, after all. No matter how hard the Greeks and Trojans worked at it, even in 10 years they wouldn't be able to kill 360 000 men, let alone in nine months.

But let's go return to Alexander; he was in Troy about one thousand years after the Trojan War, give or take a couple of hundred either way. Truth to tell, I've no time for Alexander; what good is an empire that falls apart as soon the conqueror dies, I ask you? Alexander saw himself as the reincarnation of Achilles, just as the American World War II General Patton considered himself the reincarnation of Alexander. A couple of fruitcakes.

Be that as it may, before going on to create havoc in Asia, Alexander stopped at Troy. Plutarch says he sacrificed to Minerva, goddess of war, and honored the fallen heroes. I wonder how he found their tombs but, then, any little mound of stones would probably have satisfied our Alexander. He was especially fascinated by Achilles—of course—and his friendship with poor Patroklus. Here, I will quote Plutarch since I couldn't possible do any better:

> *How happy he [Alexander] esteemed him [Achilles] in*
> *having while he lived so faithful a friend [Patroklus].*

Best friends Alexander and Hephæstion were a newer version of Achilles and Patroklus and one can only wonder if that was the real reason behind their relationship. Cicero, about 300 years later, give or take a decade or so, claims that, at Achilles' tomb, Alexander said:

> *O fortunate youth [Achilles], to have found*
> *Homer as the herald of your glory!*

Homer would have loved it. True too, because if Homer had written pastoral poetry instead of *The Iliad*, the Trojan War would be long forgotten. Rumor has it that Alexander found Achilles' armor and wore it during his Asia campaign. However, that may just have been spin by Alexander's public relations department. What was obvious was that none of them— Alexander, Cicero or Plutarch—ever met Achilles in person who, in my book, was a right bastard.

While on the subject, let's not forget Lord Byron, the great English poet, who went to help the Greeks in their revolt against the Turks in or about 1823. He is said to have swum the Hellespont but I'm not convinced. I wonder what the Greeks made of him. He died of a fever in 1824, which didn't help the Greek cause one little bit.

I was nibbling a blade of grass as the evening shadows started to fall. I looked up and there was a shape flying towards me. As it landed, I saw it was Socrates.

"Hi, there," he said. "And what may you be doing here?"

"Oh, I was looking down at the Hellespont and thinking about all that happened here and what is still to come." Socrates lifted his eyebrows. Well, perhaps not, but something along those lines.

"So, you are a seer?" he asked.

"Not at all," I answered. I wasn't about to explain anything to Socrates. "I was just wondering, you know, why do people have wars? Wars seem so senseless and I doubt anyone is better off when they're over." But then, that might not be true. Most of mankind's technological advances have occurred during or as a consequence of war. Take the airplane or the radar system—and let's not forget the microwave.

"So," he said, getting comfortable on the stone next to me. "What conclusion have you come to?" I pondered.

"Well, for all their airs and graces and their sense of superiority, humans are no different from the rest of the animal world. It's all about territory."

"Oh? And how is that?"

"All hunting animals," I continued, starting to pontificate and feeling very pleased with myself, "stake out hunting grounds. This is true of wolves, lions, owls, I dare say, and so on. And this territory they will defend tooth and nail against all comers." Socrates cocked his head to one side:

"Using the wolves as our metaphor," he said, "will they travel hundreds of kilometers to find new hunting grounds?" I pondered:

"They might."

"Will they build boats to cross the ocean to find new hunting grounds?"

"Well, no." I was starting to feel a bit uncertain.

"Do they leave the old, females and the young behind to be picked up later?"

I gritted my teeth. I really didn't know but countered with: "Perhaps."

"Do wolves manufacture weapons, bows and arrows and swords and such so they can kill more efficiently?"

"No!"

"Once they have conquered the territory in question, do they just leave and go home?"

"No!" Damn him. He'd upset my argument. Socrates looked at me in a supercilious way.

"So, do you still hold to your argument that humans are just like other animals?" I wanted to strangle him.

"I suppose not!" I snarled. Socrates looked at me in a knowing way but said nothing. He prepared to take off. "If you're so bloody smart," I shouted after him enraged, "then what's the answer?"

"How should I know?" The reply came floating back to me. "You asked the question." I shied a stone after him but, of course, it went wide. Rats!

I lazed away the rest of the afternoon, dreaming of the past, the present and the future, and trying to forget Socrates. I admit he got me very confused and I still have trouble sorting out the various bits of our conversation.

⌐ 10 ⌐

The Greeks look outside the Box

When I got back to my tree, I decided what I wanted was a good sulk. Not everyone has a tent! However, as Achilles had learnt, it's no fun making a point by keeping aloof and being outside the loop.

So one Happy Hour, a week or so later, I decided that sulking was not in my best interests, swallowed hard and trotted off to *The* Greek *Olive Tree*. There was Odysseus—and Nestor. At first, I thought I would give them a miss. Odysseus I could handle, Nestor and Odysseus together seemed a bit on the much side. However, Odysseus saw me and waved me over before I could pretend to be on my way elsewhere. Oh, well, I suppose old Nestor was an OK guy even if a bit long in the tooth. So in I went.

Eurybates winked at me as he brought my drink. His kid was fooling about and the bouncer, as usual, was asleep against the wall. I never knew such a fellow for being able to sleep upright. Odysseus made the introductions:

"Gaius, this is Nestor. Nestor, Gaius, whom I've told you about. He brought me really important information from Troy." Nestor nodded:

"Seen you around," he said. Drat it, there's no way a cat can pass unnoticed in this place. I answered:

"Hi, Nestor. Seen you too." Mutual admiration society. Odysseus put a stop to this polite chitchat.

"I suppose, Gaius, you also had a look at the purely physical aspects of Troy—walls and such."

"Yeah," I drawled. "You could get a battalion of cats, a legion of rats or an army of mice in easy. Perhaps the odd baby. Forget fire arrows, boulders, ladders, climbers; battering rams would only work on Tymbria where you could get a bit of purchase by going downhill. But you know all about that, I'll be bound." I glared at him. Odysseus nodded.

"True," he answered. "We've tried everything we could imagine and some we couldn't." My head swam. "No, I'm afraid we need to think in new ways."

"Indeed," I answered, "you need to think outside the box." Nestor's eyebrows shot up:

"What box?" he enquired. But Odysseus had already moved on. He rubbed his hands:

"I know you all think I'm a cunning old fox," Nestor and I kept quiet. We weren't about to give him the lie. Odysseus sighed when the desired response didn't come and went on. "Our only chance of getting into the city is by treachery." I was going to say this would not meet the Marques of Queensbury rules.[41] But I let it go. Odysseus cracked his knuckles. I gritted my teeth. "Now, Gaius says that the Trojans are morose, gloomy and disheartened." I spoke up:

"I suppose, Odysseus, you're going to get somewhere eventually." Odysseus waved his hands about.

"COURAGE, Gaius, ON ARRIVE." Odysseus' odd quotes really got to me. Odysseus was ready to pontificate but first he called

---

[41]   Generally accepted code of rules in the sport of boxing.

for some more drinks. First things first, as the man says. After slurping down half his mug, Odysseus began:

"Gaius tells me the Trojans are dispirited, depressed and despondent." He looked at me but I couldn't think of anything to say. He sighed and continued: "It's not easy to play tricks on people who are down in the dumps, as they will always be expecting the worst. On the other hand, happy people are pre-disposed to accept rather than reject." Nestor and I looked at each other. This was taking a long time. Nestor said:

"I suppose you intend to spread sweetness and light over the whole of Troy?" I added:

"How? Magic wand? Fairy dust?" Odysseus looked annoyed:

"I wish you wouldn't keep interrupting, the two of you," he snapped. "I keep losing my train of thought." Can't have that or we'll be stuck here until the Apocalypse. "I intend," continued Odysseus grandly, "to make the Trojans happy in three phases. Phase one—hope. Phase two—relief. Phase three—euphoria. When they reach euphoria, we've got them."

We stared at him blankly. I know I'm only a cat and haven't had much schooling—my knowledge all comes from napping on various volumes of the Encyclopedia Britannica. However, Nestor, a top-drawer academic, wasn't getting it either. Odysseus continued, walking up and down in front of the bar as if he were a professor in a lecture hall: "So, how do we achieve this?" Do tell. We sat there expectantly. He didn't. Another sigh.

"Truth to tell," he confessed, "my plans aren't fully matured—yet. But I do see a glimmering of light at the end of the tunnel." He looked heavenwards and Nestor and I did, too, but there was nothing up there. Both Nestor and I said:

"Well, aren't you going to explain?" But it seemed not. I murmured:

"Hope—a reason for confidence or expectation. Relief: lessening or removal of anxiety. Euphoria: a feeling of elation, mainly based on illusion." The three of us looked at each other and Nestor and I looked at Odysseus. "So," I continued, "that's the road you have to induce the whole community of Troy to take." Odysseus glared. Nestor looked heavenwards. Odysseus turned to him in a rage.

"Don't tell me you agree with this upstart cat!" Nestor shook his head sadly.

"My dear Odysseus, I really hope you haven't bitten off more than you can chew." Odysseus waved his finger in Nestor's face.

"My phases are entirely logical!" Nestor held up a hand.

"No doubt, my friend, but remember: each journey starts with the first step." I added my bit:

"Well, seeing the first step is hope, how, given today's circumstances, how will you make this happen? How will the Trojans take the first step leading to euphoria?" Odysseus was in a pointing mood:

"You two," he sneered, "are a pair of doubting Thomas's[xxvii]. I'll have you eat your words before too long, see if I don't. When I get to my Step Three, Troy is ours for the taking."

Nestor and I both waved at Eurybates. I needed something stronger than designer water so I asked for well-watered retsina. Pace Helen, I'll take my chance with the water. After a refreshing snort, Nestor continued:

"That may be. But, your three steps need to be implemented inside Troy. Now, let's say you actually manage to make Troy a happy town, how it will benefit us, the Greeks, camped as we are on the plain outside?" I hid behind Nestor and added a bit Odysseus wouldn't like.

"Really, Nestor, I can't see your difficulty. It's easy as pie. Once the Trojans reach euphoria, the Greeks will simply knock on the gate and will be welcomed in with open arms like long lost brothers." Nestor and I tittered; Odysseus looked like thunder and grinded his teeth. Then he suddenly relaxed and became quite pleasant.

"Gaius, you may not be as cabbage-headed as you look," he said, "That angle may have some merit." So, Odysseus went back to being all guile and cunning and we couldn't get another word out of him. We had another drink and all relaxed.

10.1 Greek Husbandry

Blimey, if next morning, Odysseus didn't prod me awake! Ignoring my bleary eyes and short temper, he started out right away:

"It's all very well for you and Nestor to mock me," he snarled, cracking his knuckles. "I know where I want to be, but I still need to work out the details." More knuckle cracking. "But my first priority is to get the High Command out of my hair, especially the frightful Agamemnon with his final solution, last push and so on." He threw up his hands: "I can't think with his voice dinning in my ears all day long."

I looked west to where the Greek camp shimmered in the noonday sun, dirty and grey, messy beyond belief. "That's the easy part," was my comment. Odysseus opened his eyes wide and smirked:

"Hoh, is that so? Do share, please." I looked at him and asked as politely as I could:

"What is an army for?" He sneered.

"To fight and conquer." I smirked to myself. Move to the back of the class. I continued:

"And when they are not fighting, what is an army for?" Odysseus jumped to his feet:

"I don't know," he shouted as if he were talking to someone beyond the Pillars of Hercules[42]. "Everyone from Agamemnon down loafs about without purpose. There are constant fights, which at least keep the field hospital busy. The soldiers don't respect their officers!" Well and why should they? "They are disgruntled and want to go home and wail about it all the time." He threw himself down on the sand again. "If the lot just had one head, I would strike if off with one blow of my sword." Oh dear, someone said it first. Caligula will be mortified![43]

---

[42] The straits of Gibraltar

[43] Caligula, Roman emperor, definitely unbalanced, born 31 AD, murdered to the relief on the whole roman world in 41AD.

"You know," I said carefully, "the secret of keeping an army in the field between battles is to set up continuous work details so everyone is constantly busy. Now, look at the camp; it's a mess." I looked at him intently and went on: "I bet anything you like no housekeeping has been done since you lot arrived." Odysseus looked put out. I continued, forestalling what I knew he would say. "Yeah, I know; what's the point, you weren't going to be here long enough . . ." I laughed my head off, well, metaphorically. I gulped and went on:

"My dear fellow, you've been here ten years; and if that's not long enough for you to start thinking of housekeeping, I don't know how long you need." Odysseus looked like thunder, clenching and unclenching his hands. Since he could think of nothing to say, I went on: "Your camp is a dump. So to get not only the High Command, from Agamemnon down out of your hair, but the whole Greek army, all you need is to get them to clean up the camp and organized along military lines. Why, I could give you list after list that would keep your lads grinding away till kingdom come." Odysseus gave me a dangerous look:

"Well, you're not going to because I'm going to wring your neck!" He ground his teeth. I replied, calmly holding up a paw:

"Forget it, Odysseus, wringing my neck would be difficult because you'd have to catch me first and anyway, even if you did it, a dead cat would solve none of your problems. Now, putting your troops to work would." Odysseus curled and uncurled his fingers. He definitely looked mad enough to kill. To show I was unafraid, I waved a paw in his face and continued:

"So here's your program of work. First, dig trenches around the entire camp; fill them with water, if you like. Behind the trenches, build earthworks, five meters high, or whatever you fancy, and about two meters wide, following the whole perimeter of the camp. At each corner, set up a wooden watchtower, whatever height or shape you fancy. Then, the whole camp needs to be quartered into straight squares, mind you, and roads of stone and gravel laid out with run offs for rainwater—well, autumn is coming soon—so the whole place won't get water logged. And you could also build storage tanks to gather rain water for washing or cooking or whatever." I was now quite out of breath and Odysseus had time to sneer and ask:

"Where do we get the wood for the towers?" I waved away this question as superfluous.

"A mere bagatelle, my dear Odysseus; send troops out to harvest wood. That should keep several battalions busy for months. Then there's the field hospital—a disgrace. Get it tidied up and organized with proper orderlies and supplies. And don't let anyone get on the sick list except if an inch from dying." I warmed to my theme.

"The kitchen—the cockroaches are so big I'm too scared to go near the place after dark. Scrub, my dear Odysseus, scrub, scrub, scrub. Then the tents need washing and mending—your sailors should be good at that, they're used to sails and so on. Same goes for the standards of the various city states." I added hastily: "Not Ithaca's of course; pristine, always pristine." Odysseus looked pleased.

"Penelope," he said fondly, "sends me a new standard every year or so. And new tents woven by herself and her maidens every two years." A guy who loves his wife. A wife who knows that the road to her husband's heart is a comfortable well run home. Be that as it may, I continued:

"And, best of all, the High Command must oversee and supervise everything. Every last Greek must be kept busy!" For a few moments, Odysseus sat quietly, chewing on a leaf from my olive tree. He rubbed his chin.

"Well, Gaius, what you say has a lot of merit. In fact, I think it's bloody brilliant. I'll get on to it right away." And he got up and walked purposefully towards *The Greek Olive Tree*. I looked after him. It worked for the Romans. Why shouldn't it work for the Greeks?

So, before I could say Jack Robinson or anything else, every last Greek footslogger was busy at tasks too many to count: maintenance work, laying stones, digging ditches. The field hospital was kept as crowded as ever due to stubbed toes, broken arms and legs from people falling off scaffolding; however, Odysseus considered this an added bonus. No shirking by the medical staff. A long movable trestle was set up on which Agamemnon marched up and down, waving a stick and giving orders that might or might not be obeyed. If nothing else, it kept him out of everyone's way. The rest of the High Command was busy supervising work in their different sectors. Peace and quiet reigned at *The Greek Olive Tree* from after breakfast to Happy Hour and Eurybates and I had the whole bar to ourselves.

Odysseus of course did not take part in all this upheaval. His camp, thanks to Penelope, her busy needle and his own well trained staff, was already neat and tidy and his second in command quite capable of seeing to the needful. Odysseus was a true leader—choose staff to do the boring bits and heavy lifting with a minimum of supervision. He himself spent most of his days on the beach, on long walks by himself, head held low thinking, I suppose, deep thoughts. The whole thing suited me fine and I reveled in getting all the naps I would ever want.

Sometimes, just for a change, I would go to the camp and do a spot of sidewalk supervision. Great fun. Everyone sweating, groaning and cursing. One day, while I was at this enthralling task, Odysseus knelt down next to me and asked:

"Will this help us win the war?" I shook my head.

"Nooo, but that wasn't really the point, was it?" He shook his head in turn.

"True, very true."

10.2 A fine Italian Hand

Odysseus shook me right in the middle of my midmorning snooze. I looked at him blearily:

"Don't you ever have a nice lie-in?" Then I suppose Odysseus thought he could always sleep when there was nothing left to be done. This wasn't then. As usual, he went right to the point.

"Gaius, what is your pal Vergil, of arbitration fame, hanging around here for?" I raised the eyebrows.

"Vergil?" I stammered. "Around here? I haven't seen him!"

"Maybe not," was Odysseus nasty comment, "since you seem to spend most of your time asleep. But take my word for it: you pal, the poet, turns up almost every day, usually at Happy Hour, and has long conversations with Agamemnon." I shrugged my shoulders.

"I really don't see, Odysseus, why this is any concern of mine. Why don't you ask Agamemnon or even Vergil himself?" I turned my back on him and closed my eyes tight. I got a few more prods but then Odysseus gave up and went away. I mean, a cat is a cat and his brain has limited capacity. To figure out Odysseus was hard enough, I just didn't feel I could take Vergil on board as well.

However, I thought I'd better check this out before Vergil sent the whole thing south, so I was back at *The Greek Olive Tree* at Happy Hour later that day. The usual lot was there but no Vergil. Eurybates served me on the quiet, which suited me fine. Incognito, that's how I like it. After mugs of raki had been handed around to the human gang, Agamemnon jumped up and started striding up and down. I knew we were in for another pep-rally.

"My fellow princes," he started out. The others looked at him with bleary eyes, quickly taking another slurp of their drinks to fortify themselves against the coming onslaught. "We have sat on our laurels long enough and it is time we were up and doing, get this war over with and go home!" Diomedes whispered to Idomeneus:

"What laurels are those?" Idomeneus shook his head sadly. Unenthusiastic grunts from here and there among the spectators. Menelaus shifted on his stool.

"As far as I'm concerned," he said in a listless voice, "we could leave this minute. All this about Helen—I haven't seen her for ten years—she's probably an old hag by now." He sulked into his raki. But Agamemnon wasn't having any.

"Nonsense," he cried. "This is no longer about Helen. It is about honor: the honor of the Greek City States. We need new ways of defeating the Trojans. New ways! New ways!" He looked around hopefully but it seemed no one had anything to suggest. Only Odysseus spoke up and he was nasty.

"If I've told you once, I've told you a thousand times. To win this war, we need to get inside Troy!" Oh dear, the Greeks were running in circles.

"And how do you propose to do that?" sneered Idomeneus. "Carrier pigeons?" There was no answer to this, although it seemed logical enough if the pigeons could be persuaded to become suicide bombers and do kamikaze runs. Odysseus gave Idomeneus a stony look that said: 'watch out!' However, Agamemnon went on:

"I," he said, laying his hand on his chest. "I, Agamemnon, have thought of a way." All faces turned towards him. "Yes, my friends. And it is a simple enough plan as even Odysseus will admit." Agamemnon thoroughly enjoyed the sense of expectation he had aroused. He went on grandly: "We will build an inclined earthen ramp that will eventually reach Troy's battlements. Then all we do is walk up and, hey presto, we're in Troy!" Yeah! And Bob's your uncle! Agamemnon's face split from side to side in an enormous grin and he spread his arms wide. Dead silence. I considered. Well, the Romans would use this strategy innumerable times. This brought me right back to Vergil as the source material. Odysseus mopped his brow and sighed:

"Agamemnon," he said in the voice one uses with small children. "Have you any idea how much earth we would need to shift? While the Trojans are on the attack? Or perhaps you plan to do it at night when they're all asleep."

"The details," answered Agamemnon grandly, "I would of course leave to you as our chief strategist!" Odysseus replied with a sneer:

"Oh, thanks!" Nestor asked:

"Where did you get this idea from, Agamemnon? It sounds quite sophisticated." At first Agamemnon wasn't willing to share but then he confessed:

"You know that guy at the arbitration? Vergil? I've met him quite often and he's been telling me how this sort of thing had been very successful where he comes from." I would have guessed anyway. Vergil's fine Italian hand stirring the Trojan stew. Odysseus looked glum. The rest went back to their booze, then they all went to bed and I to my tree on the beach. I pondered on Vergil's new agenda. Of course, it was all clear as daylight. If Vergil could, he'd derail this whole process.

I saw the two together—Agamemnon and Vergil—the following Happy Hour, in deep confabulation, with Vergil showing Agamemnon something or other on a piece of parchment. I didn't want to get involved so had a Happy Hour on my own on the beach.

Later that evening, after Vergil had disappeared and I felt it was safe to go to *The Greek Olive Tree*, there was Agamemnon expounding on the Catapult[44], the Ballista[45] and Tower[46], all tried and true Roman engines of war—in about 2 000 years' time! Agamemnon was all enthusiasm.

"Easy as winking," he said to Odysseus who looked doubtfully at Vergil's drawings. "Look. I have all the schematics! The Trojans will never have seen such engines of war! We'd get over the wall or even tear down the gates easy as winking. I especially like the tower." It would certainly have sent the Trojans running for the hills—if ever the Greeks managed (a)

---

[44]   *Catapult.* Fixed base, and an arm wound in twined hair or sinew, providing the torsion for throwing projectiles.

[45]   *Ballista*: large crossbow-type weapon that could hurl a 50-pound stone over 500 m

[46]   *Mobile tower*: covered in hide or armor, rolled up to the enemy's walls, and a drawbridge lowered from the top to allow soldiers access to the besieged fortress.

to build it, and (b) discovered how it worked. Agamemnon went on:

"Vergil has also shown me different types of battle strategies; the old hoplite one of holding the line, push and shove is quite out of fashion. There's something now called the testudo, where soldiers huddle under shields held above their heads and on both sides . . ." Odysseus sighed:

"Agamemnon, have you any idea how this works?" Agamemnon looked slightly cowed:

"Well, not exactly; as I said it's quite different from what we are used to . . ." Odysseus interrupted him:

"How long do you think it would take us to train our troops in these new tactics, taking into account, of course, that we have to learn them ourselves first?" This made Agamemnon flare up:

"Odysseus, if you are going to put stumbling blocks in front of every suggestion I make, we might as well pack up and go home. Progress, man, we have to move on, we gotta learn new ways; the future, Odysseus, the future, you gotta understand! Think in new ways; get outside the box!" Odysseus patted Agamemnon's shoulders:

"My dear friend, I'm sure that in the future warfare will change and armies will use all these new falderals. But it ain't gonna be us and not in this war. We must get through as best we can, using tactics we know; there just isn't time for all this newfangled stuff!" Agamemnon sulked, Odysseus looked put out and I went back to my tree on the beach.

I was watching the moonlight on the water when Vergil turned up and sat down next to me. I looked askance at him:

"My dear Vergil, I know what you're up to." We exchanged knowing glances. I continued: "You're trying to bugger up the Greek war effort with technology beyond their level of understanding. And while all this is going on and the Greeks are wasting their time reaching for the impossible, the whole thing will fizzle out to nothing." Vergil sighed:

"I thought," he answered, "it was worth a try, you know. Keep them busy until they die of old age. The perfect solution to my problem." He sat down and looked at the stars. He continued: "Now, the ramp thing. It might work, you know; after all, it has been used by the Romans in similar situations. Romans at the foot of a hill, enemies on top." I shook my head sadly:

"Vergil, the only similarity between Troy and Rome's enemies stupid enough to retreat to a hilltop was the hill. The Romans never faced a city with enormous walls like Troy's." Vergil sighed again:

"You're right, of course." He shook his head. "You might say that the Greeks and the Trojans are evenly matched. One of them needs an advantage if this is ever going to end." He sighed again. I pressed on:

"And all those bits you've been showing Agamemnon—it's way over their heads, man. That sort of technology will take about two thousand years to develop." Vergil sniffed:

"It would be a solution to all my problems." I wanted to pound his head into the sand.

"Indeed, my dear poet. It does you credit, I suppose, but it just won't do mainly because Odysseus will not allow it. Odysseus is too smart to take to these newfangled ideas!"

"Anything to keep the Horse at bay," came the answer. We sat there in silence for a while. Then I said:

"Sorry, Vergil, I'm afraid you must accept the facts as they are. You can't drag the future into the past; you can't change how fast the human brain develops; it must come gradually, gradually. Trust me, the time for the ballista or the catapult has not yet arrived." Vergil looked so sad I felt sorry for him. I patted his hand with my paw. He smiled wanly. Vergil didn't come off his hill for Happy Hour very often after that day, although I occasionally saw him hanging about. Fate, hubris, karma, we would have to await the will of the Gods.

I didn't really want to quarrel with Vergil so I occasionally visited him. He was usually in a funk and wouldn't talk to

me—as if the whole thing was my fault. But one day he asked me
stay. He was sitting on a stone; he steepled his fingers and asked:

"Do you want to hear my newest verses?" That answer being
no, I said:

"Of course."

Here for a full three hundred years shall be kings of the line of Hector,
till Ilia[47], priestess and queen shall bear twin sons unto Mars . . . .
   Then, proud in the tawny pelt of the she-wolf that nursed
him[48], shall Romulus in his turn take charge of the people,
    calling them Romans, after his own name . . .
     Empire unending I [Zeus] give them . . .
The Romans, the lords of the world, the toga clad nation . . .
  From this fair line shall a Trojan Caesar be born
Whose empire shall reach to the ocean, his fame to the stars . . .

I thought a while. To me, it seemed such unsubstantiated
drivel. I looked at him in disdain and said:

"You should be ashamed of yourself for coming up with this
bilge." He said nothing so I continued:

"And you've now given the Romans descent from two
Heavenly Deities, Aphrodite and Mars, as if Aphrodite wasn't
enough." Vergil looked into the distance and said:

"I think Augustus will love it. And despite your carping,
there's some good stuff there—from a poetical point of view.
As a poet, I'm pleased, as a human, perhaps not so much."
I frowned. Vergil was getting above himself. As if anyone
considers poets' feelings! So my comeback was:

"Yeah, pal, and have you got any barf bags available?" Vergil
looked at me sideways.

"No, used the last one yesterday. Seeing the way things are
going, Gaius, I really don't know what other options I have." I
eyed him askance:

---

[47] Rhea Silvia, daughter of the Alban king Numitor
[48] Now, this really freaks me out. Did Romulus kill his foster mother
and wear her hide?

"My friend, you follow the dictates of your fear, not the dictates of your conscience. May the Gods have mercy upon you."

I got up, tail in the air, and walked down the hill towards the Greek camp. No doubt, I am a coward myself but, thankfully, all my decisions are little ones—what to have for breakfast, the most comfortable chair for a snooze and so on. Now Vergil was human: he should be superior to a mere feline of the domestic variety and have a conscience. Instead of that, what does he do? Grovel! No guts!

~ 11 ~

A Horse, a Horse

One evening, as I returned to my tree after a leisurely afternoon on the beach, I found Nestor waiting for me.

"Come along," he said, turning towards the Greek camp. "You won't believe what Odysseus has come up with." Why did Nestor think I had any interest in Odysseus' shenanigans? "Hurry up," he continued, "Odysseus also has a job for you." I didn't want a job, damn him.

I looked to see if Arthur and Antonia were around and alert but I should have known they were, as usual, elsewhere. Trust a dog to make a mess of guard duty. Antonia and Arthur were probably at *The Greek Olive Tree* begging for table scraps. Dogs have no pride.

I walked behind Nestor to the Greek High Command tent. I was surprised they had one. I'd never seen them meet anywhere but at *The Greek Olive Tree*.

"Finally," said Odysseus as we came in, "we've been looking for you everywhere." Whether for Nestor or me was not clear. I looked around. All the top boys where there, including Achilles. I jumped up on a stool and arranged my tail decorously, with a sideways snide glance at Odysseus. This is a breach of contract, pal; I stipulated I didn't want to get involved with this gang of plug-uglies. In the meantime, Agamemnon and the others were bending over a trestle table, poring over a series of maps.

"Now," said Agamemnon, "this is a layout of Troy; you will see the six gates . . ."

"Yes," interposed Achilles, "and that's Chetas, where Patroklus attempted to scale the wall and was murdered by Hector." Sighs all around. One wondered whether Achilles would ever get over the death of Patroklus. He dragged his dead comrade into every conversation, no matter what the subject. Agamemnon ignored the interruption and continued:

"Now, I was thinking that if we assembled an army here by Tymbria, we could . . ." But Odysseus walked up to the table and swept the maps away. Agamemnon glared at him while the others looked cowed.

"Dear friends," Odysseus said with mock patience, "we have been through all this for longer than I care to remember. We are not going to take Troy through any of the gates or over the walls so forget it." Agamemnon looked at him fiercely but Odysseus ignored him and addressed the assembly:

"Now," he said, "I've explained we will finish Troy off through guile and psychology, not brute force. The key is to get into the city. After that, well, then it'll be another story. Therefore, we need the gates—or a gate—open. Just at present, the Trojans are despondent, without hope and, consequently, depressed. That's no good for our purposes. Depressed people aren't easily fooled. We need the Trojans to be hopeful, relieved and euphoric." I sighed. Heard that before.

"Well," Achilles sneered, "and how do you propose to do it? Puppet theatres? Free drinks? Country dances? Pie contests?" He looked around hoping for a laugh. A few tittered just to keep on his good side. One never knew . . . Odysseus waved his arms.

"Actually," he said, "Gaius gave me the idea some time ago." They all looked at me, mostly with displeasure. I sneered:

"Indeed! Do remind me!"

"Gaius," continued Odysseus, "said that the only way into Troy was by invitation. And I have now found a way of getting one. We will induce the Trojans into a happier frame of mind in three stages: Stage 1—The Greeks sail away, all of them." Everybody looked aghast. Agamemnon put on his most severe commander-in-chief face:

"You must be joking. After all this time, we just pack up and leave? What kind of tactics are those?" Odysseus patted him on the back in a condescending kind of way; this is none too bright a pupil, let's cut him some slack. One must be charitable and make allowances.

"Tactics and strategy," he said soothingly, "I leave to you. Cunning and stratagems you leave to me." Blank looks but Agamemnon cheered up at once and stood about looking important. Odysseus went on:

"So the Greek fleet will have sailed, and there will not be a Greek to be seen anywhere. However, there will be an enormous Wooden Horse standing on the beach all by itself." Odysseus rubbed his hands; I shivered. "A gift," he said, "from the Greeks to Poseidon to ensure their safe journey home." My hackles rose. The horse had reared its head. Vergil would not be happy and I was starting to feel scared. Ajax scratched his chin and said slowly:

"What Wooden Horse? We don't have a Wooden Horse."

"True," agreed Odysseus. "But we will have." Menelaus opened his mouth but Odysseus went on before he could get any words out. "And there it will be on the beach after we have sailed away." Odysseus rubbed his hands some more. "But the Horse will have a secret: it will be hiding about 30 Greeks in its entrails." He combed his hair with his fingers. Most of the Greeks looked at him in complete bemusement. Ajax asked:

"Why does anybody have to be cooped up inside this Wooden Horse we don't have?" Odysseus sighed.

"Because," he said slowly enough to let Ajax' bit of brain take it in. "As sure as eggs is eggs, this leads to stage 3—in their euphoria, the illusion of relief, the Trojans will drag the Horse into the city. Greek warriors inside the city—by invitation, so to speak." Ajax still looked puzzled.

"Why should the Trojans do that? Drag the horse in?" he asked. Odysseus rolled his eyes.

"If for no other reason, because it is there." It was clear that the whole company was befuddled; they started talking amongst themselves to see if their neighbors could make any sense of it all. Until Odysseus shouted:

"Listen, you fools! Listen! Stage 1. You are a Trojan; one day you wake up, look over the ramparts and see that the Greeks are gone, their ships are gone. All you can see is the Wooden Horse. Trojan warriors will scout up and down the coast and find not a single Greek. Stage 2. The Trojans will become wild with joy. The relief will be tremendous. Which brings us to stage 3—singing and dancing in the streets, and more important, the gates will open and many will flock to the beach." Odysseus went on dreamily: "The Trojans will love the Wooden Horse. Just the thing, they'll say, to enliven Priam Square." I bet. Kids playing around its legs. Locals putting its image on fridge magnets and tea towels for the tourist trade. I didn't like this; I didn't like this at all. I wanted to go home.

"And that," continued Odysseus, "is where they will drag it. Happy Hour will come around and they will all party; drinking and dancing and so on." Odysseus grinned. No one interrupted him but I could see the others remained befuddled. "My friends," he continued, "the Trojans will get drunk but that won't make them stupid. At sundown, they will close the gates. After all, who says the Greeks won't be back? Therefore, the Horse must be inside the city when the gates close. The partying," and he drummed his fingers against each other, "will go on to all hours, everyone will become drunk and disorderly and eventually pass out. The hangovers will be phenomenal." Nestor pulled at his beard.

"I'm starting to get it," he said. "Greeks inside the horse." Odysseus clapped his hands in delight. "Horse inside Troy."

"Bravo, Nestor. Yes, indeed. The advance party inside the horse, within the walls, will climb out in the dead of night and open the gates."

"That would mean," said Idomeneus, "we'd have, say, thirty guys there. What good will that do if the rest of us are half way back to Greece?" Odysseus clapped his hand on Idomeneus' shoulder.

"But we won't be halfway back to Greece, my friend; we will anchor just beyond Tenedos or somewhere close by—Agamemnon can decide." Agamemnon looked pleased and puffed himself up. I felt quite sick to my stomach. This adventure was fast becoming gruesome. A city of drunken citizenry. And the enemy within the walls. I shivered. Diomedes cut in:

"Well, that sounds a really good plan, Odysseus, but we can't build the horse here on the beach. Where'd we get the wood?"

"Good point," said Nestor, nodding his head. Odysseus became quite impatient.

"Please don't talk about the obvious. Of course, there's no wood here. What little there was we used for Patroklus' funeral pyre!" Everyone looked anywhere except at Achilles who looked black. "So I thought we'd build it on the island of Mitilini—that's south, just beyond the headland. We'll send a couple of biremes with artisans, craftsmen and carpenters who will build the Horse in secret and bring it back here; in the meantime, the rest will stay here and pretend to continue the siege."

"What if the Trojans attack us while our numbers are depleted?" This was Diomedes again. Another doubting Thomas. Odysseus looked ready to strangle him.

"If they do, they do and we'll have to fight them off. If we can't, well, then, they'll have won the war and it'll all be over. The Wooden Horse can then go back to Greece as a tribute to the fallen from the Trojan war."

"If that happens," said Agamemnon aggressively, "it goes to Mycenæ."

"Who cares," answered Odysseus irritated. "If we lose, you can stick it up your . . . it won't matter, will it?" Menelaus said thoughtfully:

"We could put a horse in each of the main Greek city-states. Athens, Sparta, Argos, Pylos and, of course, Ithaca." Odysseus threw up his hands. I could have told him. This lot was beyond a joke. However, they weren't finished yet. Ajax came back into the fray:

"Why a horse, Odysseus? Why not a cow or a sheep, dog or a cat? Or a bull. Now a bull would be impressive. We could . . ." Odysseus curled and uncurled his fingers and said through his teeth:

"Yeah, a wooden bull would be great, wouldn't it, Ajax? We could use your face as a model. You dunce, a pig or a cow or a dog or even a bull wouldn't impress the Trojans. Can you see them dragging a wooden sheep into the city? And what God wants a sheep or a bull? Horses, on the other hand, are sacred to Poseidon, everyone knows that. Ostensibly, we would be leaving the God an offering to ensure our safe passage home. So a horse it must be. Get serious, guys. This is not a time for levity!" Levity? That was surely quite beyond Ajax' thought process. However, they all looked chastened and there were no more objections. Odysseus went back to business.

"Now, we need someone to head the expedition to Mitilini. And, of course, an artisan to supervise the horse's construction. As it will be brought back by sea, it must come unassembled. We can put it together right here on the beach." Just like Ikea furniture, in situ. "So, what do you think?" Everyone looked at everyone else. Odysseus continued: "We need a volunteer to lead the expedition to Mitilini." This was a tricky question; they all perceived dimly that this was a crucial moment but not exactly why. Whoever went to Mitilini might miss the last battle and dying for the glory of the cause. Odysseus was fast losing his temper. "Right, can't make up your minds, I see; I'll do it for you. Diomedes, you have just volunteered." Diomedes opened his mouth to protest, I suppose, but then thought the better of it.

"Right," he said. "I have volunteered." Odysseus didn't bother answering.

"Achilles, I believe you have excellent craftsmen among your Myrmidons." Achilles nodded.

"Yes, and a really good artisan, Epeius, who could select the others. I'll get them organized." He turned to leave but Odysseus stopped him.

"Just one minute, Achilles. Guys, I can't stress the importance of security strongly enough. You must not tell anyone of our real intentions. Not a girlfriend, boyfriend, pet dog or goldfish." I heard Achilles murmur:

"What about cats?" Odysseus either didn't hear or pretended not to. He went on:

"Don't write letters, don't talk in your sleep, no interviews with the press, don't go on the nine o'clock news. This must be top secret, on a need-to-know basis: only the warriors who go inside the horse. Everyone else must believe they're on their way home; they'll be told the truth once we're out to sea. Are we agreed?" The assembly nodded. I wondered what the troops would say, after setting out for home, then told to turn right back to where they started. Mutiny in the air? But perhaps the promise of loot would pacify them.

Odysseus clapped his hand:

"Right, then, I'll just summarize: Diomedes: pack, brief the sailors and get the biremes ready. Achilles: sort out supervisor and artisans. Everyone else: let it be known we're planning to be home by Christmas." Well, the Greek footsloggers had heard this particular song time out of mind. But that was hardly my problem. The company left, leaving only me, Odysseus and Nestor.

"I don't know what you wanted me here for," I said crossly to Odysseus. "I can't row, chop wood, plane planks or hammer in nails. I hardly know what a horse looks like. And, further, you've blown my cover so our agreement is at an end." Odysseus rubbed his hands together:

"Sorry, Gaius, but I really couldn't tell this story twice. You needed to know and now you do." I left the two busy over the finer details and tottered off to my favorite tree for a lie down. I wondered what I could—or should—do. At the moment, I couldn't think of anything. After all, I'm only a cat. I fell asleep and dreamt of Wooden Horses coming out of the sea and stampeding the city walls.

Next morning, I went to visit Vergil.

"Well, my friend," I said, "the Horse has reared its head. It is to become reality." Vergil looked pissed.

"Damn and blast," he swore. We both sat there mute, looking over the sea. I must say I was getting sick of the Ægean. I longed for the Atlantic. However, suddenly Vergil perked up.

"There's many a slip," he said, "between the cup and the lip!" I stared at him.

"And what does that mean, pal?" I asked. Vergil waggled his finger at me:

"Gaius, it means that many things can go wrong with this plan of Odysseus. From the moment his biremes set off until they come back with the Horse, a lot can happen." I mussed on this.

"Storms at sea. Locating wood. Cutting and shaping. Disease. Death. Shipwreck." Vergil was right.

"What was it you said the other day? 'It's only over when the fat lady sings'. It's only over once the Horse arrives safely."

I cheered up, too.

"Vergil, you are so right. This plan of Odysseus' can spring a hundred leaks. In fact, so much can go wrong, I'd say the chances of success would be about 60% against and 40% for." We both cheered up. I invited Vergil to join me for a drink at *The Greek Olive Tree* but, as usual, he turned me down. He said he had something to do. I guessed he would be putting a hex on Odysseus and his Wooden Horse. Well, why not. If all else fails, a bit of black magic never comes amiss. However, just in case his spell called for a cat for, I took myself off pretty quickly.

11.1 A Horse in Waiting

I avoided Odysseus during the weeks that followed. I spent my time between Troy, where I hung out with Cælius and his gang of cats, dogs and assorted other beasts, and on the beach by myself. I kept away from the Trojan High Command—life was sad enough without having to listen to their eternal lamentations and watching their perpetual lack of decision taking. I didn't see Helen, either. To tell the truth, I'd had enough of human beings to last me for years.

The days wore on. Occasionally, one of Troy's gates would open and a contingent of warriors come out to challenge the Greeks who, to tell the truth, weren't really in the mood. Achilles did take up the challenge with a contingent of his Myrmidons and made short work of the Trojans. After that, even Troilus' thirst for combat seemed to wither away.

One afternoon, Cælius, Lysandra and Betsy met me at the beach for a bit of a frolic. Things were so quiet that the sparrows were enough to keep an eye on Troy; as for the Greeks, Arthur and Antonia were still on duty. I didn't tell Cælius of their shortcomings as guard dogs as it didn't really matter. At one point, Cælius and I were resting under a convenient tree while Lysandra and Betsy played a game of tag near the surf.

"Gaius," said Cælius, "I really don't know what to make of all this. The Greeks behave as if they were on a seaside holiday." And, indeed, further down the beach some were frolicking in the water, sunbathing and having picnics. "No holiday, though, for my lot." He was silent for a bit, then continued: "What you told me about the arbitration was really interesting. Imagine if they'd have come to terms. The war would have been over." I shook my head sadly.

"I'm afraid it was never on the cards. After all, when you've had a war that's gone on for nine years and more, you're hardly going to get it settled in one afternoon."

"Oh, I don't know," answered Cælius. "You might if you get into a stalemate that looked unbreakable with everyone fed up to their back teeth." He broke off as Lysandra came running up to us, quite out of breath. She pointed out to sea.

"Gaius, Cælius, look out there!" We looked.

"What?" We both said, neither seeing anything.

"To the south! Look!" And then I saw—four biremes skimming over the horizon towards us. Diomedes was back. I shivered. I wanted to run away, I wanted to hide, I wanted to climb a tree, I wanted . . . The biremes came slowly, inexorably and steadily towards us until I could see large wooden structures sticking out of three of them. So whatever spells Vergil had tried out hadn't worked. Perhaps the Gods really had it in for Troy.

"It's either the end of the beginning or the beginning of the end," I murmured, a feeling of horror taking possession of me. Believe me, knowing the future is bad for your health. Cælius looked me annoyed:

"Don't talk in riddles, my dear cat. What are you on about?"

"The Greeks are coming back."

"I can see that. They've been coming and going for nine years. What else is new?" I pulled myself together.

"Sorry, Cælius. I think I got spooked. Do tell me about your evacuation plans." Cælius settled down comfortably.

"Oh, it's all done, you know. The rats and mice could actually stay, as there are always plenty of holes to hide in. But a lot want to go with their cat. Well, it's up to the individual. The rest of us will leave at our leisure—there should be plenty of warning, you know, given the system we've set up. We've identified a couple of possible towns inland, although none as big or modern as Troy. But then, beggars can't be choosers. Of course, animal refugees will probably get a cool welcome, as the competition for food will increase. On the other hand, plenty of people take in cats—as mousers, you know. It'll take the inhabitants a while to discover that not only don't Trojan cats 'mouse', they have their own mice that also need feeding. However, all in all, I feel quite comfortable with our survival chances." I licked a paw or two and mused:

"I was thinking about the bigger animals, you know, those that can't pass through the bolt holes, horses and donkeys and dogs of the larger variety. Have you given any thought to how they will get away?" Cælius looked at me quizzically.

"When the end comes, I would expect the gates to be open. Are you saying they won't?" I squirmed a bit.

"It had occurred to me."

"Well, you seem to be the expert. What do you suggest?" He sounded quite annoyed, my dithering starting to get on his nerves. I tried to get some of my dignity back.

"I suppose I'm saying that, although you should leave at the first **sign** of trouble, the bigger animals should leave at the first **hint**." Cælius sighed, rolling his eyes heavenwards.

"Oh, boy. A sign I can deal with but what do I do with a hint?" I nodded my head:

"Don't worry, Cælius, you'll know. Indeed you will." I felt sad and Cælius looked at me curiously.

After Cælius, Betsy and Lysandra left, I watched the biremes dock and start to unload. Everyone worked hard at dragging bits of wood onto the shore. Diomedes, of course, strode away as soon as he got to land. A warrior I hadn't seen before disembarked from the fourth vessel, which I found had come from Greece proper. He was a youngish guy, all togged up to the nines. Here was a grandee, especially as he didn't help with the unloading. In fact, he had a common solider carry his kit ashore. Oh, oh. Did they really need another of those around?

"That," said a voice next to me, "is Neoptolemus. Son of Achilles." Odysseus, of course. So. 'Nough said, end of story. Vergil was right. Achilles' son was part of our timeline. Not wanting to discuss Achilles or his family, I changed the subject.

"So this," I said, looking at the bits of wooden structures now littering the beach, "is your Wooden Horse." I took a dig at him. "A bit on the elaborate side, this plan of yours, don't you think? Did no one ever teach you to keep things simple?"

"I admit it," said Odysseus humbly. "But it's very difficult, after nine years on the job, to constantly come up with new ideas that are simple as well as effective. And this one could actually run into some serious snags. For it to work, I have to assume a number of things. If these don't happen, then it'll all go down the drain."

"Do tell!" I said, my paw supporting my head, looked at him with what I considered deep interest. Odysseus sat down beside me and gave a heavy sigh—I looked at him sideways. He didn't fool me any—he just loved showing off just how clever he was. He locked his fingers around his knees and began:

"First of all, I'm counting on the Trojans believing that we have really left. Second, that the elation of our departure will induce them to become careless. And, thirdly, of the truth in the maxim *never look a gift horse in the mouth*. I can't control any of this. It either is or isn't. What have I got on the credit side? Nothing really, so I have to create something to shorten the odds. And that something is a double agent." I started to get nervous.

"Don't even think of it," I snapped, whipping my tail about in a marked manner. "No way!" Odysseus waved his hands in his usual manner.

"Will you chill out! Not you!" Odysseus sounded quite offended. "With all due respect, you'd be no good for what I'm planning. But I do have a job for you. Something really simple. Just lying around." He said, turning on the charm. "And that's what cats like doing best. Am I right or am I right?" He got up. "You know the little cove just behind that pile of rocks?" He pointed. "Meet me there the afternoon the Horse is completed."

11.2 A Horse in the Making

Next morning, the Wooden Horse, in its various bits and pieces—head and neck, torso, legs and standing platform—were still lying forlornly on the sand, like bits of an IKEA bedroom closet. Mind you, it was the concept of a horse rather than the real thing. It was made of planks—pine, I think. No attempt at realism, no fancy carvings or cunning details. The legs were square, the body a box, the neck and head more squares.

By the afternoon, however, work parties started putting the bits together and the hammering and pounding was enough to drive anyone to drink. First, the platform was assembled, then the legs screwed onto the platform. To hoist the torso onto the legs needed siege ladders, trestles and plain brute force. Ropes hoisted the head into place. Slowly, the horse took shape. It had hollow nostrils and eyes and bits of stick did duty as its mane. I wouldn't have wanted it in my garden. But then, I'm a traditionalist. Garden gnomes are good enough for me

Later on, Vergil came off his hill and we sat next to each other watching the Greeks wrestle to put the beast together. He'd lost all his sangfroid. "Of all the things that could have gone wrong, it turns out nothing did. Perhaps the Gods are on the Greeks' side after all." I had no answer to that. After a moment or so, I heard him mutter:

> *Somewhat is sure design'd by fraud or force:*
> *Trust not their presents, nor admit the horse.*[17]

He dragged out stylus and slate. I turned my eyes heavenwards. Down the ages, the phrase—*Beware of Greeks bearing gifts*—would be repeated ad naseum.

It took three days for the beast to be ready and waiting and it was huge. Now, everyone will want to know how huge 'huge' is. The answer might be: 'two football fields' or 'five greyhound buses'. But dimensions have different perspectives for cats and humans. Cats are much smaller so 'huge' to us is different from 'huge' to humans.

I asked Eurybates, who was also watching the 'fun', if you could call it that, to give me his opinion. He said:

"Well, it's not as big as Odysseus' house in Ithaca or Poseidon's temple up on the hill behind it." He thought for a bit. "And, if you were to stand on the horse's head, you wouldn't be able to climb over the walls of Troy. You couldn't use it as a battering ram because the head tops the smaller gates although you might just get it in through Antenorides, if it were open." That explained Odysseus specs. Eurybates thought some more. "All in all, I would say it's pretty big." I was sort of expecting Eurybates to say that it was two stories high and a city block wide but that concept did not exist in his reality. So take it from me—or leave it; the horse was huge. After a bit, Arthur came up, his tongue hanging out—such a revolting dog habit.

"Dog, oh dog," he said, "that is one large son-of-a-bitch. Do you think I should go and report to Cælius?" Well, I'd never thought Arthur particularly endowed with brainpower. But one must be kind to those less fortunate than oneself.

"I wouldn't worry if I were you," I answered soothingly. "There's nothing you can tell him that he can't see from the ramparts." Arthur gave a laugh:

"Are you right or are you right?" He went off, on tidbits bent I'll be bound. Of course, all of Troy was on the ramparts watching the spectacle. I wondered what they made of it. After the last nail was in, it was time to party. *The Greek Olive Tree* did tremendous business; another good day for Eurybates.

11.3 A Horse needs Backup

Once the horse was ready for action, I remembered my meeting with Odysseus. Well, I should have left well enough alone but there was something about Odysseus that drew me to him like a magnet. Call it intellectual curiosity. What would he dream up next? So, at the appointed time, I wandered down the beach to the cove indicated. When I got there, Odysseus was haranguing a young chap, blonde, blue eyed and clean cut, the epitome of the boy next door, who looked at Odysseus as if he were the Second

Coming. Hero worship. A human trait quite beyond my feline understanding. I sat down to listen. Odysseus waved a hand at me then continued with his indoctrination.

"Now, Sinon," he said to the boy next door. "In the first place, you must be absolutely sure you want and are able to undertake this task." Was Odysseus coaching a less than average football player? "If I can't trust you absolutely, you'll be no good to me. Now, I won't hold it against it you if you back out." But Sinon was all afire.

"You can trust me, Odysseus. There's nothing I wouldn't do to save that poor innocent lady." Oh, boy. Obviously, he'd never met Helen. By the looks of it, he'd have been ten or eleven when she left Sparta. Odysseus looked pleased.

"Sinon, you are a real patriot." Sinon smirked. "Now, run through your part again." Sinon took a deep breath.

"Once I see the fleet set sail, I climb the hill to the Helia gate. I make just enough noise for the Trojan guards to hear and then capture me. They will take me before the Trojan commander of the Tower." He stopped to take breath then went on. "I tell the Trojans that I am a Greek deserter whose kinsman, Anacreon, was framed and executed for a crime he hadn't committed." He stopped. Odysseus prodded him:

"What was that crime?"

"Treason! Anacreon tried to prevent the war between Troy and the Greek City States and Odysseus brought some trumped up charges against him." Sinon looked sheepish. Difficult, I suppose, to make such accusations against Odysseus to his face. You wouldn't want to give him ideas. Odysseus waved his hands impatiently.

"Good," he said. "Go on. Don't be shy. We both know your uncle Anacreon went home years ago with a broken leg. How's he doing, by the way?" Sinon said.

"Fine. Just fine. He sends his love."

"Thanks!" Sinon took up his story again:

"I tell them I wasn't about to accept my kinsman's execution. I accused Odysseus of murder and swore I would be revenged.

Odysseus became very angry and soon malicious accusations surfaced against me; it became clear that I was not going to survive to see my country or family again." Not bad, but he would need to be more forceful.

"Not bad," said Odysseus, "but you need to be more forceful. Go on."

"'Trojans'," declaimed Sinon. "'You are at war with my country and, as a Greek, I am your enemy and it would be reasonable for you to kill me. But you should know that, if you do, you will please not only Odysseus but also Agamemnon, the Greek commander-in-chief'."

"Good, good." Odysseus rubbed his hands. "At this point, there will be some discussion between the Trojans, if I know anything about human nature. Keep silent and wait until they get back to you. OK, go on." Sinon did:

"'Gentlemen, I can assure you the Greek troops have tired of this war that never seems to end. The common soldiers are mutinous and it's unlikely even Achilles would be able to drive them into battle. So, the Greek High Command decided to abandon the war unilaterally." Sinon stopped for breath. Odysseus looked at him expectantly, so Sinon continued:

"Before he left, Calchas, the seer, told the Greek High Command they would never return to Greece without first making a suitable offering to Poseidon. You can see it now on the beach'." The Wooden Horse, of course. "'As for myself, I knew I would certainly be executed before the fleet sailed. But I managed to loosen my bonds, fled and hid on the hillside. They made a search for me but gave it up in order to catch the tide. Believe me, the Greeks are truly gone'." I thought Odysseus was going to pat Sinon on the head or at least give him a lollipop. He was downright pleased.

"Wonderful," he exclaimed. "And now for the punch line." Sinon smirked. Teacher's pet.

"'I would rather die at the hands of the Trojans than give the Greeks the satisfaction of slaying me'." Odysseus danced around.

"And if they don't buy this hook line and sinker, I'm a monkey's uncle," he cried. "And I don't think you need to worry, Sinon, if I know anything about our enemies at all, you're going to live to be a very old man indeed." I sniffed.

"You have two problems," I said. I just loved raining on Odysseus' parade. "Helen and Troilus." Odysseus seemed to collapse, as if he'd been a balloon I'd pricked.

"You're right, of course," he admitted. "Troilus the hothead and Helen who doesn't believe in Greeks with or without gifts. Of the two, Helen is the more dangerous. That, Sinon, is the chance you'll have to take. You may get lucky and not see Helen at all; Troilus is another matter." He thought for a bit but I got in first:

"On the other hand," I said, "If I know anything, Troilus' stock has fallen since the arbitration debacle. He undercut Æneas' authority and made any agreement to end the war impossible. I don't think either Æneas or Deiphobus took kindly to this. Also, the Trojan court is full of bleeding hearts, starting with old Priam. Tell a good sob story and you may win them over." Odysseus slapped his thigh and turned to me: "Now, that's what I like about you, Gaius. Really, you have quite keen insight. Excellent analysis." During all this, Sinon looked a bit bewildered. Odysseus and the cat? What's this about? Odysseus saw his face and laughed out loud.

"Of course, you haven't met Gaius, Sinon. One of my most trusted collaborators. Gaius, this is Sinon. Sinon, this is Gaius Marius." Another finger-paw touch. Right. I waved a paw and said:

"There's one other thing, Sinon, you must do. If they let you lose into the general population, you must spread the story that the Greeks left the Wooden Horse as a gift to Poseidon and as such it must stay on the beach. Make sure as many people as possible know about it." Odysseus opened his mouth but no sound came out. I sneered: "Who do think, Odysseus, is going to haul your bloody horse into the City? Priam and his fifty sons?"

"I hadn't really thought about that," he confessed. I continued:

"It will be the common man, my friend, the baker, the butcher, the candlestick maker. Tom, Dick and Harry. These are the ones who need to know about the Horse."

"Gaius, of course you're right again." Odysseus turned to Sinon and waved at him with his finger. "The horse must enter the city if we are to win this game." And then: "So, Sinon. Again I ask you to decide. Are you game for this adventure?" But Sinon was all fired up.

"What d'you think I am, Odysseus? Chicken?" Hey, macho man. "But I could use a bit of back up. What if Gaius Marius came with me? I mean, not with me as such, but was around in case I needed to communicate with you." I almost bolted there and then. This I didn't need. But Odysseus loved it.

"Wonderful, Sinon. A perfect idea. Gaius is always hanging around Troy. No one will think it strange to see him there." He turned to sell me his hideous notion.

"You see, Gaius, there's an angle you don't know about. We expect, but can't be sure, that Sinon will be set free and turned loose in Troy. So when—and I say when cautiously—the Wooden Horse is inside Troy—it'll be his job to warn our ships, waiting out at sea, that they can return."

"Really, Odysseus," I said testily. "I don't see why I should get mixed up in any more of your foul stratagems. It's not as if I want Troy to fall; I like the Trojans—well, some of them—and if I could be said to be on anyone's side, it would be Helen's." But Odysseus was unstoppable.

"Of course you are," he said, "but as no one knows better than you that Helen cares neither for Trojans or Greeks. She'll just accept whatever happens, after having done all she could to wreak havoc in both camps. And it's not like you're going to be active in any capacity, you know. Your job will merely be to let us know if something happens to Sinon, making it impossible for him to do his bit." So, based on the fact that I couldn't get a word in edgewise, it seemed to be so decided and Sinon went off to take care of whatever preparations he had to make.

Odysseus turned to me: "Now, if the Trojans don't take to Sinon, decide that safety is the better part of mercy and execute or lock him up, we need a fall back plan." I stared at him. He cleared his throat: "You had better know, Gaius, that we've 'turned' a Trojan or two. The turncoat of the moment is Polydorus. We are also leaving behind a couple of our own boys, Electryon and Histiæus. We thought they would hide out *The Greek Olive Tree . . ."* I held up a paw.

"Odysseus, you've missed out a bit of the action, friend." I said. "Tell me again: all the Greek biremes will set sail." Odysseus nodded eagerly.

"That's just it, Gaius. That's the start of my strategy." I pursed my lips—such as they were—and shook my head.

"My dear Odysseus, you've left out a vital bit if your strategy is to have any credence with the Trojans." Odysseus scratched his head.

"Where are you going with this?" he asked. "If anywhere, please get on with it, will you?" Slowing things down, giving out information piecemeal—a perfect Odysseus strategy. He didn't like it, however, when the sandal was on the other foot. I was enjoying myself.

"So there you are, all you Greeks, 69 kings or whatever, sailing away—sailing away from what?" Odysseus started getting irritated.

"From what? From the Trojan shore, you moron." I laughed in a superior manner.

"And I suppose you will just leave your camp sitting there, waiting for your return?"

"Oh!" exclaimed Odysseus. The penny had dropped. "You're right, with the camp still intact, the Trojans might believe we'll be coming back." He held up a hand and said grandly: "Don't worry. I'm all over it." Having started to rain on his parade, it gave me great pleasure to continue:

"There's still another outstanding item, my friend. *The Greek Olive Tree,* where I understand you want to ensconce your turncoats . . ." I was getting too much for Odysseus now and he ground his teeth.

"So tell me, mighty Feline, what is wrong with hiding my spies in *The Greek Olive Tree?*" I thought I'd tone down the sarcasm bit; after all, Odysseus was large and brawny and I was just a middle-to-big sized cat. I so I said humbly:

"I thought the idea was that, once the Greeks were gone, the Trojans would all troop down to the sea and drag the Wooden Horse back to Troy." Odysseus nodded eagerly. "I suppose you think that the Trojans will consider *The Greek Olive Tree* private property that the Greeks will undoubtedly need on their return. Don't take my word for it if you don't want to, but my guess is a Greek bar awaits Greek clientele. So get real. Why else should it be there?" Odysseus face fell. Loved that.

"My Gods, Gaius. I hadn't thought of that. You're absolutely right." I smirked.

"So," I said examining my claws, "whatever destruction you are planning for the camp needs to extend to *The Greek Olive Tree.*" Odysseus jaw fell. He blustered.

"But where are we going to celebrate our victory if we don't have a bar?" I looked at him scornfully.

"Really, Odysseus, sometimes you're as bad as Ajax." He glared. "My friend, to get drunk you don't need a bar, which is merely a place to get drunk in. Anywhere will do. The essential part of a bar is the availability of drinkables. So if you want to keep drinkables handy, you must hide them. Bury amphoræ in the sand, take them with you—but don't drink the lot before you get back." I could see Odysseus was trying to find a way to shoot me down but could find none. At last, he sighed and I knew he had accepted my point of view. I felt quite sorry for him.

"Right you are, Gaius; I don't know why I doubted you." He rubbed his hands together: "There'll have to be a change of plans." He thought for a few moments. I sat and twiddled my paws. "Well," he said finally, "I've run out of anything really smart. So I'll place my boys right here where we are now. No one will come this far down the beach, not on that first day." He seemed satisfied and back to his old confident self. "So, all you have to do, Gaius, should Sinon be unavoidably detained, is to amble down here and let my boys know. Polydorus and Histiæus will then open the Helia gate, Polydorus taking care of the Trojan guards. So there you have it, and Bob's your uncle." I wanted to sneer:

"And Fanny's your aunt," but decided not to. I closed my eyes and shook my head to get rid of the buzzing. I wasn't at all sure I was going to go along with this last bit. A walk on the beach at night wasn't my idea of fun. But Odysseus took my silence as an A-OK and was all aflame and ready to go. Well, Odysseus could talk from now until doomsday. What really sold me on staying was curiosity, the cat's besetting sin.

11.4 A Horse in the Night

It was past Happy Hour and the light was slowly fading. The night would be dark as the moon was new. A few stray stars shone in a forlorn sort of way but not enough to see by—except for a cat. Vergil had come down from his cliff and he and I were hiding behind some sad stringy bushes. Before us stood the Wooden House, all by itself. There was activity at sea as the Greeks pushed their grounded ships into the water and those moored near Tenedos sailed close to shore. We sat quietly and said nothing for a while, watching the activity on the beach. Then Vergil said glumly:

"Well, this does it. Here is the Horse and I frankly can't see how we are to get away from the outcome we all know so well." I laid my head on my paws. I still wasn't comfortable with the existence of *The Troiad* but Vergil wasn't to be budged on that so I just had to believe him. How else had the story come down to Vergil? I could have kicked myself. I should have asked Homer when I had a chance. Imagine if I had a copy of *The Troiad* to take home! It would be the making of me! Rats! I sighed. Gone for three thousand years, probably gone for good. Then Vergil bestirred himself.

"I could murder that bastard Octavianus. No matter how hard I try, he always wins!" He got out his wax tablet and a stylus. "So I'd better get on with this horse bit." I was curious:

"Is that how you write—a piece here and a piece there? You don't start at the beginning and work through to the end?" Vergil glared at me.

"What a stupid notion. You do bits here and there and then string them together. Anyhow, here is what I propose for the horse thing." I was going to say I had a pressing engagement but then Vergil started declaiming and I was stuck.

> *War broken, rejected by fate,*
> *the Danaan [Greek] chieftains, seeing so many a year*
> *was now slipping by, with the heavenly cunning of Pallas*
> *built them a horse, in bulk as huge as a hill,*
> *whose ribs they interlaced with planking of fir.*

"Who's this Pallas person? And how did Pallas get mixed up in it? It was Odysseus' idea!" I asked rather crossly. Vergil sighed.

"I wish you wouldn't ask so many questions. I will never, while there is breath in my body, give due where it is due. It's a matter of principle." I sneered:

"I call it down right uncharitable and mean."

"Don't care," was the answer, "and Pallas is Athena, whom the Greeks call Artemis."

"Further," I continued, ignoring his last remark, "the horse is not as huge as a hill. If it was, it could never get through the Antenorides gate." But Vergil waved me away.

"I wish you wouldn't be so hung up in details," he remonstrated. "Do you really think anyone will notice or care?" I felt offended. So I turned my back on him and looked into the night.

It was now pitch black. Vergil and I where as close to the Horse as we thought comfortable. There it stood in the darkness, as if waiting for dawn. Then I saw shadows sneaking in our direction; the shadows hugged the cliff while moving towards the Horse. I whispered to Vergil:

"Move back a bit or you'll get stepped on! Get behind those rocks." Of course, Vergil had to protest and I had my work cut out keeping him quiet.

"Vergil," I whispered, "there are men moving towards the Horse. They're very near us and believe you me you don't want to disturb them." He whispered back, arguing as always:

"How do you know?" I waggled my head. These interspecies conversations can get complicated when one side has night vision while the other doesn't. So I whispered back:

"Take my word for it. I can see them." So we moved.

Slowly and silently they passed us by. I recognized some of them. Achilles and his offspring Neoptolemus, Odysseus, Idomeneus, Diomedes, Agamemnon carrying a bundle of sorts, Menelaus and so on. Each carried a sword but was not otherwise dressed for war. They gathered near the front right leg of the Horse. I heard a 'twang' and part of the Horse's leg opened. I whispered all of this to Vergil who's only comment was:

"I bet Octavianus planned it all." He looked sulkily into the darkness, his knees to his chest, his arms around his knees and his head on his arms. I ignored the comment—this idée fixe of Vergil's was getting on my nerves. I turned my attention to the Horse again. Some of the men had already disappeared inside; outside, Odysseus and Agamemnon were having an argument. I crept nearer so I could hear.

"I am king and commander-in-chief," Agamemnon was saying stiffly, "and if that doesn't entitle me to a pillow I don't know what would." He drew himself up in an effort, I take it, to look more kingly. I heard Odysseus grind his teeth:

"I don't care," he sneered, "if you were Zeus himself. There is no room for your pillow and your royal bottom will have to make do with the wooden bench like the rest of us. Now, get on with it, into the Horse you go and let's have no more chitchat." He took Agamemnon's pillow and buried it in the sand. Then I heard him whisper in the loudest whisper I had ever heard. "You stupid idiots! Will you all shut up? And stop banging those swords about. We must keep total silence." He disappeared and a second 'twang' announced that the trap had closed.

Soon all the quiet and the Horse was again alone on the beach. Waiting, waiting . . .

"What will happen," asked Vergil, "if the Trojans burn the thing down instead of taking it into the city?" I stroked my whiskers.

"Then," I answered, "our Greeks will come to a fiery end and the Trojans will have won the war." Vergil sneered:

"Too good to be true. You'll never convince me Octavianus doesn't have a hand in this." He got huffy and, muttering more curses against Octavianus he left and started up the hill.

I stayed where I was, in silent communion with the Horse. Then, just as day was breaking, a fiery light appeared in the west. I looked and saw the Greek camp on fire. A splendid sight although, as a feline, I don't care for fire. When the whole place was burning merrily, I saw a Greek footslogger running towards the water's edge where a rowboat was waiting for him. I decided that, just then, Troy was the safest place for me. As I moved towards Antenorides, I could see the dark shadows of biremes gliding west.

~: 12 :~

Troy's Gates Open

After breakfast, I was on the ramparts with everyone else, watching the last of the Greek fleet sail out of the bay, past Tenedos, into the Ægean, and then lost from view. The fire at the Greek camp had about burnt itself out but it was a magnificent sight while it lasted. Everyone likes a good fire and this had been one of the best. That Odysseus, I had to hand it to him. Fire! Why, just throw a match and the flames will do the rest. Very labor efficient. *The Greek Olive Tree* too was in flames. Only the Wooden Horse stood unscathed, down on the beach, alone, brooding, waiting. Cælius, who was next to me, asked:

"Is this the hint or the sign?" I shook my head sadly.

"A hint," I answered. Cælius turned his eyes heavenwards. He obviously had me down as a prize nut. He settled himself comfortably and prepared to snooze.

I wandered down to Priam square where the mood was festive. I saw more smiling faces in a minute than I'd seen over the past month. I sat down on a bench to watch the comings and goings. Everyone seemed to be outdoors. A load of people crowded around Antenorides, shouting for the guards to open the gate now, at once! But there were still some sensible people in Troy, and the gate remained closed. Betsy came up and reported the same situation at the other gates. Then Helen arrived, in a blue gown laced with silver, and sat down next to me.

"Now what do you think the Greeks are up to?" she asked. I shrugged.

"To all intents and purposes, they've gone." Helen sneered.

"When I can believe seven impossible things before breakfast, I might buy this story. Odysseus is up to something. And that Wooden Horse—what's your take on it?"

"It's a Wooden Horse," I answered. "A big horse made of wood. I think it's a bit of a waste myself; I mean, what's the point? It doesn't seem to have any useful purpose." Helen remained silent for a bit. Then she said:

"Did you know, they got hold of a Greek deserter earlier today? Just after the fleet sailed?" Oh, really! "I hadn't seen this one before but then he must have been just a kid when I left. It seems he's from Argos, Diomedes' little home town."

"So, what does he want?" I asked, all innocence.

"He says," answered Helen, with emphasis on *says*, "he's a runaway—he was condemned on trumped up treason charges and would have been executed before the fleet sailed if he hadn't managed to escape. A likely story!" Helen breathed contemptuously, the only person I have ever known who could pull that off.

"I would have racked him and used the thumbscrews but of course the bleeding hearts felt sorry for him and decided he was an OK guy. When I protested, the old idiot Priam said, almost tearfully: 'what could he do, one Greek among so many Trojans?' Such insufferable fools I've yet to come across. Priam then ordered the fetters removed and his hands unbound. Shall I repeat what Priam said then?" Well, she was going to whether I wanted it or not. She continued: "'dismiss your fears, forget the Greeks, become a true Trojan'. Pass me the sick bag!" Well, I didn't have one so she would have to do without.

"What did this guy have to say about the Greeks leaving?"

"That they were fed up with the whole thing and are gone for good. A fairy tale if I ever heard one. Happy endings, is it?

Beating their swords into ploughshares, forsooth!" Helen looked as if she was ready to scratch someone if there had been anyone within reach. I inched away before asking:

"Did this Greek say anything about the Wooden Horse?"

"An offering to Poseidon," answered Helen, "to guarantee their ships safe passage back to Greece. The day Odysseus believes in the Gods is the day I'll accept I'm the daughter of Leda and the swan. But all the pious oafs up in the palace just nodded sagely and said it was very proper. They also like the workmanship." Well, Odysseus' plan was working so far. And Sinon was on the loose in the city. I'd try to keep out of his way. Helen sat pensively for a bit:

"I had a notion about the Wooden Horse," she said slowly. "But I can't quite pin it down; what good is a Wooden Horse on the beach outside Troy? I don't like it, I don't like it one bit. There's mischief in the air." She hit her right fist into her left palm. And with that, she got up and sashayed off without even saying good-bye. I wasn't offended. In fact, I was pleased at having been proven correct about Helen; she really was the most dangerous person in Troy.

It was now Happy Hour and I took myself off to *The Trojan Horse*. Perhaps I should have chosen another watering hole; the name gave me the shivers. The bars and cafés in the square were heaving. Everyone wanted to be outside so it was nice and quiet inside. Marianne brought me my designer water; I toyed with my glass, watched the comings and goings in the square and meditated on nothing in particular. But of course such peace was never meant to last. This time it was Troilus.

"Don't you ever get tired of hanging around here?" he asked. No 'how are you' or 'can I buy you a drink'; a great diplomat, our Troilus. But truth to tell, I was sort of tired of hanging around. If I had had any sense, I'd have been off on the last Greek bireme. In spite of these dark thoughts, I answered:

"Oh, I don't know. One must be somewhere." OK, that's Helen's line but I'm sure she wouldn't mind my borrowing it.

Troilus wasn't listening—as usual. He was looking out of the window at the crowd in the square.

"Look at that lot," he said with a sneer. "What are they partying about? Do they really think the Greeks are gone?" He turned to me: "What do you think?" I answered cautiously.

"I can't see any, Greeks, I mean; I can't see any of their ships either. And their camp is burned to the ground."

"I can see that great big bloody Wooden Horse," retorted Troilus. "OK, so the Greeks want to placate Poseidon. But tell me, what is Poseidon going to do with that huge thing? Is he going to drag it into the sea?" I sniggered:

"Wouldn't make a very good seahorse, that one. He'd get waterlogged and warp. Curious the things people think the Gods want. Never could figure it out." But that had been a perspicacious comment of Troilus'. Sometimes he wasn't half-dumb. He scratched his head.

"There's gotta be a point to the Horse. But I'll be damned if I can figure it out. On the other hand, if they started building it before the arbitration, perhaps they had already decided to leave, no matter what the outcome." Well, Troilus ain't going to make President for sure. I made a dig at him.

"You scotched that arbitration good and proper. I hear it didn't make you popular with your nearest and dearest." Troilus waved his nearest and dearest away.

"Bunch of pussycats. Sorry, no offence meant." I let it pass. "But if I hadn't been there, Æneas would have given everything up without a whimper. Couldn't have that, you know. Honor of the side and all that." Yep. This world's Troiluses keep the fat cats of the military-industrial complex in business. I said:

"Well, you must be the only one in Troy today who isn't celebrating—albeit there seems to be degrees to the merriment—some letting it all hang out while others are more cautious. Why not join the crowd? Party it out. Have a drink—dance in the street. If it all goes south tomorrow, at least you'll have had a good time tonight." As usual, he wasn't listening. Pearls before swine, talking to Troilus. Silk purses and sows' ears. He suddenly changed the subject.

"D'you know, they caught a Greek this afternoon on the hillside? Spying or I'm a Dutchman! I wanted to execute him immediately and for once Helen backed me up. He told us this sob story about Odysseus ill-treating him and wanting to execute him. That alone should have been enough to condemn him. If Odysseus wants you dead, dead you are, an affidavit[49] won't do." Troilus chomped on his lower lip for a bit. I pondered. Troilus was spot on. But who's going to believe anything this bull-in-a-china-shop says? His actions and decisions have too often ended up having the opposite effect of what he meant. That's the trouble with being a hothead. When the wolf actually turns up[50], no one believes you. He continued:

"He said the Wooden Horse was to be left on the beach until the Greeks reached home. If the Trojans were to drag it away or, say, burn it, both Argos and Mycenae would be destroyed." He would have spat if he hadn't been well brought up. "Well, even Æneas and Deiphobus were doubtful about that. As for Helen . . ." Then, as suddenly as he'd come, he was gone. I sipped my drink thoughtfully. Odysseus' plan didn't seem to have much going for it at the moment. There were still a lot of imponderables. I hadn't seen Sinon around, either. Perhaps they'd decided to keep him locked up after all.

Then Æneas took Troilus' place at my table. Really, Happy Hour should be savored in peace without an endless succession of bewildered Trojans needing comfort and drink. But one must be polite.

"Æneas. Pleased to see you. Take a load off. Sorry about the arbitration." Æneas called to Marianne for 'Retsina and go easy

---

[49] *In Law:* a declaration in writing made upon oath before a person authorized to administer oaths, esp for use as evidence in court [from Medieval Latin, *affidare*— to trust].

[50] The Boy who Cried 'wolf' so often that when the wolf did come no one believed him and the wolf ate him.

on the water'. Helen's drinking habits were becoming popular. He didn't say anything until his drink arrived and he'd taken a couple of swallows.

"Hades, that was our one chance of coming out of this thing in one piece. That damned idiot Troilus. I could skin him!" He was truly pissed. "And Helen would have gone along with whatever was decided—I felt really good when you came up with that power-of-attorney. Bloody Hades, of all the miserable luck." I tried to placate him.

"But the Greeks are gone now. So it seems to be all over, anyway." Æneas wrung his hands.

"I don't like it. Just too good to be true," he answered. Yeah, as we say at home, when the Saint finds too much money in his collection box, he becomes suspicious. Æneas scratched his head. "I've looked at this from all sides, and I just can't see the downside. That doesn't mean there isn't one, though." He became confidential.

"I'll tell you something. Deiphobus and I have decided to open the gates tomorrow." He held up a hand. "I know what you're going to say—is it wise? Well, maybe not but there's no avoiding it. If we don't, the populace will tear them down with their bare hands. No one can stand being cooped up in this town any longer.

"There are moments in government," he went on thoughtfully, "when the people won't be governed. This is one of them." I thought about this. Lots of examples in history. Ask Louis XVI (France), Charles I (England), Nicholas II (Russia), Saddam Hussein (Iraq) and Omar Gadhafi (Libya). If any of them had had any sense, they would have taken the money and run. Æneas was right; the next step would be mob rule. Roll out the tumbrels. I should have brought my knitting.[51]

Æneas continued:

---

[51] A reference to the French revolution and executions by guillotine. the old women watched the heads roll while doing their knitting.

"I've been thinking, you know, and I've decided that this king business is the worst kind of government possible. Just look at Troy. Priam has been king for time out of mind. He should have gone to pasture long ago. He's outstayed his usefulness, no doubt about that. Don't get me wrong, he's a nice old guy but we wouldn't be in this mess if we'd had a different regime. Say, one ruler for four years, chuck that one out and get somebody else. It doesn't do to let the guy in power get too comfortable."

Was Æneas looking into the future and were these the first seeds of the Roman Republic? I thought of Vergil. And of my own world. Without Æneas, my world and Vergil's wouldn't exist. And I sort of like mine, I don't say it couldn't be improved upon but it's the best anyone has come up with so far. So, sorry, Vergil. Fish out your tablet and stylus and get cracking. However, Æneas hadn't finished:

"Priam indulged Paris; he was the golden boy and so on. Nothing was too good for him. And when he came up with this hare-brained scheme of abducting Helen, Priam smiled and said: 'boys will be boys' and 'he's just sowing his wild oats'." He drummed his fingers on the table and continued: "Hector might not have been so soft—on the other hand, Hector, although a great warrior and wonderful with horses, was no great shakes as a disciplinarian." He stared gloomily into nothing. I felt like patting him on the head and saying it would be all right on the night and not to worry. But I hadn't the guts. So I called for some retsina. I felt in need of something stronger than designer water.

I dossed with Cælius that night. I'd gone with Betsy on her rounds of the gates but had found no sign of Sinon. Perhaps Troilus got him after all. Well, I wasn't going to worry about it. And I didn't want to worry about tomorrow either or that ominous Wooden Horse down on the beach. All things considered, I slept more or less soundly. Just as well; who knew what the new day would bring? Cælius and I woke up fairly early, had a bit of breakfast and then thought we'd go to the ramparts and watch the action.

By the time we got to Priam Square, the whole of Troy seemed to be on the move. Girls in bathing suits under sundresses, kids with buckets and spades and beach balls, parents lugging beach umbrellas, deck chairs and picnic baskets, all headed for Antenorides. Some especially eager youths were already hammering on the double gates. The guards opened them and the Trojans streamed out; who could blame them after being virtually locked up for nine years. I saw what Æneas meant when he said he couldn't have kept the gates locked even if he wanted to.

Families headed for a day on the beach; adolescent boys were all over the battlefield on the Dardan Plain, picking up trophies, broken armor and weapons that had once been a proud warrior's war gear. There was quite a crowd around the Wooden Horse and kids were climbing over the bits they could reach. The Wooden Horse didn't seem to mind. It stood there quietly, silent, sinister, waiting. When Cælius spoke, I almost jumped out of my skin:

"You said yesterday the Wooden Horse was a hint. Does that mean you think our larger members should leave Troy now? Take advantage of the open gates?"

"I think," I answered slowly, "that it would be a good idea. After all, if nothing happens they can always come back."

"I see," said Cælius. "Sort of precautionary." I nodded.

"You got it."

"Right," said Cælius, getting up and swizzing his tail in a business-like manner. "You may be crazy but I would hate myself later if you actually turned out to be right. So I'll be off and get things organized." And off he went. I felt a lot better and I settled down for a snooze. It was some time later that I felt a presence at my side. I woke up immediately—as cats do—you don't catch a cat napping and that's what catnap means—and there beside me, leaning on the next crenulation, was Sinon.

"So there you are," I exclaimed. "I was wondering what had become of you." Sinon looked into the distance.

"I thought I should lie low for a bit," he said. "I almost copped it yesterday. You were right, that Helen is one dangerous lady. It was just bad luck that she should have been there when they dragged me in. Of course, she didn't believe a word I said although I'm sure I sounded convincing enough since I was dead scared. There was a younger chap there, too, a hothead who wanted me thrown off the ramparts." He shivered at the memory. We both brooded for a bit. It was now mid-afternoon. There was a lot of movement around the Wooden Horse, people shouting and laughing. Some men where bringing up wooden rollers.

"Those rollers," I asked Sinon, "did Odysseus leave them there on purpose?"

"I wouldn't put it past him," replied Sinon. Yeah, he would have outfitted the horse with wheels. But that might have been a tad too obvious. "Look. I think they mean to move it." Sturdy lads were digging a trench in front of the beast, putting down rollers and then the whole crowd pushed and pulled and the horse moved forward an inch or two. I could hardly bear to watch, it was so unnerving.

"Lor' luv'a duck," I exclaimed, "I believe they're actually going to do it."

"Ef . . . ing Hades," exclaimed Sinon. "They might as well skip the next act and start digging their own graves."

Once the Horse moved forward, the rollers dragged to the front and the pushing and shoving recommenced. Some bright young things had gotten rope from somewhere—perhaps Odysseus had left that lying around, too, wouldn't put that past him either. The crowd danced and hollered as they tied the ropes around the horse's front legs and pushed and shoved and pulled. Then there was a commotion at the gate and we saw an oldish guy in the flowing white robes of a priest hurrying through the crowd, followed by some of the more gentile Trojans, among them Helenus, Deiphobus and Æneas. The old guy started waving his hands and shouting at the crowd. He had a loud carrying voice. I bet even the folk in the last row could hear him during Sunday services.

"You fools, what are you doing? Get away from that horse! It is a Greek horse. It is accursed!" Wrong tone altogether. Some smarty-pants in the crowd answered:

"What does it look like, old man? We're taking it back to Troy. Then it'll be our horse!"

"Yeah," yelled someone else, "then we'll see how the Greeks fare getting home!" Loud yells, guffaws and much laughter. But the old guy went on, even though the mob clearly wasn't with him. He didn't make it better by continuing in an officious tone:

"Is this is a toy made especially for you? When have the Greeks ever given us gifts? Can't you see it has a purpose? And Greek purposes bode ill for Troy!" The crowd responded:

"Yeah, they're going to roll it up to the wall and climb over the ramparts standing on its head!" Shouts and dancing around. Since the Wooden Horse wasn't anywhere near as high as the city walls, this was thought a fine joke. The old guy went on, raising his hands to heaven:

"Burn it, throw it into the sea. But do not take it into the city! This horse may contain the destruction of Troy." The crowd was now no longer in the mood to listen to him at all. Someone gave him a shove and he fell and rolled away down towards the sea. The last I saw of him was by the water's edge, getting to his feet unsteadily, two young men giving him a hands up.

Æneas was now close to the horse, too, but he did nothing. The crowd was beyond anyone's control. Slowly, inexorably, the Wooden Horse moved towards Antenorides and the city. Then I heard a sound at the next gate, Troien. Craning my neck, I saw a mixed troop of horses, donkeys, mules and large dogs heading out, turning right to avoid the crowd and the Wooden Horse. Betsy was last. They rounded the corner of the city and were lost to view. Cælius had heeded my warning. The hint had become a sign had become a warning.

I had persuaded Vergil to come to Troy with the argument this would be his last chance to see the city. We strolled around a bit. I asked Vergil what he thought.

"A bit primitive," was his comment, "we've come a long way since then. That knucklehead Octavianus has made Rome into a city of marble, in honor of himself, you may well believe." We looked at the marble statues and even dragged ourselves up all those steps to the temple of Athena. A marvelous building; I was especially impressed by the mosaics on the floor—colorful and superbly inlaid and fitted. Vergil sniffed at my praise; at first, I was miffed but then remembered I had never seen Rome in all its glory, just the bits and pieces that survived down the ages. I invited Vergil to climb the ramparts—for atmosphere—but he declined.

"I don't need atmosphere," he drawled, "since as a poet I am only interested in Troy's destruction, not its past glories." I shushed him, afraid someone might hear. I'd never be able to explain. So we went and sat down on a bench in Priam Square to watch the natives in their natural habitat. Then who should join us but Æneas; I reminded him he had met Vergil at the arbitration and Æneas nodded but I could see his mind wasn't on it. He shook his head.

"I don't like this, Gaius; I don't like this at all. Something is wrong, very wrong. I mean, after ten years of war, the Greeks just go off leaving a Wooden Horse behind! Man, it just doesn't fit their profile!" Vergil and I exchanged glances. Æneas was oblivious. "And strange things are happening; the priest Lacoon and his two sons are missing. No one seems to have seen them since the scene at the beach when Lacoon exhorted the Trojans to burn the Horse."

"I saw him and his kids fooling around on the beach near the water line," I said. "Perhaps they drowned or something." Æneas shuddered.

"I hope not. He was a good man and had the interests of Troy at heart." He got up to go, saying emphatically; "One thing

I can assure you; those gates are being closed at sundown come Hades or high water." He went off. Vergil's comment was:

"Come Hades or high water, I shall be out of here before the gates close. What about you?" I shook my head.

"Closed gates are not a problem for me, pal. Lots of ways for a cat to get out." Vergil looked dubious.

"I think you would be well advised to come with me." He went off to *The Trojan Horse* and got himself a snort full that he brought back to our bench. He offered to share but wine isn't my thing. He said:

"What do you think happened to poor Lacoon?" I shrugged. How should I know? He continued: "I've just thought of some good lines for him." He took out his tablet and stylus, quoting as he wrote:

> *"Laocoon, follow'd by a num'rous crowd,*
> *Ran from the fort, and cried, from far, aloud:*
> *'O wretched countrymen! what fury reigns? more*
> *than madness has possess'd your brains?*
> *Think you the Grecians from your coasts are gone?*
> *And are Ulysses' arts no better known?*
> *This hollow fabric either must inclose,*
> *Within its blind recess, our secret foes;*
> *Or 't is an engine rais'd above the town,*
> *T'o'erlook the walls, and then to batter down."*

I looked at him doubtfully.

"Well, my friend, I grant you Lacoon was into conspiracy theories. However, you've got some facts wrong, if you will forgive me. The Horse cannot look over the walls; as for containing secret foes, Lacoon didn't mention that. In fact, none of the Trojans has considered it at all. Except, perhaps Helen." Vergil closed his tablet with a sharp snap.

"Don't care," he said. "In my epic, this is the way it's gonna pan out." I didn't say anything but thought: 'Trust not the poet if you love the truth.' But from previous experience with Homer, I knew it was pointless, fruitless and bootless to expect a poet to care for truth. Of course poets believe in truth; their truth. Homer and Vergil had a lot in common.

"Is there anything—or anyone in particular—you would like to see?" I asked. After all, a lot of these people would figure in his epic. Vergil shook his head.

"No, I can already see them in my mind's eye, what they are like and the part each will play in my epic. The reality would just ruin it for me." I was disappointed but it figured. Vergil then went off for more drink and I asked him to bring me some water.

12.1 A Horse in Priam Square

It took the mob almost all afternoon to get the horse inside the city. I was surprised they didn't give it up as a bad job and chuck the thing into the sea. It was arduous and sweaty and, especially, thirsty work. But at length it was done. Just in time for Happy Hour and, boy, those Trojans took to Happy Hour like ducks to water. Every available table in the outside bars was taken, as were all chairs. More tables were dragged out from peoples' houses and those who couldn't steal a chair, sat on the ground. There were enough mugs to go around, although I did see a couple of guys sharing.

In the midst of this hullabaloo, the Horse took up its place serenely near the south lion in Priam Square. From the top of his marble column, Tithonius had a good view of him. Penny for his thoughts! The kids were all over it. They played around the legs and rolled about on its platform. Some tried to climb up the legs but will little success.

Then Sinon turned up just as Vergil came back. I introduced them without bothering much with personal details. Sinon looked at Vergil and saw straight away he was not a Trojan. He whispered to me:

"Who is this guy?" I patted his knee.

"Don't worry, pal, you're quite safe here with us. You see, we are just a couple of tourists; we don't belong to Troy." That didn't satisfy Sinon:

"I have no idea what you are talking about," he said. Vergil put in:

"Go get yourself a drink, friend, and top up mine while you're at it." So there we were, watching the Trojans going at it hell for leather, laying the foundations for their way to Hades. I said to Sinon once he got back:

"You'd better drink, too, pal. If not, you'll stand out and someone might find it strange." Sinon looked at me in surprise:

"Are you mad? I can't get drunk tonight." I answered shortly; I was feeling very jumpy.

"Of course you can't but you can pretend. Get some wine, water it well and keep watering it. Just make sure you have a mug in your hand all evening. Go and dance with the girls. Slap the guys on the back. Be a hail-fellow-well-met chap and the life of the party." Sinon saw the sense in this and went off. Presently, there he was, carousing with the best of them.

As the sun started to set, Vergil got up.

"You may hanker after high drama," he said, "I won't say I don't, but only of my own invention. So I'm off. Come with me. We can watch it all from my camp." But I declined.

"I really want to see a bit more, Vergil, but I'll probably join you at some point." So off he went.

The gates closed at sundown—shutting the chicken coop with the fox inside. Quite a few Trojans, who wanted to continue partying on the beach, protested. But Æneas was adamant.

"Party if you like, where you like," he said, "but the gates will remain closed until morning." Some wag said:

"Maybe he doesn't want the Horse to run away!" Guffaws from his mates. I never learnt what happened to those who stayed on the beach.

I sat sedately on my bench watching the Trojans making utter fools of themselves. And one thing it did teach me: the humans

217

in Troy had lost all sense of danger. After a bit, Cælius turned up and sat next to me. I asked him:

"Tell me, Cælius, had you been king of this city, would you have brought that thing in?" He thought a bit then shook his head.

"Nooo," he said slowly. "I would not."

"And why not?" I enquired.

"Because," answered he, "I don't know what its purpose is and I wouldn't want to find out and not be able to run away." That's what I mean. A sense of danger. All animals have it but humans, with all their civilization, writing and so on, have lost it. Cælius continued: "Tell me, Gaius, I take it we are beyond a hint and this is now a warning?" I looked at him meaningfully:

"If I were you, I would get my lot out before midnight or thereabouts." Cælius nodded:

"The time has come." He ambled off. Cælius never hurried, no matter what the circumstances.

Suddenly, who should sweep up to my bench but Helen with Deiphobus in tow. Stunning as usual, in her best blue gown, this time with gold trimmings. She stood, arms akimbo, and stared at the Horse. Deiphobus sat down next to me, looking somewhat bemused. I asked:

"Where's Paris?" Deiphobus almost jumped. He looked embarrassed.

"Paris?" he repeated, very uncomfortable. "Must be around somewhere." Silence. "To tell the truth," he at last confessed, "Helen and Paris have split up. Helen and I . . . Well, Helen and I . . . I've liked her for a long time, you know . . ." That Helen. And chalk one for Odysseus. SOB is always right. Oh, and Jonathan.

Meanwhile, Helen stood in silent communion with the Wooden Horse; they stared at each other, neither moving a muscle. Then she walked around it. After each couple of steps, she called out a series of names:

"Odysseus. . . Anticlus . . . Demophoon . . . Idomeneus . . . Menelaus . . . Podalirus . . . Diomedes . . . Philoctetes . . ." I looked at Deiphobus:

"What on earth is she doing?" Deiphobus shook his head.

"She seems to think these guys are somewhere near at hand and she's trying to flush them out." He looked round the square. "I can't imagine where, though." I suggested Odysseus might be masquerading as Tithonius on his column but Deiphobus didn't think that likely. Helen continued walking and shouting:

"Achilles . . . Thalpius . . . Leonteus . . . Neoptolemus . . . Eurydamas . . ." This went on as she walked three times around the Horse. Then she went up to it and rapped on its leg:

"Odysseus, what do you think Penelope is doing? Still at her weaving? But perhaps not. Diomedes, what about your fair Cressida? Is she just waiting for you, twiddling her thumbs? Achilles, what about dear Brisies or was it Crisies?" She stopped and put her hand to her mouth. "Oh dear, I forgot, I do apologize—Patroklus, that's it isn't it? And that horrid Hector killed him thinking he was you. Now don't feel guilty, sweetheart, there are plenty of pretty boys about just dying to share your tent.

"Eurydamas, how's sweet Daphne? But of course you haven't seen her for ten years—I hear she's taken up with that nice Spanish tennis pro. Meriones, Ialmenus, did you like your 'Dear John' letters? Were you surprised? How long did you think Chloë and Zoë were going to hang around waiting? . . ." And so it went on.

"Well," I said to Deiphobus, "if this doesn't bring out some Greek to strangle her, nothing will." I paused. "Or they may truly not be here." Suddenly, Helen stopped and listened. Then she came running over to us.

"Gaius, I thought I heard a sound somewhere close by! A sort of strangled cry! Did you hear anything?" I shook my head. Cats have excellent hearing but, to be frank, I hadn't picked up anything coming from the Horse.

"Sorry, Helen, not a thing. What with all the noise around, I'm surprised you did." Helen sat down next to us, a dejected look on her face. She made fists of her hands and hammered on the bench.

"I know something is different," she exclaimed. "I can feel it. Women's intuition, you know." Surprising how many people see things with their subconscious minds but are unable to make any sense of it. Helen knew her Greeks and she'd have had the answer to the riddle of the Horse if she'd trusted what she called her feminine intuition. To bring it to her conscious mind, she only needed to hit the right buttons. I've always felt intuition to be a matter of self-confidence and lack of this commodity was hardly Helen's problem. And then, the inevitable happened.

Cassandra turned up. What had taken her so long? She was all fluttering garments as usual, still greys and browns. A terrible combination. Her hair was all over the place, and since she didn't seem to have washed it for a bit, there was a definite Medusa[52] look about her. Her madness was becoming more and more apparent. She stood in front of the Horse and gazed and gazed at it, as if she expected it to say something. It returned her stare in a serene sort of way. Then she turned her back on it, spread her arms and cried out:

"Trojans, hear me. This is an unhappy hour. You have brought death into the city. Get rid of the Wooden Horse, take it back to the beach, burn it, drown it! Trojans, cease your merrymaking and return to guarding your city. We are all in peril of our lives. The city is in peril of its very existence. We are all doomed, doomed. Fire and blood! Fire and blood! Have you not seen the portents?"

"Portents?" I asked Deiphobus. "I haven't seen any." Deiphobus shook his head sadly. But Cassandra was not done raving.

---

[52] **Medusa:** Anyone who looked at her head, even after death, was turned to stone.

"Have you not seen the statues of the Gods shedding tears of blood? Do you not hear groans from the graves or felt Troy's walls tremble? Trojans, listen to the night birds and their dismal cries! Or to the wolves and jackals howling on the hills!" Well, it sounded good but, frankly, I think Cassandra must be hallucinating for no one else had seen or heard any of this. "Look at the sky!" she wailed. "Where are the stars? Where is the moon? It should be near full tonight. Instead, blackness covers Troy. Oh, my countrymen, take heed, take heed!" Of course, no one took her seriously. One very merry fellow offered Cassandra a drink that she refused out of hand. Another guy shouted:

"Sister, we've listened to you for nine years, give or take a few months. When are you going to give it a rest? No one has ever believed you. No one wants to believe to you. No one will ever believe you. Go get yourself a nice husband and five kids and stop bugging us." Loud cheers rang out and suggestions on how Cassandra could skip the husband as it was easy enough to get the five kids without one. More laughter, everyone had another drink and went back to their business of getting pie eyed. Cassandra looked crestfallen but soldiered on:

"You fools! Can you not see fire and blood and death within Troy? You are doomed, each and every one of you." And then she suddenly ran forward and, picking up a double headed axe someone had thrown down, made for the horse, axe held high over her head. However, a few likely lads intercepted her and took the axe away. Someone else cried out:

"I bet Cassandra has been around the Greeks' camp with her prophecies; they didn't believe her either and that's why the fools left." General laughter. Cassandra doubled up, weeping, pulling her hair and tearing her clothes. Helen put her arms around her, bringing her back to our bench. They both sat down. There was sorrow and kindness in Helen's eyes. She smoothed Cassandra's hair and said soothingly:

"Why are you so worried? What reaction did you expect from these scurvy people? Remember: sufficient to the day is the evil thereof. Forget the future; it will take care of itself." Good line but definitely defeatist. Not like Helen at all; if she'd come to this, things definitely did not look good. She then turned to Deiphobus:

"Come on, I need a drink." The three went off to *The Trojan Horse*, the other one, that is. I shivered. For the life of me, I couldn't have faced the inside of any horse, Trojan or otherwise. This was not a night for drinking or merrymaking.

At long last, Troy fell silent. Most of the revelers had gone home to sleep it off. The hangovers in the morning would be horrendous. After all that noise, the stillness seemed uncanny. An hour or so passed; then Cælius come running up.

"We're out of here, Gaius. This is it. The end of Troy." Out of curiosity, I asked:

"How do you know, Cælius?" Cælius replied:

"Everything's too quiet; I can smell disaster in the air. And where are the stars? Can you see any? No, pal, this is it, finis. Come on, let's go." I felt totally paralyzed and unable to move so I procrastinated:

"I'm going to wait a little longer," I said. "I'll catch up." Cælius shook his head:

"Take my advice. Don't hang around here too long." Then he was gone. I saw shapes of various sizes scurrying along; the gate cats with their mice and rats, Lysandra, who waved at me to join her, Herakles bringing up the van. But before bolting, he limped over to me; I could see Phillip clinging to his ear. As usual, he was all gas and gaiters:

"Good show, jolly good show!" he said approvingly. "Ready, are we? Go, is it? I'd stay and fight, too, Gaius. But my rats and mice depend on me and I can't let them down. So, duty before pleasure. Have at it, Gaius. Show those bastards up! Win one for the cats, one for the rats and one for the Gipper[53]." He limped off

---

[53] Geroge Gipp, 1895-1920, American Football hero. Ronald Reagan, who played him on the screen, used this quote during his run for the American presidency in 1980

and not before I was ready to see him go. Troy was now empty of its animals.

I started to shake; I felt a panic attack coming on. I should go, too. I could smell danger in the air. What did the silence indicate? A lull before the storm? I managed to pull myself together, jumped down from the bench and started walking towards Antenorides. The gate was closed; the guards slumped over their spears, fast asleep. Naturally, they weren't supposed to have been drinking but then, as Priam would have said, boys will be boys. I supposed it was the same at the other gates, the guards lost to the world. I shivered. Why was I still here? But there were the bolt holes. I'd be OK, just take in a bit more of the action, then be off and read all about it in *The Æneid* curled up in my favorite armchair. I went back to my bench. Something swooped down and perched itself on the back of it. I almost jumped out of my fur. It was Archimedes.

"D'you think," he said, "it's OK to hunt mice now?" I almost welcomed him. Someone to vent my anger and fear on.

"Your one track mind is disgusting," I raged. "Here we are, the whole of Troy's fate in the balance, and you talk to me of mice!" Archimedes looked offended.

"One's gotta eat," he said huffily and made ready to fly off.

"If I see you swooping down on as much as a cockroach," I screamed after him, "I swear I'll claw you until you haven't a feather left to your name!" As he became airborne, I heard him mutter:

"Jeez, talk about bad tempered cats!" I looked for something to throw at him but there was nothing to hand except, of course, the Horse. How can anyone be such a glutton? It made me sick. I lay down and must have napped. I woke up to an eerie silence. It was still deep night, neither moon nor stars visible, but I could sense dawn was not far off.

12.2 A Horse comes to Life

Presently, Sinon came sliding up to me.

"It's time," he whispered, "it's time." He carried a large torch, still unlit. I followed him with my eyes as he moved across Priam Square. Then, a few minutes later, I saw a blaze of light in the uppermost level of the Tower, waving slowly from side to side, the flames fluttering in the breeze. The signal would be seen way out to sea, by eyes watching from the bridge of the biremes hidden beyond Tenedos. I imagined the oars dipping carefully into the water and the vessels starting to move slowly and stealthily towards the shore. The flames on the tower went out. Sinon came running back across the square and towards the Wooden Horse. He struck on one of its leg three times then stood waiting. As I watched, the Horse's belly gaped open—giving me a shock that almost sent me into the middle of next week although I knew what was coming—ladders were dropped and, led by Odysseus, the Greeks clambered down. Odysseus came up to me and said, as if continuing a conversation we'd started on the beach:

"I tell you, it gave me a turn when Helen started shouting at us. It took all my guile to keep the guys quiet. Diomedes wanted to jump out and have at Helen then and there, and I just about had to sit on his head to keep him quiet. Fortunately, Menelaus helped me. After all, there's nothing Helen could say to offend him, seeing what she's already done. Some of the others became restless too—what fools men are, did they really think Helen, who has been away from Greece for ten years, knows what their wives or girlfriends are up to?" I thought: the eternal male conundrum. Odysseus rubbed his hands. "What a night. I really don't want to live through another like it, cooped up in a tiny space with a lot of sweaty guys." He then went back to his former subject. "Tell me, what on earth got into her? Helen, I mean. Could she possibly have guessed?" He looked perplexed. I shook my head.

"She didn't guess but she knows you and how your mind works and what kind of plots you're capable of dreaming up," I answered. "You've all short-changed Helen. She's worth more than all those petty arrogant puffed up princes of yours. Take my word for it. She was within a whisker—if I may use the expression—of sussing you out."

"If so," said Odysseus, "then most grievously would we have paid for it." I kept silent. Boys, you haven't had the full bill yet. Gird your loins and get your checkbooks ready. I couldn't resist taking another poke, though.

"As for Helen not knowing about your women back in Greece, don't be too sure. She's a woman and she knows how women feel and react when abandoned year after year. Look to yourselves when you get back home." Odysseus didn't like this.

"I'd put my hand in the fire for Penelope's virtue." I sighed. How often have men said that and lived to regret it? But I said no more. I'll leave Euripides and Æschylus[54] to sort out the Greeks' homecomings.

Everyone was now out of the Wooden Horse. I counted about 30 warriors. After stretching their legs and touching their toes to get the stiffness out, they made a circle around Odysseus. Diomedes asked:

"Well, here we all are. What's next?" Odysseus answered impatiently:

"We've discussed our plans and strategies to exhaustion. You should all know your postings and the gates you will be expected to control: Mycæneans: Antenorides; Sparta: Dardan; Cretans: Troien; Chetas: Phthia; Helia: Salamis. So get yourselves organized and we'll take it from there." Of course, Ajax had to ask:

"What about Tymbria?"

"Tymbria," repeated Odysseus. "Keep away from Tymbria if you value your life and those of your warriors. It's right on the cliff edge and we don't want any idiots falling off into the

---

[54] See the plays: The Odysseus, Agamemnon and The Trojan Women

Hellespont. Tymbria needs to stay closed because it's the one point where the Trojans may try to escape. That and Helia." Nods but no one spoke so Odysseus went on: "Remember we have a very small window of opportunity before the Trojans realize we're inside their city. And further: we want the nobility alive so they can be ransomed. So don't let your boys kill too many of them." He turned to Nestor: "Nestor, you and I will set up a command post under the column in the center of the square. Agamemnon," he interjected before that gentleman could protest, "I know your dearest wish is to lead your troops in the field. And that's where we need you. In the center of the action." The Greek High Command dispersed and Odysseus and Nestor, with their seconds-in-command, moved to their positions by the column of Tithonius.

Discretion being the better part of valor, I climbed a tree just in case. I looked towards Antenorides; a couple of Greek lads were taking out the guards—cutting their throats as cool as cucumbers. I gagged.

Then I heard the great gates creak open and fully armed Greeks streamed into the city. The biremes were back. Their commanders tried to steer them this way and that but with little success. Everyone was intent on doing his own thing. To my horror, they started killing off the drunks lying around in the square, stabbing them with their short swords where they lay. My acute cat's hearing picked up the slurp of the swords going in and coming out of the bodies.

Oh, Lord of Cats. I hadn't realized . . . Was this Odysseus' strategy? His battle plan? But I knew only too well: once the action starts, strategies and battle plans fly out the window.

If killing became indiscriminate and general, what about my own chances? If nothing else, my coat would get sticky and icky with blood. Surely, Odysseus had not planned this wholesale slaughter. I felt sick. I should have gone with Cælius. I want to go home. I want my own bed.

∴ 13 ∾

Fire, Blood and the Art of Survival

13.1 Hector's Farewell

I looked towards Odysseus' command post. He and Nestor were in deep confabulation but I was either too sick or scared to concentrate on what they might be planning. I became acutely aware this was not the place for me. All my feline instincts were aroused and shouting: flight, flight. Gaius, it's time to move or curiosity may well kill this cat. I looked around. The butchery had not yet reached my part of the square. I flew down the tree, streaked across to the palace and hared up the marble steps, my paws barely touching the ground. Lots of places for a cat to hide in a palace. I flew through the portico and atrium . . . and came to a screeching halt in the main hall where I found I was not alone.

Æneas stood with his back to me, stock still, facing an archway three steps above him. My fur stood on end. On the top step, a pale shimmering shape faced him. Slowly, slowly, it took on the form of a man and slowly, slowly, it became Hector. Æneas gasped. I gasped. Hector as he had been upon his funeral pyre: his body black with dust, his feet swollen from the ropes that had dragged him behind Achilles' chariot round and round Troy's walls, his hair matted with dry blood and dirt. Fresh blood flowed from all the wounds he had received in his country's defense, dripping onto the floor. Tears were flowing down Æneas' cheeks. I would have wept, too, except cats don't. I've said that before? Sorry. I was overwrought. Then Æneas broke the silence, his voice a mere croak:

"Hector, champion and mainstay of Troy, how we have missed you, how we need you now! Have you come back from Hades to support us in the hour of our greatest peril?" Hector's ghost looked at Æneas sadly. It said:

"My dearest of friends, I have come to warn you. Troy is doomed and cannot be saved. Don't throw away your life in defending what is indefensible. The Greeks are within the gates and swarming through the city. My friend, leave this horror and destruction behind, leave the killing and the fires that are to come. Your duty is done and there is no more you can do for your country and your people.

"If a mortal man were fated to save my father's life, throne and nation, I would have been he. I and I alone. As I am no longer of this world, Priam's city will be no more. Go far away from this unhappy place, Æneas. Take the memory and values of Troy with you and, in a distant land, build a city that will last for thousands of years, ensuring the survival of Troy's soul."

And, as he had come, so he slowly faded away. Æneas and I remained rooted to the spot.

Then the outside world encroached upon our bemusement and we returned to the world of the living. We could hear a low moan escalating and escalating until it seemed to cover the whole of Troy. Then war whoops and the sound of thousands of feet running and the clashing of steel upon steel. We became aware of a glow in the sky although dawn had not yet come. And then the wailing increased, going from strength to strength—the lamentation of women who had lost—or were about to lose—husbands, fathers, sons and, as I was to learn, their own lives.

We both sprang back to life and rushed out onto the terrace. I jumped onto the balustrade, Æneas leaned over it, and we looked down upon the city. Horror of horrors; the sight before us was Tartarus[55] come to life. Before us, Antenorides' gates were on fire. Æneas pointed to the east.

"Look, Gaius; every one of the gates is burning. All exits from the city are now blocked." Clearly, the Greeks, in their rampage of destruction, weren't planning on taking prisoners. The fires illuminated most of Priam Square, where the dead were starting to pile up. Greeks covered in blood ran everywhere, cutting down anything that moved. Other fires were beginning to spring up in various parts of the city. Æneas whispered:

"The fire has spread to the city itself, to the temples and great houses." He gripped the balustrade so hard his knuckles turned white. "That I should have lived to see this day, such wanton destruction. The Greeks have gone insane." Well, thinks I, what did he except—the war has gone on for nine years, everyone exasperated, fed up to their back teeth and now totally out of control. But I kept silent. What was there to say? "Over there," cried Æneas, pointing: "that's Deiphobus' mansion in flames—and Helenus'! And see how brightly the sea shines with a splendor not its own but borrowed from Troy!" I looked at the Aegean. The Greek biremes where anchored in the bay, as if they'd never sailed away. New clamors arose, more cries, trumpets blared. Æneas turned suddenly and rushed off. I called after him, whining:

"Æneas, where are you going?" I was going to add: what about me, but this didn't seem to be the time. He turned and there was a glint of madness in his eyes.

---

[55] **Tartarus**: a deep abyss under Hades used as a dungeon for torment and suffering of the wicked after death.

"If my city dies," he cried, "I will die with it; with my sword in my hand, fighting to the last drop of my blood, to the last breath in my body." In panic, I looked out over the city again. The burning gates meant no bolt holes. The fire was spreading fast. Although Troy was mainly of stone, roofs were wooden and burnt a treat, to say nothing of furniture, clothing and curtains and so on. Flames were everywhere, greedy, licking upwards, dancing and sparkling.

In the middle of Priam square, the Wooden Horse continued its silent vigil, shadows and light flickering on, over and around it, for all the world like some macabre SON ET LUMIÈRE[56] spectacle. Now that I think of it, most spectacular. But me, what about me? What was I to do? Where could I to turn? If only I'd stayed down on the beach or gone into the hills with Vergil. If only I'd left with Cælius. My life had boiled down to all the wrong decisions I'd taken in the last 20 minutes, but regrets would not get me out of my present predicament.

OK, Gaius Marius, I said to myself. All this weeping and wailing is not going to get you out of here. But what would? Then I saw it: two people for sure would survive the sack of Troy: Helen and Æneas. Now, I didn't know where Helen was, perhaps the Greeks had already killed her in revenge for taunting them or as payback for ten years of misery. I shook myself. Don't be stupid, Gaius. You know she's coming out at the other end, unscathed in body if not in mind. Both Homer and Vergil say so and, at this moment, I had to believe it or I'd go bonkers. But with Helen out of reach, the remaining option was sticking close to Æneas. Come, Gaius, let's go, let's go. I sprang from the balustrade and leaped down the steps where Hector's ghost had stood. My luck held. Æneas had stopped to buckle on his armor. The Deiphobus and Helenus came rushing in, both armored, both holding bloody swords.

---

[56] **Sound and light show**, a form of nighttime entertainment usually presented in an outdoor venue of historic significance.

"What hope is there?" cried Æneas. "What more can we do, where shall we make our last stand?" Helenus shook his head sadly.

"Troy is no more, Ilium is no more. The day so long foretold has finally arrived when Troy becomes a Greek city. The fires are everywhere and the Greeks are everywhere." Deiphobus continued:

"There are many more Greeks than we thought. They most have picked up warriors along the coast as they sailed back." He sighed. "There were Greeks inside the Wooden Horse, you know. Sinon betrayed us. Troilus was right for once, we should have executed that slimeball as soon as he appeared." Elementary, my dear Deiphobus. But what is done cannot be undone. Helenus added:

"The Greeks are fanning out, killing men, small children and old people. The younger women and older children are being herded together; for the slave markets, I'll be bound. I tell you, no one is going to get out of this burning Hades." Deiphobus snarled:

"At least we warriors can die with dignity and make sure of taking as many Greeks as we can to the underworld." Æneas sprang up.

"What are we waiting for? Let's go, those of us who are still standing. To the ramparts, to the ramparts!" They rushed off. This didn't bode well for me. Unfortunately, Æneas wasn't going to take Hector's advice and cut and run.

I slunk into a corner, trying to make myself invisible. I stayed there as quiet as a mouse. The long day wore on. I napped when I could but the clamor in the streets grew louder and louder, only subsiding slightly as dusk came, oh, so slowly. Then I heard many feet running into the great hall. A band of Greeks streamed into the palace, bloody and disheveled, swords in hand. They were back in a trice, dragging poor Cassandra with them; she was crying and begging for the gods' mercy.

A young Trojan suddenly appeared with drawn sword to defend her, but the Greeks were too many for him and he was cut down. He lay where he fell. The Greeks left, three dragging Cassandra along, the others loaded with booty.

I was alone again, except for the corpse. I wept even though I was a cat. Cassandra! Cassandra my friend! Odysseus, this is not right, no, it's not right! I hate you! I hate you!

In spite of my terrors, I must have fallen asleep for the next thing I remembered was the dark, the darkness of three o'clock in the morning, and don't talk about the black night of the soul, I'm not in the mood. There were faint sounds coming towards me. A bit of light, too. Both sound and light came closer and closer. I couldn't creep further into my corner without passing through the wall and I'd have to be Hector to do that. But then I realized these were Trojans, I could smell their dejection and despair. In they came, Æneas—and was I happy to see him, perhaps he'd be sensible now and leave—followed by Deiphobus, Troilus, who immediately threw himself on the floor, and some others I didn't know. Deiphobus took a torch and came over to look at my companion, the corpse.

"It's Coræbus, our kinsman from the north," he said sadly. "He came to us in our need. And see how he has been repaid." Æneas sat down then called out:

"Gaius, I know you're here. What happened?" Well, of course I was, it was no good pretending I wasn't, so I answered:

"The Greeks took Cassandra. This fellow tried to defend her." A chorus of sighs.

"Our poor sister," said Deiphobus. "And Helenus, too, is gone. But he's dead—perhaps he's the lucky one." I remembered what Helen had said about Cassandra's fate and shivered.

"I suppose," said Troilus from his prone position on the floor, "the only bit of luck we've had tonight was when that company of Greeks fell in amongst us."

"Androgeos," added one of the others, who turned out to be Dymas. Troilus continued:

"It was before we met up with you, Æneas. Androgeos took us for Greeks. He started berating us: 'Why in Hades did it take you so long to get here? I've been holding this position for hours and I was promised relief ages ago.' He was one pissed-off Greek. 'I suppose you've been looting and squirreling stuff away. Well, you can get on with the fighting now. Me and my lads are out of here.'" Troilus laughed bitterly. "Well, we soon corrected his mistake. They tried to put up a fight but we were too many for them. Now that's one lot who won't be going home laden with Trojan loot." There were murmurs of appreciation and a few 'well dones' from the party. Troilus went on. "We thought it might be a good idea to put on Greek armor and weapons so we stripped the corpses. In fact, it was Coræbus' idea; he was in the midst of it then. I don't know how or when he got separated from us and how he ended up here." Dymas took up the tale:

"We've been all over Troy and made sure quite a few Greeks won't be going home. It was the Greeks' turn now, you see, to be careless, thinking it was all over bar the shouting. But then we ran into a spot of real trouble. Friendly fire. We were looking for Greeks at the base of the tower when some of our own guys, barricaded in there, mistook us for Greeks and rained rocks down on us; we had to get out of there fast." A guy named Ripheus said:

"Then some Greek suddenly shouted that we were Trojans not Greeks, he could tell by our accents. We lost quite a few of our boys in the subsequent melee. And that's when we met you, Deiphobus, and Æneas."

Deiphobus rubbed his chin:

"That must have been about the time the Greeks found there was still resistance inside Troy. Ajax got a unit together and charged us. Unfortunately, we were too few and too badly armed to withstanding them. And so we came here." A period of silence followed. Then Æneas said:

"My brave friends, although I don't see how we could have done better, given the odds, it has, alas, been in vain. Troy's plight is truly desperate and the gods have abandoned us.

How can we, the few that are left, save the city against so many enemies, to say nothing of the raging fires! Let's go back out into the streets. And not to the alleys or byways but into the public squares, face to face with the best the Greeks can throw at us."

13.2 *The Panic Room*

Off they went and there was no way I was going with them. My hall was decidedly not safe; if all the noise outside was any indication, it would soon be filled with stabbing, slashing and thrusting men and dead bodies. No place for a cat. I tried to move further into the shadows and I pushed myself backwards even when it was obvious I'd run out of space, when suddenly the wall gave way and I fell into a void. Being a cat, of course I landed on my paws, for that's what cats do. Looking up from where I had come, I was just in time to see a stone slip into place in the wall above me and I was alone in the dark.

Being alone wasn't so bad, not just then. In fact, it might be a good idea to stop here until the whole thing was over. On the other hand, there might be a problem with getting out. I had obviously touched a hidden spring but I couldn't see one from this side. I turned and saw a long passage snaking its way into the gloom. Well, secret passages always lead somewhere. But still I hesitated. What if it led to the one place I didn't want to be—Priam Square? I procrastinated. I might get myself entombed until Herr Schliemann dug me out sometime in the 19th century. Long time to wait. So, better the death you know than the one you don't.

I gathered what was left of my courage and moved off, listening to the silence; silence was good. After I had wandered for what seemed an hour, but was probably only 10 minutes, I reached an impasse—the passage ended at a blank wall. I stared at it. Bad news. The secret passage went from point A to point B. What now? I decided to tap on the stones and, after an eternity, or thirty minutes, sure enough one stone slid silently backwards and then sideways. I heard low voices; I made sure they were not Greeks and then crept out as quietly as I could.

Fortunately, my particular corner was in darkness. I stayed in the shadows, looking around and saw I was in a smallish cozy chamber containing six people: Priam, Hecuba, Andromache and her son, Astyanax, as well as Priam's youngest children, the twins Polyxena and Polytes. The room was richly furnished with couches and chairs covered in pillows, the walls had frescoes of mythological inspiration and friezes with geometric designs. There were no windows and I couldn't see any doors. This had to be Priam's Panic Room.

The old man was moaning about his fate. Pal, after nine years, all I can say is, live with it or move on.

"Can you hear them?" he asked plaintively to no one in particular. "I think I hear the noise of battle coming from the tower." Well, I could too, but as there didn't seem to be any direct link between the tower and this chamber, I felt safe—for the moment. I suppose the Trojans should have a good chance of holding out if they'd managed to secure the tower. Priam started to sniffle.

"I should never have turned the command over to Deiphobus and Æneas. Look where it has led us. Memnon, Memnon of Ethiopia would have saved us. Who was Helen to deny us? She's just a woman! I should never have allowed it." Old fool. As if he could have done any better! As if he were man enough to oppose Helen! She'd have made mincemeat of him. Hecuba, a look of pity and compassion on her face, leaned forwards and patted his feeble old hand. Did she know what had happened to Cassandra? If she didn't, ignorance was indeed bliss.

"I'm certain there are no warriors braver than ours," she said. "I have full confidence in Deiphobus; he was always such a bright boy." Her eyes started to water. I wondered how many sons she'd lost since I'd seen her last. Priam continued speaking as if he hadn't heard her.

"How often have I looked from the ramparts down on the Greek camp where, in happier times, our herdsmen tended their flocks and the peasants sowed and harvested. Gone now, as if the wind had swept around Troy and blown it all away. My country, my Ilion, home to so many heroes and good and loyal people, of so much beauty and grandeur. Troy that should have gone from me to my sons and from them to their sons. And where now are my sons?" Polytes jumped up.

"Father, I'm here. Let me go and fight." Typical young scallywag. No sense of danger. But Hecuba shook her head.

"No, Polytes, you are our last hope; if Troy is to survive, you must survive." Sorry, honey, ain't the way it's going to go.

Polyxena was playing with Astyanax. Andromache watched them; I could see into her heart. Her husband was gone and she knew Astyanax would soon follow him. Doomed, all doomed. I tried to keep a few sniffles back, which proved to be my undoing. Hecuba heard and called out.

"Gaius, is that you?" Well, it was, and I came out into the light and sat down in the middle of the floor. Astyanax pointed a finger at me:

"It's a kitty cat!" What a wise little boy, to be sure.

"Gaius, do you know how the battle is going?" Well, I did and I didn't. I knew it was going badly but I didn't know how much worse it was going to get. So I temporized:

"I saw Æneas and Deiphobus not so long ago," I said. "And Troilus. They told me it's been rough but they'd had some success. They were all OK." Hecuba and Priam both sighed. Please don't ask me about Cassandra. Or Helenus. Andromache sighed:

"I wish we had sent Astyanax out of Troy; he should have gone long ago to my kinsmen in the North." She looked sadly at the kid who was, as kids usually are, oblivious to what was going on around him. It must be nature's way of protecting the innocent. Hecuba said:

"So many regrets, my dear Andromache. So much we should have done and didn't do. I should have protected my children, too, and I didn't. And as my sons died I should have become wiser, but I didn't." She got up and starting pacing: "My poor Cassandra, scorned and ridiculed. Hector, who destroyed himself for honor. Honor, a mother's bane. More sons have been lost to honor than to any known disease. That, Andromache, is what you must teach Astyanax. Honor serves no purpose except a hero's death"

Easy to be wise after the event. However, although I sympathized up to a point, doing nothing for nine years was a grievous fault indeed and grievously were the Trojans paying for it. There was really only one thing they could have done and that was to get rid of Helen. Priam suddenly came to life, turned to me and said:

"Gaius, there's a secret way from this chamber leading straight up to the Tower. I know it's a lot to ask but could you run up there and see what's going on?" He added hastily: "I would go myself but you're so much smaller than I am, also, your legs are younger and so much faster. Just so we'd have some idea of what is happening." Hecuba added her bit:

"Please, Gaius. It would be such a comfort." Could be for her although there didn't seem to be anything in it for me. But how cowardly and selfish can one get; there are limits even to a cat's indifference to others' sufferings. So I agreed with ill grace.

Andromache went to the wall and pressed a slab. It slid silently backwards and then sideways. Another secret passage. I bet the whole place was honeycombed with them. The opening was just big enough for a man to crawl through; a dozen cats could have made it easy. Andromache said:

"You'll see a lever to your left as you go in. That's how you open the passage from the inside." I insisted on trying it out a few times before I set off. As I went and heard a click behind me, I debated whether I should just go to sleep in the dark and the silence; however, if the whole palace collapsed, I'd really and truly be stuck. And I'd already had this discussion with myself before. So I padded on. I hadn't gone very far when I heard sounds of scratching. I stopped.

A rat came out of a tiny hole I wouldn't have thought a cockroach could squeeze through. He squeaked:

"Hi, I'm Mortimer." I raised my eyebrows. I wasn't surprised. There is no such thing as a city, village or hamlet without rats. I answered courteously:

"Well, Mortimer, and what on earth are you doing here? Why didn't you leave with Cælius and the others?" Mortimer sat down. He seemed ready for a long chat.

"I don't really know; I suppose I wanted to see the last act. You're Gaius Marius, aren't you? I remember you from that meeting of the Committee." I acknowledged that I was indeed he. Well, Cælius had said that the rats should be all right no matter what. I said:

"I'm going up to the tower, Mortimer, just to have a look-see." Mortimer squeaked.

"I'll come with you. I've wanted to but I was scared of going on my own. Here, I know an even better way than this one."

"If it's that beetle passage you came out of, forget it. Couldn't even get my paw in." Mortimer squeaked in merriment. One thing about rats, at least those in Troy, they thought everything was a joke.

"'Course not. C'um on, I'll show you." Mortimer ran up the passage a little way and then turned into what seemed to be solid wall. But when I got there, it wasn't. The opening was just wide enough for a cat my size to squeeze through. I hoped I wouldn't have to turn around at any point. The ground slopped upwards; Mortimer ran on ahead. At one point, I started hearing unpleasant noises—shouts and rumblings, and heavy objects being pushed this way and that.

13.3 The Trojans' last Stand

Then suddenly we were out on the Tower platform. There were men leaning over the crenulations, others behind them passing boulders and vats of burning oil. There were also women there, working as hard as the men. Nothing like the prospect of slavery to focus the mind. Paris was very busy with his bow and arrows. Whatever his other faults, Paris was one of the best archers in Troy. Æneas, of course, was the man in charge. He saw me and cried out in surprise:

"Gaius, what are you doing here? This is no place for a cat. If we don't fall over you, step on you, drop a stone or burning oil on you, the Greeks will get you." Mortimer thought this was oh so funny. I said to him sourly:

"Don't know what you're laughing at. It goes for you, too." Mortimer gulped his snickering down and said soberly:

"There's an opening just over there where we can look down." I wasn't too keen. "It's OK; it's like a little balcony. Come on." He ran between the legs of a guy carrying an enormous stone. I followed a bit more cautiously. A small section of the lower parapet under the balustrade had crumpled away so there was just room enough for us without falling over. I settled myself in snugly and looked down. To my left was Priam Square, the four bronze lions completely oblivious of the mayhem going on around them. The Wooden Horse, too, was where he should be, untouched, as yet, by flames. Trojan warriors were all over the place, exacting a heavy payment for whatever spoils the Greeks took from Troy. Really, these Trojans might not be top drawer in the planning department but when action was called for, they were the best.

Straight below us, a contingent of Greeks were trying to batter their way through the heavy wooden tower door, not an easy task as stones and boiling oil kept raining down on them. The Trojans on the ramparts were now using their swords to hew wooden beams from walls and ceilings to use as ammunition. The Greeks would break through eventually but it was going to be a costly business in terms of lives. As each barrage descended on them, forcing them to retreat, at least one more Greek would not rise to fight again. But more Greeks always arrived to take the place of the fallen. It seemed that the

Trojans would run out of anything throwable before the Greeks ran out of warriors.

During a lull in the action, I saw the Greek warrior who'd come ashore with the Wooden Horse: Neoptolemus, Achilles' son. Suddenly, leading what looked like a whole company, he started raining blows with his axe on the Tower gate; other Greeks joined him, forming what so to speak a human battering ram. One mighty push . . .

"All together now," cried Neoptolemus. You could hear the wood groan. Neoptolemus went back to using his sword as an axe and then I heard the hinges starting to yield; the double bars gave way; the gate to the tower had been breached.

But our attention was diverted by things hotting up in the square; a company of Trojans, led by Troilus, engaged a group of Greeks. Then I saw Achilles; he had jumped up on one of the bronze lions and was exhorting the Greeks—Myrmidons, I would guess—to finish off Troilus and crew. He was wearing his golden armor cleaned, I hope, after Patroklus died in it. His arms raised, head thrown back, sword in one hand, shield in the other, he looked like the Achilles of legend. Then I heard a zing—an arrow sped from the tower with such force it transfixed Achilles, going into his back and coming out of his chest. For a moment in time, for a moment sublime, he stood there, erect, rigid, arms stretched out, for the world as if he was preparing to fly straight to Olympus, before he slowly toppled forwards. A gasp of incredulity rose from Trojans and Greeks alike, those in the square and those beneath the tower and those on the ramparts. As he fell, the crowd fell silent and for a minute or so all activity stop. Then a scream, followed by a keening wail, seemed to blanket the city. I'd heard that voice before. Thetis. Achilles, the magnificent, the superb, the golden; Achilles, the son of the sea nymph Thetis, was no more.

Æneas shouted:

"Oh, good shot, Paris." The understatement of the year. After that minute's lull, the full fury of Neoptolemus blazed forth. He shouted:

"Greeks! Our greatest warrior is dead, downed by a Trojan arrow. Fight, Greeks, fight to avenge our fallen hero! Raze the palace, the temples, kill them all, no quarter, no mercy, no surrender!" He continued, holding his axe high: "Myrmidons, take Achilles' body and carry it down to our ships; we will perform the sacred funeral rites once not a stone remains to show where Troy once stood." Then it became business as usual, sword on shield, hacking and stabbing. A mighty crash told me Neoptolemus' gang had finally broken through and were inside the tower. The Greeks stormed in and we could hear them thundering up the stone steps. Æneas jumped back:

"Trojans," he shouted. "There's nothing more we can do here. They're in the tower and will be in the palace soon enough. Let's go and make their victory as difficult as we can for them." He rushed off, everyone running after him. Mortimer and I looked at each other. Mortimer was all excitement.

"Come on," he squeaked.

But before either of us could move, Mortimer started to shake and pointed to the ramparts below with a trembling front paw. I looked. There was Laodicea, the golden haired, the ice maiden. Flames were hungrily making their way towards her and I could see that the wall she was standing on wasn't going to hold very much longer. Laodicea wore her best dress, a brightly colored flowing garment, her long golden hair blowing in the wind and fanned by the flames below. She wore a wide diadem of gold fillet with seven golden chains hanging to her shoulders. She raised her arms, her face towards Olympus and cried:

"Oh, you Gods of Troy! Have pity on me and take me, spare me defilement at the hands of my enemies! Let me die where I was born. Let me stay in the earth that is my homeland!" Mortimer and I were transfixed. And then the wall under her gave way, great boulders crashed down, taking Laodicea with them. Once the dust cleared, there was no sign of her. She was entombed under the great stones of Troy's walls, where she will probably rest for all time for who will ever move that lot? Mortimer and I hurried away.

"I tell you, Mortimer," I said and there was a catch in my voice, "the women of Troy are something else again. Had they been in charge, none of this would have happened." Mortimer just sighed and shook his head. He led the way back to the little passage and just about flew down it. I followed at a slower pace. I didn't feel any particular urgency. No sense in breaking a leg or twisting a paw. We'd get there soon enough.

When we arrived back in Priam's panic room, we saw one wall had been smashed in and Priam, Hecuba and Andromache, with Astyanax in her arms, were being herded through magnificent chambers into the large hall where Æneas and I had met Hector's ghost. Mortimer and I followed cautiously, keeping as deep in the shadows as we could. In the main hall were a number of Greeks, Neoptolemus in the lead. He signaled one of his warriors, who immediately tore Astyanax from Andromache's arms. Astyanax started wailing. Andromache screamed, fell on her knees and held her arms out.

"Your father killed my father and my husband. They may have been guilty in his eyes and in yours but my little son is an innocent babe. Leave him to me, oh, leave him to me!" Neoptolemus sneered:

"I know just where this little tyke belongs!" And the Myrmidon holding Astyanax darted off. Andromache stayed on her knees and buried her face in her hands. A wild scream came from her; blood starting running down her neck and dress and I saw that she had scratched long gashes in her face with her nails. I shuddered. A primeval reaction of a mother deprived of her young. Mortimer cowered behind me and I thought I was about to faint. Then Andromache screamed.

"Take me quickly, throw me from the tower, from the walls of Troy, pierce me with your blade, spit me on your lance. There is nothing, nothing left for me on this earth." But that would have been too easy, especially with Neoptolemus in control.

"Take her down to my ships," he yelled. "She's mine! And if Odysseus interferes, kill him!" It took about four Myrmidons to drag Andromache away. I heard later that Astyanax had been thrown to his death from the highest part of the tower. Sad, but it wasn't on the cards that Hector's son would be allowed to survive. I could only wish Neoptolemus joy of Andromache. Myself, I'd as soon have taken a tiger home with me.

In all this confusion, poor old Priam had managed to get hold of a sword and was waving it about in an ineffectual sort of way. Hecuba cried out:

"Husband, husband, have you lost your senses? Do you think you can fight the son of Achilles? Even if Hector were here, he would know we need other weapons now." She went to the old man and embraced him. "Come; let us face our destiny together." A Greek warrior wrenched the sword out of the old man's hand. Other prisoners were herded past, the women screaming and trying to hang on to furniture, hangings, columns, anything, but to no avail. Then a young man just about fell through the door.

"Found him on the palace steps," the Greek following him said. "Thought you might want him." Neoptolemus looked at Polytes—for that was who it was—with interest. Then, springing forward like a tiger, he lifted his spear and pierced Polytes with so much force that the spear came out of the poor lad's back. Polytes fell down dead. Neoptolemus, his eyes burning with hate and lust for maiming and killing, glared at Priam and Hecuba who, aghast, looked at their dead son. Hecuba whispered:

"He was just a boy!" Looking at Neoptolemus, I thought: what a charmer, our Neoptolemus, just like his daddy, when his daddy finally came out of his tent. Cruel, bloodthirsty and treacherous. Hecuba threw herself on her son's remains, wailing, her body racked with torment. At the sight, the fear of death left Priam and he faced his son's murderer. He turned savagely on Neoptolemus:

"The gods will surely punish you, barbarian that you are, for delighting in murdering a son before his parents' eyes. But the apple doesn't fall far from the tree and like father like son. Your father, too, enjoyed killing; no morals, no ethics; he sold me my son Hector's body for gold, yes, gold, and then went back to the safety of his tent!" Priam lifted his frail arms: "I curse you both! May you be damned forever!" He grabbed a javelin from a nearby Myrmidon and cast it at Neoptolemus. However, Priam's unsteady hand did not have the thrust necessary to pierce Neoptolemus' armor. This futile gesture enraged Neoptolemus beyond all measure. At a gesture from him, one of his soldiers pulled Hecuba away from her son's body. He grabbed Priam and threw him on the corpse.

"You and my father can discuss all this when you meet in Hades!" he cried, driving his sword through the old man's heart. "Go and join your sons." And so died this king who had once held sway over all of Asia, who had seen his sons cut down one by one in a cause I wouldn't have touched with a ten foot pole. What a waste! What a terrible waste!

The Greeks then herded whoever was still standing out, including the sobbing Hecuba. Mortimer and I stayed where we were as if glued to the floor. Now it was just us and the dead.

~ 14 ~

Æneas and his Family

Before we could get ourselves to move, Æneas came in, covered in blood and gore from head to foot. Mortimer shook all over and I had to quiet him down. Wish I'd had some brandy. Oh, no, I wouldn't have given him any. Too young!

"Oh, ye gods," exclaimed Æneas, staring at the sight before him. "Will the horrors of this night never end? Priam and Polytes. Father and son." Then suddenly another reality appeared in his mind and I'd swear I saw his hair stand on end. "I'd quite forgotten my own family, father, wife and son. My father's white hair won't save him as it didn't save Priam. As for the wife and kid . . ." Better not speculate. The answer was all over Troy. He looked at the two of us. "Where is everyone? Where are my companions?" What could one say? "I'm going mad. They're all gone. Some of my comrades became so desperate they threw themselves off Troy's ramparts!" He shook his head. "That it should all have come to this! That it should all end thus!" Then he seemed to pull himself together. "Come on, let's get out of here." I looked at Mortimer:

"Perhaps you're better off staying," I said. "It should be nice and cozy back in your rat hole." But Mortimer shook his head.

"I'm not staying by myself with all those corpses. I'm coming with you". I shrugged. Between the living and the dead, I'd trust

245

the dead anytime. But to each his own. We followed Æneas out of the chamber of horrors.

Æneas didn't use the front entrance of the palace. The walls had been breached in so many places we were spoilt for exits. We kept to the shadows, such as we could find. Priam Square was littered with Trojan dead, young and old, warriors or waiters. The Greeks were having a great time—they'd gotten into Troy's cellars and there were drunks all over the place. Fires raged everywhere and night had turned into day but the square itself was mostly untouched. I had a horrible feeling the Wooden Horse was looking at me. We slipped down an alley that lead towards the great walls. The going was slow since we had to hide whenever a Greek patrol came by; at least, Aeneas did, because who would care for a cat and a rat out for a stroll? Although I kept in mind there is sport in tormenting a cat to death, especially among the yobs. In fact, the Americans claim tormenting cats is the first sign that a nasty little boy will become a serial killer.

We finally got to the Chetas gate area where the better streets of Troy were once to be found. Since the flames from the gate still burned furiously, the Greeks hadn't bothered to post guards. No one paid much attention to us; a lone man, a cat and a rat. So much had happened that night that a man and a cat and a rat going off together would have seemed quite commonplace.

We passed behind the temple of Pallas Athena. We could hear shouts as the Greeks sacked the place. Well, the best of British luck to them, thinks I. And much good it will do them when they get home. Those that do. We passed a house where we could hear people screaming, as they burnt alive together with their home. In another, the corpses of two children lay in the garden while the husband dispatched his wife with a sword, which he then drove into his own heart. I shuddered.

Then, as we neared the Troien gate, we saw a lone female figure sitting on a pile of fallen stones. It was Helen, all huddled up in a cloak, her hair covered with soot, her dress torn and filthy, her arms and legs covered in mud and blood. The fires cast weird lights and shadows over her, giving the illusion that sometimes she was there, sometimes she wasn't. Vergil will say she was afraid of the Trojans finding and killing her but I don't agree. I think the Greeks would have a bone to pick with her, too. But my money would be on Helen any time in a contest against either. Æneas stopped looked at her.

"I hope you are satisfied!" he said grimly. "You are truly the curse of both Greeks and Trojans. What can you hope for now? What else is there for you to destroy? " Helen looked at him balefully.

"Don't think you're going to blame this whole thing on me," she snarled. "It's all your doing, you men with your appetites and desires and ideas of honor and glory. What do I care for any of you when none of you cared for me?" Æneas became really angry at this and I can't say I blame him.

"No one cared for you!" he shouted. "How dare you say that when so many have died to protect you!" Helen jumped to her feet, eyes blazing and screamed back at him:

"Protect me! Protect me? When did I ever ask for protection? What good did any of it do me? Tell me! Tell me!! What did I get out of it? Where's my percentage? All I got were curses and scorn and hatred! I was called a slut, a trollop, a whore! I was derided. I was used as an object to feed the Trojans' idea of glory and a reason for the Greeks' greed." She faced him, furious. "Don't talk as if it all happened for my sake! What choice did I ever have? My father gave me away as it suited him and then I was abducted—sort of—by that pretty boy. I'm the victim here!" Æneas took a step back. Helen in a temper was scary. Finally he said:

"Perhaps Menelaus will kill you and put you out of your misery!" Helen laughed hysterically.

"Menelaus? Menelaus kill me? Oh, spare me! You think he has the guts? Not he! He'll come crawling, begging me to go with him back to Sparta." By now, I didn't know which of the two was the more livid.

"So that's it," Æneas shouted. "You're sailing away to your splendid palace, with a retinue of admirers, a complaisant husband, while Troy burns and Priam's corpse lies rotting in his own palace!" He reached for his javelin and raised it. Helen looked at him defiantly, without moving.

"Go on," she taunted him. "That's right. Kill me. That's all men are good for. Kill me and see how much honor and praise you will get for having slain Helen. The bodies of all your dead friends and comrades will rise to applaud you." This was getting serious. To be frank, I had no idea what to do to separate those two. I looked at Mortimer. He shrugged his shoulders. I was debating if a few bites and scratches would turn Æneas' mind to other things. I wish I could say something clever or that something extraordinary would happen—and then it did!

A shimmering of light appeared from the shadows of the temple. Oh, dear, I hoped it wasn't Hector again—all those gaping wounds would bring up my dinner if I'd had any. But, no. It was a woman; youngish, modishly dressed. Æneas gaped.

"Mother," he cried. Well, at least she seemed to have died a natural death. Helen turned her eyes towards the heavens.

"A ghost, give me a break. I'm out of here." And off she went. Æneas' mother, like mothers in all times and places, started to lecture her son.

"My son," she said, "what is this rage that has taken hold of you? Have you forgotten where your duty lies? That you have a father, a wife and a son? Do you know what is happening in your house? What if the Greeks are there, even now, spreading death and destruction?" As mothers went, this one didn't seem to be too bad. "This war," she continued, "came from the gods, not from Helen's face or Paris' actions. Æneas, don't waste your time any further on this hopeless cause. Hurry, hurry, to the family who needs you." Having had her say, she slowly dissolved and was gone. Æneas stood stock-still. The dreadful sounds of battle came closer. The sky lit up as fires spread to buildings nearer and nearer to where we were. Then we heard a tremendous crash—part of the outer wall near Antenorides had collapsed. Æneas suddenly came to life.

"She's right, my mother's right, there's nothing more for me to do here. The city's dead, nothing can save it. Come, to my house, come." He sprinted off. Mortimer and I just sat there for a minute. Should we go? Should we stay? Should we hide? Now, that would be sensible. Mortimer, however, couldn't seem to get enough excitement. He started running.

"Come on, follow me!" We set off. Mortimer stayed in the shadows, ran in ditches and along inside walls where available. As we sped along, we saw—and heard—the agony of the city. Fires were now everywhere; we could hear the screams of the dying and wounded. I don't have to say that the city administrators had not planned on how to care for the wounded; there were no field hospitals, ambulances or guidelines for mass evacuations, to say nothing of centers for psychological counseling for survivors, but survivors were at best a moot point. Everywhere there were Greeks, looting, drinking and killing, just for the fun of it.

We could see Æneas' shadow ahead of us. He'd had a head start but a human can't outrun a cat and a rat. Whenever we left the safety of the walls, we tended to slip in pools of blood. We did a lot of jumping—over corpses, fallen masonry. We passed Cælius' favorite wall. The fire had reached the house behind it and red ghosts seemed to be dancing in the ruins. Remind me not to travel to a besieged city on my next holiday; it's not much fun.

Æneas turned into a side street that slopped gently upwards. The roadway was slick with pooled blood. He dived into what had once been a fairly stately home; the fire hadn't reached it yet but the war had. The gate was smashed, the door hung on its hinges, broken furniture thrown into what had once been a tidy and well-tended garden, the mosaic floor looked as if someone had taken a sledgehammer to it. We ran through the atrium, empty except for wrecked household objects; in a back room, three people were huddled together: an elderly man, a woman and a small boy, I would imagine about 10 years old.

"Father, Creusa, Ascanius!" cried Æneas. The kid ran to him.

"Dad, dad, you've come to save us! We've been so scared!" Æneas hugged the kid. The lady, Creusa, made a face and pulled her skirts around her.

"There's a rat over there and a cat. Why doesn't the cat kill the rat? Where's my broom?" Lady, you have other problems than rats and cats. Live with it. Æneas said:

"Oh, that's Gaius Marius and Mortimer. Never mind them." He continued. "I don't know how you managed to stay alive since the Greeks have obviously been here." Creusa started sobbing:

"Æneas, they've taken all our good stuff. The pewter and those plates Priam gave us for our wedding and my mother's teapot!" How like a woman: about to be skewered on a Greek sword and here she was worrying about kitchen appliances. The kid interrupted her:

"We hid in the garden, Dad," he said. "You know that huge tree back there with those enormous roots you've been planning to get rid of for I don't know how long? A good thing you didn't. It was the perfect hiding place." The old man spoke for the first time:

"They were bent on looting when they came here, not killing."

"Right, everyone," said Æneas briskly, "we've got to get out of here. Sorry, Creusa, but you can't take anything; put on your best and warmest clothes and see if there is any food around. Come on, let's get moving." But the old guy shook his head.

"Son, I'm too old to run. This is my home, my city. Let me die here. You are young, you may still have a future. Go! Our enemies will help me die, I don't doubt. As for my tomb, I leave that to the gods. I miss your mother. I think it's time I joined her." Cries and protests from the human contingent. Personally, I think the old guy made a lot of sense. I can't remember what happened to Anchises on Æneas' travels but I know the whole thing would be a frost. Now, here we have one of the central problems of humanity. Humans cannot say when they've had enough of living and feel it's time to go. Other humans protest. The family wails. Strangers gather in large numbers with placards, and so forth and march around protesting through bullhorns. My opinion? Well, we can't, unfortunately, control our birth. But it should be the fundamental right of any living creature to control his or her death. OK, Gaius, get back on track.

"Father," cried Æneas. "I can't, I just can't go off and leave you here. What would life be without my father? If this is your decision, then I will take up my armor and sword again and go and find an honorable death among our foes!" Get real, Æneas. You've forgotten the wife and kid. Æneas continued: "Is it your intention to stay knowing that nothing will remain of Troy? Did I leave the battle, facing our foes in the streets, seeing our citizens ruthlessly cut down, dead and dying everywhere, to reach my home just to witness the slaying of my father, wife and son?" Anchises held up his arms to heaven:

"My son, don't you see this is too much for me? My city destroyed, the king whom I served for so long slain? If the gods wanted me to enjoy an old age, they could have saved Troy. It is your duty, Æneas, to save the few Trojans who remain and lead them to a place where they can take up their lives and where a tiny piece of Troy may survive." By this time, Æneas had lost it. He picked up his sword again and turned to the doorless opening, bent on returning to the streets and the fighting. He was sure to find a Greek compliant enough to kill him. But then Creusa threw herself in front of him, stopping him by hanging on to his knees. One could but feel for her, her husband was about to go off and abandon her and their son in quest of a glorious death. If we all survived, I would consider introducing her to Helen.

"Husband," cried Creusa. "You can't leave us here—at least let your wife and your son go with you so we may share your fate." She sobbed and for sure she had reason to. "How can you leave us, where is the love you pledged to me and the protection

your son is entitled to expect from you? If you leave now, you
will never know what happened to us, left alone in these ruins;
and, if you survive alone, how can you live with yourself? How
can you ever forgive yourself or rest knowing that we are dead
and unburied or enslaved? Your father makes his own choices
and I accept your abandoning me here but your son deserves a
better fate." Well, all things being equal, I had a lot of time for
the ladies of Troy. Any one of them was worth five of the men.
Now, in telling this tale, I decided to leave out all the gods and
goddesses although Vergil will probably disown me—tough, pal,
but cats just don't go for all that stuff.

But again, something happened—I won't say the gods were
responsible but I won't say they weren't—I keep an open
mind. The sky lit up and a comet—or a god, depending on
your orientation—raced across the heavens, trailing stars of
light. We all gasped and Mortimer tried to hide under my tail.
We watched until it disappeared over the horizon. There was
general speechlessness. Then Anchises came to life:
   "A sign from Olympus," he proclaimed. Me, I wasn't about to
contradict him. "My son, my path is now clear; you are right. Let
us leave this place at once." Well, that was a turnaround if there
ever was one. Anchises got busy. "Get up, Creusa and Ascanius,
let's get ready." So they picked up a few garments, found a crust
or two and some old cheese, wrapped the lot in a handkerchief
and before you could say Jack Robinson, we were all outside on
the portico. Anchises looked up to heaven and lifted his arms
upwards: "You gods of Troy, into your hands I deliver all our
fates." And, putting his hand on the kid Ascanius' head, he
continued: "guard this relic of the Trojan race, this small child."
And so we all left, me and Mortimer bringing up the rear. We
ran down to the main thoroughfare. The fires blazed stronger
than ever, spreading fast and furious: a strong wind had sprung
up to fan them along. There were people everywhere: the quick,
the dead and the dying. Women wailing over their children;
wounded trying to drag themselves out of harm's way; looting

Greeks and Greeks dragging girls into alleyways—at least they had some sense of shame. The noise was deafening and the crush of bodies overwhelming. Mortimer and I kept to the gutters; I tried not to think what I was stepping in; it was all gooey and wet—ye gods; this was not a time for squeamishness. Æneas was having trouble keeping his family together. He supported his father on one shoulder and kept tight hold of Ascanius' hand. Creusa struggled behind as best she could. Æneas kept up an encouraging flow of words to his father:

"Come, father, hang onto me. Whatever the outcome, we shall either win through or die together. I'm holding on to Ascanius, too. And Creusa is following close behind us." We all hurried along. Æneas continued to me: "We are heading for the ancient temple of Ceres, Gaius. You'll recognize it by a cypress as old as Troy itself. If we lose each other, that's where we'll meet." Well, the Temple of Ceres was not one of the sights on my list so I had no idea where it was but I trusted Mortimer did.

At first Mortimer and I tried to keep up with Æneas but this was too much for Mortimer and by the time we were on the main street, he stopped and gasped, really fagged out; he was after all quite small with short little legs. Once he got his breath back, he said:

"We can't go Æneas' way, his legs are too long and he will have to keep to the main streets. I know a better way. A short cut that starts at the end of this alleyway." Well, I didn't have great faith in shorts cuts; trusting unreliable friends, I had often ended up lost and desolate. I looked down the alley; it was dark, a good thing as it meant the fires hadn't reached it yet. And Mortimer was right. If we followed the main streets, horses could step on us, chariots wheels run us over or stabbed—by either side—in the excitement of battle. Even a stray arrow would put paid to us. So Mortimer's short cut it would have to be.

"Right," I answered. "Lead on, Mortimer my boy."

Mortimer's short cut was made of water culverts, holes in walls, sewers—open or closed—underground passages, some of them rat sized so I barely managed to squeeze through. Not the route a fastidious cat would choose but, as the man said, beggars can't be choosers. Thank Gods cats' bodies are so flexible. The theory is that, if a cat can get his head through, the rest of him will be able to follow. Some openings I doubted I could handle, they were really tiny. One was so small, I hesitated. What if I got stuck and couldn't move either forwards or backwards? Mortimer was jumping and squeaking and refused to go first. I sat looking at this minuscule passage until I heard the wall behind me starting to fall. All doubts gone, I squeezed through and just managed to grab Mortimer by the tail before the masonry came down. Mortimer sat looking at me shivering.

"I thought," he said, "you were going to eat me!" I rolled my eyes.

"Not even to please you. Let's go!" At another point, I had to submit to the indignity of Mortimer pushing me through a hole, which made us about even. After that, we both needed a rest so we stopped and lay there panting. We found a shallow pool where we had a drink, making sure, first, that the water wasn't liberally sprinkled with blood. But the war hadn't reached this far into Troy's slums only fit for rats, other creepy-crawlies and the dregs of humanity. After a bit, we went on.

Mortimer's short cut suddenly ended and we faced the prospect of having to skirt—or, worse still, cross—Priam Square where there was still a lot of action; fires raged, the roof of one of the government buildings caved in with a crash, sending sparks everywhere with humans running hither and thither for their lives. Only the Wooden Horse, still untouched by fire, stood silent as if awaiting further events. I shivered at the sight. Uncanny, to say the least. An island of stillness in what seemed the anteroom of Hades. We left. At first, we skirted the square, keeping close to the buildings and making ourselves as small as possible. But then we were faced with a conundrum. We needed to go down an alley we could only reach by cutting across one corner of Priam Square, meaning we should be in the open. I reconnoitered carefully but there was no other way.

"Right, Mortimer," I said, "best foot forwards and don't stop until we reach the temple steps." So we set off at top speed. And then I stumbled. I looked and saw I had fallen over a corpse. In fact, I had almost fallen into a great gash in its chest. I gasped when I recognized him. Troilus! Oh, Lord of Cats. The dead I don't know I can handle. The dead I do know unnerve me. I wanted to lie down on Troilus and wail: 'forgive me, forgive me for thinking so many nasty things about you. I did like you, why, perhaps I even loved you in my own feline way'. Mortimer pulled my tail urgently.

"Come away, Gaius. We can't stay here. You can cry later on. Not now, not now." So I struggled on, leaving what had been Troilus behind. And so by byways and highways we finally spotted ancient cypresses and knew we were near the temple of Ceres. We hurried on, and suddenly there it was.

⁓ 15 ⁓

The Temple of Ceres

The temple of Ceres was far from the center of Troy, a forgotten nook set amidst ancient groves and woodland. It had an abandoned look; lichen and creepers covered the temple's marble walls and once stately columns; what had once been well-tended gardens now overgrown with weeds. A small crowd of frightened people—who had only one thing going for them: they were still alive—huddled together. Not too long after we arrived, Æneas struggled in with his father and Ascanius.

"Where's Creusa?" I asked. He looked behind him. But there was no one there.

"Oh, ye Gods," he cried in panic. "We've lost her." He deposited Anchises and Ascanius and rushed off. I looked around. There were about 60 souls there, all of them dirty, all of them ragged.

I searched for familiar faces and was happy to see both Marianne and the old waiter from *The Trojan Horse*. Marianne was not her usual well-groomed self; her hair looked bedraggled and needed both a wash and a comb. Her dress was torn and filthy. I didn't recognize anyone else. I went over to Marianne. She looked at me.

"Hi, there. So you made it this far, too." I nodded.

"And I'm glad to see you, Marianne. And the waiter."

"Oh, yes, Demosthenes. I tell you frankly, I'm not quite sure how we got here. It was sheer luck, it was." She shivered. "My room is—or rather was—over the café with a view of Priam square. I was really spooked by that Wooden Horse, let me tell you. I was on the beach when the old priest, Lacoon, rained curses down on the townsfolk for dragging it into the city. And then later I heard Helen walking around it calling out strange names in that weird way. So I didn't sleep easy; I kept getting up to look at the thing. I was at the window when I heard a snap, saw the Horse open and shadows climbing out." Talk about spooky. "So I threw on a few things, got Demosthenes and we set out." She stopped. "I wanted to bring my dog, too. You remember Antonia." Indeed I did. "But she didn't come when I called her." She started crying. "I didn't want to leave without her but what could I do!" Marianne had shown herself more faithful to Antonia than Antonia to her; I'd seen Antonia leave with Cælius' group. I put a paw on Marian's arm.

"Don't worry about her," I said soothingly. "She's OK. Call her when you get outside the walls. I'm sure she'll come." Poor Marianne blew her nose on her skirt. No hanky, just like a woman. She continued bitterly.

"Bloody coincidence, wasn't it, my café being called *The Trojan Horse*. My husband set the business up—with my dowry, mind you—and insisted on that ill-fated name. I should have known nothing good would ever come from anything he did. He said it would please Hector." She clenched her fists. "A right bastard he was, too," her husband, I take it, not Hector, "always going for the bottle and flirting with the girls while I wore myself to the bone working." Scratch any Trojan woman and you will find a man hater. "Then he decided to go for a soldier and never came back. Good riddance." I kept politely silent. Marianne went on with her story. "Anyhow, me and Demosthenes had a head start; just as well, as *The Trojan Horse* became the Greeks' first pit stop. I saw them break in as we looked back from the palace steps." Sacking a town is thirsty work, sunshine. "We spent most of the day hiding in ditches

and abandoned houses, working our way towards this temple."
I asked:

"Was there any pre-arrangement that Trojans should head
this way in case of trouble?" Marianne shook her head. "This
is just the loneliest bit of Troy; off the beaten track, so to speak.
I figured the Greeks would be busy elsewhere before getting
around to this place."

"That's quite a story, Marianne. I gotta hand it to you Trojan
women, you don't really need men, they just seem to be an
encumbrance."

"You're damn right, pal," she answered. "What I say is I
just can't afford having a man; always wanting their teas and
dinners and clothes washed. Would you believe mine had
a garment he called his dirty work tunic, as if he ever did
anything that would require it!" There it was, Marianne's story.
Strange to have seen her so often yet known nothing about her
at all.

We looked up at the sky. There was a glimmer of dawn, a
rosy light just discernible in the east. The day was not long off.
I felt as if a year had passed since me and Sinon had sat on that
bench in Priam Square, only two nights ago. That's how long it
took to destroy a city that had stood for a thousand years, give
or take a hundred or so either way. Then it occurred to me: in
the 20th century, humans had become much more effective. In
World War II, cities were leveled, too, but that only took a few
hours of intensive bombardment from the air. How long did it
take to destroy Hiroshima? Twenty minutes to half an hour, I
believe. Now, that's real progress, and in the same war, too, if
you please. The next step will be to destroy the planet in five
minutes. And don't think they can't or won't. Too many nutcases
around with their fingers on buttons. I went back to where
Mortimer was curled up and curled up myself.

Then Æneas returned—alone. He came over and slumped down
beside me.

"I couldn't find her, Gaius. I've been through the main streets and squares, up alleys, hidden corners and everywhere I called her name. I went all the way back to our house to see if she'd gone there. Well, she hadn't but the Greeks were all over it, I can't imagine what they wanted since they'd already taken everything of any value. So they set the house ablaze. And why not, I ask you, if the rest of the city is being burned to the ground? If my father and Ascanius hadn't been here waiting for me, I would have stayed and given them lessons in good manners. As it was, I had to fight my way out." He stopped.

"I've been to the palace; it's a burning inferno and the roof has caved in. At the temple of Juno, I saw Odysseus and Nestor set up like a pair of tax gatherers, collecting the loot and totting up figures." He sighed then continued: "I never really knew how rich a city Troy was until I saw the spoils those two had accumulated. And that's not counting what the ordinary footslogger has put in his pocket." Well, you may not have known, Æneas, but I'm certain the Greeks made up their little wish lists long ago. Æneas went on.

"Golden cups, Gaius, purples vestments, marble statues of the gods painted in gold, all the treasures of Troy." I didn't say anything so he continued: "Then I saw the prisoners: children, women of all ages. No warriors, though. I did hear some fighting still going on but I believe most of the Trojan warriors have been slain." He started sobbing. "It was unbearable; I looked for Creusa among the women. If she'd been there, I would have rushed those guards and we could have died together. But she wasn't. I saw Polyxena, Cassandra, Andromache—but not Astyanax—and Hecuba, and so many, many others." He now wept openly. "To this has our arrogance brought us; and all for a paltry woman—I should have killed her when I had the chance."

"That would hardly have made things better," I admonished him.

"But I would for sure kill Paris if I could find him. He, more than Helen, is responsible." Well, as for responsibility, to my mind there was enough to go around and then some. We sat

259

quietly until, suddenly, Mortimer squeaked and pointed with his paw.

In a small grove of cypresses, some little way from us, a light was shimmering. Another ghost. I must confess that, by this time, I was getting used to ghosts and, believe you me, just then I'd rather meet any number of them than living Greeks. The three of us got up and walked quietly towards the light. As we came nearer, it took form.

"Creusa," Æneas whispered. "So you are dead. All is now lost." But perhaps Creusa was on my wavelength. Better to be a ghost than a slave. She became more and more distinct. She said gently to Æneas:

"You mustn't fret, my love, for I'm now somewhere far far better than anywhere I've ever been before. It was not my destiny to leave Troy. Don't fret, my Æneas. Neither tears nor woe relieve the dead. And you, you have responsibilities that will not allow you the luxury of sorrow. The gods have given you a great task that you must carry out."

My, that's telling him. No nampybampy stuff from Creusa, even in death. She raised her ghostly arms to the heavens.

"I have seen your future in the skies. You will wander far, your labors both on land and sea will be hard. But one day you will reach a land called Latium, through which runs a great river; there you will find green fields and flower filled meadows. And there your labors will cease, my Æneas. There you will establish a peaceful kingdom and restore the Trojan line through our son, Ascanius." I swear Æneas tried to embrace her but it goes without saying that all he managed to do was fall over.

"Creusa," he cried. "I don't even know how you died!" She answered:

"As if that matters! Let it be enough that you know I am not a slave or servant in some Greek household. I am free and have found peace with the gods. So, weep no more for me, Æneas, weep no more . . ." and she slowly vanished.

I looked around for Mortimer but he'd disappeared. I turned my attention back to Æneas who was sitting on the ground sobbing. My, he was in a bad way. I tried to give aid and comfort:

"Æneas, what Creusa said really makes a lot of sense." I thought of Tennessee Williams—*the dead are lucky*[57]. Something to think about. But that would not help Æneas just now. I soldiered on: "As far as we know, you are the only Trojan leader still alive and it is your duty to look after the survivors. So, pal, pick up your burden like a good 'un." Æneas sniveled.

"D'you think there's anything in what she said about my reaching that quiet and peaceful land?" I replied:

"I don't think, Æneas. I know. And the city you will found will be a great power one day, much greater than Troy ever dreamt of." I didn't bother to tell him he would have to fight for this land and kill its present inhabitants. Then it would be peaceful and green. However, when peoples move about that's what happens. Remember the Saxons in Britain and the People of the Sea in Greece, to say nothing of the Europeans in the Americas.

However, the future must look after itself. I got Æneas back to the Temple and had him lie down for what was left of the night. It wasn't much.

---

[57] *The Glass Menagerie,* play by Tennessee Williams

❦ 16 ❦

The Scæan Gate

When we woke from an uneasy sleep just after dawn, a lot more Trojans had managed to make their way to the Temple of Ceres. There were now about 200 souls, all much the worse for wear. Æneas made them pool whatever food they had and saw it distributed equally so that everyone got something to eat. A little stream behind the temple served to quench their thirst. Mortimer and I shared some of my cat food. Then Æneas got the Trojans organized into teams; he must have had something in mind but by the time he was done, he just stared at them helplessly.

"This is all very well," he said. "But how do we get out of here? The latecomers tell me that all the gates are manned by the Greeks." Right. What kept the Greeks out for ten years was now keeping the Trojans in. Then help came from a most unexpected quarter. Mortimer was squeaking excitedly next to me.

"Guys," he said. "If you continue through the woods behind the temple, you'll come to a spot where there's a stone missing in the wall. We rats know about it because it's been very helpful in our comings and goings. I think the humans might be able to dig out a few more stones and just crawl out of Troy."

Æneas said thoughtfully:

"The Scæan gate! I've heard of it but never knew where it was. Legend says it was blocked up decades ago." Since no one had anything better to suggest, Æneas led the way through the wood, following an excited Mortimer. We were stopped by a thick and mighty hedge covered in thorns. Sleeping Beauty's castle—let's say, at year 51 out of 100. I looked at Mortimer.

"Any more bright ideas?" He answered me crossly:

"What d'you mean, can't you see?" Since it seemed no one could, he continued: "Very well, come with me!" And disappeared into the hedge. "Come on, Gaius," his voice came from within. I sighed.

"Mortimer," I said as patiently as I could, "I would if I could! But I don't see . . ."!

"Squeeze under the hedge, you ninny!" Well, the little nobody was now getting above himself so I squeezed under the hedge just to teach him a lesson, getting multiple scratches for my pains. When I reached him, he was sitting smugly in a clearing; I waved a paw at him.

"Now you listen to me, young Mortimer," I said severely. "You seem to forget that you are a rat and I am a cat and therefore above you in the food chain . . ." But then I looked around. The clearing was close to Troy's wall. An archway, hidden by the hedge, was in fact a tunnel leading to the wall itself. Now, as I've said exhaustively, Troy's walls are very thick—a mile they say, although I don't know what a mile is. If true, Mortimer and I must have walked about 95% of a mile through the archway before reaching the outer wall. Mortimer looked at me, pleased as punch. He cried:

"Come with me." Why, this rodent was getting more uppity by the minute and I really thought I needed to teach him his place. I pounced on him but he wasn't there. Then I saw. Down near the ground, a smallish flattish stone was missing and that's how Mortimer escaped my claws. I heard his voice floating in:

"Come and get me!" I wasn't going to accept that kind of challenge from a mere rat so I went after him. I just managed to squeeze through on my tummy, front paws stretched out, back ones too but in the other direction. For a moment, I thought I was stuck but Mortimer hauled on my front paws—with more strength than one would think possible—and I ended popping out like a cork from a bottle. Not dignified. But then I looked around in amazement. I was outside Troy. Mortimer was skipping around for pure pleasure. I decided to forgive and forget.

"Jolly good, young Mortimer. Now let's head for the high ground." Mortimer looked at me severely.

"I think not!" he exclaimed. "What about the others?" I shrugged.

"What do we care? They're just humans." Mortimer frowned and said sternly:

"They are our friends," and disappeared back into the city. I sighed and followed. I arrived as Mortimer was explaining to Æneas about the tunnel, the missing stone, dancing around. Didn't he ever stand still? Æneas looked at me quizzically.

"Is this on the level?" I just nodded. Æneas scratched his chin. "We need to get through the hedge first," and went at it with his sword, several of the others falling to, while the women and children cleared away the fallen branches. In no time, the opening was wide enough and Æneas stepped through, looking in wonder at the archway and the tunnel. With Mortimer running in front of him, he reached the wall and Mortimer showed him the missing stone. Æneas saw the possibilities at once.

"We'll have to remove some more stones before we can get out and that won't be easy." However, there was nothing for it but set to: the men with swords or knifes attacked the surrounding stones. It was a long and tedious job, especially as we had to be sure the Greeks didn't wise up on what was going on. Mortimer and I slipped out and lay down on a convenient large stone just outside, while Ascanius and some other kids sat on the ground just inside, passing our messages along to the grownups. Of course, the odd Greek patrol came by but all they saw was a cat and a rat lying on a stone, which caused them enormous merriment.

"Did you ever see the like, Polydeuces," exclaimed one guy to his buddy, "a cat and a rat together as if they were best mates." The s.o.b. threw a stone at me but of course he missed. "Hey, cat, you're supposed to eat that rat." The patrol shrieked with laughter. Such yobs. Do they really think I would lower myself to eat an uncooked rat? And you can't eat someone you're on first name terms with. Anyhow, off they went and the Trojans continued with their backbreaking work. Just after dusk, the job was done; the opening large enough to allow a man through, if he crouched. However, Æneas decided not to leave the city until it was truly dark. Then, again, Mortimer and I kept watch while one by one the Trojans scrambled out and, as silently as possible for humans, ran towards the hills and disappeared into the undergrowth. As Marianne came through, we heard an excited bark not far off. And, sure enough, Antonia came gamboling up to her. Idiot dog, she might have woken the whole Greek army up with her barking. Lucky for her they were probably all drunk. Marianne bent down and hugged her.

"I knew you wouldn't abandon me!" she cried, in her turn doing her best to bring the Greeks down on the refugees. Mortimer and I looked at each other.

"Human and dog," I said, "difficult to decide who's the most ham-fisted." Marianne waved a cheery goodbye to us, all smiles now, Antonia wagged her tail, and off they went.

"Perhaps Antonia will be the ancestor of a race of dogs who will rule over the dog world," said Mortimer in his innocent way. I shuddered at the thought of meeting some of them in my future. The last to go was Æneas.

"Gaius and Mortimer, come with us," he said. But we shook our heads.

"Just don't forget us," we said. "We won't forget you." To be sure. All we would have to do was pick up *The Æneid* and we would walk with Æneas in Troy again.

"Yes," squeaked Mortimer. "When you get to Latium, send us a postcard." I got a hug—hate it—and Mortimer a pat. And then Æneas passed into the night, into the hills and out of our lives.

⌁ 17 ⌁

Goodbye to Troy

After the horrors of those nights, Mortimer and I finally struggled down to the beach in the early morning. I've never been so tired in my life. Mortimer dragged himself along behind me. *The Greek Olive Tree*, or rather, what had been *The Greek Olive Tree*, was heaving. Laughter and shouting fit to wake the seven sleepers. A load of Greeks was dancing in the sand. Eurybates was raking it in just as I had predicted. I said to Mortimer:

"I hope you don't mind but I don't want a drink. I don't want to celebrate."

"Neither do I," said Mortimer. "Let's go get some sleep." We crawled to my favorite tree and collapsed under it. Just as I was dropping of, a raucous noise reached me. I looked up blearily. The Greeks were all assembled at the raising of the Greek City State flag. Then they burst into their national anthem.

Oh, say can you see by the dawn's early light
What so proudly we hail'd at the twilight's last gleaming?
Our banner flying o'er the Greek city states
From the Acropolis high,
To far o'er the Ægean sky,
Gives proof of our Greek superiority.
May it forever wave
O'er the lands of the Greeks!

A terrible noise, especially since everyone was inebriated and off-key. After that, I think we both passed out. The sun was high in the sky when we woke up. Mortimer and I breakfasted on some of my cat food. Afterwards, I looked back at the city—what a difference a day—or three—makes. The tower in ruins. Smoke lay thick over the city and drifted out towards the sea.

Walking along the beach later, I came upon Odysseus looking out to sea more or less as he had that first day we had talked. He seemed pleased to see me.

"I came," he said, "I saw, I conquered."[58] I sneered.

"Sure ya did, it just took ten years." It was my turn to sit down next to him. I was not pleased with him at all. "Well," I snorted, "here you are. I hope now you are satisfied!" And I meant it to sting. "A nice mess you made of it," I said severely. "Even Agamemnon couldn't have improved upon your handiwork."

"My dear cat," he answered, "if you think for one moment that this was what I had in mind, you are not as smart as I thought." He swept his arm towards the city. "All this destruction is completely nutsville. What good are these ruins to us—or anyone else for that matter? I wanted to make Troy a Greek city. New name and so on; under new management, you know." He shook his head.

"The truth, Gaius, is that no military plan survives the first five minutes of battle." Odysseus shook his head sadly. I sneered. Heard that one before. "Such a waste," he went on. "We'll have to build a new city from scratch and we won't be able to use this site, too many memories and curses." He thought a bit. "The other side of the Hellespont, I think would be a good spot." Indeed. The Greeks did build a city there, but it took them a bit of time to get around to it, 800 years, give or take a few decades.

---

[58] May 47 B.C., Julius Caesar moved against Pharnaces of Pontus, an area by the Black Sea. . Caesar claimed the battle lasted four hours. To inform the Senate of his victory, he wrote, *veni, vidi, vici* ..

A city that still exists into the 21st century, although by then it been through quite a few hands and name changes.

"What about your wealthy prisoners and all the ransom you were going to get?" I asked. He looked sad and said philosophically:

"Even if I had gotten any, there's no one left to pay."

"You should have thought of that before you destroyed the whole bloody place," I sneered. "And what became of the Wooden Horse?" Odysseus chuckled.

"It burned down with the rest of Troy. Wasn't worth much, anyhow, mostly pine. Agamemnon can take the ashes back to Mycenæ if he wants to. Why, I'll pay for the urn myself." Well, Agamemnon deserved not to get anything he wanted. So that was OK. I said:

"I was sort out of the action for most of the time so I don't really know what happened. I saw Priam killed and one of his sons and I saw Cassandra being dragged off. And Achilles shot dead. That was Paris, you know. Fine archer, that lad. What happened to the rest?" Odysseus replied:

"I'm afraid, Gaius, not many of the Trojan warriors survived. Paris is dead Deiphobus, too. Don't know what happened to Helenus. Or Æneas for that matter." I looked innocent and he pierced me with his gimlet eye, then let it go. "Our worse loss was Achilles, as you might have guessed, but, truth to tell, I can't say I'll miss him." I answered:

"I met his son, Neoptolemus. A nasty piece of work, does his daddy proud."

"You're right," Odysseus nodded. "The less I see of that young man the happier I'll be." I went on.

"We met Helen, you know, about two nights ago. She was all alone near the temple of Juno. It drove Æneas mad; boy, did he get worked up! He wanted to kill her there and then. Helen stood up to him, too, no wilting lily-in-the-field she; no begging for mercy; just her usual spit-in-your-eye attitude. I really thought he was going to run her through with his sword and she was going to claw his eyes out. But then we got separated. What happened to her?" Odysseus was playing with a stick, drawing lines in the sand.

"She made it out all right. In fact, I don't think anyone saw her at all, except you lot. Some of the lads were out to get her, you can bet, they're still seething over the comments she made in Priam square. She's down there." He pointed with his stick.

I found Helen sitting on a piece of driftwood on the beach, the picture of beautiful desolation. I sat down next to her. I said:

"I see you made it out OK." Helen scowled.

"I'm always OK. Fate made me not only beautiful, but indestructible." For a few moments, we sat in silence, each nursing his and her own thoughts. Then, for the first time, I saw Helen cry. Not just ordinary sobs, but deep shattering wails that seemed to take over her whole body.

"Oh, what have I done? The Gods gave me the power of beauty and I have turned their gift to evil. Oh, Gaius, why did I come to Troy? Paris? I never cared for Paris or for any of them, Trojan or Greek. What was I looking for? Gaius, I hate my beauty and what it has done to me. And so I used it to destroy—destroy everything I touched! And this is my reward!" She went down this path for some time. I patted her arm with my paw until she calmed down. Neither of us had a handkerchief so she blew her nose in her dress, or what was left of it. Then I said:

"Helen, two thousand years from now, a great poet will write about you and this is what he'll say:

> *Was this the face that launch'd a thousand ships?*
> *And burnt the topless towers of Ilium*
> *Sweet Helen, make me immortal with a kiss.*
> *O, thou art fairer than the evening air,*
> *Clad in the beauty of a thousand stars."*[59]

Well, I like the lines but I've never figured out what they are doing in Christopher Marlowe's *Dr Faustus*. I watched Helen as

---

[59] Christopher Marlowe, *Dr Faustus*, 1606

she listened and the tears started again. But then she got herself together. She looked at me and said:

"Gaius, those are beautiful wonderful words; if I am remembered this way, even by one single person, I feel my life may not have been a waste after all." I replied with feeling:

"Helen, no matter who will be forgotten from this war and time, you will live forever in the minds and in the imagination of people yet to be born, in lands still to be discovered. Helen, the incomparable, Helen, the most beautiful. And I shall remember you as Helen, the most brave." Helen dried her tears surreptitiously, pretending she hadn't been crying at all.

"Gaius, you are such a comfort. Come back with me to Sparta so I'll have at least one friend." I shook my head:

"Helen, I miss my home and my friends and I want to get back to them." She enquired:

"Where do you live, Gaius?" Now, that would take some explaining so I kept it simple:

"Far away in space and time." Then Menelaus came up to Helen, for all the world as if she'd been on a business trip and he was picking her up at the airport.

"Let's go home, Helen," he said, stretching out his hand to her. Helen ignored the hand and stood up on her own.

"Why not," she said, "after all, one needs to be somewhere."

And then they started leaving. The biremes came close to shore and the rowboats came and went. Agamemnon left, dragging poor Cassandra with him and carrying an urn. I said to him:

"Agamemnon, a word of warning: taking Cassandra back with you is a really bad career move. Leave her behind. Take the advice of a neutral party." Agamemnon looked at me with a supercilious look:

"Odysseus may take you seriously, cat. I don't." Cassandra cried out to me:

"I've told him he's carrying death back with him but of course he doesn't believe me. And, you know what, Gaius? For

271

the first time, I'm glad not to be believed." And so the great Agamemnon went to his doom and Cassandra to hers. Screw you, Agamemnon. Of all the Greeks involved in this disaster, your guilt is the greatest because it was based on greed.

Andromache, of course, belonged to Neoptolemus, a fate worse than death. I hope she never learnt what happened to Astyanax but she could have guessed that the son of Hector would not survive. Then Ajax and Diomedes and Nestor went. I hope Diomedes married Cressida and lived happily ever after. Amazing that almost all my sympathy was with the women. Men are supposed to be able to look after themselves. I followed Helen and Menelaus down to the beach. Helen picked me up and gave me a hug. I did a bit of purring. Hmm . . . won't complain about that.

"Come and see me in Sparta, Gaius," said Helen again. "I'll make sure there's a regular supply of mice for you." This idée fixe of cats eating mice is starting to get on my nerves. I'll chase mice for sure but only if they insist. Good for the waistline.

"Goodbye, Helen," I answered. "Forget the mice. I like fish-based cat food. Safe journey." They got into the rowboat and Helen left Troy. Ten years ago, she'd come to a wonderful, beautiful and rich city. Life sucks.

Odysseus and I had a last drink at the embers of *The Greek Olive Tree*. Eurybates told me he was all packed up; the wife and kid had gone on ahead on another ship. Lucky for them. Vergil says somewhere in his epic that Æneas picks up a survivor from Odysseus' shipwreck. I do hope it was Eurybates.

As Odysseus was boarding his ship, he called out:

"Gaius, come with me. You'd make a wonderful ship's cat." I waved at him.

"Not this time, Odysseus. Bon voyage." After all, a cat lives 15 years, give or take a year or so, and I wasn't about to spend the next ten of mine with Odysseus. But Mortimer squeaked:

"I've always wanted to travel. I think I'll join him." I looked at Mortimer doubtfully.

"You might not want to go all the way," I warned him. "If I were you, I'd get out on Calypso's island and stay there. It's supposed to be really nice. Sort of like the Caribbean."

"I'll remember that," he said. "So long, Gaius, great to have known you."

"Good bye, Mortimer. If you're ever in Rio, look me up." So off he went, into the bowels of the bireme, I imagined. I felt quite sad. Amazing. I'd never thought I'd miss a rat.

I went up the cliffs and saw Vergil off. He was in a bad mood, of course; Homer had turned out to be right and now he had to write as ordered by Augustus.

"Well," he said, "that was quite a show the Greeks—and Trojans, of course, put on. Night was like day so I had a splendid view." It sounded like he'd been to the theatre. He scratched his chin. "Pity I'll have to wrap it all up in God and Goddess stuff to please that poltroon Augustus and confirm his divine descent. Can't be helped, though." But for all his bad humor, he was nice to me:

"I've really enjoyed meeting you, Gaius. Although I wish you'd change your name." I shook my head.

"Sorry, my friend. I love you dearly but once a cat has been given a name, it can't be ungiven, so to speak. Look it up in any decent cat care manual. I hope you have a good trip home. Good luck with your poem and keep your matches dry." Vergil called me back:

"Before you go, I have the first verse of Æneas' journey from Troy to Latium." I sat down patiently and Vergil rose to his feet and took the poet's favorite stand:

> When Heav'n had overturn'd the Trojan state
> And Priam's throne, by too severe a fate;
> When ruin'd Troy became the Grecians' prey,
> And Ilium's lofty tow'rs in ashes lay;
> Warn'd by celestial omens, we [Trojans] retreat,
> To seek in foreign lands a happier seat.

I applauded.

"Sounds great, Vergil." But then couldn't help adding. "Although Troy only had one Tower—albeit a big one." Vergil waved his hands:

"Now, don't get hung up in details, my dear Gaius. Poetic license, dear friend, poetic license. And, anyhow, who will ever know how many towers Troy had." Sighs. "Now I just have to do the other bits. Getting Æneas from Ilion to Latium will take many lines of verse." He added cheerily: "Perhaps Augustus will die before we get there—perhaps I will die before we get there." I answered moodily:

"Hope springs eternal!" It would be a long epic—about 100 000 words in 12 books! I continued: "I'm glad you've met the real Æneas so you know what a nice guy he is." But Vergil shook his head sadly:

"Sorry, Gaius, but if Æneas was really the ancestor of that arch villain Caius Julius Cæsar and his rascally nephew, the bastard Octavianus-cum-Augustus, he has to be a downright S.o.b. Stab first, ask questions later—if at all." He sighed. "As if you didn't know that this is how all nations originate—with war." Well, I couldn't quarrel with that—all too true. So Vergil was going to drown the noble saga of the founding of Rome in blood and gore. I suggested:

"You could kill Æneas off, you know, then he would never get to Latium. Say, instead of Dido, queen of Carthage, committing suicide, stabs Æneas for the faithless lover he is." Vergil cheered up immediately. "What a good idea," he said. "I'll certainly consider it." We knocked fist and paw. As he was leaving, he said:

"I hope that the memory of our friendship will be everlasting!" Then he disappeared over the hill.

After they were all gone, I looked back at the city. The fires still smoldered, the walls breached in so many places, the gates open to all the world, broken, burnt, hanging from twisted hinges. From the ruined tower, the Trojan standard—scorched, blackened and ragged—fluttered dismally in the breeze, the final proof of the city's agony.

And it came to me that this had once been a land of grace and beauty with its palaces, temples and groves of olive trees and cypresses, famous throughout the known world as Troy, the many-gated city. And here a people had taken their last bow: heroes and their fair ladies, common folk and peasants. Look for it no more for it is but a dream remembered—a civilization gone with the wind . . .

And so I turned away and left Troy.

Endnotes

i **Pyrrhus (319-272 BC), king of Epirus.**

> Accepting the invitation of the Greek city of Tarentum in Italy to lead the Italian Greeks against Rome, he won battles in 280 and 279 BC but was unable to establish himself in Italy. The expression 'Pyrrhic victory', a victory gained at too great a cost, is ascribed to Pyrrhus after the battle of Asculum (279 BC) when he routed the Romans but lost the best of his army: "One more victory like this and we are undone."

ii **All for Love (Epilogue)** by John Dryden (1631-1700)

> ….
>
> Yet, if he [Mark Anthony] might his own grand jury call, By the fair sex he begs to stand or fall. Let Cæsar's [Octavianus] power the men's ambition move, But grace you him who **lost the world for love**!

iii **The New Testament**

> **John 4.44**
>
> For Jesus himself testified, that a prophet hath no honour in his own country.
>
> **Matthew 13:57**
>
> And they [the apostles] took offense at him. But Jesus said to them, "A prophet is not without honor except in his own town and in his own home."
>
> **Mark 6:4**

Jesus said to them, "A prophet is not without honor except in his own town, among his relatives and in his own home."

Luke 4:24

"Truly I tell you," he [Jesus] continued, "no prophet is accepted in his hometown".

iv   **The New Testament (King James) - Luke 15:10**

Likewise, I say unto you, there is joy in the presence of the angels of God over one sinner that repenteth.

v   **Luke 15:11-32 - The Parable of the Prodigal Son**

11 A certain man had two sons:

12 And the younger of them said to *his* father, Father, give me the portion of goods that falleth *to me*. And he divided unto them *his* living.

13 And not many days after the younger son gathered all together, and took his journey into a far country, and there wasted his substance with riotous living.

14 And when he had spent all, there arose a mighty famine in that land; and he began to be in want.

15 And he went and joined himself to a citizen of that country; and he sent him into his fields to feed swine.

16 And he would fain have filled his belly with the husks that the swine did eat: and no man gave unto him.

17 And when he came to himself, he said, How many hired servants of my father's have bread enough and to spare, and I perish with hunger!

18 I will arise and go to my father, and will say unto him, Father, I have sinned against heaven, and before thee,

19 And am no more worthy to be called thy son: make me as one of thy hired servants.

20 And he arose, and came to his father. But when he was yet a great way off, his father saw him, and had compassion, and ran, and fell on his neck, and kissed him.

²¹ And the son said unto him, Father, I have sinned against heaven, and in thy sight, and am no more worthy to be called thy son.

²² But the father said to his servants, Bring forth the best robe, and put *it* on him; and put a ring on his hand, and shoes on *his* feet:

²³ And bring hither the fatted calf, and kill *it*; and let us eat, and be merry:

²⁴ For this my son was dead, and is alive again; he was lost, and is found. And they began to be merry.

vi "**Delenda** *est Carthago*" ("Carthage must be destroyed")

Latin oratorical phrase in popular use in the Roman Republic in the 2nd Century BC during the latter years of the Punic Wars against Carthage, by the party urging a foreign policy which sought to eliminate any further threat to the Roman Republic from its ancient rival Carthage, which had been defeated twice before and had a tendency after each defeat to rapidly rebuild its strength and engage in further warfare. It represented a policy of the extirpation of the enemies of Rome who engaged in aggression, and the rejection of the peace treaty as a means of ending conflict. The phrase was most famously uttered frequently and persistently almost to the point of absurdity by the Roman senator Cato the Elder (234-149 BC), as a part of his speeches.

vii **Romeo and Juliette—William Shakespeare—Act III, Scene 1**

Romeo: Draw, Benvolio; beat down their weapons. Gentlemen, for shame, forbear this outrage! Tybalt, Mercutio, the prince expressly hath Forbidden bandying in Verona streets: Hold, Tybalt! good Mercutio!

Tybalt under Romeo's arm stabs Mercutio, and flies with his followers

Mercutio: I am hurt. **A plague o' both your houses**! I am sped. Is he gone, and hath nothing?

viii   The Lady is a Tramp from the 1937 musical Babes in Arms. Rodgers and Hart

> I get too hungry, for dinner at eight I like the theater, but never come late I never bother, with people I hate That's why the lady is a tramp
>
> I don't like crap games, with barons and earls Won't go to Harlem, in ermine and pearls Won't dish the dirt, with the rest of the girls That's why the lady is a tramp

ix   Gaius Marius - Born: 155 BC in: Cereatae, Latium, Died: 13-Jan-86 BC

> Roman General and consul of plebeian descent, son of a small farmer of Cereatae near Arpinum. Served in Spain under Scipio Africanus. In 107, was elected consul for the first time. Marius was recognized as the ablest general of the day, and appointed commander against the Cimbri and Teutones. Marius, out of unpromising materials and a demoralized soldiery, organized a well-disciplined army, inflicting two decisive defeats, the first in 102 at Aquae Sextiae (Aix), the second in the following year on the Raudian plain near Vercellae. In 101 Marius was elected consul a fifth time (previously in 107, 104, 103, 102), hailed as "savior of his country", and honored with a triumph of unprecedented splendor. He had himself elected consul for the seventh time, in fulfilment of a prophecy given to him in early manhood. Less than three weeks afterwards he died of fever, on the 13th of January 86.

x   Jean de La Fontaine The Monkey And The Cat

> Bertrand was a monkey and Ratter was a cat. They shared the same dwelling and had the same master, and a pretty mischievous pair they were. It was impossible to intimidate them. If anything was missed or spoilt, no one thought of blaming the other people in the house. Bertrand stole all he could lay his hands upon, and as for Ratter, he gave more attention to cheese than he did to the mice.

One day, in the chimney corner, these two rascals sat watching some chestnuts that were roasting before the fire. How jolly it would be to steal them they thought: doubly desirable, for it would not only be joy to themselves, but an annoyance to others.

"Brother," said Bertrand to Ratter, "this day you shall achieve your master-stroke: you shall snatch some chestnuts out of the fire for me. Providence has not fitted me for that sort of game. If it had, I assure you chestnuts would have a fine time."

No sooner said than done. Ratter delicately stirred the cinders with his paw, stretched out his claws two or three times to prepare for the stroke, and then adroitly whipped out first one, then two, then three of the chestnuts, whilst Bertrand crunched them up between his teeth. In came a servant, and there was an end of the business. Farewell, ye rogues!

I am told that Ratter was by no means satisfied with the affair.

And princes are equally dissatisfied when, flattered to be employed in any uncomfortable concern, they burn their fingers in a distant province for the profit of some king.

xi **Heinrich Schliemann (January 1822—December 1890)**
German businessman and a pioneer of field archaeology, an advocate of the historical reality of places mentioned in Homer. Schliemann excavated Hissarlik, now presumed to be the site of Troy, along with Mycenae and Tiryns. His work lent weight to the idea that Homer's Iliad and Virgil's Aeneid reflect actual historical events.

xii **Hannibal Barca, (264—146 BC) Carthage general.**
Hannibal led his army and elephants over the Alps to attack the Romans on their own soil. For many years, he led his victorious army up and down what is today Italy. Unable to stop Hannibal in Italy, the Romans

took the fight to the Phoenician colonies. Hannibal was lured to North Africa -- supposedly for peace negotiations -- where Roman troops were finally able to defeat him.

xiii Kilkenny cat: a tenacious fighter

"There once were two cats of Kilkenny,
Each thought that was one cat too many;
So they fought and they fit, and they scratched and they bit,
Till excepting their nails and the tips of their tails
Instead of two cats There weren't any..."

xiv Alexander III (July 356 — June 323 BC)

Alexander the Great, Ruler of Macedon, and creator of an empire that included Greece, Persia, Egypt. Tradition says he wept 'when there were no more worlds to conquer'. This may originate from Alexander' reaction to a discourse about an infinite number of worlds that made him weep. "Is it not worthy of tears, that, when the number of worlds is infinite, we have not yet become lords of a single one?'

xv Hamlet (Act I, Scene II), William Shakespeare

Ham: Is it not monstrous that this player here,
But in a fiction, in a dream of passion,
Could force his soul so to his own conceit
That from her working all his visage wann'd,
Tears in his eyes, distraction in's aspect,
A broken voice, and his whole function suiting
With forms to his conceit? and all for nothing! **For Hecuba! What's Hecuba to him, or he to Hecuba, That he should weep for her?** What would he do, Had he the motive and the cue for passion That I have? He would drown the stage with tears And cleave the general ear with horrid speech, Make mad the guilty and appal the free, Confound the ignorant, and amaze indeed The very faculties of eyes and ears.

xvi The labors of **Herakles**

1. Slay the <u>Nemean Lion</u>.
2. Slay the nine-headed Lernaean Hydra.
3. Capture the Golden Hind of Artemis.
4. Capture the Erymanthian Boar.
5. Clean the Augean stables in a single day.
6. Slay the Stymphalian Birds.
7. Capture the Cretan Bull.
8. Steal the Mares of Diomedes.
9. Obtain the girdle of Hippolyta, Queen of the Amazons.
10. Obtain the cattle of the monster Geryon.
11. Steal the apples of the Hesperides (He had the help of Atlas to pick them after Hercules had slain Ladon).
12. Capture and bring back Cerberus.

xvii   New Testament, Book of Revelations. 6:1-8

1 And I saw when the Lamb opened one of the seals, and I heard, as it were the noise of thunder, one of the four beasts saying: Come and see.

2 And I saw, and behold a white horse: and he that sat on him had a bow; and a crown was given unto him: and he went forth conquering, and to conquer.

3 And when he had opened the second seal, I heard the second beast say, Come and see.

4 And there went out another horse *that was* red: and *power* was given to him that sat thereon to take peace from the earth, and that they should kill one another: and there was given unto him a great sword.

5 And when he had opened the third seal, I heard the third beast say, Come and see. And I beheld, and lo a black horse; and he that sat on him had a pair of balances in his hand.

6 And I heard a voice in the midst of the four beasts say, A measure of wheat for a penny, and three measures of barley for a penny; and *see* thou hurt not the oil and the wine.

⁷ And when he had opened the fourth seal, I heard the voice of the fourth beast say, Come and see.

⁸ And I looked, and behold a pale horse: and his name that sat on him was Death, and Hell followed with him. And power was given unto them over the fourth part of the earth, to kill with sword, and with hunger, and with death, and with the beasts of the earth.

xviii Publius Vergilius Maro (October 70 BC—September 19 BC)

One of the greatest Roman poets of the Augustan period, known for three major works: Eclogues, Georgics, and the Aeneid, considered the national epic of ancient Rome. The **Æneid** follows the Trojan refugee Æneas as he struggles towards the shores of Italy and—in Roman mythology-- the founding of Rome. Virgil's work has had deep influence on Western literature, most notably Dante's Divine Comedy.

xix Lucius Cornelius Sulla Felix (c. 138 BC—78 BC)

Roman general and statesman, twice consul. He was awarded a grass crown, the most prestigious and rarest Roman military honor. A gifted and skilful general, he revived the office of dictator, which had not been used in over a century. In poor health, he stunned the world (and posterity) by resigning his near-absolute powers, restoring constitutional government in late 81 BC. After seeking election to and holding a second consulship, he retired to private life and died shortly after.

xx Augustus (September 63 –August 14 AD)

Founder of the Roman Empire and its first Emperor, from 27 BC until his death. Born Gaius Octavius, in 44 BC he was adopted by his maternal great-uncle Gaius Julius Caesar. Augustus restored the outward facade of the free Republic. In reality, however, he retained his autocratic power as a military dictator, holding a collection of powers granted to him for life by the Senate. He rejected monarchical titles, calling himself Princeps Civitatis ("First Citizen"). The reign of Augustus initiated an era of relative peace, the Pax Romana (Roman Peace). He reformed of taxation, developed networks of roads and an official courier system, a standing army, the Praetorian Guard, police and fire-fighting services, and rebuilt much of the city. Augustus died at the age of 75, succeeded by his adopted son (also stepson and former son-in-law), Tiberius.

xxi **Loch Lomond**—Lady John Stott (1810—1900)

By yon bonnie banks, and by yon bonnie braes,
Where the sun shines bright on Loch Lomond,
Where me and my true love were ever wont to be,
On the bonnie, bonnie banks of Loch Lomond.
Oh, you'll take the high road, and I'll take the low road,
And I'll be in Scotland afore ye
But me and my true love will never meet again,
On the bonnie, bonnie banks of Loch Lomond.
I mind where we parted in yon shady glen,
On the steep, steep side of Ben Lomond,
Where in deep purple hue the Highland hills we view,
And the moon coming out in the gloaming.
      Oh, you'll take the high road... etc.
The wee birdies sing and the wild flowers spring,
And in sunshine the waters are sleeping,
But the broken heart will ken no second spring again,
And the world does not know how we are greeting.
      Oh, you'll take the high road... etc.

xxii **Rudyard Kipling, Anglo-Indian author, 1865-1936**

"The White Man's Burden: The United States and The Philippine Islands"
Take up the White Man's burden, Send forth the best ye breed
Go bind your sons to exile To serve your captives' need;
To wait in heavy harness, On fluttered folk and wild--

Your new-caught, sullen peoples, Half-devil and half-child.
Take up the White Man's burden, The savage wars of peace--
Fill full the mouth of Famine And bid the sickness cease;
And when your goal is nearest The end for others sought,
Watch sloth and heathen Folly Bring all your hopes to nought.
Take up the White Man's burden And reap his old reward:
The blame of those ye better, The hate of those ye guard--
The cry of hosts ye humour (Ah, slowly!) toward the light:--
"Why brought he us from bondage, Our loved Egyptian night?"
Take up the White Man's burden, Have done with childish days--
The lightly proferred laurel, The easy, ungrudged praise.
Comes now, to search your manhood, through all the thankless years
Cold, edged with dear-bought wisdom, The judgment of your peers!
Take up the White Man's burden, In patience to abide,
To veil the threat of terror And check the show of pride;
By open speech and simple, An hundred times made plain
To seek another's profit, And work another's gain
Take up the White Man's burden, No tawdry rule of kings,
But toil of serf and sweeper, The tale of common things.
The ports ye shall not enter, The roads ye shall not tread,
Go mark them with your living, And mark them with your dead.

Take up the White Man's burden, Ye dare not stoop to less--

Nor call too loud on Freedom To cloke your weariness; By all ye cry or whisper, By all ye leave or do, The silent, sullen peoples Shall weigh your gods and you.

xxiii   Mary Howitt (1799-1888)

"Will you walk into my parlor?" said the Spider to the Fly,

'Tis the prettiest little parlor that ever you did spy;

the way into my parlor is up a winding stair,

and I've a many curious thing to shew when you are there."

"Oh no, no," said the little Fly, "to ask me is in vain,   for who goes up your winding stair -can ne'er come down again."

xxiv   Reginald Heber (1783-1826). Missionary Hymn,

From Greenland's icy mountains, from India's coral strand; Where Afric's sunny fountains roll down their golden sand: From many an ancient river, from many a palmy plain, They call us to deliver their land from error's chain.

What though the spicy breezes blow soft o'er Ceylon's isle; **Though every prospect pleases, and only man is vile?** In vain with lavish kindness the gifts of God are strown; The heathen in his blindness bows down to wood and stone.

Shall we, whose souls are lighted with wisdom from on high, Shall we to those benighted the lamp of life deny? Salvation! O salvation! The joyful sound proclaim, Till earth's remotest nation has learned Messiah's Name.

Waft, waft, ye winds, His story, and you, ye waters, roll Till, like a sea of glory, it spreads from pole to pole: Till

o'er our ransomed nature the Lamb for sinners slain,
Redeemer, King, Creator, in bliss returns to reign.

xxv   **Croesus (595 BC-c. 547?), king of Lydia**

Croesus consulted Delphi before attacking Persia, and
was advised, "If you cross the river, a great empire will
be destroyed." Believing the response favorable, he
attacked, but it was his own empire that ultimately fell.

xvi   **Marathon: A village and plain of ancient Greece,
northeast of Athens.**

The site of a major Athenian victory over the Persians
in 490 BC. Legend says a messenger ran from
Marathon to Athens to announce the victory . A
Marathon today is a cross-country footrace of 26 miles,
385 yards (42.195 km).

xvii   **Doubting Thomas:**

Sceptic who refuses to believe without direct personal
experience—a reference to the Apostle Thomas, who
refused to believe that the resurrected Jesus had
appeared to the eleven other apostles, until he could
see and feel the wounds received by Jesus on the cross.

Lightning Source UK Ltd.
Milton Keynes UK
UKOW03f0823060314

227660UK00002B/141/P